HERE GOES NOTHING

ALSO BY STEVE TOLTZ

A Fraction of the Whole
Quicksand

HERE GOES NOTHING

A NOVEL

STEVE TOLTZ

HERE GOES NOTHING

First published in 2022 by Melville House

Melville House Publishing
46 John Street
Brooklyn, NY 11201

and

Melville House UK
Suite 2000
16/18 Woodford Road
London E7 0HA

mhpbooks.com
@melvillehouse

ISBN: 978-1-61219-971-9
ISBN: 978-1-61219-972-6 (eBook)

Library of Congress Control Number: 2022931505

Typeset in Adobe Caslon by Midland Typesetters, Australia

Printed in the United States of America

1 3 5 7 9 10 8 6 4 2

A catalog record for this book is available from the Library of Congress

FOR MY PARENTS

HERE GOES NOTHING

Nobody was ever thinking about me.

Now that I'm dead, I dwell on this kind of thing a lot: how I often made life choices to avoid the disapproval of those who hadn't even noticed me standing there; how I longed to be liked by the very people I disliked in case finding me objectionable was contagious and would spread throughout the general population; how—and here's the sad truth—if all my reversals of fortune had been private, I'd have been mostly fine with them.

That's not all I lament; why hadn't I seen more of our world? Why did I never skydive or sexually experiment? Why exactly was I so uninterested in touching a dick? So what if I was heterosexual? Don't most vegetarians eat fish? And why was I so convinced that every supernatural belief was just an embarrassing throwback to the pre-scientific age? I had my irrational fears, of course: of mannequins and steep slopes and being stared at, but never of the dark, of the dead, or any kind of afterlife. To me, heaven was a childish dream, purgatory an obvious metaphor, hell credible only on earth, and the very notion of an immortal soul was only a way to avoid facing our imminent trip to Nowhere.

It's humiliating how wrong you can be.

ONE

'Danger is near . . . We must creep into a very tiny space.
If we can, we must creep into an orange. You and I!
Or even better, into a grape!'

Federico García Lorca

1

The beginning of the end—

Huge iron-grey cloud banks lay motionless above our little house, the dawn skies fading. The finger of a nervous stranger in a flannel shirt lingered on the doorbell.

This was arguably the most significant moment of my life.

I wasn't there.

My side of the bed was cold and empty. Gracie woke afraid and irritated because I hadn't come home again. Staggering off the bed, she threw on her robe, clomped down the stairs and flung open the front door: the short, balding man on the porch was in his late sixties, owlish with thick eyebrows, his forehead shiny where the hairline receded.

'Sorry to bother you, miss,' he said. 'My name is Owen Fogel, and you don't know me.'

'I *know* I don't know you,' Gracie said, annoyed. 'You don't think I know who I don't know?'

'I don't know.'

'What do you want, my money or my time?'

'I grew up in this house. Forty years ago.'

'My time, then.'

'Mind if I come in?'

'Did you leave something here?'

He couldn't tell if she was joking. 'I'm just wondering if I could come in and look around, you know, for old time's sake.'

Old time's sake? Gracie couldn't see how that expression related to a stranger demanding access to her private home.

'Haven't you ever gone somewhere,' he said, 'just to get a sense of where you came from?'

'Nope.'

'You never went back to an old school or an old job or the place where you lost your virginity?'

'I lost my virginity in the back of a bus.'

'I retract my example.'

Gracie gazed across the quiet street, then back to the blushing stranger now smiling with his tight mouth. 'Visiting the past because you're nostalgic is like drinking sea water when you're dying of thirst. It'll only make you thirstier. And it's gross. Why would you do it in front of a complete stranger?' she asked.

'It's a long story and I'd rather not tell it on the front steps.'

'Oh well. Next time you'll remember to cut it short.'

Gracie heaved the door shut. Fuck that guy. What an odious intrusion. She eyed the couch, lusting for sleep.

The doorbell rang again.

Through the peephole, the man's desolate figure was sulking in the patchy sunlight, his finger jabbing the doorbell insistently. Gracie grew frightened.

'I'm calling the police!'

'I'm dying.'

'What?'

'You heard me.'

Now he crept forward a little. 'I'm sorry to be intruding,' he said through the door. 'And I'm sorry that pretty soon I won't be bothering anybody ever again. Most of all I'm sorry that my *dying wish* is to come and look around this stupid house and remember my mother and father.'

Gracie opened the door and steadily regarded the visitor; his body may have fallen on hard times, but he looked robust enough to survive the morning. 'I don't like you looking at me like you've come to collect a debt,' she said, pressing her lips together, 'but you can come in.'

'Should I take off my shoes?'

'Don't bother. You won't be staying long.'

2

The dying visitor stood in the middle of the living room, as if unable to choose a direction to walk in.

'Go on, then. Have a look-see.'

He crossed the creaky floorboards from the TV to the potted cactus under the corner window. He made a cursory inspection of the floating shelves, the wallpaper map of the world, the cracked leather couch, the armchair, the enormous industrial fan. He stared at the odd religious paraphernalia—a Star of David that hung over a faded painting of Ganesh next to a wooden pentagram—and then fondled the fibre-optic Christmas tree with palpable sadness.

'If it isn't taken down by July,' she said, 'it makes sense to keep it there until December.'

He didn't nod his head so much as waggle it.

'What did you say your name was?' asked Gracie.

'Owen. Owen Fogel,' he said and then muttered, almost to himself, 'So much happened here.'

'For instance?'

'Puberty. I did a lot of violence to my body in those years.'

'Terrific.'

He spoke in a strange, faraway voice: 'Life is a funny thing.'

'How banal.'

He eyed her, transfixed, as if he'd had a sad insight and was resisting a powerful urge to share it.

'What?' she asked, suspiciously.

'Was I staring?'

'Like you're a lip reader waiting for me to say something.'

He laughed. 'Sorry. It's just sometimes, when you're not prepared, a beautiful face can be startling.'

Gracie froze, suddenly self-conscious to be wearing only a robe, disturbed by the possibility of what she had ushered into her house. Owen had sinewy arms that could easily overpower her. She heard a low-level ting and realised it was coming from a beige hearing aid in Owen's ear. So what? That didn't mean he wasn't a monster.

'My husband will be home any moment.'

'It's so early. He didn't come home last night?'

She dug her fingernails into her palms. 'No, I mean . . .'

'Has he done that before? I'm sure he just fell asleep on a friend's couch. Isn't that what they always say? "I must have passed out." Or, wait, "I was too drunk to drive and it was too late to call." Classic.'

She swallowed a *fuck you*. 'Are you even dying?'

'I am. Truly.' He caught the panicked glint in her eyes. 'Wait. Am I making you anxious?'

'Yes.'

'*Please* don't be.' There was only sorrow in his voice. Maybe the worst that would happen was that she'd be forced to endure his story or attend to a seizure.

'Just keep three feet away from me.'

'I only know the metric system.'

'Are you kidding me right now?'

'May I continue the tour?' he asked in a placating voice. Gracie nodded warily.

He moved skittishly around the room, sighing at the cracked walls, the peeling wallpaper, the blistered paint. He fingered the dust that covered the broken jukebox and even squatted in the corner, as if to get a child's point of view. That he only seemed dimly mindful of Gracie's presence somewhat alleviated her fears.

'Is it okay if I go that way?' he asked, gesturing to the kitchen.

'I guess.'

In the kitchen, Owen brushed his hands along the cabinets and the countertop while sneering at the apparent smoke damage from stovetop fires. He moved into the damp laundry and tromped down the steps to the pitch-dark basement. Gracie fished a corkscrew out of an ice bucket and slipped it into the pocket of her robe. Owen emerged from the basement and walked to the sunlit studio at the end of the house before circling back to the living room.

'May I look in the bedrooms?'

'Wow. Rude.'

'Is that a no?'

'Oh, whatever. Help yourself.'

Owen smiled politely then disappeared down the stained-carpeted hallway. Gracie made a coffee and smoked two cigarettes while imagining Owen masturbating on her bed. She thought: He'll come on my pillow soon and leave. Or he'll fall over and sue us. Something absurd will come of this.

Now she could hear a clatter in the bathroom and the sound of phlegm hawked into the sink. She made a mental note to incinerate the handtowels.

He returned to the living room combing what little hair he had with his wet fingers.

'How long have you lived here?'

'Two years.'

He moved around the room at the speed of someone trying to walk up a down escalator. Gracie fondled the corkscrew in her pocket and said, 'I can't remember if we were supposed to get the best house on the worst street or the worst house on the best street.'

'I don't think this one's either.'

Gracie was still uneasy. The only sound was the *chit-chit-chit* of Mrs Henderson's sprinklers, which were turned on in defiance of the water restrictions.

'Well, thanks for stopping by,' she said.

'What do you do for work?'

'I'm a marriage celebrant.'

'Interesting!'

It occurred to Gracie that Owen's grin seemed bogus, an instant red flag; when you've just met someone, you shouldn't be able to tell their fake smile from their genuine one.

'Newlyweds are refugees fleeing single life,' she said. 'Most people totally misrepresent themselves and enter into legally binding, lifelong marital agreements dragging a trail of half-truths. They'll do anything to grow old with someone overnight.'

'Huh?' An astonished look crossed his face, but it seemed routine, as if it was his tendency to be surprised. 'How did you get into this profession?'

Her nervousness prevented her from escaping this conversation, which had now run away from her.

'It's kind of a funny story.'

'Is it?'

'About ten years ago, my best friend Tara asked me to officiate her wedding. I had to do a one-month course at TAFE. Now that I'm saying it out loud, it's not really that funny a story at all, is it?'

'Not really, no. You get clients?'

'Every weekend. Mooney videos the weddings. We're a one-stop wedding shop.'

'What's a Mooney?'

'Angus Mooney. My husband.'

'The missing husband.'

'He's *not* missing.'

He made a 'poor baby' pout of his lips. 'Do you enjoy marrying people?'

'I'm usually freaked out that I'm going to ruin their special day, but I love it.'

'Do you?'

'It's my calling,' she said, earnestly.

She fished the corkscrew out of her pocket and fingered it openly, looking Owen directly in the eye. It was time for this lonesome, death-haunted man to get out of the house. 'Anyway, as I said, thanks for stopping by.'

'You're welcome.'

'Where's the next stop on your nostalgia tour?'

'Nowhere. This is it.'

'Have you seen everything you want to see?'

An abrupt smile appeared on Owen's face, as if he had just suffered an unwanted spasm of good cheer. He sat on the cracked leather armchair and eased back into it.

'Not quite,' he said.

3

Until my death, I had never had what could be described as a mystical experience. What I had instead was a sneering contempt for the supernatural, which I blamed on a childhood inundated by believers of all persuasions and levels of fanaticism. Everyone was convinced of one fool thing or another. Nobody around me was a sceptic; kids and adults alike were having 'experiences', although never in the presence of a corroborating witness. It was hard not to be suspicious.

At the age of three, my birth parents abandoned me—the shits—after a seemingly minor skirmish with community services. By my eighteenth birthday, I had been fostered, but never adopted, in four strangers' homes, every one of them by a major freeway, every arrival arbitrary, every departure inevitable.

The first house I can barely remember but for a mother figure at the bedroom door tolerantly explaining that, 'There is nothing in the dark that wasn't there in the light.' It made perfect sense to me, but that logic had no effect on the inconsolably panic-stricken twin brother and sister in the adjacent bunk bed who'd flick on the lights, climb into the same bed and cry themselves to sleep. Each night, the same dismal routine, and never the lesson learned: the dark had sinister potential, sure, but it never delivered.

The second house was a red-brick bungalow tucked away in a cul-de-sac where I shared a narrow bedroom with a sad-eyed foster sister, Emma. We used to cry at night together—they called us 'soblings'. I remember the hoarse-voiced foster mother on the edge of my bed telling me that 'everything happens for a reason', that it was 'meant to be' that my parents couldn't take care of me, and that 'karma' would get them in the end. Emma, meanwhile, rattled on about the literal monsters lurking under the floorboards. I was resistant to the whole idea. If monsters were real, I argued, why had we never seen a single one caught, killed and paraded on the news? It was only at night, when she lay in bed immobilised with fear, that I could get any rest.

At the age of eight, I was moved into a weatherboard house in Kensington with the Brocks, an old couple who were almost *too* kind and sympathetic, as if they'd mistaken foster care for palliative care. There was nothing scary in that house other than Mr Brock shouting 'Breakfast!' like a carnival barker, one 'uncle' always looking at me ominously as he applied lip balm, and a grandfather who'd seen a UFO one September night twenty years earlier—a pulsating orange globe—and would often recount the time he'd been visited by the vessel's alien pilot. 'I woke up to find it at the foot of my bed,' he said, in a throaty whisper. 'It didn't say anything, but its superior alien intelligence was clear. He wanted me to know we are not alone.' Sometimes he would read from his favourite book, *Chariots of the Gods,* whose author travelled interdimensionally to uncover the true history of the universe; other times he would just wave it at us and say, 'When the alien returns to take me with them, it might take you too.' There was always one silent child who listened with the force of a scream. I'd think, why would an alien visit *him* of all people, and not someone famous, powerful or wise? I read the faces of the other adults as he told his stories and learned for the first time what it was to feel embarrassed for another person.

Of the fourth house, in Meadowbank, two blocks from the Parramatta River, I remember the always-expired milk in the fridge, the apricot bathroom tiles smudged with dirty footprints, and the Virgin Mary and baby Jesus garden sculpture in the backyard that I'd often stare at through the leadlight windows at the end of the hall. The house belonged to a paediatrician, Dr Fitzsimmons, and his wife, Beverly. Their wedding photos showed they got married barefoot. Above the fireplace was a plaque that read: *If you lived here, you'd be home by now*. Their own child had died from meningococcal disease. My first night in their home, three days before my twelfth birthday, a kid named Ernie told me the child's ghost moped in the dusty corner of the room.

Ernie also tricked me into swallowing tadpoles, then told me that frogs would grow in my stomach unless I took a powerful laxative to shit them out, and made me drink the MiraLAX that was for Dr Fitzsimmons's upcoming colonoscopy. I emerged from the toilet two hours later to find Ernie doubled over with laughter.

'That was hilarious. You okay, Numbat?'

'My name's Angus. People call me Mooney.'

'Yeah but Numbat's better. Ever seen one? It's the termite-eating pointy-faced marsupial you look like.'

I shrugged it off. Being called names has never particularly bothered me. I find insults amusing if they aren't true, and a free life lesson if they are.

'Ernie!' Dr Fitzsimmons was standing at the bedroom door. 'Don't say things like that. You are *all* beautiful children.' I thought: why does everyone on the planet earth *have* to be beautiful?

What kind of value system is that? He said: 'Remember, Ernie: "Do not neglect to show hospitality to strangers, for some have entertained angels unawares."'

Ernie gave him the finger. Dr Fitzsimmons smiled and said, 'Oh, you!' Then he bowed and turned off the light. It only now occurs to me how accepting he and his wife were of our ingratitude.

The shadows looked like cold animals crouched in the dark. Ernie crept across the room and perched on the edge of my bed. I was scared—I thought he'd come to torture me—but he whispered, 'Don't worry, Numbat. Things will get easier with time.' (Now I understand: *of course* things get easier with time. That's how desensitisation to pain works.)

Ernie soon schooled me on the way things were run in the Fitzsimmons house. Mild physical abuse was defined as horseplay, nobody respected anyone's toothbrush (I kept mine in our bedroom), games of hide-and-seek were only a means to abandon someone, and if you wanted to steal a cigarette, your best bet was Beverly Fitzsimmons, who went through a pack and a half of Horizons a day. A steady smoke rose from her and, from behind, it looked like her head was made of dry ice. She wore cat's-eye sunglasses inside the sunlit kitchen and read all our horoscopes like a town crier. She believed her dreams were prophetic yet only recounted them *after* the events they predicted had come to pass. If one of the kids fell off the roof, she'd say, 'That's so amazing. I dreamed last night that you were falling.' You just had to stand there like a dolt and pretend to believe it.

It was Beverly who made me suspect that even so much as wishing upon a star was an act of self-aggrandisement. It was also Beverly who often called me an old soul. I never took it as a compliment. To accuse a child of wisdom beyond their years is to imply they're abnormally devoid of youthful enthusiasm and naiveté. I mean, what's so great about saying to a kid, 'Hey, old man . . .'?

Meanwhile, Dr Fitzsimmons always consoled us about our fucked-up biological families by saying, 'The Lord works in mysterious ways.' That made no sense. It's pretty easy to understand why the devil is wily—but why must God be too?

I put up with a lot during my childhood, and the Almighty was just another nuisance. I remember a Sunday when seven of us children were forced into itchy suits and herded down to St Michael's, where Beverly was being confirmed. Over breakfast, Dr Fitzsimmons had presented her with a silver crucifix and explained to us that even though Beverly had been born into the Church of England, from this day on she would be a Catholic.

'How does that even work?' I asked.

'What do you mean?'

There was never anything so inexplicable to me as those who could switch between incompatible eternal truths without breaking a sweat.

'There's only two directions in life, Angus,' she said. 'A turn towards God and a turn away from Him.' I already knew then that I'd prefer to go around.

At St Michael's, the bishop stood at the pulpit beneath an ostentatious cross, carrying on melodramatically like he was a character in an Agatha Christie novel. It's always the same with these guys. They never let you forget that Jesus is dead, that it was foul play, and that you're the main suspect.

At some point I fell asleep and had to be shaken awake to see the bishop touching Beverly's forehead with his bent finger, saying, 'Do you reject Satan and all his works and all his empty promises?'

She said, 'I do.'

He went on about the risen Christ, how he was there in our very midst, and how Beverly belonged to Jesus now. Then he gently stroked the side of her face and said, 'Be sealed with the gift of the Holy Spirit.' That was it. She was a Catholic now.

The bishop smiled with the seedy delight of a lothario who'd just notched another sexual conquest. I looked at the newly confirmed congregants. Their souls didn't seem eternal. They didn't even seem like they'd last the week.

'Glory be to the Father, and to the Son, and to the Holy Spirit; as it was in the beginning, is now, and will be forever.' The parishioners all said 'amen' at the same time and I resisted the urge to say, 'Jinx.'

Ernie pulled a Sharpie out of his pocket and drew a pentagram on the back of the pew.

'They're going to see you,' I said.

With his right hand he gave me the sign of the devil.

Ernie was a goth and an amateur Satanist. He and his depressing friends wore black, smudged their eyeliner and tried to contact the dead with a homemade ouija board. (These séances were a chaotic mess; someone was always bursting into nervous laughter or silently fingering someone else under the table.) Otherwise they drew pentagrams in the dirt and sat around bonfires and got fucked up.

The devil never made any sense to me, conceptually, and still doesn't; for me his motivations are just too evil to be believable. Personally, I never met a torturer who wasn't well-meaning.

Dr Fitzsimmons was diagnosed with cancer six months later. It was vaguely embarrassing to watch his struggle. He'd sit at the kitchen table and say, 'Don't worry, everybody. I'm too young to die!' I immediately understood that Death is an abusive partner, gas-lighting you with sunshine and dawns.

We were all present for his final breath. Beverly said it comforted him to have us all sprawled across the dusky room, though I doubted he noticed; he was wafting in and out of sleep. When it happened, he wheezed, his face registered a complaint, then he was gone. Everyone reported a different version of observing the spirit leaving his body. Somehow, I was the only one who didn't see anything at all.

The following Saturday night, Ernie held a séance. I watched the stupid, solemn faces of him and his friends bursting with a power they did not possess. They thought they had the kind of shoulders ghosts like to cry on. As we clasped sweaty hands, Ernie said, 'Dr Fitzsimmons, I feel your presence. Are you here among us?'

I whispered, 'Sorry to call at such a late hour.'

'Shut up, Numbat,' Ernie said.

Frankly, nothing said about ghosts ever made sense to me. Why moan? A voice in the dark saying plainly, 'Hey. Nice to see you,' would petrify me more. And why are they always stuck in their murder houses like convicted criminals with ankle monitors on house arrest? And why did ghosts stop rattling chains at the same time in human history that men stopped wearing hats? And why don't ghosts appear so much in the day? It never made sense to me that ghosts, as well as being dead, are reputedly night owls.

'He's here,' said Ernie, grinning. 'I can feel him. Can you feel him too?'

I could not.

'Can you hear him?'

I could not.

In my opinion, most paranormal phenomena are debunked by the spiritualist's own shit-eating grin. It annoyed me how people professed to believe in the unseen world and then bored you with how they'd seen it. To make it worse, they looked at you with pity, as if they were born with superior antennae and you were too physically and mentally underdeveloped to perceive the invisible.

The summer I turned sixteen, Ernie and I were arrested inside a neighbour's house. We'd broken in when they were at work to raid their booze and play video games, and we'd made the crucial error of forgetting to not pass out drunk. We were both sentenced to community service in an aged-care facility in Ryde, where we witnessed the daily tragedy of people who'd come to the end of an unforgettable journey only to have completely forgotten it. It wasn't just disturbing that these terminally confused folks had some very dirty things to say about destiny but that almost all of them believed the dead were alive and the past was the present. They resurrected their loved ones right in front of you, or *inside* you, and were distraught when you couldn't play along. It was painfully clear that these mistaken beliefs were the result of either damage to or deterioration of the brain. I took that as yet another lesson that the subjective experience is unworthy of respect.

Soon after that, the era of relying on the kindness of strangers came to an end. Ernie moved out into a share house in Dulwich Hill. I turned eighteen shortly after and moved in with him, sort of: my home was a corrugated iron shed in his backyard. It didn't have a bathroom but I could piss in the bushes, shower under a garden hose, and shit in the McDonald's up the road. Unbelievably, I lived there for most of my twenties.

Ernie had hooked up with his housemate, Lisa. They were disgustingly in love. The worst thing about them as a couple was how they would feed each other over dinner; the worst thing about Lisa as an individual was how she mistook every banal coincidence for synchronicity and honeyed with meaning whatever blew across her path. She wouldn't shut up about how everything in the universe was connected and how she was at the epicentre of it. She really was the empress of us all; her gods were working hard for her. 'Even you were sent here to me,' she said one night. It was Lisa who gave me the first clue that 'spirituality' could be a splashy form of self-obsession.

One night we were drinking in the garden beside the firepit and I told her about my birth parents abandoning me. Lisa closed her eyes and made a face as if she were on the precipice of confessing someone else's darkest secret. I didn't want to hear it. She said, 'The universe is telling me that they are ready to ask for your forgiveness.'

I said: 'I doubt it.'

She said, 'This is something that's going to change your life, Mooney.'

For all my life I'd hated my birth parents as if it was my profession, but was this the time to search for them? I was eighteen—not a man, exactly, but some form of adult. I said, 'Yeah, no. That's bullshit. Not interested in those fuckers.'

Lisa laughed and said, 'You're trying to not be born.' I laughed too, even though it was the most serious thing that anyone had ever said to me.

The woman at the foster care agency gave me the address. Their names were Joel and Dawn Mooney, and unless they were brother and sister or father and daughter, the news that I had been given up by a married couple sent me into an even angrier depression.

They lived on Giffnock Avenue in Macquarie Park. It took me only forty-five minutes to get to their perfectly ordinary and pleasant-looking house. It was galling. I could've grown up there.

I pounded on the door. When it opened, an old leathery woman with white chin hairs shouted, 'What do you want?'

I smiled apologetically and gave her a brief summation of my quest. While I spoke, the old woman just stood there smoking, ash falling off her cigarette onto her bare foot.

'They're dead,' she said.

So that's what an axe to the chest felt like.

'Both of them?'

'One after the other.'

'When?'

'About five years ago.'

'How?'

'Does it matter?'

'Well . . . yes.'

She sighed. 'Your father drank too much piss and drowned in the Hawkesbury. Two years later, your mother went through her own windscreen. Stupid girl hadn't worn a seatbelt for twenty-five years.'

'Then aren't you . . .?'

'What? Your mother was my daughter. Is that what you're getting at?'

My eyes grew too large to contain the tears. 'Doesn't that make you my grandmother?'

'All right, Einstein. So what?'

Every fibre of my being felt rejected. This terrible woman who was my grandmother heaved an impatient sigh and said, 'We done?' then slammed the door in my face.

Maybe my anger and bitterness from that encounter contributed to the regrettable way I lived the following decade.

It started trivially: getting blackout drunk and into fights. Committing juvenile, pointless crimes so dumb you couldn't in good conscience call them crimes—they were more like pranks that occasionally pulled a small profit. Then Ernie and I started smashing car windows for loose change and breaking into houses, where we thought everything was worth stealing—there's no doubt we had a hoarder's taste for larceny. We also took stupid quantities of amphetamines and barely noticed the transition from using to selling. I won't say that I never soiled myself.

I never entirely forgave Lisa for getting my hopes up about my parents. She continued 'communicating' with bogus otherworldly presences, and if she said, 'I felt something,' I'd just say, 'Me too.' When she said, 'My dream came true last night,' I'd say, 'So did mine! So weird, right?' It drove her crazy. Her other most repeated expression of mystical power was the prophecy that, one of these days, Ernie and I would go too far. Obviously she wasn't the oracle she thought she was, but she also wasn't wrong.

It was a bit of a blur, but here were the ingredients: a drizzly Saturday night, us stone broke and lurking on Victoria Street, an oily businessman hailing a cab, Ernie grabbing his briefcase and twisting his arm behind his back.

'This is a bit unfriendly,' the victim said, before elbowing Ernie in the groin.

Whatever it was Ernie did with his fists, the man went down hard. His head hit the gutter with an audible crack; there was a distressing amount of blood. A young kid shrieked from inside a parked car and I remember thinking: here's an indelible childhood memory for you. People rushed out of their houses and we darted off, not knowing if our victim was alive or dead.

To my absolute surprise, a few days later Ernie dragged me with him into the church on Harrington Street. Next to the altar and rough-hewn statue of Christ, there was a confession booth. Was he serious? Apparently so.

After Ernie's turn, I slid back the curtain and entered. It was cool inside. The priest's silhouette was rocking gently. I didn't know the etiquette that surrounded this corny transaction, but here he was: a master of silences, practising his art. The temptation to say *cunt fuck shit* was almost overpowering.

'Take your time,' he said, amiably. I could hear him smiling through the grate.

I had a hundred petty confessions as well as this big one, the line I'd recently crossed, but I hesitated to utter any of them aloud.

How could I know this priest didn't have a legal obligation to inform the police? Or, worse: How did I know he wasn't gathering material for a novel?

The priest leaned forward in anticipation. I thought that what the confession booth had the most in common with was the peep show, or the partition dividing a cab driver from his potentially lethal client. 'I know I said to take your time,' the priest said, 'but I do have an appointment at two.'

'On second thought, Father, why should I tell you anything?'

'For God's forgiveness.'

'So *you* say.'

How reliable was this guy? Maybe he'd *say* I was forgiven, but maybe when I died, I'd wind up boiling in a lake of fire, thinking, 'Wait until I get my hands on that priest!'

'You must have faith.'

'Piss on that.'

I left the confessional and sat watching the priest. He had to dress in black, even in summer. He moved about the world with everyone thinking he was a paedophile, or at the very least broke bread with paedophiles.

The other people scattered in the pews were an enigma to me too. Who kneels in a church on a Wednesday afternoon? It seemed to me that if these folks just had someone to look them in the eye they would be fine. Why were so many people susceptible to God and I was not? And who even wants to be? I always hated how, even on his best days, He could be merciful but never actually kind.

Ernie sat down next to me, loud-whispering about scoring speed, and I realised I had to distance myself from him or I'd wind up dead or in jail. A priest nearby was talking about his old bugbear—sin. 'What a load of shit,' I heard myself say.

Back then, I couldn't hide my intolerance. The way I saw it, faith in the Lord was like walking around in a suit of gold that looks fancy but weighs you down, Satanic worship was a tragic teenage affectation, belief in magic, ghosts and monsters was inversely proportional to one's ignorance of the natural world, and mystics were more or less method actors who forgot they were playing a part—the humourlessness of the mystical experience itself the signature giveaway. I thought that the people who thought 'God' was not a noun but rather a verb should just look for a different word. And, my crucial mistake: I thought that the afterlife was for those who couldn't abide ultimatums.

4

With growing impatience, Gracie gestured at the wide-open front door. Her husband had been gone two nights with no explanation, and now an unwanted visitor was picking his teeth on her armchair and refusing to leave. Owen switched on the TV and began flicking through the channels.

'Make yourself at home, why don't you?'

Owen landed on a news story about a white amputee who had 3D-printed a black hand for his at-home transplant surgery.

'What do you think?' asked Owen.

'About what?'

'The state of things. Fake news bots. The rise of autocrats. Phones spying on their owners. Sonic attacks. The two seasons on earth now being just Fire and Flood. Something's gone wrong on a global scale, don't you think?'

'You said you came here to look around.'

'What keeps you up at night, Gracie? If you had to pick one thing.'

'Hacked sex toys. Vibrators that can be reprogrammed remotely to kill their user.'

'For me, I'll go with non-state actors in possession of weapons-grade plutonium in hand-me-down warheads from old Russian stockpiles,' he said, then looked back at the TV and cringed. 'Now look at this one: they're massacring dogs in Greenland.'

Gracie looked at the TV to see dogs, haemorrhaging and howling, crammed into wire cages, and soldiers lining up to shoot them. It was a sickening scene.

'Why?' she asked, aghast.

'Global warming. All the ancient permafrost is thawing. The dogs are sick with a virus linked to that Pleistocene wolf that they found embedded in ice last year. By overheating the planet, we have ceded ground to the virosphere and—Jesus.'

The howling of the tormented dogs was cut off by gunfire followed by the wailing of their devastated owners. Gracie glimpsed the gruesome extermination through her fingers. 'How about a warning, CNN?' she cried. 'Fuck!' She switched off the TV.

Owen sank back into the cushions and hummed softly to himself. Gracie was almost impressed by this impudent stranger's audacity.

'Owen, it's really sad you're dying, but —'

'Thank you, Gracie.'

She hesitated over her next move. 'Have you tried non-traditional healing?'

The lines on Owen's weathered face deepened. 'You mean like lying to myself that a completely ordinary substance has rejuvenating properties? Or do you mean letting someone with zero medical expertise wave their hands above my body in vague motions?'

'A cynic, then.'

'A realist.'

'I imagine dying really fucks with your head.'

'It does.'

'Makes you feel like nothing you do matters.'

'Nothing does.'

'And I suppose it hurts even more that you're past the age of it being unfair.'

Owen huffed and removed a packet of Marlboro Reds from his pocket. 'Can I smoke in here?'

'You can, but should you?'

'Definitely.'

He lit up and deep-dragged and exhaled the smoke in a deflated sigh. He got up and walked to the back door and stared through the small window at the garden as if he had some holy devotion to it.

'Owen. I think it's about time you leave.'

'I was just thinking about my father.'

'What about him?'

'He's dead.'

'I'm sorry.'

'It was a long time ago.' Owen sucked hard on the cigarette, then exhaled. 'He died because of his pockets.'

'What do you mean?'

'Always walking with his hands in his pockets, as if he hadn't a care in the world, whistling some inane tune. And when he tripped, because his hands were in his pockets, he couldn't reach out to break his fall. He cracked his head open on that stone there.' He pointed to the three stone steps that led down to the infrequently used, evil-smelling outside toilet.

Owen jerked open the rusty-hinged back door and stepped onto the deck.

'Watch out,' Gracie said. 'There's a missing plank.'

He walked over to the leaf-strewn fire pit, where a dented bicycle rested.

'We had a swing set there. I remember jumping off it and running over to him. The hole in his head was too big to stop the bleeding. I didn't know what to do, so I didn't do anything. He took such a short time to die. Maybe three minutes. Seemed longer though. I was sixteen.'

Fresh tears came to Owen's glazed eyes. Spooked, Gracie gazed at the stairs, imagining them bright with fresh blood. Owen straightened up, as if perfect posture would arrest the tears. He wiped them with an awkward laugh.

'This is embarrassing. I haven't cried about that in thirty years.'

'Come inside and sit down.'

She guided him back to the living room couch and poured two whiskeys. Owen raised his in a toast.

'I lived in the past. I feared the future. I wasted the present.'

'I'll drink to that.'

Owen downed his whisky, eyeing Gracie through the bottom of the glass.

'God, you're beautiful.'

'Don't start that again.'

'I'm not starting. I'm continuing.'

Morning light gushed through the window and everything went soft. Owen stared dumbly at his reflection in the television set.

'Can I be honest with you? There's something else I want,' he said. Here comes the indecent proposal from hell, Gracie thought. Was he going to ask to lick her feet? 'And it's going to sound . . . peculiar.'

5

To explain where I was when Owen was bothering Gracie, we need to go back four years, to the low-key summery afternoon when Ernie and Lisa got married in their backyard. Chickens roamed, the dress code was 'picnic casual', and uninvited neighbours were peering over the fence. I arrived late and missed the walk down the frangipani-strewn aisle, taking my place on one of the white plastic seats that dug unevenly into the wet grass.

Because the ceremony was already underway, I had not yet grasped the bewildered and even disapproving silence of the guests. The nervous couple stood on a portable aluminium stage: Lisa took exaggeratedly deep breaths, Ernie looked like he'd just dismounted from a horse. And standing between the bride and groom, there she was, my future widow. She was short, verging on tiny, with dirty-blonde hair piled up as if to give her more height. She wore a gratuitously low-cut denim jumpsuit and comically high platform shoes. With every spoken phrase she poked her finger at the couple aggressively.

'You've decoded each other's confusing signals, haven't you? You've overcome your ambivalence, right? You saw no viable alternative, did you? Well, maybe you did, but you both elbowed competitors out of the way. And now, despite totally reasonable qualms and misgivings, you've closed the door to other romantic possibilities for the medium-term future. Congratulations, bitches. It's an arranged marriage, and you arranged it.'

I'd never heard anything like it. What was this? I looked around and spotted the mother of the bride staring acidly at Gracie.

'You weighed the pros and cons and concluded you probably deserve each other, yeah? Whatever intersections of self-interest have brought you here, you two free individuals have made some sober calculations and decided to marry. Nice one. Now you're freshly configured and you each have someone to help you out of vicious loops. It's virtually *guaranteed* that you'll not go days without hearing human voices. And, most importantly, you've just improved your health! The chronically single have depressed immune systems, and by this union you will have higher white blood cell count with which to fight foreign intruders. Let's take a moment to acknowledge that your life expectancy went up today, okay? Statistically, by four years. That's not nothing.'

The bride and groom gave each other a look and braced for the unknown direction this ceremony was taking.

'If you settled for each other, that's okay!' Gracie was now yelling. 'If you woke up this morning and said, "This is madness!" that's okay too!' The father of the bride shifted to the edge of his seat, like he was about to rush the stage. 'Love is a miracle only if you don't understand what the word miracle means.' Gracie paced in a slow arc around the couple. 'Marriage is not without its difficulties, right? Holy shit, it's complex. If you want privacy, you've come to the wrong institution. Your life together will be defined by accidents, arguments, unexpected windfalls and poor decisions. I promise you. This wedding will be the least pivotal moment in your whole marriage.'

She draped her arms over their shoulders.

'But listen up, you guys, don't kid yourself about this union's infinite duration. Marital bliss can be revoked by either party. Once the romance fades, worthy substitutes abound. Think of it this way: a wedding is like a tetanus shot. Later, when a wound is infected, you'll discover the immunisation was only good for five years.'

There was an arduous minute of silence. Gracie seemed to be deliberately working uncomfortable pauses into the ceremony.

'One day, you'll find mealtimes growing silent. There will be pugnacious mornings. Brittle nights. You'll farewell the loving gaze and welcome the era of the stabbing eyes. You'll start to think about the alternatives your life choices excluded, and those unlived lives will cast dark shadows that singe the very ground you walk upon. You will plan escape routes. Divorce, aka *cutting your losses*. One day, maybe, I guarantee you, one of you will dream of taking a photo of your spouse on the edge of a cliff, telling them, "Just step back a little. No, further. Just one more little step . . ."'

I couldn't imagine where she got the nerve to stand in front of a crowd and say such things. Some of the guests were delighted, others were slack-jawed and visibly contemplating relieving her of her duties. The whole thing felt like I was watching a parody of something, but of what?

'Right. Here are some survival tools: The enemy of love is impatience and eye rolling. Even gentle mockery is corrosive. Learn how to defuse the other's ticking bomb. Notice what the beginning of a negative spiral looks like. Prioritise snoring remedies. Don't exaggerate hurt feelings. Have more morning sex than night sex. Identify which of your partner's faults are unfixable and devise a workaround. In marriage it is survival of the deafest, okay?' She was shouting right in their faces. 'No bathroom lightbulbs over forty watts! Deciding what to eat will constitute three-quarters of your marriage so, when it comes to menus, always state strong preferences! And remember, you're there to soften the blows *even when you're the one delivering them*!'

As Gracie went on haranguing the betrothed, I felt something tense up inside me, as if I was eavesdropping and about to get sprung.

'All right!' she shouted. 'Now hurry up and switch glittery trinkets.' The rings were exchanged with a sigh of relief.

Gracie clapped her hands and announced to the assembled guests: 'True love has come to pass. Unblock the fire exits. The damage is done.' She turned to the couple. 'I now diagnose you husband and wife. You may kiss the groom, and vice versa.'

The overlong kiss was met with wild applause, but I was staring at Gracie with lost wonder. The couple were happily dragged off by the photographer, while the guests, beaming at each other with damp eyes, shared a laugh that verged on hysteria. Weddings are crazy.

I crossed the yard to the drinks table, where Gracie had stationed herself. She was talking to a wizened, great-aunt-looking woman, and I heard her say: 'When someone tells me they want their ceremony to be dignified, I think, This will end with one of them not leaving the other a forwarding address.' The great-aunt giggled and left.

I sidled up next to Gracie. She had a soft face and big mascaraed eyes and vivid lips. Tattoos crawled down both her arms (spiders, howling wolves that turned into flowers, endless knots, seascapes). It was hard to know what not to stare at. She looked at me blankly, swirling the champagne in her plastic flute.

'That was really something,' I said.

She mock-curtsied. 'You're a friend of the bride or groom?'

'The groom and I grew up together for a few years in the same house, even did joint community service when we were sixteen, at an aged-care centre in Ryde. We used to ransack the patients' rooms when they were aqua-healing or lunching or taking their forty-five-minute shits.' Her eyes widened in mild surprise. I casually leaned on the bar table, making it tilt. 'You know the thing I remember most about that place? The purple, splotchy, elephantine things that were once human legs and feet.'

What had I just said? I've always been envious of anyone with a free and easy manner, but when I try to emulate them, it comes out wrong. The look on Gracie's face was unreadable. Behind her, a queue of guests was waiting to fawn over her.

'Take it from me,' I said. 'When people talk about the horrors of old age, they should mention the legs.'

With that, I made a hurried exit, manoeuvring my way through the crowd to the married couple. Ernie wanted to know why I was sweating, and I glanced back—Gracie was gazing at me with curiosity. I hoped to impress her later on the grassy dancefloor, but she ghosted before I had a chance.

Later that night, drunk, I flopped onto the cold centre of my bed with my laptop. I wanted to see if could find anything about her online.

Turns out, I could find out almost everything.

From the posts, updates, tweets, photos and videos that she'd littered along the peaks and valleys of her social media landscape, Gracie Adler disclosed to her 4000 followers and 5000 friends a mind-boggling amount about herself. Her childhood hero was Eeyore from Winnie-the-Pooh, she'd suffered from cluster migraines since the age of six, and she got a new tattoo every three months. She loved cherry blossoms, horror movies, playing chess, Diane Arbus, and her Ventolin inhaler. She was a self-confessed mouthy, Jewish ciswoman who endeavoured to return every sexual favour that was ever given to her and whose sexual orientation had been fluid but now, for better or worse, had solidified into heteronormativity.

'I believe the only thing worse than being sexually objectified is not being sexually objectified,' she posted.

Her parents had named her Gracie to upset her Orthodox grandmother, she'd had a cervical tumour removed, she seemed devastated when any musician died, including seven whom she called 'the soundtrack to my youth'. She was electrocuted in an abandoned building in her late twenties, she was an actual Marxist and she couldn't find a relationship. She posted: 'I suspect I might be dating Buddhists. All the men I'm going out with are really into non-attachment.'

She was involved in three road rage incidents (in two of them she was the aggressor), went to—and sometimes led—lucid dreaming workshops, didn't own a calendar because 'my face and a mirror are the only timepieces I need', and declared that of the top ten problems in the world, male violence was eight of them. Her favourite stories as a child were ones in which a time traveller predicts an eclipse and freaks the fuck out of the villagers, her superpower was 'never hating to disappoint someone', she believed the greatest thing about Australia was the rock pools dotted along the coast, and every day she found herself in the glittering water where the 'boundaries between worlds are their most porous'.

She semi-regularly took ayahuasca and mushrooms, and had a shaman named Tina who prescribed a bi-monthly ego-death. She completed a bachelor of communications degree majoring in cultural studies, semiotics and phenomenology, wrote her thesis on Nazi fetishes, and had a brief stint as an adjunct professor, though it wasn't clear if she quit or was asked to leave. She posted: 'My idea of optimism is to hope that I'll always be a psychiatric outpatient and never an inpatient.'

She adored videos of customer meltdowns and soldiers returning home to their dogs, was obsessively in love with her own golden retriever, named Ziggy, and was politically vocal on almost every conceivable topic, though most of all on asylum seekers, gay marriage, women's reproductive freedom, sexual predators, animal cruelty, racial injustice, structural inequality, women's rights, the patriarchy, and rape culture. She was torn 'between wanting to blow it all up and wanting to burn it all down'. She wisdom-bombed her followers with quotes from Krishnamurti, Chuang Tzu, Fritjof Capra, Ram Dass, G.I. Gurdjieff and Madame Blavatsky, and wrote a series of blog posts for a women's health and spirituality website called *Goddess* that tackled the big questions: *How did our ancestors love? Is cheating genetic? Are your genitals clairvoyant? What does it mean to be spiritually fluid? In which psychic crawl space hides the soul?*

It was clear from her posts that our era of drone terrorism, nanobot murders, hurricane firestorms and utter global chaos stressed her out. She often made the sour acknowledgement that she had not yet lived up to her reproductive potential and probably never would. She posted: 'I think I'm destined to be a childless stay-at-home mother.'

She was also lost career wise. She posted: 'The universe doesn't want me to sit on my hands, but what the hell am I supposed to do?' Then, in her late twenties, her best friend Tara begged her to officiate her wedding and, with little else to do, Gracie enrolled at North Sydney TAFE and completed a certificate in celebrancy. After she nailed the ceremony at Tara's wedding, receiving both enthusiastically positive reviews from friends and scornful disapproval from Tara's grandparents, she posted: 'Guess what, bitches? My calling called and I answered. I'm bringing people in love together.' She clarified: 'Turns out I'm good at giving people feelings. The sad fact is people go through long periods where they don't feel human, which is, you know, a business opportunity.' She came clean: 'And now my selfless devotion to love is paying the rent!'

Within months she was booked solid every weekend and felt herself to be at the beginning of a happy and fulfilled life.

Yet this dizzying read didn't end there. She posted a photo of a crumpled-faced old woman: 'A year ago my nana moved into a retirement village. I always visited at mealtimes, nap times, or when half the residents were dead and the new ones had yet to arrive. Some eyed me suspiciously, others hungrily. Today, I arrived just as an ambulance was carrying my nana out. She'd died in her sleep.'

A month later, she posted: 'Sorry for my unsolicited white tears, but my father died today.' She described him as 'a beautiful, complex, distant, homophobic man' and posted a blurry, orange-tinted photo of herself at age seven, sitting on his shoulders. She posted: 'Even towards the end, he looked shyly away. Didn't he remember that we once lived together for twenty years?'

After his funeral, she and her dog Ziggy set out in her van, 'The Black Tarantula', to travel around the country. She had only just exited the abandoned railway tunnel in Newnes National Park when she got a text message informing her of her mother's death, about which she posted: 'I lost my best friend today. Just found out my mother died of a heart attack. Or grief. But probably heart attack. Last time I saw her I told her she looked pale, like unpasteurised milk.' Then: 'Buried my beautiful mother today. ☹ Lodged in memory: how the heels of her feet were so badly chapped, when she walked barefoot it sounded like she was wearing wooden clogs.' And: 'WTF to do w/ these mixed feelings. Just found out the sale of my parents' apartment + their life insurance = a deposit on a house.'

A series of posts followed that documented Gracie's search among dozens of overpriced dwellings and her losses at auctions, until she bought a house in Maroubra 'only a frantic twenty-minute power walk to the beach'. It had a dead front lawn and a wild overgrown back garden, an embarrassment of natural light, and a working fireplace. From the front verandah she could smell the ocean and, on silent nights, faintly hear it.

She posted: 'I've come far, people: from spending three days living in a storage facility to sleeping in a friend's kayak in his backyard to renting minuscule studio apartments geographically the furthest possible distance from any convenience store, supermarket or restaurant.'

A single woman buying a house—the triumph of it! There were dozens of photos of her grinning and Ziggy panting outside her crumbling little yellow house, a single palm tree on the front lawn.

Was she happy? A series of posts about the neuroscience of loneliness suggested otherwise. She made it explicit: 'I've really never gotten over the plight of being the only child of two only children.' Growing up, it saddened her that she'd had no siblings, no aunts, no uncles, no cousins, and now, while taking a selfie beside her parents' twin cemetery plots, she realised that, in terms of her bloodline, there was nobody at all. She posted: 'I have nobody except my dog and a city-full of under-interested strangers.'

The next post was an anguished plea for help. Ziggy had disappeared! She plastered signs all around the neighbourhood and roamed the streets calling his name. She posted: 'Over the past month, I've come across a hundred golden retrievers who could've played mine in a movie.' When he was eventually found, dead on the side of the Princes Highway, it exacerbated Gracie's terror of being alone. The frequency of her posts increased from daily to every three or four hours. In her most recent, about the stabbing attack in

Sydney's CBD that resulted in eleven fatalities, she posted: 'I hate when, after some horrendous tragedy befalls a family, someone tells me to hold my loved ones tight. I'm all alone, fuckstick. Now I feel bad for them *and* for me.'

I closed my laptop, exhausted and amazed that there was seemingly no limit to what a person in this disintegrating world might disclose. That night, I sent her an instant message.

'Hi.'

'I don't know you.'

'Yes you do. It's Angus. From the wedding today. I haven't stopped thinking about your speech.'

'The connoisseur of old people's legs.'

'That's me.'

'What's your full name?'

'Angus Mooney. People call me Mooney.'

'I probably won't.'

'Angus is fine.'

'Where do you work, Mooney?'

'DHL.'

'What's your address?'

'400 Denison Street Camperdown.'

'What's the postcode?'

'2050.'

'Thanks.'

'Should I say something now?'

'You don't feel anything? I'm internet searching the shit out of you.'

'Uh-oh.'

'Wait for it.'

'Maybe we should have a drink while I wait?'

I had to wade through a four-hour pause before she answered: 'Bay Hotel. 5pm. Tomorrow.'

It was a dull afternoon and clouds were in a mad rush overhead. Gracie was already on a stool in the hotel's prized window seat, scribbling on a beer coaster and hesitating to demonstrate how she'd mastered the sexy, distracted chewing of pencils. I took the adjacent stool, there was a brief awkward silence, and then she said, 'I like your beard.'

'Thanks.'

'Tell me something embarrassing you've never told anyone.'

That was easy. 'When I was a kid, I thought an orgy was a naked human pyramid.'

'Mooney, you've got a criminal record.'

'That's true.'

'I don't want to pry but, on the other hand, I'd rather not get murdered by a degenerate.'

'Understandable.'

She turned her thinly drizzled smile to me, waiting for an explanation.

'You know the expression "I know a guy who knows a guy"?'

'Yeah.'

'I was the guy.'

'Which guy?'

'The *second* guy.'

I gave her the briefest summary of my partnership with Ernie and explained that, while in theory I was not averse to an honest day's work, I just never had one of those professions for which an honest day's pay was enough to feel genuinely worth my time. I'd been a taxi driver, a bicycle courier, spent six months behind a car-rental desk. Eventually, you make the calculation, and I made it by the time I was twenty-one: 984 shifts or do one little job. How can anyone who knows basic arithmetic not slip, from time to time, into a night of crime?

'What did you do?'

'Nothing too violent. Shoplifting. Minor drug-dealing. A few home invasions. The occasional mugging.'

'Jesus Christ.'

'You've got to be careful what tricks you pick up in adolescence. You know what I mean?'

'No.'

'Skills are even more dangerous than habits.'

'How so?'

'When you go out in the world, not excelling at anything for years on end, you crave the satisfaction of a job well done.'

Her inscrutable stare upset my equilibrium. 'And now?'

'It's in my past. Definitely.'

'Why?'

'To tell you the truth, I got involved with some pretty bad people. I was in way over my head, and I needed to get out.'

'What kind of people?'

'Men who threaten to fuck you in your exit wound.'

Sometimes when talking about myself I feel like I've cut and pasted someone else's life onto my own. Nothing I say feels earned or believable. 'And I was nearly getting caught all the time. It's fucking hectic, sprinting back to a getaway car to find your driver blackout drunk, then having to sit on his lap as you drive away with either bullets or thrown bricks shattering your rear windscreen.'

Gracie drank from her glass, her eyes narrowing in deliberation.

'I'm only a danger to myself these days. I promise.'

I felt exhibitionistic, like I'd just unpeeled myself in front of her, waiting for her verdict, which she delivered by ordering more drinks. We sat at that window for hours, watching the palm trees turn black against the darkening sky, beginning in earnest the conversation that would continue until the day I died.

We left the pub at last drinks with locked arms, and she hurried me along the street, making me feel like I was being recruited to work for a foreign power. It was a warm night and the moon's halo was ragged at the edges. Four blocks over, at her crumbling yellow house, we trod the path through the vegetable garden, which I knew from social media boasted carrots, basil, mint and tomatoes. By the time we reached the front door, I felt so at home I almost checked my pockets for the key.

'It's a bit messy,' she said, and we entered the house with a distinct no-turning-back sensation.

I am not a neat person, but at least my messes make sense. There was an armchair, a cracked leather couch, mismatched art deco floor lamps, dozens of half-read books carpeting the floor, a giant industrial fan, and a single wall covered with a renaissance map of the world. Later, I learned that she furnished the place with items from auction houses and deceased estates. We stood in the doorway, swallowing in silence.

'Don't just stand there like a Mormon, come in.'

She made her way around the room and lit a number of cheap Virgin Mary candles. Prayer beads hung from nails on the walls along with an ornate wooden crucifix, a Buddhist prayer wheel, paintings of Shiva and Ganesh, a wooden fish, a pentagram, a yin yang decal, and a ceramic Star of David.

'This is a genuinely confusing room.'

She stayed close beside me as I examined the mismatched iconography. It all had such an odd, cumulative effect—making me think of so many things at once—that my mind was, for all practical purposes, empty.

'What do *you* believe?' she asked.

'Not much.'

'You must believe in something.'

'Must I?'

Did I?

Most of my beliefs were about beliefs, but it was difficult to put them into words. I explained that it had always been wacky to me how belief comes in strange yet predictable pairings. How those who are into angels and ghosts are also often anti-vaxxers convinced the moon landing was faked, just as the individuals who insisted that crop circles were forms of extraterrestrial communication had an equal faith in trickle-down economics.

Gracie looked at me curiously, as if she was still waiting for the sound of my voice to reach her ears.

I always believed, I went on, that nearly all the people on earth are self-mythologising liars who only have premonitions in hindsight. (If you told them, 'Hey, someone was murdered right here in this house,' it was only *then* they said, 'Yeah, I knew I felt something.') I said I believed that most paranormal occurrences are either too far away to perceive or too close up to focus on, and that it's very suspicious that almost nothing supernatural exists at a critical distance.

Her eyes seemed to be staring in the direction of my mouth.

I said I also believed that life was meaningless but not worthless, and how that distinction had been enough to get me out of bed in the morning. I believed that gullibility was akin to a disability and should be treated accordingly. And that if everything happens for a reason, those reasons are chance, luck and chaos.

The words seemed to be breaking free of my face almost of their own volition. It was very quiet in the room. Gracie edged closer towards me.

I said I believed that spontaneous combustion was only evidence that, if some fucker is determined to set you on fire and sneak off without being seen, he was certain to do so. That there was no such thing as a reliable human witness and that all mystical visions were self-generated, which is why Buddhists didn't get visions of Christ, Christians didn't see the Buddha, and there's not a single solitary instance recorded of a rabbi visited by Mohammed. Mainly, I believed that the very people who think they have special powers lack even the ordinary ones.

Then I said, 'You know what else I believe?'

'What?'

'Women don't care about men's bare shoulders like men care about theirs.'

Her t-shirt had fallen off her left shoulder, revealing a milky slope. I kissed it, and we didn't even make it to the couch; we had sex against the wall and then on the hardwood floor.

The unfamiliar feeling of getting what I wanted was almost overwhelming, and it put me off my game. I tried not to be too hard on myself. Sometimes sex just doesn't quite work. She said, 'Slow down. It's like you're trying to do fifteen things at once.' I slowed down, but so much so that I made myself unobtrusive. That wasn't right either. We were fucking at cross-purposes.

'That wasn't amazing,' she said afterwards.

The second attempt was better, and the third time more or less life-changing.

I remember noting, as we lay naked on the hallway runner, that each having a decent amount of belly flab meant that our physical imperfections were evenly matched and would probably keep us both at ease. Then she stood and walked so erect and straight-backed to the bathroom, it was almost a military march. That told me something about her I wouldn't have otherwise guessed: only ashamed people walk with that much dignity.

It was only a few months later that we negatively formulated our own marriage proposal. We were treading the chalky blue water in the Mahon rock pool, facing out towards the misty horizon, when I said, 'You wouldn't want to marry me, would you?' She said, 'Wouldn't I?' Discussions went from there. It was crazy how easy it felt to take this decisive step. Two months later we were married.

About those first years, I'll say this: for the first time in my life I felt sorry for guys who weren't me. I always thought a human's natural state was mutually assured isolation, but here I was, feeling unalone and like I had suddenly moved over to the leisure class, as if I'd retired after a long working life.

We didn't just live together—we started working together, too. Gracie taught me how to make wedding videos. During the week, I'd be editing the previous weekend's ceremony while she wrote sermons for the approaching ones. Fridays she would be struck by her mortal fear of public speaking and spend the day with her head in the toilet, surfacing only to rehearse excuses to back out, but come the weekend, she was in her flow state, gyrating around whatever gazebo or garden she was in, haranguing each nervous couple with the most absurd and remarkable things I've ever heard anyone say.

The genuine shock of it all was that my whole existence had overnight become intensely livable. True happiness, however, puts you on the edge of your seat. Was I going to fuck it up? I didn't see how. Other than the minor problem that a light sleeper probably shouldn't marry another light sleeper (we were constantly waking each other), our only real difficulties were financial: the income from our small business, which operated only on weekends, was pitiful. We were haunted by the spectre of not making the mortgage payments.

'Why won't anyone marry on a Tuesday?' Gracie would moan. 'Or after work on a Thursday? You can't convince them! I've tried!'

I suggested we find a more lucrative business, but marrying people was her vocation, and ultimately she wasn't as obsessed about our financial woes as I was. I did the worrying for both of us, even though money wasn't the only cause of my persistent unease.

I knew Gracie liked my 'do no harm, take no shit' philosophy but, other than that, I couldn't work out what I'd done to win her over. She kept saying I'd 'saved her', but never specified how. We were a couple, on equal footing, but some days I felt vaguely chaperoned—over dinner she would gaze lovingly at me, but also as though something didn't quite add up, as if I was a secret that she would get around to uncovering after figuring out all the other, more profound secrets she was trying to get to the bottom of.

I had to admit, it was a little odd that after my years of disdain for a wide spectrum of beliefs, I was married to a woman who often posted on social media about having borne witness to the supernatural and whose religious epiphanies were publicly accessible. In her defence, her beliefs did not seem self-serving or ornamental or solipsistic, but were more of a sort of thinking out loud, and she was never evangelical for her position. Even when she'd judge someone for their astrological sign or tell me something absurd, like how she'd once been cursed and had defeated the curse with a counter-spell she found on the internet, there was an uncertain tone to it all that I found endearing.

Mostly I found Gracie's belief structures to be refreshingly provisional and admirably slippery: the universe *could* be a process of unfolding; there *might* be patterns; everything *may well* be connected; humans are *possibly* component parts of some greater whole. *Surely* we're on a path, and that path *probably* has a direction, and that journey can *likely* only be seen from above. She was a total fence-sitter.

Sure, some days she totally believed in a God, though that belief was not imbued with a sense of gratitude but with suspicion.

What's in it for Her? I found her ideas invigorating if never convincing. I appreciated that, to Gracie, nothing was *that* sacred. It's true that, after a lifetime of deeply mistrusting these kinds of viewpoints, I'm rationalising, but there's no mystery to my hypocrisy; when you resolve to adore someone, you develop new blind spots as you go.

She deceived herself about me, too; 'spirituality' and 'mysticism' were core to her sense of self and, although I worried that it bothered her to be with a total and shameless sceptic, somehow it didn't; she'd convinced herself it was an amusing opposites-attract kind of situation.

No, the real problem for us wasn't spiritual—it was biological.

It surfaced two years into our marriage. It was midnight in the backyard and the starry sky looked like a cheap screensaver. Gracie was missing it, lost down the rabbit hole of her phone, her face bathed in screenlight. She was watching a video that came with the sound of barking.

'Can you put down your phone?'

'No.'

'The truth is, I've hated technology ever since it was just a rotary phone. Imagine how I feel now.'

'What?'

Here's the thing. Gracie had her flaws. The sound of a straw broom against a concrete floor set her into an exaggerated fit. She constantly said, 'I really should meditate twice a day,' yet I had never seen her meditate once. She lost as many wallets as she overflowed bathtubs, often said the words 'tick-tock' to hurry you up, and couldn't go to a stranger's house without judgementally watering their plants. But her worst habit was: she couldn't put down her fucking phone. And, worse, my wife had a 'social media presence'.

Ostensibly, this was how she publicised our business, and it was true her incessant posts were the reason we had weddings booked every weekend. But she was also an addict, unable to go two minutes without connecting with 'friends' who were, in my opinion, only marginally better than hallucinations, and often markedly worse. Over time she made a few online enemies, mostly from passive-aggressive little spats and misunderstandings that didn't seem altogether adult.

'Gracie. Why not make a resolution to only look at your phone on Sundays?'

'Sundays? Are you crazy?'

Maybe I was, but browsing the internet and connecting with old friends seemed like a sweet thing to do on a Sunday afternoon, like hobbies of old, such as stamp collecting. Nobody looked at their stamps every six minutes. Social media only seemed good to me if you no longer thought earth time was precious. And not *one* single argument in favour of it—keeping in touch with friends, being socially aware, staying politically engaged—addressed why you should check it thirty-seven times a day or why your online persona needed to be hyperbolic or cheery to the point of sinister. Not to mention how mortifying and degrading it was to have every detail of our misadventures made public.

'Gracie.'

'What?'

'What *are* you looking at?' I asked.

'I prefer to watch dogs see themselves in mirrors than children. Humans just fall in love with their image at first sight; dogs want to kill their double.'

'Do you miss Ziggy? Do you want to get another dog?'

'That's not what I was thinking.'

I knew what she was thinking.

From then on, we did a quick inventory every morning and always found the headcount was one off—there was a child missing.

A couple, no matter how close, is not a family unit. According to Gracie, a family unit is three. Personally, I was unconvinced. But for almost a year we tried casually, then insistently, then graspingly, to get pregnant. Sometimes the sex was aggressive, like I was trying to catapult a baby into her or she was trying to yank it out of me. It felt nothing like making love and everything like a tug of war. Other times, it felt like we were fucking as asexually as plants.

Gracie's defence mechanisms handled this frustrating and disappointing period for her. 'Oh well,' she'd hear herself say. 'The world is going to hell anyway. Wanton environmental destruction, irreversible biodiversity loss, the risk of runaway AI and robot-dog soldiers, white supremacist massacres and the global caliphate . . .' She was so convincing, I almost wanted to end it all. Eventually, this catastrophic line of thinking backfired on her too. 'The world is turning back to times when people had a dozen children because you never knew who'd make it through the winter,' she realised. 'Yet we can't hatch a single one!'

It finally dawned on us that we might have a problem conceiving. It was a hard thing to admit; failing to do something on purpose that so many have done by accident was humiliating.

IVF is not a poor man's game; in this biological gamble, there was no five-dollar table. We weren't just trying to harvest eggs and grow life, we also had to find a way to pay for it. I had two jobs—three if you count distributing leaflets, which is hardly a job by anybody's standards. If you knew us then, you'd swear we were emanating a desperate little hum wherever we went. The hormone injections, the countless blood tests, the workmanlike procreational humping, it was all taking its toll—and for nothing. We were trying to fuck our way onto the Great Chain of Being but kept sliding off.

Online, Gracie was trying to counteract the shame by over-sharing. Although the sight of my own private turmoil splashed on her feeds made me recoil in horror, I could plainly see that Gracie needed to do it, so I didn't complain about her posting the details of our failures. In the meantime, what else could we do but keep trying to have a baby? We had nightly meetings about starting the long process of adoption, almost impossible with my criminal record. International adoption was prohibitively expensive, and surrogacy was illegal in Australia. The obstacles didn't just *seem* insurmountable—they absolutely were.

All of this was the reason I was away the morning that Owen Fogel first arrived at our house. This failure to have kids had been corrosive, bringing us to the dawn of estrangement; two days earlier, I had told Gracie I was heading out for another all-nighter of mushrooms and video games with Ernie. She took it as me avoiding having sex with her.

'You've been out the last three nights,' she said.

'I told you. Ernie's been going through some shit, and you always said, mushrooms help you clean out those hard-to-reach spots.'

That was two back-to-back lies. Ernie was still deliriously happy with Lisa—those fuckers have never had a bad patch—and we weren't planning on taking shrooms.

Even when we missed a mortgage payment, Gracie had been anxious about me 'using my old contacts', as she put it, and expressly forbade it. Yet how else could we afford adoption or IVF treatments?

I left the house flushed with guilt. Lying to her made me miserable. Three nights running, Ernie and I had gone out to clubs, pickpocketing on dancefloors and from those cramming at the bar for a drink—it wasn't too hard to snatch a wallet from someone already being shoved from all angles. Only a few of our 'donors' were people we approached in alleyways, which required a touch of force. Nothing to be proud of, but we'd accumulated enough cash over the past three nights to buy a couple of eggs.

That night, Ernie had product to move. I spent most of the evening in a shadowed corner of a half-deserted street, helping my foster brother unload little plastic baggies of amphetamines, moving within whispering distance of prospective clients and throwing my voice like a ventriloquist; to sell to people who gave off the aura of a ruined life, I stayed away from streetlights and moonbeams, and didn't look any customers in the eye for fear of embarrassing them. Nobody wants to be seen on their way to rock bottom.

A bald, tattooed man signalled me over, and we ducked into an empty side street. The transaction was smooth. It's amazing to me how everyone, regardless of education, knows how to expertly palm a banknote. Once we were done, he pulled a knife on me.

'Empty your pockets,' another voice said.

A second, thicker, stiff-armed man appeared from behind me. It was a set-up. They looked unpredictable, and not above committing a casual homicide to make a point. I had to make a move quickly; I'd been in plenty of fights, and the only weapon that ever worked for me was the element of surprise.

'What do you want,' I asked. 'The wallet in my sock?'

When the man with the knife glanced down, I punched him, kicked the one behind me, then sprinted away, my mind wiped clean with fear.

Running for your life restores you to factory settings. Their heavy footsteps pounded in my ears. I glanced back—they were in close pursuit, both now armed with metal poles. I could tell they didn't mind witnesses. They would beat me as long as their attention span held.

I ran with a crazed intensity, beset with visions of Gracie's face—seen from a hospital bed or the witness stand. I was taking great gulps of air and heading east, because when I am running for my life it is always to Gracie that I run.

6

'I need to ask a favour,' Owen said.

'I don't know you well enough.'

'Think of it as granting a handsome stranger a dying wish.'

Owen winked at her. He must have thought it was endearing. 'Dying wish is . . .' he said, in a slow drift towards a complete sentence. 'If it would not be too much trouble, that is to say, I would be forever grateful . . .'

'Spit it out!'

'I would like to die in the house I grew up in.'

'You what?'

'Please, Gracie. Let me die here.'

'You can't die here.'

'Why not?'

'Because your death is *your* unsolvable problem, just as mine will be mine.' Her grandfather, before he caught a lethal cold, had told her that. 'And I don't want your fucking ghost wandering around my home.'

Owen chuckled abruptly, then stopped. That's how he laughed—in instalments.

'I've seen a ghost,' she said, solemnly. 'When I was fifteen. At my best friend's father's farm, the night his brother Terrence died.' Owen waited for the story, but she didn't tell it. 'There are things out there we can't see and can't understand.'

'Unexplained phenomena, you might call them.'

'That's right.'

'Ghosts. Spectres. Wraiths. Phantoms. Apparitions. Spirits of the dead. I still maintain that I don't know if they're real, but because you insist *you* know, you're actually saying there is no such thing as unexplained phenomena because you've just explained them.'

He looked soothed by the defiant logic of his own thoughts.

'Owen, do you know what the Vietnamese say?'

Owen looked surprised. 'What?'

'The frog at the bottom of a well believes that the sky is as small as the lid of a cooking pot.'

'I *love* that you know what the Vietnamese say.'

Gracie gave a tight-lipped smile and stared across the backyard. 'I died once,' she said, her voice low. 'It's a long story, but I was electrocuted inside an old factory.'

The darkness, she recalled, had felt like a long pause. The silence, like a calm sea. A soft light appeared above her. It was, she instinctively felt, a searchlight, looking for her. She began to move towards it. Or rather: the terrestrial world pulled away. If anything, it felt like she was sinking, but the light grew larger, brighter. She apprehended that going towards the light was an illusion—in reality, the light descends towards you.

'Don't you think it's mysterious that all these people, from all walks of life, experience the exact same thing?' she asked.

'There's nothing mysterious about a human being reaching for a cliché.' Owen's voice was full of admiration for his own point of view. 'I'll tell you what happened to you,' he said, dully. 'Oxygen deficiency triggered hallucinations. Release of endorphins gave you the calming effect. The light isn't real, it's just an ophthalmologic phenomenon created by the optic system. It's a common reaction to mental and physical stress—women during labour often report the same symptoms. If you lie down, with a one-hundred-millilitre injection of ketamine, I can show you the same bright tunnel of light. You heard of REM intrusion, Gracie? When the mind awakens before the body, sensory information overloads the visual cortex. *Or.* You know about infrasound? Extremely low-frequency sounds can induce hallucinations and engender feelings of acute fear. Perhaps the machines in the factory —'

'What do you believe?' asked Gracie, bored of his rant.

'Absolutely nothing.'

'Neither does my husband.'

'What I mostly don't believe in is God.'

'Why not?'

'Neonatal strokes.'

'What's that?'

'Newborn babies get strokes. And we're supposed to praise the Lord? I don't think so. Make up your minds, humanity. Either killing babies is inexcusable *or it is not.*' His angry grimace made his face so taut she felt worried for it. 'However, now that I'm dying, I look at believers like yourself and I'm sick with envy.' He lowered his head, as if in prayer, and turned his heartsick smile towards her. 'I want to believe, but I can't do it without the tiniest, infinitesimal hint of proof. If I could see for myself.'

'See what?'

'A voice. A whisper. A shadow. Gracie, if I stay here, maybe you can convince me.'

'Owen, I only want to convince you of one thing.'

'What's that?'

'To get the fuck out of my fucking house!'

The sun was still only halfway over the trees. I had removed my shoes to sneak into the house quietly when I heard Gracie's scream; I charged in barefoot and, seeing an unknown man looming over my wife, grabbed him by the wrist and started hauling him out.

'Go easy! He's harmless!' she said.

'What are you screaming for, then?'

Gracie couldn't put it into words. I angled my head and looked at the stranger squirming in my grip, half on his knees.

'He's dying,' she explained. I loosened my grip and he fell to the floor. 'And he wants to die here.'

'What do you mean, *here*?'

'In this house.'

It was true, he fizzed with death. I thought: The poor homeless bastard must've bumbled in off the street, looking for somewhere dry to die.

'You should go next door,' I said. 'They have air conditioning.'

'Owen grew up here. He wants to die in the house he grew up in.'

'In my old bedroom,' Owen said. 'The room at the end of the hall.'

That made me think this Owen wasn't homeless but some brutal combination of insane and alone. Whatever personal tragedy had preceded his mystifying decision to barge into our home and demand to die here, I didn't want to know. Worst, his distress was slow-moving. That's for families to deal with—or non-profits.

I asked her, 'Do you want him here?'

Gracie deliberated. Owen was looking at her with a pleading smile.

'No.'

'Say goodbye, Owen.'

I began the miserable task of hauling this dying man out the door. It was like trying to move the sorrows of a whole town. Owen resisted fiercely, and we wrestled for control of his arm.

'Come on, mate. Let's go!'

'No!'

'Wait! He's got cancer!' Gracie shouted.

'That's okay,' I said, grunting. 'It's not a force field.'

I tossed Owen outside onto the rotten floorboards of the porch. He lay in a forlorn heap, labouring for breath, and eyed me coldly. Gracie called out from the living room, 'Bye, Owen! Good luck!' and went into the kitchen to make herself a consolatory cup of tea.

Outside, it was cold and blowy and damp. The violent act made me feel ashamed. Owen was staring darkly at Gracie's carrots, planted in neat rows in the garden. The tiny next-door dogs ran unleashed on their dead lawn. Owen got to his feet and leaned heavily on the porch railing.

'What kind of cancer do you have?' I asked.

Why was I still talking to this man? Maybe because he was dying, and because he was only five foot four—I understood the discrimination short men suffered, and whenever anyone told me to 'check my privilege', I always thought: white and tall.

'I never said it was cancer.'

'What is it?'

'Creutzfeldt-Jakob disease.'

'What the fuck is that?'

'A fatal brain illness.'

'Sucks to be you.'

Owen smiled sadly and made himself small and creaturely.

I asked, 'Isn't there any hope?'

'No, no hope.'

I could smell lemon tea on his breath. He looked to be weakening with every passing tick of the clock.

'But medical science is making groundbreaking discoveries all the time,' I said.

'Medical science isn't even in on how often it's best to wash your hair,' he said, ogling our house and the garden, and sighing languidly, like he had all the time in the world. 'Young couple like yourselves in a place like this, you must have crushing mortgage payments.'

'We get by.'

'As a wedding videographer?'

'It's not the worst job in the world.'

'You know who you remind me of?'

'Who?'

'Myself as a young man.'

'Thanks.'

'It's not a compliment.'

Owen's cold smile persisted. This was outrageous. My head was pounding—I'd barely recovered from running for my life—but now he raised his finger to indicate he had more to say.

'I want to make a deal with you guys,' he said.

'I don't want to hear it.'

'I don't want to hear it either,' Gracie said, stepping onto the porch.

He stroked his chin like there had recently been a beard there. 'If you let me die here, in my old bedroom, I'll leave you everything I have.'

'No chance!' said Gracie.

'Hang on, Gracie,' I said. 'This "everything" that's going to be left to us. How much is that, exactly?'

'I own an apartment in Watsons Bay.'

'How many bedrooms?'

'Mooney!'

'Three.'

'And what else?'

'A car. A '69 Mercedes. It's parked on the street, if you want to look at it.'

'How many kilometres?'

'Oh my God!' Gracie said.

'One hundred and thirty thousand, but it's in perfect condition.'

'Is that all?' I asked.

'Yeah,' Gracie said, 'have you got any gold teeth my husband can wrench out of your mouth once you're dead?'

Owen laughed. He seemed to be in good spirits now. 'No gold teeth,' he said, 'but about $120,000 in stocks and bonds.'

I whistled. 'And when will you be dead, exactly?'

Gracie slapped my arm. 'Now that's just impolite.'

'Two months,' Owen said, flatly. 'Maybe three.'

'Owen,' I said. 'Why don't you go inside, into your old room, and give us a minute?'

'With pleasure.'

'Or with pain. We don't care.'

With the rain falling and the morning sun still hidden by low cloud banks, Gracie and I sat in the front garden, on the charred wet pews scavenged from a church fire. I went first: 'This is a golden opportunity. And when opportunity knocks, you have to answer.'

'We answered,' Gracie said. 'And now opportunity wants to die in our bed.'

'So? The worst-case scenario is after Owen's death we'll be baffled for a while and objects will take on a new vividness. Apples will look shinier, leaves greener.'

'What kind of people would we become?' Gracie asked. 'Egging on death, cashing in on brain disease? And I don't want an owl-faced stranger dying in our house and then haunting us from beyond the grave. Won't it be scary going to the bathroom at night? What will we do when our home becomes that eerie house the neighbourhood children dare each other to enter?'

Owen was staring at us grimly from our bedroom window, parading his illness. Gracie looked faint.

'Are you okay?'

'You know how I can lie *unless* you ask me a direct question, and then I have to tell you the truth?'

'Yes.'

'Well, in the same way, I can ignore my fellow man's suffering all day every day—unless he outright asks me for help. Then I can't say no.'

'That's unfortunate for us.'

'I know.'

I admitted my own reservations. After foster homes in my childhood, share houses in my twenties and doss houses and halfway houses in my thirties, I'd sworn I would never live with a stranger again. 'But that dying sad sack can pay off the mortgage, dig us out of crippling debt, fund our baby, and allow us to enjoy what's left of our youths.'

'You're forty-two years old,' she said. 'How long is this youth of yours expected to last?'

Her eyes unexpectedly filled with tears.

'What's wrong?' I asked, knowing what bothered her; my secrets were fatal to us as a couple, and she saw through them anyway. I had to come clean. 'Okay, okay,' I said, 'I've been working with Ernie.'

'You promised.'

'I know. It's just, I've been making a nest egg to buy eggs.'

'Oh, baby,' she said.

'What?'

'I've been waiting to tell you,' she said ominously, 'but you didn't come home for two days.'

'Tell me what?'

'I'm pregnant,' she said, laughing.

The world went mute, the heart in my chest no longer held in place. The yearning that had consumed us was gone, just like that, and replaced by some entirely new version of itself: a longing for the exact thing we had.

Owen had moved to the couch, where he was sprawled with his eyes closed, as if sailing off into a dream.

'How are you feeling, Owen?' Gracie asked.

'Gracie, this disease is characterised by rapidly progressive dementia,' he said, opening his eyes again. 'I've got some muscular coordination issues, my memory's shit, and my judgement questionable. And thinking—I can't even think about it. Not to mention impaired vision, insomnia, depression and—it's not exactly a medical term—but I just feel weird all the time.'

I donned a haughty professional voice. 'Have you recently undergone any treatment?'

'There is no treatment for CJD,' he said, plainly.

'That's going to get messy, right?' Gracie said, in a quiet, fretful voice.

Owen's throat tightened. He opened his eyes again and sighed deeply. 'As the illness progresses, my mental impairment will become severe. I'll develop involuntary muscle jerks and I'll probably go blind. Eventually I'll lose the ability to move and speak and then I'll enter into an irreversible coma—if pneumonia or other infections don't kill me first.'

Owen took a long hard look at us. Gracie seemed positively enraptured. I was smiling too, thinking about how my foster parents never looked me in the eye. They modelled anger or they modelled fear or they modelled distance, but none of them were big on eye contact.

All through our attempts to get pregnant, I had been secretly ambivalent about the whole notion of parenthood, but in that moment I had no great plans in this whole long life but to be a father and to look our child in the eyes as often as possible.

Owen snapped, 'What?'

Gracie burst out with it. 'I'm pregnant!'

'Apparently we're going to have a baby,' I said. 'I just found out.'

'Oh,' he said. 'Congratulations.'

'You too!' I said. 'I mean, condolences. I mean . . .' I considered for a moment. 'Theoretically, Owen, or should I say hypothetically . . .'

Gracie noisily exhaled and asked: 'How the hell will we take care of you?'

With a show of effort, Owen lifted his head, then settled back into the cushion. 'You won't have to do anything,' he said, every word catching in his throat. 'You just sit back and let nature weave its black magic.'

Poor sick bastard. He gave Gracie a weak smile, full of gratitude, and I felt genuinely sorry for him—at the time, of course, I hadn't the slightest idea that he would outlive me.

TWO

'It is better to say "I'm suffering" than to say "this landscape is ugly".'

Simone Weil

7

That first morning, I woke naked in a forest clearing with the odd sensation that I was inhabited by another version of me, one holding his breath. I'm no outdoorsman, but even I know that a naked man in the wilderness is not atop any food chain or pyramid—he's about on par with a gazelle.

I got to my feet and spun in circles, trying to see everything at once. Nearby was a squat, slate-tiled building with high windows of glinting black glass, and I made a run for it. Even though I didn't know where I was, I thought: I hope I don't run into anyone I know.

Inside was a single cavernous room that looked ransacked. I groped among empty tables and open cupboards and sat on a swivel chair with a creeping sense of unease. I quickly scanned my body—red blotches on my inner thighs, painful lumps in my armpits and, when I touched my face, my beard was gone. I felt licked clean. I gazed down at my arms—my tattoos were gone too. That should've drawn me closer to an answer, but it didn't. My mind was a tour de force of what the fuck.

I stepped back into the clearing under that bloated monster of a sun. The knotted trees and the wildflowers gave off a weird stink. I felt harangued by the silence and the light. An orange flash blared in the sky above me and I started running wildly, as if someone behind me had released the hounds.

Not all who wander are lost, but most of us are.

With every step I alternated between feeling weightless and too heavy to move. I resisted calling out, in fear I wouldn't recognise my own voice. I clambered down a rocky slope onto a dirt road and, reasoning that you can't be stranded if you keep in constant motion, kept on walking. It unsettled me to think who might come along. The sun was still high and garishly bright. My vision kept fogging up, like a windshield on a freezing cold day. Every breath felt like unfinished business.

In the hazy distance, I spotted a vehicle moving towards me. It grew closer: it was a bicycle rickshaw. The driver stopped in front of me and I was surprised to see a family of four squeezed into the back. The father greeted me with a mad stare while the doughy mother and their two children simply gawked. My mood: unconditional surrender.

'Speak English?' asked the driver.

'Yes,' I said. My voice came out in a whisper.

'You should've stayed at the centre,' the driver said. 'Someone would've picked you up.'

I didn't know what to say to that—I was preoccupied with my nudity.

'It's shameful,' the mother said.

'System's understaffed and overburdened,' said the father.

'Stay right here on this road,' she said, kindly. 'Someone will be by soon enough.'

I tried to look harmless, a negligible presence.

'I'm cold,' I said.

'What do you want—the clothes off our backs?' asked the father.

'Sure. I'll take those.'

'Can't spare any.'

'What about a lift?' I asked.

'Got the kids with us,' he said.

The father poked a finger at the driver's neck, impatient to get moving, and the driver started to pedal.

The little boy stood up and pointed at me. 'You're dead!'

'Don't be rude,' said his mother.

'He is, though!'

I scowled at the little shit.

'Good luck,' the father said and lifted an arm in farewell. The mud-stained rickshaw raised dust as they sped away.

The sun didn't seem to be going anywhere. Maybe it would be midday forever. I sat on a flat grey stone on the side of the road and dry-heaved. My mind was relieving itself like a bladder. I always thought I would be slowly driven crazy, but I *totally forgot* about psychotic breaks.

Then—coming along the road was another rickshaw. It didn't slow, and I was afraid it wouldn't stop, but it jarred to a halt at the last moment. The driver, a grey-haired man of indeterminate age, was panting as he leaned on the handlebars.

'I see you brought the good weather with you.'

'What?'

'Too soon?'

'What?'

'You should've stayed at the centre.'

'So I've heard.'

'Ride to town?'

'Please.'

'Let's go, come on. Vamos.'

I climbed onboard.

'Under the seat there's some activewear.'

I lifted the lid under the seat and picked out a grey cotton hoodie and tracksuit pants, slipping them on.

'How was your passing?'

'You mean, my . . .' I said, my voice faltering.

'Never mind. Buckle up.'

The rickshaw jerked forward and tossed me around as I frantically searched for the seatbelt. The driver turned back with an amused glint in his eye. 'That's only an expression. There are no buckles. Just hold on.'

The driver laboured to drive the rickshaw up out of the valley, up an absurdly steep rise. The road flattened out and then we were atop the mountain range, navigating treacherous hairpin turns. From the crest of the ridge, I looked down at the valley, a river far below. Then—a sad stretch of dusty, crabby road with no trees, nothing but mist rising from the large expanse of packed dry soil that looked like salt plains. It was an inhospitable nowhere of a place.

We reached a long dirt road with ploughed fields. It was desert hot but there was snow on the ground. I felt nauseated from the violent sway of the rickshaw and my mind was berserk and insensible with questions. I concentrated on the grass, the trees, the iron sky. Then—civilisation. Overgrown fields dotted with houses, rotting telegraph poles, chain-link fences, water tanks, dilapidated factories and, in the cool and glary dusk, a small village.

'What's that place?'

'Doesn't matter. That town's full. I'm taking you to the next one. It's much bigger.'

I sat stiffly, as if I had no moving parts.

My mind was a mess; it felt like, inside me, something new had scared off something old.

'Hey, buddy. Wake up.'

I let out a yawn that should've broken my jaw. Had I even been asleep? It was now night, and a dark-haired woman was shaking me. To the driver, she said: 'I'll take him from here.' She worked her mouth into a smile and said to me, 'Come on, sleepyhead.'

I scrambled down and stood dazed in the rickshaw's headlights. It looked like I'd arrived in a town square. There were people watching us from doorways. Were they defenceless strangers in a strange land too?

'I'm one of the welcome clerks and I'm here to get you settled,' she said. 'How was your passing?'

'It was traumatic.' I held out my trembling hands. 'I'm still shaking.'

'That'll pass,' she said. She handed me two pills and a bottle of water.

'Anti-virals.'

'What for?'

'Shingles. Nearly everyone gets them.' I popped the pills into my mouth and downed them with the water. 'Sorry there was no one to greet you at the arrival point.'

'Was there supposed to be?'

'You've died at a bad time.'

'I did?'

'All right. Let's get down to it. Can we walk and talk?' She took out a black notepad, poised her pen, and started moving off. I had to break into a trot to keep up with her. 'Name?'

'Angus Mooney.'

'Date of birth?'

'Twenty-third of May 1983.'

'Date of death?'

'So I am dead?'

'You're definitely on the spectrum.'

'What?'

'Joking. Do you remember the date?'

'The eighteenth, I think. May.'

'How did you die?'

'I don't want to talk about it.'

I didn't even want to *think* about my final moments; it was unbearable for too many reasons.

She hesitated, then gripped her pen tight. 'Occupation?'

'Wedding videographer.'

She wrote that down with a faint sneer.

The streets were alive with angry voices, strange accents, unfamiliar languages, tense arguments. My hearing went in and out; it felt like someone was wrapping and unwrapping my head in cotton wool. At an intersection, the pedestrian light was a red thumbs down. A man prodded my shoulder and said, 'Welcome, brother. How was your passing?'

'It sucked balls!'

He let out shouts of laughter and ducked into a doorway.

She said, 'I suppose you have some questions. You can ask them on the way.'

She hurried me down twisty, congested streets that all looked alike. Everywhere people jogged, staggered, eyed us from windows. I wondered if it was pragmatic to just fear the worst. There was a tumult of bells as we made our way through a mounting congestion of bicycles then turned down a long tree-lined avenue of skinny houses with darkened windows. 'Have I had a complete psychotic break?'

'I sure hope not,' she said, laughing. I laughed too, with delusional intensity, then stopped. Was that supposed to be funny?

'So I'm not in a persistent vegetative state?'

'No, Mr Mooney.' She seemed to mimic my smile rather than come up with one of her own.

We crossed a footbridge and then headed down a crowded cobblestone street washed in amber streetlights. Even though we were walking on a level road, I felt like I was making a backbreaking ascent.

I had avoided my real question, but now we had to get down to it. It was time to jettison a lifetime of non-belief. How embarrassing. Was I about to meet God face to Face? Or the Devil? Into which afterlife had I arrived? I couldn't see any souls flying forth in joy, and this certainly didn't feel like divine bliss, but there were no towering beasts with razor sharp fins or teeth either. Or were there?

'Have I gone to a better place?'

'Better than what?'

'Is this the Kingdom of Heaven? Or am I rotting in hell?'

'Neither.'

'Is this Purgatory? Or limbo?'

'Wrong on both counts.'

'Are we the damned?'

'That's subjective.'

'Did I go through a tunnel of light?'

'I don't know. Did you?'

Did I? I couldn't remember. 'What day is it?'

'Wednesday.'

'Does the Day of Atonement fall on a Wednesday?'

'What does that mean?'

'How did I get here?'

'You materialised.'

'Is this the same body I had before?'

'You are your quintessential shape.'

We passed a sidewalk café, a Vietnamese noodle place, a barbershop, a kebab joint, a nail salon and a bar, all of which were open, despite the late hour. 'Can I get back to my life?'

'No, but good for you.'

'Good for me?'

'Heidegger says that questions are the prayer of human thought.'

Heidegger? I'd had enough of this. 'Can I die here?'

'Obviously.'

I saw a man on a bicycle carrying a refrigerator on his back. That was some Cold War, Soviet-level shit.

'But if this is death, and you can die in death, where do you go from death when you die?'

'We'd all like to know the answer to that one.'

'So you're saying that non-being maybe isn't even a thing?'

'Mr Mooney,' she said, 'when I said a few questions . . .'

She looked stressed, overworked. She was guiding my elbow through another tangle of alleyways and narrow streets crammed with foot traffic. Were there more men than women, or more women than men? Did death have a gender bias? I saw glazed eyes, constipated smiles, hungover faces; I heard laughter, sneezes, whistling, bellyaching, mournful singing from broken apartment windows; in other words, the human race.

'I don't understand the laws of physics, but if I did, would this be within my expectations?'

She winced at that. 'Listen, you're not my only arrival. Can we get moving?'

I was trying her patience and she was trying mine. We hurried past a decrepit old man sucking the little bones off some kind of cooked bird and calling for his mother, a woman who I very much doubted was in the vicinity.

I couldn't stop myself from unleashing a barrage of questions: Did I have the same blood type? Where were my beard and tattoos? If souls were the ghosts in the machine, were we the ghosts, or the machines? Had I gone through a wormhole? Was this a simulacrum? Was I on the royal road to the unconscious? Was I a butterfly dreaming that I was a man? Did this have something to do with quantum weirdness? Was I both a wave and a particle?

She threw me a sidelong glance of disgust. 'Your questions are ridiculous. And by the way, before I forget, I have to inform you that smartphones and internet aren't consumer products and exist only for government and military use. So please don't beg me for a phone.'

'Do most people?'

'Hell yes.'

'Is my other body in a coffin somewhere in the ground?'

'How am I supposed to know that?'

'I mean, not all the dead are here.'

She breathed deeply and tried to regain an air of professionalism. 'That's right. We get approximately three-fifths of the world's dead.'

'Where's everybody else?'

'Could you shut up for a minute? You're asking a lot of questions, and things are really out of control here right now, and I'm not —'

'You don't know anything!'

'We know some things.'

My crotch began to itch. I had a rash where my thighs met my balls. 'Do you age?'

'Yes.'

'So there's disease. Like cancer?'

'Not *like* cancer. Cancer.'

'Is there free healthcare?'

'Yes.'

'Are we living inside a hologram?'

'No.'

'Will I see my wife again?'

'I don't know.'

I began to feel a rising tide of anger. I said: 'I'd be super satisfied with a gross oversimplification of what this is.'

'My job is to get you settled for the night. Can I just do that, please?'

It was exhausting holding back tears; pining for Gracie was already an intense, physical calamity. What was she doing right now? Checking my pulse, cradling my head, failing to resuscitate me?

'This is you,' the woman said, grinding her teeth and motioning to an eight-storey concrete building with an ominous lightning-shaped crack in its facade.

It felt like a trap. An old man squatted in the doorway, rocking to and fro. I hoped he wasn't defecating. He licked his lip in a way that made him look like he wanted to lick mine too.

'Excuse us,' she said, with mock cheerfulness. And to me: 'Watch your step, please.'

The lobby reeked of sweat and fried meat. In the murky light, a couple were fondling on the steps of a steep, circular staircase. The air was damp and hot. Shirtless, inebriated residents sat on the torn and stained couches—mostly black, Chinese and Middle Eastern men with stony gazes. I had a terrible feeling this would be a dorm situation.

'Do I get my own room?'

'Yes. Don't expect too much, though.'

The elevator doors glided open, revealing a small anaemic man who glared at me but didn't make a move to exit. He appeared to be living inside the elevator. Old books and records were piled from the floor to the ceiling, and against one wall was an army cot. There was only room for one other person.

'You take it,' the woman said. 'I'll meet you on the third floor.'

I got into the elevator. It moved grindingly slow. My claustrophobia was intensified by the elevator man's witchy smile, which had a veiled meaning I didn't want to get to the bottom of.

He said, 'Would you believe me if I told you that, if I had just expanded one quarter inch in every direction, I would have reached my potential?'

'I don't know what that means.'

'Don't you?'

On the third floor, the elevator doors opened and I hurried out, as if from a narrowly averted fist fight. The woman was waiting impatiently for me and resumed the tour before I was even by her side. 'The kitchen's communal. It's on the first floor. Showers are at the end of the hall. Garbage chute the other end. Recycling is optional.' She hurried me down the long dark hallway and opened an unlocked door. 'This is you.'

The cracked doorframe showed evidence of forced entry. That wasn't encouraging. It was a simple room with mustard-yellow walls and coal-black curtains to block out the sun, a kitchenette, and separate nook for the bed. At the far end was a sloped ceiling to bang my head on.

She motioned to a doorless toilet. 'Don't flush anything larger or harder than a shit.'

Beyond the curtains was a balcony too small for anything other than a child's foot.

She spoke so quickly her sentences practically overlapped. 'Air conditioning ducts are taped shut for a reason—do not remove the tape. As I mentioned, there's a cafeteria downstairs and you may eat there for two weeks. You probably won't be able to hold down any solids for a few days.'

From the floor above, I could hear the creaking of footsteps.

She snapped her fingers. 'Okay, let's finish up so I can get the hell out of here.' She fumbled in her bag for a thermometer and stuck it in my mouth. 'Ninety-eight point six,' she said approvingly, then attached a cuff to my upper arm and took my blood pressure. 'Ninety over sixty—a little low. Drink a lot of fluids today.'

She opened an ink pad and her notepad. 'Right thumb here,' she said, as if I hadn't been fingerprinted multiple times before.

After I made my thumb print, she tore off a carbon copy from the notebook and gave it to me. 'Interim Death Certificate. Keep this on your person at all times.' I looked at the paper—the writing was so small I couldn't even read it. Was it in English?

She handed me an envelope. Inside were discount restaurant vouchers, ads for massage parlours, brochures for clothing stores, and a plastic credit card.

'Anyway, you must be tired. And thirsty. And horny. Eager to masturbate.'

'Well, I —'

She looked like she no longer wanted to breathe the same air as me. 'I'll leave you alone so you can attend to your needs.'

She headed to the door.

'Wait.'

'What?'

I wanted to say that I felt embarrassed—I had put all my eggs in the basket of bodily death and personality extinction, because faith was so human, and humans so defined by self-deception, and the human mind programmed only for survival and not for truth, and I had always been certain that the fine tuning of our solar system producing life on earth had been a total fluke, so it was shocking to now discover, so late in the day, that my *soul* existed and even had enough value not to have been tossed in some cosmic shredder. I didn't even know if any of this made a supernatural intelligence more likely, and even if it did, if it had a name, and if we could put a face to the name.

Instead, I just said, 'Do you have a cigarette?'

'Tobacco doesn't grow here,' she answered, moving rapidly out the door.

I crossed the rickety floorboards to the small window that looked out over the town with glimpses of a river. It looked like the earth I knew, but I supposed it wasn't. I still wasn't convinced this wasn't a bad dream or some kind of Matrix. I concentrated hard, hoping to trigger a clairvoyant episode. I felt tense and exposed. I also wanted to brush my teeth.

On the small table was a radio. I turned it on. The voice said, 'Warlords in the area defying orders of senior military figures began their campaign . . .'

I turned it off and sat motionless in the cold light, gazing around the suffocating room. In the dull silver of a wall mirror I looked at myself and thought: I can't even take my own face at face value.

I collapsed on the bed, on its too-soft mattress, and panted like a dog after a run. It had been a while, but it was time to bring out all my childhood fears and be afraid of them again.

8

I woke blinded by the cloudy sunlight. It was a double dislocation—waking from one dream world into another dream world. Out the window, a brown river, narrow streets, and the coloured rooftops of squat buildings. 'Oh, that's right,' I said to myself. 'You're dead, motherfucker.'

In the shower stall in the communal bathroom, an unspeakably tough-looking pubic hair lay on the drain. There was one humungous tap. I turned it—no water. I stood naked, staring up at the dry showerhead, thinking anyplace without Gracie was the very bowels of hell.

A man with a thick face came into the bathroom. He gave me an indifferent smile.

'Morning,' I said.

'Hey,' he said, groggily. He removed his robe and entered the shower stall next to mine and put a coin in an oblong metal box I hadn't noticed before. Oh—the showers were coin-operated. He turned his tap and water sprayed out.

I said, 'Brother, can you spare a coin?'

He fondled his long, narrow dick ostentatiously and, without looking at me, reached over to his metal purse with his other hand.

'Just one.'

'Thank you.'

They weren't coins, but tokens that operated the tepid shower for a minute and a half with minimal water pressure. That ninety seconds still dragged on, however, because I spent the whole time failing to think of something that wouldn't upset me.

I no longer believed I was the victim of an elaborate prank—I was actually dead, and mistaken about everything. I dried my uncanny body with a small coarse towel. It had always seemed to me that eighty to ninety years of consciousness was more than plenty. Now what? The mind is like a radio you can *never* turn off? The concept was ungraspable. I wanted to hide under bedcovers and shoot heroin.

I got back to my room to find a short piggish man standing awkwardly by my window, silhouetted by wide shafts of bright daylight.

'How was your first night's sleep after the upheaval?' he asked.

'What do you want?'

'Just a minute of your time. I'll make it quick. You're due at orientation before your CEA appointment.'

'CEA?'

'Central Employment Agency.'

'I have to get a job?'

'You weren't told?'

He made a note of that in a small notebook. He'd come, in fact, to evaluate the clerk who had processed me. He wanted to know if I felt welcomed, if she'd managed my terror and confusion, and what I would rate her professionalism out of 5000. I said in the high 3700s—that seemed plausible. I just wanted the surveyor out of my apartment.

'I should go, then, so I don't miss orientation.'

'You can catch a later session if you miss today. Did she tell you this accommodation is temporary and you might be resettled?'

'No.'

'You must be screened and evaluated. You'll be allocated to the appropriate region, depending on current quotas and resources. And we need you to be self-sufficient as quickly as possible. Tell me, did she answer all or most of your questions to your satisfaction?'

'Not even close.'

'Please name the questions she was unable to answer so we are better able to assist you.'

I repeated the unanswered questions, and added a few supplementary ones: Was I going to meet God? Was sin a thing after all? Was redemption pointless? Did *most* people feel dissatisfied with their lifespan? And what was the etiquette here? Should I offer condolences to everyone I met? And where were our whereabouts? Had we left earth or hadn't we? Did universal laws apply—did all states still drift towards entropy? Were *any* of the major religions even in the ballpark? Did the soul regenerate a body from memory? What was our death expectancy?

He said, 'Woah, we got a live one here.'

I kept going: 'How much of me is me? Is my genetic material identical? Have my fingerprints changed?'

'Why would you want to know that?'

I didn't know. I just couldn't stop myself. Was this where the hidden knowledge was hidden? Was I still human or was I just in human form? Did this have something to do with the singularity? What about the ninety-nine percent of species that became extinct—were they here? Mammoths? Sabre-toothed cats? Giant sloths?

He gazed at me as if he'd discovered the source of all human headaches.

'Oh, forget it,' I said. 'Where's orientation?'

He told me, and I headed off into the ordinary town—nothing heavenly about it. There were powerlines and storm drains and stop signs and garbage trucks and pot holes and men catcalling women. There were bicyclists ignoring traffic signals and pedestrians avoiding buskers and drunks yelling at nobody. There were old men with sunburnt faces sitting on milk crates drinking espresso and women walking with linked arms, loud-talking over each other. For about two minutes I wanted to shout howdy to everybody and applaud wildly. We had all died, and yet here we were. Somebody's *good riddance* hadn't worked on us—that was something!

At the end of a large, tree-lined avenue, I found the sandstone town hall where orientation was taking place. Men and women poured down the steps, shell-shocked, agape or breathlessly chattering. An unshaven official with a beer gut was perched on a stool, barking 'Good luck!' at everyone. He was flanked on either side by sentries in military uniforms, rifles in their hands.

'Is this where the orientation is?'

'Was. It's over.'

'When's the next one?'

'In two hours.'

'Okay.'

'But it's full.'

'When's the next one after that?'

'In four hours, but that's full too.'

'When's the next one that *isn't* full?'

He looked like a man who had to work on Christmas morning without holiday pay. 'That's going to be tough,' he said. 'We're over capacity. It's been crazy around here.' He leaned forward with his mouth half-open, as if considering whether or not to launch into a rambling monologue, but settled on adding, more sympathetically: 'You died at a bad time.'

'So I've been told.'

'Come back later and check in, see if someone else misses theirs.'

Not knowing what else to do, I roamed the town and its strange districts. This place was architecturally confused: grey, narrow streets, buildings tall enough to induce vertigo, strange labyrinths of little squares, old stone houses, dingy cafés, hidden alleys, wide leafy boulevards with ornate street lamps and upmarket restaurants next to neighbourhoods that looked to have been going downhill for years, unpaved backstreets of cracked terrace houses with shuttered windows, sinuous mud pathways, brick walls on the verge of collapse, terminally ill trees. It was as if the whole dumbfounded place wanted to be all things to all people, and failed. Commercially, there were the usual suspects: supermarkets, coffee shops, discount furniture stores. It was an afterlife without a single unheard-of business venture. I heard French, Spanish, Mandarin and Urdu. I saw Nigerians, Koreans, Egyptians and Mexicans. Each member of this human fog looked robust and healthy and made an excessive amount of eye contact. A common destiny didn't make anyone smile. In fact, this world seemed populated entirely by people who used to laugh more.

I moved through a landscape of metal fences, rows of dead yellow flowers and gaunt trees against the blue-grey sky. The footpaths were grimy and cracked, and laundry was drying in the windows of small houses set in plots of brown grass. A guy in overalls pushing a broom gave me a cute little wink and I thought: Wow, imagine dying and then transmogrifying into a flirtatious streetcleaner.

I walked up a hill to a small park and sat on a wrought-iron bench and watched the creep of clouds above. I was still hoping to catch sight of an angel. And what about biodiversity? There were mobs of men and women, but where were the flocks? The gaggles? The herds? The packs? Where were the ant armies and clouds of insects? I hadn't seen a mosquito here, or a fly, or a bee. The complete absence of birds was ominous. This seemed to be the type of place where there'd be more human centipedes than centipedes. I wanted a drink, a cigarette, and twin sets of bosoms to cry into. I wanted someone to take my hand and say, 'I'm so, *so* sorry you are dead.'

For a few silent minutes in the lazy warmth of that blaring sun, I thought how far away Gracie felt—not just in space, but in time—and yet I couldn't shake the feeling that if I reached out blindly in the right direction, I could touch her. Was this hell after all? I stood and looked squarely at all the passing faces—did everyone look like unrepentant killers or child molesters? I couldn't tell. I felt like I had outsourced my internal locus of control, but to whom? Or was I being too sensitive? Were they just walking, or were they on some kind of murderous prowl? The feeling I had was of incomplete horror, like this might be my worst nightmare or it might be just fine.

I left the park and wandered through the streets. In a shop window, I pressed my face to the cold glass and thought about all my lifetime guarantees that had just expired. The teenagers inside the shop made faces at me. I gave them the finger and they returned the gesture. It was the first interaction since arriving that I had completely understood.

The smell of fried cheese drifted through the open doorway of a café. I was starving. I ran inside a supermarket crowded with languid shoppers. Basket in hand, I threw in bread, cheese, peanut butter, strawberries and processed slices of unspecified meat. It was so weird to be dead and running errands. I couldn't help feeling limited, human, dirtbound. My past life was only yesterday. Already I understood that, in an eternity with oneself, familiarity breeds contempt.

At the check-out, I glanced at the newspaper headlines: SECRETARY ACCUSES MINISTER TESHIMA OF SEXUAL ASSAULT, BRYSON RETURNED TO JAIL, REDLAND REPELS INVASION, THOUSANDS BURIED IN MUD SLIDE. I wasn't up for this unexpected level of reality and it set off a dizziness, an unspooling sensation. The man behind me was breathing hotly on my neck.

I turned and asked him, 'What's this town called?'

'Lagaria.'

I handed over the card to the cashier, a man with half-closed eyes.

'You have insufficient funds for all these items,' he said.

'What can I get?'

'Just the loaf of bread. And the raisins.'

'How do I buy the rest?'

'How do you think, genius?' the man behind me said, and I knew the answer, I just didn't want to accept it.

9

The employment officer's mouth was so small, I couldn't imagine how it functioned as an orifice. I thought of all those people who had worked themselves into an early grave and were then marched from the cemetery right back to the office.

I said, 'Isn't there any kind of welfare I could apply for?'

'Not anymore,' he said. 'Budget cuts. It says here you were a wedding videographer. That won't come in handy. You have what we call a non-transferable skill set. Tell me what other positions you held.'

'I don't want to tell you what I did because I don't want to do them again.'

'That's unacceptable.'

'I'm sorry.'

We were already in an uncomfortable stand-off. Behind him were shelves that were empty except for a pile of bulldog clips and a coffee mug. I thought: This netherworld is inconceivable—in that, who would conceive of a place so banal? There was nothing mind-boggling about it; it was petty, bureaucratic. I thought: I worked my guts out all my life and never really derived a sense of purpose from it. Working, for me, meant never being equal to any assigned task, never being up to scratch, and clocking off with the suspicion that I was living the wrong life.

He said, patiently, 'Perhaps you can help with the war effort?'

'What war?'

'I don't have time to give you a history lesson. How about landscaping?'

'Meh,' I said.

He slumped in his chair as if I'd already broken his spirit. 'Tell me your *entire* employment history. Everyone has to register their professional qualifications and degrees. And please be honest. You'd be surprised how many people lie about their education and credentials. We can't exactly check records or contact references, but you will be tested and vetted thoroughly, so please don't say you were a surgeon if you were in fact a nurse—you'll only wind up in jail, or worse. Full compliance is as much for your benefit as it is for ours, Mr Mooney.'

In the silence that followed, I wished I'd had the presence of mind to begin this afterlife under an assumed name. What even were my skills, besides basic carpentry, shoplifting, card shuffling and getting extra life from batteries by turning them around? And what was my dream job? I couldn't recall a single wild employment fantasy.

'Well?'

I remembered that I used to imagine being a friend/butler to a wealthy philanthropist, visiting charities and consulting with the needy to make sure their needs were met—that seemed like nonsense now.

The employment officer was breathing hard, and I wondered if he ever contemplated the irony of working in the Department of Employment when his own job seemed a massive, dull mistake.

'Tell me, Angus. Did you leave someone behind?'

'A wife. She's pregnant.'

His face softened with gentle concern.

'There are communes in the outer zone that you are welcome to join,' he said.

'Communes!'

'A collective community, much like a kibbutz. About forty miles to the west. You'd work the orchards, or the fields, and in return you'll be housed and fed. You live and eat with others. It's easier to form attachments there than here in town.'

His voice drifted off, and I almost fell off my chair. I felt as if my brain had shrunk and motion was causing it to hit the sides of my skull. My jaw felt cumbersome. And had my exposure to the overbright sun here left a psychedelic residue on my retina?

He leaned heavily over the desk and asked: 'Are you still experiencing issues of synchronisation? Perceptual hallucinations, audible mistiming, tidal-motion balance issues?'

'Yes. What is that?'

'You should have learned all this in orientation.'

'I missed orientation.'

He sighed loudly. 'Your soul—for want of a better word—has not aligned with your body in perfect synthesis. You're carrying quite a cognitive load. Your whole physiological apparatus is askew. Recalibration doesn't happen overnight. Therefore, action is required: anything that concentrates the mind and is also mindless. Physical repetition of the mechanical kind aids with reconstitution. You don't want your interim state to become permanent.'

'I have no idea what you're talking about.'

'And I don't have time to sit here and interrogate the meaning of work. Take mind–body realignment as work's specific objective for today. Tomorrow will take care of itself.'

'What do you mean?'

'Until we find the right position for you, I'm going to start you off making umbrellas.'

'Umbrellas? You're shitting me.'

I felt like this was a punchline to an easy joke, and I didn't get it.

10

There were a dozen workshops in the constructibles factory in the industrial sector, making everything from kettles to toothpicks. About twenty of us were assigned to the umbrella division, and it was plain to see by the muddled expressions that my co-workers were equally mystified as to why they were making umbrellas, of all things.

'I'm glad you all made it,' the supervisor said. Did he mean to the factory, or to the afterlife?

The supervisor explained we'd be divided into four groups to do the job: the first would narrow birchwood shafts down to fit the handle, the second would bend wire into a triangular shape and hammer it flat, the third would attach the ribs to the shaft, while the fourth would sew the canopy to the ribs of the umbrella. We all stood there in smocks, like, Who are we right now? It was hard to know if this was day one of eternal punishment or if we were lucky to be in gainful employment. Nothing was clear. Were we answering for our crimes right here, right now? We had wasted our lives—must we waste our deaths too? The banality was almost titillating.

The floor had a thin layer of sawdust that got stirred up when anybody moved. We eyed the supervisor suspiciously—surely we were deserving of an almost supernatural amount of sympathy, yet he made a real show of not caring. One of the workers touched me gently on the back and said, 'Stay close.' He seemed to be under the impression we were in some sort of concentration camp. That opened the floodgates, and we quickly bonded over our complaints: the sun was despotic, our living quarters back in town were cramped, the drinking water tasted like old fingernails, and where were we anyway? On a planet? In a dimension? A petri dish? Nobody was sure. Even those who insisted we were 'here for a reason' admitted the whole thing felt arbitrary.

We introduced ourselves and I immediately forgot all but three names in our odd group. Kira was an Irish woman who wouldn't stop taking deep breaths and repeating the words 'stay calm, Kira'. Joseph was a thirty-year-old from Nigeria who paced the room incessantly, using the sound of his own footsteps as a sort of incantation. Farhad was a middle-aged Iranian who kept saying, 'Let's just get to work,' thinking that further punishment awaited us for dawdling.

Everything was a source of confusion, from the constant grating sound of machines from adjacent workshops to the resinous, unplaceable odour that filled the workspace.

'Why are we even doing this?' Kira asked no one in particular. 'Why are we doing what we're told?'

I suspected that our souls had been taken from us and we had to work for their return, but I kept this to myself.

Farhad waved a hammer in the air. 'I was exceedingly busy for forty years. I never said no to a single request. So let's just get to work. It is what it is.'

Stoic people exhaust me. I needed to see the slightest touch of hysteria in someone's response to an emergency or I just assumed the person was a psychopath.

Joseph clasped his hands on Kira's shoulders. 'You look tense. Would you like a massage?'

'Hey, bossman! Get this creep's hands off me!' She metoo'd him and it wasn't even ten in the morning. Joseph held his wrists behind his back, as if to prepare for handcuffs. It seemed we were all doing cruel impressions of ourselves.

We spent the morning learning how to shape the wooden shaft to a precise diameter of 12 millimetres. We worked in silence, a bunch of scared strangers from all walks of life making umbrellas like it was our sacred destiny to do so, an outcome so bizarre that all morning I wondered if I wasn't being controlled somehow. Was I operating under my own free will or was I, in reality, just some rando's avatar?

Nobody wanted to be alone. When someone went to the bathroom, the rest of us had to resist tagging along. We didn't want to admit that the afterlife felt like a demotion. And the employment agent hadn't been kidding—we were all misaligned; a feeling of incongruity hovered over everything and, every now and then, one of us would lose our balance and fall over or freeze catatonically to the spot.

'Just clap your hands loudly in his ear,' the supervisor said when Joseph was frozen in place. 'That'll restart his engines.'

On our lunch break, we sat in a carpeted vestibule area and ate noodles drenched in orange sauce and eyed each other curiously. Were there any conclusions we could infer from the demographic make-up of our little group? We were men and women, white, black, Middle Eastern, Asian. The youngest was in their twenties, the oldest mid-seventies.

All were obsessed with the sad circumstances of their deaths—I was no different. A sad-eyed Spaniard had been the victim of someone with a literal axe to grind. Joseph was a war zone surgeon; his hands were so badly burned he couldn't operate, his last moments spent instructing a twelve-year-old girl how to remove shrapnel from a lung.

'Now look at them,' he said, holding up perfect, unblemished human hands.

'It's a miracle,' Farhad said, himself having succumbed to an antibiotic-resistant staph infection.

Out the window we watched men in combat fatigues, guns slung over their shoulders, move down the street. Were they on our side? Was this a place of nations? Of states? What about the grotesque spectacle of patriotism? How had people arranged themselves tribally? I hoped nationalism was dead. Of all the arbitrary distinctions made between people, the longitudinal and latitudinal happenstance of birth always seemed to rank among the most meaningless.

I asked, 'Does anyone know the form of government here?'

'Democratic,' Joseph said.

'Oh, okay.'

'You prefer fascism?'

'No, democracy's fine.' It might've been nice to have an enlightened despot for a change.

For the remainder of the workday, my questions persisted: Was consumerism still the axis by which the world revolved? Were too-young girls still eroticised to sell products? Were white people still afraid of black violence? Did a predatory free market set the rules? What the fuck was the social contract here anyway?

At four p.m. the supervisor said, 'Great work, everybody. Now follow me!'

We were herded down a staircase to a fluorescent-lit room with rows of computer terminals. We were ordered into seats and shuddered at the sight of our uncanny faces reflected in the computers' blank screens.

'Listen up,' said the supervisor. 'At the end of every day, you will come down here and spend one hour answering questions with brutal honesty. And I mean brutal. Don't hold back, now.'

He started the timer. We put on headphones and a soft, monotone voice came through: 'This is your Evaluation of Record. There will be one hundred and seventy thousand questions to answer unselfconsciously—not all today. Ha-ha.'

I turned to Joseph: 'Did your computer just laugh at its own joke?'

He didn't hear me. A barrage of questions came through, appearing on the screen simultaneously. I was struggling to answer one when the next question popped up.

Were you more afraid of (a) a claw, (b) a beak, or (c) a palsied hand? What percentage of your proudest moment was you play-acting with your transitory self? The questions were perplexing, clumsily worded, and oftentimes leading: *Name a single life choice not born of imitation. What age did you first contemplate suicide not as a reason to punish loved ones? Is there anyone you wanted to have sexual relations with but didn't for fear of an indelible moral stain? What form of salvation were you least repelled by? Other than orgasms, what is your preferred method of self-soothing? How often did a guilty conscience cause you to act worse, and not better? Which platitudes did you most commonly utter yet didn't comprehend? Describe a moment your moral backbone either bent or snapped entirely due to reflexes or group pressure. Which of your preferred sexual positions could be also interpreted as antisocial behaviour?*

It was exhausting. An hour later, we were escorted to the exit, where we entered our credit cards into a slot in a large triangular prism. It emitted a low hum and when the card slid out I was

$112 richer. I moved quietly away, up the back staircase and out of the factory.

It was raining, sort of—an intermittent rainfall reminiscent of an air conditioner leak. My body felt like slush. There was a chlorine taste in my mouth, my skin exuded a white foam, like the residue of sunscreen, and I felt hot, as if the day's sunlight was trapped inside my body. I was barely in control of myself, as if all my nerves had come loose and were flopping around like live wires.

It wasn't the worst workday I'd ever had, but then on my way home I got stuck on a tram with a bunch of former Make-a-Wish Foundation teens who were critiquing each other's wishes.

I needed a drink.

11

My neighbourhood bar, the Bitter in Soul, was run by a Scotsman named Cragg who hated bars and human voices. It was a bare-bones space with empty beer kegs for bar stools and a louche, bad-tempered clientele who nursed their terrors with hard spirits. I couldn't name half the accents, nor could I recognise a quarter of the languages.

I sat at the bar and ordered a Moscow mule. The alcohol quickly got to the point. The guy on the adjoining stool had been a history teacher and, even though he'd been dead for a year, he was still bitching about his students. I shuffled down a few stools and drank until I was enveloped in a warm mist.

'Being dead is emasculating,' I heard a man say. A whiny, high-pitched voice added: 'I travelled from earth to here and I've never even been on a plane.'

At the pool table, a fight broke out. A man with heavy eyebrows shouted, 'You cunt!' and his pot-bellied companion replied, 'Don't speak ill of the dead!' Both men erupted in laughter. This was the perfect place for me: a dimly lit, mirrorless room where the drinks were cheap, the popcorn on the house, and the dead gathered to contemplate their lot.

At two a.m., everyone ran outside for a drunken game of soccer in the starlit, dusty street. As we kicked the ball around, a fight broke out between those with differing accounts of their rebirth. Some people claimed they saw a tunnel of white light, some swore they passed through a lake of fire, another said she was carried up and dumped here by a gigantic wave. It seemed like each hour we discarded more weird ideas than we'd had in our entire lives.

Back inside, we drank with increasing urgency. We formed a loose circle and played 'Last Words', an impromptu game in which we revealed our final, dying words.

One drunk woman: 'Be right back.'

A gap-toothed man: 'I just need to sit for a minute.'

A sick and fascinated laughter erupted. This was a pretty funny game. Last words are, by their very nature, futile; I suppose that's what makes them funny. Voices on the verge of hysteria uttered a few more: 'Leave him alone.' And: 'Nurse!' And: 'Hurry up.' And: 'I can reach it.'

Then it was my turn.

'I think I just said, "Gracie, Gracie." I was calling for my wife. She was downstairs while I was being murdered upstairs.'

This only elicited a few chuckles.

The young red-eyed man next to me recounted his last words: 'I said, "Run, child, run! Find your mother!"'

Nobody laughed. The mood turned maudlin. The manic drowning of hard spirits continued, but the game didn't seem so funny after that.

THREE

'The idea that the world exists is not acceptable to me.'

Ghalib

12

Let's go back—

'Get him a glass of water,' Gracie said.

'You think that's some kind of medical breakthrough?' I said. 'A glass of water?'

Through the walls, our dying guest's hacking cough was getting on our nerves. A minute later, his bed was squeaking.

'What's *that* noise?'

'When you've eliminated the impossible, whatever remains, however improbable —'

'He's masturbating?'

'Elementary.'

The squeaking continued with tragic insistence. Gracie cringed painfully. 'I've heard about dying men's libidos. They want to fuck everything.'

'Let's tell him to keep his hands out of his pockets.'

One week in and living with Owen was already intolerable.

He was a lousy house guest in all the normal ways people are lousy house guests—a compulsive midnight eater who emptied the refrigerator one yoghurt at a time, a slob who left pubic hairs on the soap, a son of a bitch who squashed a huntsman spider with our wedding album—but he was also a lousy house guest in his own particular way.

Around midday, he would plod down the stairs, swaddled in a blanket that dragged on the dusty floor, and stand in the kitchen like he was in a queue. Afternoons, he would pace the living room denouncing western medicine, or he would squash himself into the armchair, sucking his way through a packet of Werther's Originals, watching TV and commenting on developing news stories: the global recession picking up speed, arsonists in Canada setting fire to solar-power fields of artificial sunflowers, doctors throwing up their hands and declaring the official end of the antibiotic era, the canine virus spreading to parts of Scandinavia and as far east as Latvia. Now foxes, coyotes, wolves and jackals were being exterminated as the virus reproduced itself across canine species. Owen watched this latest shit show with a mix of dull horror and glee.

At dinner, he would stare miserably at us with the look of a man who endlessly rotated through the same exact three negative thoughts. At night, his insomnia was chronic; he would surprise us by bathing at two a.m. with the lights out or lying half-naked on the couch or trudging through the dark house, catching his bathrobe on a door-handle and causing doors to slam and lamps to tumble from sidetables.

Often, he sat grim-faced outside in the dark, on the tree stump or on the very step where his father died. The old fool had fallen into the sinkhole of dying with no bucket list at all, apparently, and he was content to bide his time on the porch with a thermos like he was paid to be there, our own night watchman. When I stepped outside to join him, he looked at me as if I was out of my jurisdiction.

Sometimes, when Mrs Henderson's hairless dog barked from over the fence, he barked back. That's the kind of man he was.

Clinging to an overall feeling of shame was the only thing keeping him afloat. He asked us to turn up the TV because he had psychogenic urinary retention—a bashful bladder—and couldn't pee when others were in earshot. When we caught him staring at himself in the hallway mirror, he said how he felt 'mortified to no longer be associated with all that I had once personified', whatever that meant. Later that day, in the kitchen, he tasted one scoop of ice-cream from the carton then tossed it on the floor because he found it 'embarrassing to have entered a mental space in which all gratification is unsatisfying'. And most humiliating of all, he said, looking at my list of last year's New Year's resolutions stuck to the fridge, was the whole concept of self-improvement. 'Ugh. To have once been in thrall to one's potential!'

'Jesus Christ, Owen,' I said. 'What *don't* you find embarrassing?'

He thought about that. 'At the end of a human life, the only thing that is definitely *not* embarrassing are the compromises,' he said. 'Thank God I folded on that issue, didn't hang on to that idea, was not too trenchant on this or that position. Thank God I bent . . .'

Now, the bed in the adjacent room stopped squeaking, leaving a fraught and terrible silence.

I said, 'We should've limited him to the ground floor.'

It was deathly quiet—as in, maybe he was dead. Someone had to investigate.

I nudged Gracie. 'You go.'

'*You* go.'

'We'll both go.'

We crept like cat burglars down the hallway and double-dared each other to peek through the door's crack. Owen was alive and squinting at what looked like a CT scan or an X-ray flattened against the lampshade. He turned his sad glare on us, which we took as an invitation to barge in. He smiled bleakly yet avoided eye contact. The medical images pinned up against the lampshade gave the room an eerie quality.

'Shouldn't these be with your doctor?' I asked.

'I am a doctor.'

We let that sit for a moment—who ever heard of a doctor not announcing their credentials within the first thirty seconds of conversation?

'You didn't tell us that!'

'I retired a year ago.'

Owen flopped on his bed and tried to get comfortable; he flipped on his side, then on his back, then angrily sat with his knees bunched up to his chest. Gracie squatted down beside him. 'Are you okay?'

'Far from it.'

She placed her hand on Owen's forehead. 'You're not warm.'

'You don't really know anything about brain disease, do you?'

That wasn't unfunny—yet nobody laughed. Owen's smile looked like a wound that had sealed over. I noticed him gazing at Gracie's cleavage like he was considering it for his final resting place.

'Could you make me a ham and cheese sandwich?' Owen asked Gracie. 'In my condition, it's difficult to —'

'With pleasure,' I said, quickly. Why shouldn't I wait on this creep hand and foot? You get tired of being lazy. I made a bow of exaggerated servility and, as I trudged downstairs, I predicted that the phrase *In my condition* was how his sentences would increasingly begin.

In the kitchen, I made him a sandwich without washing my hands, then took it upstairs. I stood outside Owen's room, eavesdropping on his conversation with Gracie.

'The doctor is dauntingly neutral,' Owen was saying. 'He has no skin in the game. For him, the difference between *it's terminal* and *it's benign* affects only his mood on his evening commute home. Anyway, as far as I remember, I called Dr Kosinski's mother a whore, whimpered in the elevator, and on the street grabbed a shopkeeper's hand. That was the extent of my mourning.'

'This reminds me of my grandma,' Gracie said. 'When they told her that she had stage-four lymphoma, she went to the beach and slept all night on the sand.'

'You must have had an easy life.'

'Why do you say that?'

'Anyone whose biggest trauma is the passing of their grandparents had an easy life.'

'You don't know the first thing about me.'

'You're right, sorry,' he said, and switched to talking about how he had learned how to manage his own expectations too late, but that he didn't regret not raising children, *and* that he never had a pug as a substitute, so that was a victory of sorts, didn't she think?

Not that I needed any more clues, but it was clear that our dying house guest was infatuated with my wife, and hitting on her in his own sad way. In fact, other than placing a bowl of potpourri in the bathroom, his main contribution to the household was a suffocating atmosphere of sleazy panic.

'You should stop drinking so much tea, Gracie. Lead isn't good for the foetus.' He adopted a clinical tone that sounded like a foreign accent. 'I've noticed that by ten a.m. your caffeine intake already exceeds the recommended two-hundred milligrams.'

Gracie brought the conversation back to her grandmother's cancer—how her post-chemo wig had lice, how she grew offended when Gracie's mother hung pine-tree air fresheners around her bed, and how, as the end grew near, she faced it bravely, just like Owen was doing now.

'Gracie, I know you mean well, but would you please stop comparing my death to the death of some old lady?'

'Sorry.'

'No. I'm sorry. I'm in a strange mood tonight.'

For the record, Owen had said, 'Sorry, I'm in a strange mood tonight,' four nights running.

There was a loud clatter. 'I'm going to miss watching people drop their phones,' he said, wistfully. 'Why are you always holding your phone, even in your house?'

'I don't always.'

'Yes. You do.'

'Any dying wishes before I go to bed?'

'Just one.'

'What it is?'

'Can I see your breasts?'

'No, you can't, Owen.'

'Then nothing. Thanks.'

Gracie abruptly exited and literally bumped into me in the hallway, and I almost dropped Owen's sandwich. When I entered his room, he had a surly look on his face.

'You took your sweet time,' he said, taking the plate from my outstretched hand as if we were master and servant in a story set in the distant past. He took one bite of the sandwich then tossed it aside. 'That's the irony of life. Just when you no longer care about watching your weight, you lose your appetite.'

I stared too long into the freaked-out mirrors of his eyes. All my own thoughts arrived nowhere. I said, 'Any dying wishes before *I* go to bed?'

Owen made a leave-now motion with his hand.

When I got back to our bedroom, Gracie was hunched over her phone in the dark, the white glow on her face. I said, 'About the deal we made with Owen.'

'What about it?'

'We should've haggled.'

'Maybe.'

'I wish he'd die so fast he leaves a cloud of dust.'

'He won't.'

'Why can't he say, *And without further ado*, and then keel over?'

'Mooncy.'

I snapped my fingers. 'Why don't we go up to Lennox Head, rent a place? The deal didn't specify that we needed to remain in the house. We leave for two months and come back when he's dead. Call in the coroner, then a fumigator, and it'll be like it never happened.'

It was weird we hadn't thought of that earlier. Why should we hang about, waiting for this stranger to die? Our deal was the location of his death, not that we bear witness to all his final agonies.

'We have to be with him,' she insisted.

'Why?'

'Because no one else will.' Gracie picked up an unlit cigarette. 'Everything in life is fifteen percent worse without smoking.' She started sucking on it pointlessly. 'I think Owen's still in shock.'

'From what?'

'His diagnosis.'

It made perfect sense that one might sustain more trauma from a fatal diagnosis than a fatal illness itself, but something else occurred to me. How come we hadn't known he was a doctor? I reached for my laptop.

'Why haven't we googled him yet?'

Google informed us that Dr Owen Fogel MD attained his medical degree at the University of Western Sydney, interned at Westmead Hospital, co-owned a private practice in Redfern East with a

Dr Nilesh Patel, lectured part-time at the University of Sydney, and received an average review of one star from the website Rate My Doctor.

'One star!' Gracie said. 'That's shit.'

'You sure it's him?'

'Look.'

The striking young man in the photo was unmistakably Owen—he had the same cold, glassy eyes that came with the implied warning: *Disturb at your own peril.* The review headlines—AVOID. SUB-PAR. WTF?!—were unpromising. For the next half-hour, we read bad review after bad review. For example:

> So many red flags. He walked into the examination room hyperventilating, as if he was coming down from a fit of rage. And he's extremely suspicious. When you tell him your symptoms, he looks at you as if you're trying to rope him into a pyramid scheme. Avoid this doctor at all costs. One star.

> Dr Fogel was dismissive of my complaint, asked no questions, and while taking my blood he went off on a long monologue about how much he resents Dr Patel, the other doctor in his practice. When my screening test came back positive for Lyme disease, he said, 'C'est la vie.' Never going back. One star.

> I came in to have a cyst lanced. He groaned with impatience and boredom, as if he had already diagnosed me the previous night in a dream. Then I told him I drink eight beers a night, every night, and he wrote down 'social drinker' and winked at me. One star.

Gracie, over my shoulder, said, 'Here's a positive one.'

> I want to say something about the other reviews here. It's true Dr Fogel is a man who always seems to be in his saddest hour, and sometimes looks at you as if you are the ghost of his childhood bully, but Dr Fogel is an absolutely phenomenal diagnostician. He can recite my medical history by heart even with a year between visits. By far one of the best doctors I have ever had. Just don't be surprised if he cries. Three stars.

I said, 'This weird creep is living in our house.'

'*Dying* in our house.'

'I can't say for sure, but he seems the type of man who'd train his dog to bark at people of colour.'

'You don't know that.'

We didn't know anything. It was weird to make a man's acquaintance at the very end of his life; whatever personality he had left was strictly residue.

Gracie fell asleep and I lay awake for another hour, going deep down pathetic internet rabbit holes, watching videos of otters taking baths, penny-farthing bike races, et cetera, all the while unable to dislodge the unsettling feeling that we had invited something nefarious into our house and that the price to pay would be way out of our emotional and psychic budget.

Before I shut down the computer for the night, I took one last look at his Rate My Doctor page. Here is another review I came across:

> He did everything right. He was courteous and he diagnosed my condition right away. He prescribed the right medicine and sent my test results as soon as they became available.

> But since my visit, I've had three bad dreams about him. I don't know. It's three a.m. and I just woke up from another nightmare. Fuck this sleepy town. And fuck Dr Owen Fogel MD. One star.

That was the weirdest one yet.

13

Was it a week after that? It's hard to remember. All I know is that I was dead less than a month later. I was downstairs in the cellar, at my desk, doodling anchors on letters from debt collectors, when I heard Owen shout: 'Gracie! Gracie! Here we go!'

I raced upstairs to find Owen sitting crookedly on the armchair, hands clasped together at his crotch; he looked pale and shrunken, and exuded a stink of sadness and decay. He was rolling a butterscotch lolly in his mouth. Through the window, I could see Gracie outside in the garden, watering and belittling the carrots.

'What is it?' I asked.

'Don't listen to the environmentalists. Biodiversity is the worst!'

'What are you talking about?'

'The news, dumb-arse. It jumped the species barrier. Humans have been infected!'

On TV, people in yellow hazmat suits were establishing a biohazard containment circle around an apartment building in

Stockholm. The media were calling it the Siberian Flu, or Man's Best Virus, or the Good Boy Disease, but scientists referred to it as the K9 virus. So far there were three hundred suspected cases and eighty-four reported deaths in northern Europe.

Owen wiped sweat off his stubbly neck; his breathing sounded like wind whistling through trees. 'All the world's greatest diseases have been zoonotic,' he said, shaking his head. 'We've always been looking at the birds and the monkeys and the pigs—the last pandemic put bats on the shit list—but we let our guard down with the dogs. We let them get too close.'

He flipped the channel. On another news program, a reporter wearing a surgical mask was discussing the analysis of blood and faecal samples taken from twenty-five dogs to obtain viral sequences.

'I've always said that letting your dog lick your face would lead to trouble,' Owen said. 'Granted, I was thinking about inappropriate relations, intimate dog-on-human stuff.'

I wondered if it would spread to Australia from northern Europe. The last pandemic had been bad enough: all that gruelling isolation and silly panic buying and overeating—the Fattening, they'd called it. The only thing we learned was how to hide from deliverymen. Was this the beginning of that again?

Owen seemed to be mulling over the thoughts in my head. I snatched the remote from his hand and turned the TV off.

'Why are you sitting in here?' I asked.

'It's the sitting room.'

'That's all you do.'

'I've done everything in life there is for a curious man to do, Angus. Truth be told,' he said, 'I'm trying to decide if dying is the second worst thing that ever happened to me or the third.'

I caught an unexpected whiff of what I imagined was his brain disease. I opened the window.

'Aren't you going to ask me what's the —'

'Nope.'

I called out to Gracie in the garden. 'What do you feel like for dinner?!'

'I don't know. Chinese?!'

'No!'

'I don't feel like Chinese?! What do *you* want?'

'You choose!'

'*You* pick something.'

'Whatever you want!'

'You're so indecisive!'

'So? What's great about being decisive when you also have bad judgement?'

Owen groaned. 'A boring couple is not two times but *ten times* more boring than a boring single person.'

It was true. Damn it.

'At the moment, cognitive dissonance is working in your favour,' Owen said. 'Gracie has justified to herself the reasons for being with you, and has, for the time being, minimised your obvious flaws.'

'I don't know what you're talking about.'

'Don't you know how cognitive dissonance works?'

'Vaguely, but not really, and I don't care to know.'

Here's the thing: I didn't understand cognitive dissonance, nor did I know how a jet engine worked, nor could I calibrate any settings, nor recite chemical compounds nor name galaxies nor explain fractals nor list more than a couple of prime numbers and I couldn't tell you the etymology of a single word. Even after all these years, television seemed like sorcery to me, and I enjoyed it that way.

'Let me explain it to you.'

'Don't you dare.'

Moreover, I disliked when anyone tried to give me knowledge non-consensually; I wanted to protect my ignorance, the most underrated of the human rights. Even when you mutter, 'That's okay, I don't need to know,' people still talk at you as though they're an expert witness called to the stand. It's a mortifying spectacle of unbearable pomposity.

'Normally, when a person has heavily invested in something, they have a cognitive bias to justify their investment . . .'

Sometimes I wondered why people bothered bathing and getting haircuts and wearing nice clothes when they were also always talking to you in a way that painted them in such an unflattering light. Besides, information doubles exponentially in size every second on this chaotic and confusing planet. What are you going to do? You can't keep up. You might as well live clumsily in a fog—you're going to botch it anyway.

When he noticed I wasn't listening, Owen closed his eyes and said in a faraway voice: *'Like a secret tradition on the road to perdition/ To think and talk in mediocrities/ Fake philosopher, you are bluffing, "I know I know nothing"/ Fool, Ignorance doesn't make you Socrates.'* He opened his eyes. 'That's the poet Thurlow Olcott.'

'Ugh.'

'What?'

Whenever I hear someone reciting a poem, I also hear the hours of practice they put into memorising it *just* for the occasion of saying it to you. It's excruciating.

'Nothing,' I said.

Owen sneered. He stood and his left leg buckled; he grabbed hold of the edge of the couch.

'What's the matter?'

'You're so boring you put my foot to sleep.'

'That's on you.'

'Whoops. Here she comes,' Owen said, mostly to himself.

Gracie hesitated at the doorway with her head buried in her phone, feeling her way inside like a blind person. Owen fell back into the armchair melodramatically and loudly sighed.

It worked. She looked up from her phone. 'Owen, are you okay?' she asked.

'Don't you two *dare* use my death to teach you a thing or two about life.'

'Don't worry, we won't,' I promised.

'Consciousness is a tour of duty, and there's nothing sad when the tour ends. It's a cause for muted celebration and gratitude.' He then went on a grating tirade about not wanting a funeral parlour to use cosmetics to make him look like he's sleeping. When he was dead, he said, he wanted to look dead. If a make-up artist was required, they should only *add* gore and decay. In his opinion, a man's loved ones should not remark upon his peaceful countenance; at a minimum, they should gasp.

'Speaking of loved ones, where *is* your family?' Gracie asked. 'Where are your close friends?'

He just shook his head; it was too pitiful to contemplate. It was weirdly easy to imagine him long-dead and forgotten. It was also strange to be feeling pity for someone who was so odiously leering at my wife. Why I didn't sense any real danger from him is now beyond me.

'What about your mother? Is she still alive?'

'What do you want to hear about first? The severe emotional abuse? Or the appalling neglect?'

'I don't know,' I said. 'Let's go for severe emotional abuse. That sounds the most interesting, right, Gracie? Is that what you would've picked?'

'Owen, you don't have to tell us.'

'Good, I won't. But I have been meaning to mention something.' He stroked his own hand like a cat. 'As I mentally degenerate, please play along with my delusions. That's how you respect brain disease and its attendant dementia.'

'What is it you want us to do?'

'I want you to step into my reality, whatever that is.'

A belated addition to the contract was *role-playing*? Who knew what sordid lies we'd be obliged to tell? Would we have to help Owen deceive himself that it was 1962? Was I going to have to pretend to be his kid brother or his dead father? This was madness.

'Whatever you need us to do,' Gracie said, piously.

'Thank you, Gracie,' he said with such heaviness that an awkward silence followed, which I contemplated breaking by telling him that I noticed a sweat stain on the bathroom mirror that could only have come from his rested forehead. Instead, I made a grand announcement to my wife. Since my life had been a disjointed series of false starts, I said, and since—if I was to be totally honest—filming weddings was more stressful than a heist in broad daylight, and the fear of getting caught by the police was nothing compared to the terror of missing a key moment and disappointing a happy couple, I wanted to never again film weddings and instead become a househusband and stay-at-home dad. Frankly, I'd be thrilled on two fronts: to be the kind of parent I never had, and to get the fuck out of the workforce for at least five years.

'Wait, really?'

Gracie turned and scrutinised my face for evidence of a joke; I saw her suspicion give way to understanding and a mixture of tenderness and pride. 'That's exactly what should happen,' she said, agreeing that she would continue to officiate weddings and that I would stay home with our child.

It was a good moment, and during this conversation that entirely excluded Owen, he trudged up to his room, closed the door, and didn't come out for three whole days when, to our surprise, Owen had an actual human visitor.

14

A short Indian man with an uneasy smile stood noncommittally at the front door, his skin gleaming like it had been recently moisturised. He was holding a bottle of Devil's Springs Vodka. He cleared his throat before he spoke. 'Is this where Dr Owen Fogel is staying?'

'Regrettably,' I answered. 'Would you like to come in?'

For a moment, it looked like he might politely refuse.

'Nilesh?' Owen emerged from upstairs in his dressing-gown, and his face made a crinkled smile I hadn't seen before.

'Owen. There you are. Came to see how you're getting on.'

They shook hands stiffly.

'Is that for me?' asked Owen, and took the bottle.

'Strongest vodka on earth. I thought you might need some anaesthetic.'

Owen actually laughed. 'This is Dr Patel,' he said to me, with atypical civility.

'Pleased to meet you,' I said.

'What's this? What's going on?' Gracie shouted, curiosity physically propelling her down the stairs.

'This is Dr Patel,' I told Gracie. The same doctor we read about online, who had once shared a practice with Owen.

'Nice to meet you,' Dr Patel said. 'You're a little pregnant, aren't you?'

'I am,' said Gracie. 'Thanks for noticing.'

Since this was Owen's one and only visitor, we gave them no privacy. The four of us drank coffee and ate biscuits in the living room.

'You look better than I expected,' Dr Patel said.

'What were you expecting?' Owen asked.

'A corpse of some kind.'

'You came a few weeks too early.'

They seemed to have come to some kind of unspoken agreement: Dr Patel would try to sound upbeat, and Owen would attempt to conceal his discomfort. I could tell he desperately wanted to berate us for sticking around but held back in front of his old colleague.

'How's the practice?' Owen asked him.

'The usual. Cough twice. Piss into this.' He then switched to a Transylvanian accent. 'I *vant* to take your blood.'

'Putting out fires in the human body.'

'That's right,' said Dr Patel. 'Still reading those mysteries?'

'They're my only source of pleasure,' Owen said.

'That's still the saddest thing I've ever heard.'

'I doubt that's true.'

This was their version of banter. It didn't come to much. Owen was the type of host who behaved like a hostage, as if his guests were keeping him in his own home against his will. Dr Patel kept glancing over to me and Gracie, clearly wondering why we were just sitting there contributing to the oddly strained atmosphere by bearing mute witness to it.

Dr Patel leaned forward as if in a panic. 'Owen. You've heard about the crisis overseas.'

'A few isolated cases.'

'More than a few. I'm on a scientific advisory committee.'

'You? I would imagine it's just virologists and epidemiologists needed.'

'For the time being. But they're contacting everyone in case we have to mobilise. The hospitals will be overwhelmed. I thought you might want to put your name down for pitching in, should it come to it.'

Owen remained blank-faced. 'I can't understand why you're bothering me with this fantasy. I'll be dead in a few months.'

'It might never reach Australia, that's true, but it did last time, so it might again—in a year, or Monday morning at nine o'clock. A third of the world's population infected now seems like a conservative estimate.'

'That's a shame.'

'Owen, why are you smiling?'

'I'm enjoying your tone of voice.'

'It's going to be all hands on deck if this hits our shores.'

'I suppose so.'

'The government's trying to get on the front foot, should the worst happen. They're even considering shutting the airports.'

'Oh dear. No more cunts coming in, no more cunts going out. How will we ever survive with just the net number of cunts currently here?'

Dr Patel looked stonily at Owen, then burst into laughter. 'Our borders are vulnerable.'

'Globalisation was always a poison pill. And if K9 virus really does make it through quarantine, the left-wingers with their open-border fetish will get a nice surprise.' Dr Patel gave him a look. 'In case you haven't noticed, Nilesh, I'm sort of dying myself.'

'I'm aware of that. You can still be of use, and I would think that might be how you prefer to go out.'

Who did Dr Patel think he was talking to? This was the only man I knew who had turned dying into a form a masturbation.

'You did a lot for the community,' Dr Patel said, as if to contradict my inner thoughts. 'You took over when I was unavailable, not charging patients who were struggling financially, making house calls . . .'

Owen was irritated and embarrassed by these revelations 'Why are you asking me this when it's *you* who owes *me* the enormous favour?'

Dr Patel grimaced and made an ungainly gesture with his hands that was impossible to get the meaning of. He said in a chilly tone, 'Do you know how quickly the K9 virus would spread through this country?'

'I can well imagine.'

I couldn't, and I would've liked to hear some estimates.

'Do you understand what it does? To the human body?'

'From what I can gather, it's a kind of Ebola–Marburg–West-Nile combo, with a twist of scrub typhus, and a touch of Hantavirus Pulmonary Syndrome.'

'Precisely. And we're going into summer. That means mosquitoes. We're not as prepared as they're making out.'

'Have you ever read the *Decameron*?' asked Owen.

Dr Patel looked surprised. 'Boccaccio.'

'One of the world's most famous literary works was written during a plague. That's my answer. It wouldn't be the worst thing in the world.'

'For art, you mean.'

'Yes.'

'But not for people.'

'No. For people it would be devastating.'

Dr Patel was incredulous at Owen's stone-hearted posturing, while for me it only confirmed something I'd long suspected: Owen was a sadist.

'Are you a lost cause, then?'

'I certainly hope so.'

Dr Patel held his breath for a few seconds, then let it out. I think that's just how he breathed. 'It has an eighty-nine percent fatality rate. They're not even close to a vaccine. Two billion people will be dead. Just think of it. You can't! It's unthinkable.'

'Speak for yourself. I can think of it just fine.'

'And?'

'And these pessimistic projections are just a tease. You're just trying to get my hopes up. The whole world dying at the same time as me? I couldn't possibly be that lucky.'

'So I'll put you down as a definite no?'

'That's correct, Nilesh.'

'And you're sure I can't change your mind?'

'Jesus Christ. Tell Sarah I said hello. Wait, perhaps it makes more sense if you tell her I say goodbye.'

Dr Patel sighed sadly and then smiled, as if he'd expected Owen's refusal to help all along. 'Okay. Okay.' He fixed his gaze on Owen's shoes. 'I brought you something else. May I go out to the car and get it?'

'Please.'

Dr Patel ran out into the blowy afternoon.

'He seems fun,' Gracie said in the silence that followed.

Owen didn't respond. We all felt buried under the accumulation of whatever sick thoughts were piling up inside his head.

Dr Patel swept back in holding a violin and a cello.

'You're kidding,' Owen said.

'I'm afraid I'm going to have to insist.'

'One last time, is that it?'

'It need not be the last.'

Owen glared at me and Gracie. 'Would you two *kindly* leave us alone so we can play in privacy?'

'Not a chance,' I said.

'Afraid not,' Gracie added.

He gave a pinched smile. 'As you like,' he said.

The two doctors picked up their instruments. Owen rested his chin on the violin like he wanted to tell it a sad story. Dr Patel extended his arms, as if it was safer to keep the cello at a discreet distance. He said, 'This is an Erwin Schulhoff duo for violin and cello.'

'Can't wait,' Gracie said.

Owen picked up the bow and sawed at the instrument with an anxious freneticism while Dr Patel made his cello sluggishly groan out a low cry for help. This strange interplay of sounds went on for seven minutes at an irregular tempo, the cello's loose, bowel-like moans versus the violin's sharp and violent shrieks. There was nothing unified about the performance; the whole thing sounded like two battling solos, totally out of sync. Their complete confidence was mortifying to me. I thought: So this is what an utter lack of natural talent sounds like. If this had been a school concert, and one of these guys was your kid, you'd go home afterwards and sell his instrument.

After the gloomy crescendo, Gracie applauded. The two doctors smiled triumphantly at each other. Another win for subjectivity.

15

For reasons unknown, Dr Patel's visit plunged Owen into a deeper depression. For five days he no longer gave unbidden lectures or tried to belittle me, and he even stopped contributing intrusively to conversations that were none of his business. He took up residence on the couch in the living room, unable to make it upstairs to his bed, and when he tottered to the toilet, he returned to the couch without flushing or washing his hands.

I had a bad feeling. Not only from Owen; Gracie's eyes were clouded by schemes. I could tell she felt obligated to alleviate his suffering and interfere with his terrified rush into the eternal darkness.

Gracie plopped herself beside Owen on the couch and studied him closely.

'What?' he asked, annoyed.

'What's wrong with you?'

He sighed. 'I feel so exhausted that it seems pointless to have ever felt rejuvenated.'

'Drink! Enjoy! For tomorrow you'll be literally dead!' she said. 'You still have a working body and a good mind.' Owen made a mournful, whimpering sound, and I didn't blame him. People are always trying to count your blessings for you, but their arithmetic is way off.

Gracie tapped Owen's knee gently. 'You're not a body with a soul but a soul with a body, and soon you won't even have this sad one-piece you've been wearing. You'll be free.'

'I envy you, Gracie. I was never able to lose touch with reality.'

'When we first met, you told me you wanted to believe.'

'Yes. When is *my* great spiritual flowering, dammit?'

'This is what I'm trying to tell you,' she said excitedly. 'I'm going to help you begin it.'

From then on, Gracie made it her personal undertaking to find Owen proof that there was more to heaven and earth. That night, Gracie gave him a seminar on weeping Christs, ghost trains, seed biology, Venus transits, past-life regression, phantom hitchhikers, after-death communications, and bi-location. Gracie even inundated Owen with blurry internet photos of ogres, werewolves, and Bigfoot. Fucking Bigfoot!

'Fucking Bigfoot, Gracie?' said Owen.

'We have to be methodical here, Owen. Even a stopped clock —'

'Yes, yes. Everyone knows about the stopped clock.'

She wanted to show him that his disbelief was nothing more than a force of habit.

'Do you think every single caterpillar *wants* to become a butterfly?'

'How would I know that?'

'Owen, you are an infinitesimal speck living on a microscopic blue dot, right? Didn't Carl Sagan say something like that?'

'About *me*?'

It was dispiriting how these conversations went on.

Over the next few days, the two of them went to a so-called haunted hotel, a so-called mind-reader, a so-called tarot reader, and a so-called mystic, who actually said the word *abracadabra*. Even Gracie had to admit that most of these people had shit for brains.

The last outing—on the very day I died—was to a self-proclaimed shaman who did interdimensional healing on a houseboat moored on the Hawkesbury River. This time, they allowed me to tag along. As we stepped inside the boat, I wondered, why is it that wherever you find crystals you also smell tantric sex? The shaman and his clairvoyant wife gave off the vibe of having met on Craigslist that very morning. The dishevelled clairvoyant's frizzled hair indicated the remnants of a former beehive. Owen made a show of trying not to look disdainful, but then he spotted a crystal ball on a side table.

'Crystal ball! That's not just a prop?'

'No, it's not,' she said, explaining that she could just as easily stare into clear water in order to see the future or the past.

'The medium is the message,' Owen said.

'I've never heard that one before,' she said, dully.

The shaman and his wife said they'd be happy to help Owen get to know his interdimensional self and took turns talking about chronobiology and harmonic convergence for almost forty-five minutes. Every word seemed to contain a subtextual childish taunt: *My higher self is higher than your higher self.*

'The sun is setting on your human form,' said the shaman. 'The blood has gone tepid in your veins, your organs have soured, yet your soul will pulse forever. Have you loved your body?'

'Not much.'

He laid his palms on Owen's head. 'What do you feel?'

'Embarrassed for you.'

The shaman seemed annoyed. The clairvoyant took over. 'Would you like to have a reading or speak to a loved one who passed?'

'No thanks,' Owen said.

'What about your father?' Gracie said, then made an aside to the clairvoyant: 'He died in our home!' I saw Owen tense up. 'Go on,' Gracie said. 'Don't you want to talk to him?'

Owen pretended to be gazing at the crystal ball. 'My father . . .' he said slowly, being careful with his words, 'once squashed a whole case of empty beer cans on my forehead, one by one. He had no control over how angry he allowed himself to get, including the time he tried to smother me with a pillow. And my mother never raised a finger to stop him. So no, Gracie, I don't want to give either of them a call right now.'

That was news. He'd never revealed anything personal about his upbringing, and it gave everything that came before it the feeling of a lie. At the same time, hearing this dying bastard's revelations of childhood abuse made me almost sick with compassionate regret.

'Could I just have a reading?' Gracie asked. She didn't want to miss out on her spin of the paranormal wheel.

The clairvoyant stroked the tops of Gracie's hands, as if wiping off specks of mud. 'Silence now, while I concentrate,' she said, and channelled that uncanny faraway look in her eye that clairvoyants pretend to get. It was quiet, the only sound the splash of a pelican diving for fish. I could tell by Gracie's stillness that she was all-in.

A flicker of concern crossed the clairvoyant's face.

'So, what do you see?' said Gracie.

She gave her a vaporous smile. 'I see that you are pregnant.' There was a twinge of anxiety in her face.

'What? Is something terrible going to happen to me?' Gracie said, laughing.

'Not at all! What? No!' The clairvoyant squinted at Gracie's hands, as if reading an inscrutable text.

This purposeful accentuation of mystery no doubt was a precursor to upselling her services—yet the reading ended there. Gracie looked stressed out by the ploy. Isn't there a code of conduct, or a clairvoyant's oath to do no psychic harm? Sure, we all have terrible futures, but was whatever was going to happen to her going to be *especially* terrible?

That night, I had a dream in which I was trying to turn towards a window but my head wouldn't move. That was the whole stupid dream. Gracie kept saying, 'Look outside. You won't believe it,' but I couldn't budge.

In the morning, we were woken by the sound of whooping and the clapping of hands. Downstairs, Owen was standing on the couch in his muddy shoes.

'Every hospital ward in New York is an isolation ward! The response teams in Washington are all infected! Mass graves are being dug outside of Paris! Pakistan's got it! Mexico too! I can't believe my luck!'

The TV was showing footage of medical personnel being vaccinated against the Good Boy Disease by men and women in hazmat suits.

'There's no way that's the right vaccine!' Owen said, laughing. 'Okay, so it still hasn't hit here yet, or Asia or Africa or South America, so global containment is theoretically possible, but I wouldn't bet on it. Is this or is this not the best thing to ever happen to a terminal case in the history of the world?'

I said, 'Can you stop being a monstrous cunt for just a minute? I can't hear.'

The co-anchor was talking to someone off-screen. 'To kill a dog is one thing, but to kill nine hundred million dogs and dispose of their bodies without touching them?'

The other anchor slapped his forehead cartoonishly. 'What don't you get about this, Debbie? It doesn't matter about the dogs anymore.'

'He's right,' Owen said. 'Saliva, cough droplets—it's airborne. And even mosquitoes can carry it!'

Owen was actually giggling. Of all the soul comfort Gracie had tried to give him, the man had made no great spiritual gains—his ennui was still deadly, his fear still palpable, his impenetrable gloom still tedious—yet watching the world unravel was putting a genuine smile on his face.

By afternoon, Gracie couldn't take any more. She leaped from the couch and announced she was going to her safe space, Mahon rock pool, to submerge her body in the ocean with the sound of waves drowning out all thought. She didn't take her swimmers, which meant she would be going down those mossy steps into the water in her underwear or, if there was nobody about, completely naked.

Maybe it was the sleazy way Owen watched Gracie leave the house, or a thought triggered by his earlier revelation about his father's cruelty, but I suddenly had an epiphany so obvious and so overdue, I leapt to my feet and swayed there, gaping at him.

'What?'

'Nothing.'

I ran into Gracie's study and found the phone number for Wayne Morris, the man who'd sold Gracie the house.

'Hello?'

'Hey, Wayne, it's Angus Mooney. My wife Gracie bought your house.'

'You watching the news?'

'Yes. But that's not why I'm calling. I just wanted to know if you could tell me who you bought the house off.'

'Oh, sure. It was the Khourys. Nassim and Yasmin.'

'Do you remember how long they'd been in the house?'

'What's this about?'

'It's a long story. How about a number for them?'

'Can't help you there, but I do know they share a medical practice. They're both doctors, can you believe that?'

'Why wouldn't I believe that?'

'How's she doing, anyway?'

'Gracie? She's great.'

'I meant the house. How is she?'

'Oh . . . sturdy?'

I rang the Khourys, who informed me the previous owners had died; they gave me the phone number for their daughter, an entertainment lawyer, who had prepared the paperwork for the sale. She led me to Arthur Johnson, who led me to the grandson of the Crabbes, the original owners and architects.

Everyone I spoke to missed the old broken-down place and seemed to take personal credit for rising property values in the street, and each prolonged the conversation with DIY reminiscences: the addition of the sunroom and deck, the upstairs bathroom renovation, the construction of the outdoor toilet. I even spoke to the original owner, an amateur architect, who wanted to know how we enjoyed his vaulted ceilings.

Not one of them carried the name Fogel, or rented to a family by that name, or had heard of anyone named Fogel, or a boy named Owen, or a father who died in the backyard. A couple of hours of slapdash investigations and I'd unravelled his whole story.

Why hadn't we checked it out earlier? The answer was obvious and mortifying: the lure of easy money.

Is there an activity more satisfying than furiously throwing somebody else's things into a suitcase? I crammed in socks, underpants, shirts and pants as carelessly as possible, while humming a little tune. Books, X-rays, magazines, toiletries—the suitcase didn't close, but that wasn't my problem.

'What are you doing?' Owen stood motionless in the doorway, staring hard at me.

'You didn't grow up in our house.'

'I know that.' He looked at me with boredom.

'You admit it?'

'I can see you know it's true.' Now I detected a smidgeon of relief, and a superior glint in his eyes, as if he couldn't believe how long it had taken us dunces to cotton on. 'Does Gracie know too?'

'She will.'

I pulled out my phone.

'Wait. You have to let a man explain.'

'Are you really dying?'

'Yes. I mean, I've played with the timeline a little. I was diagnosed two years ago. But yes, I am.' He spoke with impatient exasperation, livid that I had forced him into the indignity of a confession. 'After being diagnosed, I hit rock bottom. Only when you receive a death sentence do you finally understand how much you dislike yourself. You go from thinking, "No one will mourn me," to "I wouldn't either, if I was them." Hobbes's description of life as nasty, brutish and short could also, I realised, describe me as a person. That's some kind of sick-making insight, I can assure you.'

This was already the worst personal anecdote I'd ever heard, and I sensed he was only at the beginning.

He went on: 'I had money, but nothing to spend it on. I agonised over my solitude. One night I woke up and looked online and felt an overwhelming feeling of peaceful delight. So what if I was dying?

Had I forgotten that the world was burning too? Even before the K9 virus, there was Islamist and white ethno-nationalist terrorism, all those wonderful opioid overdoses, the thriving suicide rate, hit-and-runs by self-driving cars, the increasing selfie-death rate, the video-game deep-vein thrombosis dead, the phone users strolling into traffic—every time I looked it was a hundred dead, ten thousand dead, a hundred thousand dead. I couldn't get enough! It really perked me up. Then I went on social media so I could revel in everyone I knew whining about it, and I stumbled upon a friend's post about getting a speeding ticket. There was a single comment: "Australians' most serious ideas about injustice involve the locations of speed cameras and the unfairness of breathalyzers." It made me laugh out loud. I thought: Who *is* this person?'

I could see where this was going.

'I found myself on her page, where she had just linked to a story about Aboriginal deaths in custody with the comment: "The arc of the moral universe is long, but it bends towards . . . oh, shit, it broke, never mind."'

'Gracie.'

'Yes.'

'It's amazing what you can find out about a person these days.'

He'd gone down the same route I had.

'I didn't even need to request to follow her. All her posts are public. I spent hours reading her every thought and utterance. I learned everything about her: her childhood, the death of her parents, her relationships, her dead dog, her buying this house, her mystifying infatuation with you, your struggles with IVF. And despite her self-consciousness and how sadly performative her life was, there was no diluting the almost preternatural brilliance of her mind, her sexy way of being alive, her straight-up astonishing beauty. I mean, I don't have to tell you.'

'You really don't.'

'I *was* content to just stalk her online . . . until one day.' Now he pitched his voice so low I had to lean in to hear. 'I was at home and there was a knock on the door—it was a disgusting old woman and a snot-faced young man. The old woman said she'd grown up in my apartment and wanted to show her grandson around. I told them to fuck right off. But that's how I got the idea to pretend to have grown up in Gracie's house. That was the plan. I didn't have an inkling that it would work. In the same way that very few people can talk about their grandparents' grandparents, nobody knows the history of their house. Well, some do. You don't.' He took a few steps backwards, as if in retreat. 'I know this old-fashioned love obsession is pathetic, but who am I harming? She has a soothing presence and being in her company is all the palliative care that I require.'

He had a solid argument, I had to admit, but it wasn't enough to sway me. 'Sorry. Deal's off. It's too fucking creepy,' I said. 'I'll have your things sent to you.'

'Have a heart.'

'Nup.'

He gave me a pleading look; his health had already begun to nosedive, and it wouldn't be long in the grand scheme of things. Still, I couldn't have him leering at us a moment longer. I was done with his soft-toned insinuations and watchful presence and discouraging odours.

'Out with you. Come on, let's go. Shoo.'

'You fucking appendix.'

'Did you just call me—an appendix?'

'A vestigial organ that has lost most of its ancestral function, yes. That's what you are to Gracie. You could be removed and all she'd have is a thin, barely visible scar, with zero loss to her, in terms of functionality.' He took threatening steps towards me. 'I was unlucky in life, Mooney. The women who loved me in dribs and drabs, I didn't love back. And the woman I loved—and I really shovelled it out—didn't love me at all. There was no damn crossover. I never had a real conversation of hearts. The best I can hope for as I breathe my last is to be near Gracie. But I can't get near enough. I want to get into her bed. I want to get into her clothes.' He spoke as if suddenly out of breath. 'I want to be absorbed into her bloodstream.'

That was too much. I turned away and texted Gracie, *Guess who wants to be absorbed into your bloodstream lol*.

Before I could hit send, I blacked out.

16

The floor was rolling like the deck of a boat. The ceiling fan creaked and wobbled as it turned. Black flies beat against the screen door. The air thinned, like on a mountain top. Owen stood over me, looking vaguely frightened, as I drifted between deep sleep and deep space.

'You're bleeding out,' he said in a thick whisper. 'Maybe we can say it was a hunting accident.'

Blood dripped from the base of the lamp he gripped in his hand. I took a lungful of air and it hurt. I reached out to him for help and he looked at my outstretched arm with horror, absorbed by my predicament. Or, as he probably saw it, *his* predicament.

'It looks like I've permeated the blood–brain barrier and an epidural haematoma is compressing your brain,' he said. 'To save your life I'd need to drain blood from the foramen magnum, but . . . maybe I won't?'

Owen was sucking on one of his detestable butterscotches and staring at me with dour inevitability. 'You still with us?' he asked sourly, his voice cracking a little.

After that, all I could hear was the wall clock's heavy ticks and my own flailing heartbeat. I looked at the room's dark yellow curtains and the curtain rod's faint metallic polish; through the small window, I could see the moon lurking behind a bleak veil of leaves. The whole scene was inconsistent with reality.

Owen placed a seashell to my ear. 'I thought you'd like to listen to the sea.'

He held up a poster of Bosch's 'Ascent of the Blessed', an image of the dead drifting towards a shining corridor of celestial light.

'Is this what you see? Do you see a light? A distant brightness?'

I didn't see anything during that long Indian summer of death.

Downstairs, I heard the front door open. Gracie was home. She made so much noise slamming doors and rattling pans it was like she was playing it for laughs.

'Where are you guys?' she yelled.

My heart wobbled at the sound of her voice. I called out weakly, 'Gracie, Gracie.'

'This really shouldn't be taking so long,' Owen said. 'It's inexcusable. I'm sorry for the delay.'

He put his hand over my mouth and pinched my nose.

What happened next is difficult to put into words. Think of a sea mist that's entirely black. Now picture that black mist blooming inside you. Now consider how it would feel to change places with a shadow. Then visualise your heart circling a drain. Now imagine you're a plant at the moment it's pulled up by the roots. Following that, envision being a dawn in reverse and your lungs being erased atom by atom while your head is lowered into a pit of mud. Now conjure up an immense all-consuming silence. It is difficult to put into words, but you can see where this was going, and where it went.

Reader, I was dead.

FOUR

'For me, a desert island is no tragedy—and neither is a deserted planet.'

Peter Wessel Zapffe

17

Sometime much later, in the course of my soul's long wanderings, I learned many unpalatable facts about Gracie's life without me. She had always said that we're endlessly running ahead of ourselves, down our own paths, whatever that meant. And as much as my instinct leans towards whining solely from my own viewpoint, I have to admit that this is *our* story, not just mine. In a very real way, Gracie is writing this chronicle with me.

At the time I could see nothing of what she was going through, of course, but eventually I was given a thorough debrief that contained more repugnant details than I ever wanted to hear. Most of them are painful to report even now.

For instance, I learned that, the morning after my murder, Owen came down to breakfast and found my widow worrying about my unexplained absence; he did nothing but sit beside her, noisily stirring his tea.

'Is he out all night again?' he asked blithely.

'I'm calling Ernie.'

The phone call elicited no useful information—Ernie hadn't seen me in two weeks.

'He probably went for a really long walk,' she said, uncertainly.

'Probably,' Owen agreed, still sticky from the sweat of the previous night.

For Gracie, my unexplained absence became missing, missing became presumed dead, and presumed dead became categorically deceased when two uniformed police officers turned up at the house with tragic news: her husband's body—*my* body!—had been found in a wheelie bin in an alley behind the Mandalay on Darlinghurst Road.

While I had died from asphyxiation, I'd also suffered a blunt head trauma and every bone in my body was broken. Yet there was no blood at the scene: it was obvious I'd been killed elsewhere and then dumped in the bin.

The officers did a hurried and shoddy search of the house. They asked, 'Was he dealing drugs again?' Gracie said I wasn't, though not with a great deal of certainty. The officers' questions about my criminal background had a clear implication: I had got what was coming to me, right? They were weakly apologetic that they had no leads, nor suspects. Because police resources were stretched by contact tracing overseas arrivals and investigating credible threats of bioterrorism, the case would be put on the backburner.

Frankly, Owen had murdered me at a good time.

Even Gracie had to wonder if I was up to my old nefarious activities. Or, as corny as it sounded, had the past finally caught up with me? What Gracie *wasn't* thinking was: How had diminutive, enfeebled, weak-gripped Owen got my body out of the house and dumped it on the opposite side of the city? And why were my bones broken?

For almost a week, Gracie resolved to solve my unsolved murder herself. She went howling to the damp alley where my body had been discovered; hysterically interviewed everyone within a two-block radius; blundered around the surrounding streets, harassing my old contacts; tore into known drug dens and pointlessly interrogated strangers and acquaintances alike, a chaotic force, desperate for someone to fuck with her. When nobody did, she thought: You generally reap what you sow. Did Mooney sow this or did he not?

At midnight, she returned home and grilled Owen: 'Are you sure he didn't say where he was going?'

'He didn't,' Owen said tetchily.

For a week she went back to that alley—she even slept there two nights—until one morning the sun rose and with the warm air came a breathless epiphany: In my misspent youth I had inflicted physical and psychological damage on my fellow human beings and I was well within my rights to get murdered in this way. My violent end may have been an anachronism, but it was also cosmic justice.

She returned home and confessed these dark thoughts to Owen.

'I think that's the right way of seeing it,' he said, looking like a crustacean pulled out of a boiling pot at the last minute. He had got away with murder.

18

It was late afternoon in the crematorium. This was arguably the most significant moment of my death.

I wasn't there.

There was a decent, standing-room-only sized crowd, and though their condolences were sincere, Gracie wanted to scream at the assembled mourners: *Even if she's pregnant, don't tell the widow she's glowing, you dumb shits.*

Obscenely, my murderer stood beside her, wearing a vintage suit and a plastic smile. The nervy, solicitous chaplain began with a request to turn off electronic devices, then delivered a short sermon that was a little about the eternal love between me and my devoted wife, but mostly about the burdens of being a chaplain, with a special emphasis on drumming up future business.

When he stood down, Ernie took his sombre place at the podium.

'Why does death have a dress code? Mooney was never comfortable in a suit. It looks as if he's going to heaven for a job interview.'

He stared down into my open coffin. 'Everyone is afraid to laugh in a corpse's face, but look at him, lying there. What a dummy.'

Ernie, for the record, denied any knowledge of the circumstances surrounding my murder; he knew that some mourners present considered him a suspect even though he'd been cleared by the authorities and had an iron-clad alibi, being that he was already in custody for public drunkenness.

Next he recounted several inappropriate anecdotes from our misspent youth: the time we stole dogs and returned them to their owners for the reward; the time we stole luggage from baggage claim carousels in the domestic terminals; the time we hit a few toy stores and sold Hot Wheels garages to desperate dads on Christmas Eve—that one caught in his throat.

He stepped down and leaned over the coffin. 'See you, Numbat,' he said, and planted a wet kiss on my cold, waxy cheek.

Gracie stepped up to the podium and explained that the coffin was a repurposed old door. 'You can't imagine how long I struggled over whether the doorhandle should be on the inside or the outside.' She gave a hopeful glance at the open coffin as if it might change my condition.

She said, 'He took stupid chances, and I'm not sure why.'

The mourners could actually hear her resentment towards me for allowing myself to be murdered with a baby on the way.

With a sullen air, she recounted scolding me for getting her toothbrush ready. 'He'd put the toothpaste on my brush, then hand it to me as I walked in the bathroom, and I was mad about that. What's wrong with me?' she wondered aloud. 'What kind of person is afraid of devotion?'

She kept her gaze fixed on my cold face. 'I think he once nearly killed a man himself.'

If people weren't paying attention before, they were now. There was a murmuring throughout the church—it was scandalous, a widow confessing her dead husband's worst sins, a betrayal of sorts. It just wasn't done.

'All right, so he might have killed someone. But he was too hard on himself. He felt really bad about it all the time. I told him once, being killed could've happened to anybody. And, in the end, it did. It happened to him.'

Gracie went silent then. She gave the mourners a dark look, as if accusing them of a prurient interest in the cold case she herself had just reopened. 'Fuck it. Let's just do this.'

Gracie wanted to be the one who lit the match, but cremations don't work that way. The slowness of the conveyor belt made everyone uneasy, my coffin moving towards eternity at a glacial speed.

At a cremation, Gracie thought and later posted, it's kind of a bummer that nobody is blinded by the glare of firelight.

19

As for me, I woke crying from the terror of a night plagued by obscene, violent dreams—mostly of Owen's leering face and the sensation of a throatful of blood. The sound of arguments and the honking of bicycle horns got me out of bed. I leaned heavily against the window, peering down into the tangle of alleys, the garbage piles, the zigzagging bicycles, the ceaseless flow of men and women living with gusto and delirium. It looked like a parade after the sound of gunfire.

I went to the toilet and took a constipated shit. The ordinariness of it was faintly distressing. I sat there, straining, thinking, Really? *This* again?

After a drip coffee and a brief, unsatisfying shower, I dragged my feet to the factory for an eight-hour shift during which the entire umbrella division only worked when the supervisor came near.

My co-workers and I had fast developed an unexpected intimacy with one another, like adults at a court-ordered driver's education class.

When we weren't working, we were speculating. Joseph wondered why, in lieu of Oblivion, death wouldn't just reveal all the juiciest details about life. Was it that all secrets were classified and we didn't have security clearance? Kira whined that in our whole lives we could've been dead at any moment, and now, at any moment, we could be dead again. Farhad posited that existence was probably a series of interlocking temporary conditions; we were all being kept under observation, and any day now he expected a voice to boom, 'Heaven is ready for human trials.'

He also wondered if God even knew we were here. If, by remaining alive after death, we'd undermined his authority. I still hadn't made my mind up either away about the existence of such a being, but if there *was* a God, it was clear he had an avoidant personality.

There was a further hypothesis by Haruto, a fifty-year-old Japanese man who hadn't spoken up until now, that the soul was both mortal and immortal, and that the immortal part was the soul's excess. Depending on how exuberantly one had lived, the dynamic, over-excited part of our souls refused to die. Our immortality was merely stubbornness, like a child who refuses to go to bed.

Kira liked this idea. She said, 'Heaven must be full of only the most excited beings. That's what *makes* it heaven.'

'With all due respect,' Joseph said, 'if you call this place heaven one more time, I'll kick you in the pussy.'

She pretended not to hear him and said, 'Imagine for a moment that God exists. At this point, what could his motivation even be?'

No one had an answer. We all agreed that the universe was indecent, especially considering the disgusting number of unanswered prayers floating out there. At this point, could there be anything viler than purporting to know the meaning of eternity? Could we ever again trust anyone in a position of religious authority?

After exhausting ourselves theologically, we got personal.

Joseph grew morose. 'I thought I was at a turning point in my life, but maybe I wasn't. I thought I was going to turn things around. Maybe I would have, but I doubt it.'

For Joseph, all up, things had turned out quite well. His wife hadn't loved him for years, but they couldn't afford the divorce. He kept talking about his debts, the web of lies that was catching up with him, and now here he was, home free. 'I'd ruined my life by the time I was twenty, yet I lived on and on in my ruined life, wondering how to get out of it. As it turns out, the solution was always there, waiting for me.'

Farhad had been arrested and was awaiting trial 'for some bullshit'. He hated being taken from a life he hadn't yet put the finishing touches on. 'My whole life, I felt a resistance to everything I tried to do, from getting a job to finding someone to love.' He wasn't alone. We all had the general feeling that the universe was pushing back at all our natural instincts. He said: 'I was frightened of too many things, none of which killed me.'

That was another common theme—how none of our fears had done us in.

Priya, a quiet woman with soulful eyes, slapped her hands together. 'What are you all whining about? This is the best thing that's ever happened to me! I'd been very sick for so long. Parkinson's. I tried every therapy in the book. Now I'm all clear.'

'It has to be said,' Kira agreed, 'death has an unambiguous upside.'

It was a startling discovery—death had no adverse health effects, and was, in fact, a cure. You woke up here purified of whatever disease had plagued you in life. The maimed had limbs returned, the disembowelled had their entrails back, the Alzheimer's crowd had normal cognitive abilities, the asthmatics could breathe easy, the alcoholics had virginal livers, the cancerous were benign, the HIV-positive had perfect immunity, the irritably bowelled were regular again, the epileptics no longer lived under the threat of seizure, and the muscularly dystrophied were in a state of gratitude, always flexing their calm, steady hands in amazement. Those who had stunk of the decay of a long illness were now intoxicated by the perfume of their own vitality. Similarly, the disfigured were reconfigured, the formerly pustular and badly scarred could not keep from staring admiringly into mirrors, all tangled nerves were straightened, all spleens unruptured, all prolapsed anuses reverted to their inverse state. You get the idea.

I'm not saying I understood everything—don't ask me about the decapitated or the insane. Did death have its limits? You could still see plenty of bug-eyed and moon-faced and hook-nosed people walking around. I guess even death can't change who your parents were.

By lunchtime, we had exhausted our rants; we sat on the roof and ate without speaking, as if our mute sadness was a ritual silence. I thought about Gracie and how, eventually, she would paw through my secret drawer in the old desk in the basement and find my sketches and plans for unrealised heists. Why don't we burn our shameful documents when we have the chance? I guess we're always outwitted by our own optimism.

After work, we headed down the steep metal stairway to sit at the computer terminals and answer more absurd and penetrating questions about existence. They seemed to be getting harder and more personal. *In what ways did you most routinely flatter yourself? Did you ever extol frankness as a virtue as a means of exercising cruelty? Did you ever alter your sense of well-being in order to display an ostentatious sadness to elicit sympathy or to outmanoeuvre a fellow being? Name three whisper campaigns you were involved in. Which of the worst life events of your three closest friends were you the common denominator of? Which of your most valued principles were you unable to live up to? Which of your worst attitudes towards yourself and/or which terrible life decisions did you blame 'the culture' for?*

So it went.

After work, I went back to the Central Employment Agency and took a seat in the vestibule, feeling gormless and blue. The tiny-mouthed employment officer saw me through the glass wall and opened his door.

'You don't have an appointment.'

'Can I change jobs?'

'Not yet.'

'When?'

'I don't want to get your hopes up,' he said and softly closed the glass door.

I didn't have the energy to move and sat there for another hour. I also felt overwhelmed with emotion, wondering if not getting my hopes up was the nicest thing anyone had ever done for me.

20

People who hadn't made casseroles for a decade made casseroles. They offered Gracie their cleaning services and took out her recycling bin. They also said 'Everything happens for a reason,' and 'I understand what you're going through'. They also said 'In time . . .' and 'Just give it some time . . .' People spoke with pretentious authority about time right before unleashing an anecdote about how their family pet passed away after a long illness.

In some cultures, widows shave their heads or are buried with their husbands. They're expected to howl like tornados or wear black forever or marry their brother-in-law. Here, they're expected to drink cups of milky tea and have a lie-down.

For the first month, my poor widow mourned the only way she knew how: she screamed into pillows, threw loving glances at my toothbrush, stood at the fridge mindlessly, fogged over windows with her breath, pulled out the armchair's loose stuffing, watched television from a crouched position with the sound off, and wondered if it was possible to turn into a hunchback overnight. When she found the bath drain blocked with my hair, she pulled out a clump, kissed it, then returned it to the drain. It was maddening that she couldn't take sleeping pills or drink herself into oblivion or even smoke a fucking cigarette. How incredibly stupid to be pregnant at a time like this!

Then the first case of the Good Boy Disease was reported in New Zealand, and the Australian news anchor was unable to contain his schadenfreude. Gracie stared grimly at the TV screen, too afraid to speak, while Owen bounced on the couch. 'That's our neck of the globe. It's time to get ahead of the game!'

On the TV: '. . . outbreak is under control and squashed, the infected are effectively isolated, every citizen other than essential workers is in a twenty-one-day quarantine . . .'

'It was only one case,' said Gracie.

'If something happens here, it'll happen fast. Best we stockpile now. You should get to the shops.'

Gracie didn't move, in fact seemed incapable of movement. Owen disappeared into his bedroom for a few minutes and then came back.

'You can't stay inside forever. A shopping trip will do you good! Here's a list.'

Gracie took the paper without even glancing at it. 'I'm also going to give you some prescriptions to fill.' There were forty-two pages left in Owen's prescription pad, and he filled them with enough scripts for antibiotics, painkillers, sleeping pills, muscle relaxants and anti-depressants to get through a year.

Out in the world, traffic was a nightmare. Shopping centres had a manic, Christmas Eve vibe, and there was a conspicuous endgame of stash and hoard going on. Word was out that the unthinkable was inevitable, and people were once again readying for the adventure of staying home, tapping into their animalistic drive for tinned foods and toilet paper.

It was strange to be in the company of people who had not just undergone a life-changing tragedy. Gracie trudged the supermarket aisles amassing non-perishable foods and listening to the other customers distract themselves from the global emergency with talk that was unendurably small. Gracie resolved to tell everyone who tried to engage her in conversation that her husband had died.

They said 'hello' and 'good morning'.

She said: 'My husband died.'

Then they said: 'Oh Jesus. I'm so sorry. When?'

When? That question carried within it a clear limit. She could almost hear them insisting: This death better be *fresh as fuck.*

When she responded with the truth—a month ago—she could see them calculating whether she was still within her rights to make a big deal about it. Mostly she could see them thinking: It's a cushy job, being sad, and our hearts have been mistreated too—who will let *us* walk around visibly shaken?

A couple of braver souls asked, 'How?' which Gracie understood was their way of asking, *Could it happen to me?*

21

I sat in the dankly lit Bitter in Soul, already sick of my new grievances and feeling so vulnerable that I warned the bartender, 'Don't frown at me—it'll leave a mark.' The snatches of conversations around me flew in and out of my head. ('I wouldn't be caught dead, but I was.' 'Killing myself was career suicide.') The man next to me picked up a beer bottle using only his teeth. A woman laughed hysterically at a joke she was in the middle of telling. None of us looked like a person anyone would take a warm, personal interest in ever again.

I said, 'Turns out, time wasn't of the essence after all.'

The bartender said, 'Are you talking to me?'

'Never mind.'

I tried to boost my mood with a mindless smile that hurt my jaw. Then for a while I cradled my head in my arms and listened to myself breathe like a thirsty dog. A woman's voice whispered in my ear, 'How did you die?'

'Murdered,' I mumbled.

Her hand on my neck triggered an unexpected shiver of delight. She asked, 'Is anyone relieved that you're dead?'

'The prick that killed me.'

'Did you deserve it?'

'I didn't think so, but now I'm not so sure.'

The hand began to pinch my neck hard until it became a violent squeeze. I tilted my head up to the culprit: it was the woman who had shown me to my sleeping quarters.

'I remember you,' I said.

'You complained about me.'

'No, I didn't.'

She gave me an accusatory look. 'People should have the guts to criticise you to your face.'

'I didn't say anything to anyone.'

'You got me fired.'

'I ranked you in the high 3700s!'

'Is that all? No wonder!'

'How was I supposed to know the metrics?' I said. 'I'm sorry.'

The bartender set more drinks down derisively. The woman lit up a cigarette with a green plastic lighter.

I said, '*You* told me there were no cigarettes here.'

She blew a smoke ring that didn't really coalesce.

'It's a synthetic,' she said, exhaling green puffs of smoke. 'Very bad for you. It's got more chemicals than tobacco.' I snatched a cigarette from her pack and put it in my mouth. 'It causes cancer twice as fast and I'm told you go blind as well.'

'Got a light?' I asked.

I lit up; a perfectly bright sphere of light flew into my eyes and a suction sound roared in my ears. I took one of those shingles pills from my pocket and downed it with vodka.

'That shouldn't be mixed with alcohol.'

'People have been telling me that my whole life.'

She made a real show of contemplating my face.

'You need to sleep.'

'I can't.'

Her heavy lips made the faint trace of a sympathetic smile as I explained how, since arriving here, I'd had a restless, disturbed, encased-in-ice feeling: my ears were filled with lonely little sounds that I couldn't deduce the meaning of; sleep, when it finally came, was a dark immensity that opened like a toad's mouth and soaked me in lurid, prurient nightmares of my final moments; I woke up with Owen's sour breath on my face and the urge to rage-vomit.

An emaciated man on the next stool leaned over. 'When I was alive, the big plan was to stay alive.' He sighed. 'I suppose it's still the plan.'

'Nobody's talking to you!' I shouted.

'You seem angry.'

I erupted: 'That's because it turns out that every one of my life choices was unrelated to this outcome. There's no cause and effect. Everything's the same. You still have to take food in, and you still have to shit it out!' The other drinkers began to listen. 'The universe is like when a friend says, "I have a secret, but I can't tell you," and you ask, "What is it?" And they say, "I really can't tell you, but it's an amazing secret," and they wear an expression like they're desperate to spill the beans but they don't so you give up and spit in your friend's face, they're so fucking boring.'

The woman I'd got fired regarded me squarely. 'So this is where the fun people drink?'

'Yep.'

She let out a series of drawn-out sighs. I didn't blame her. Everything I'd been saying sounded like it had been translated from an infant's shriek.

'Looks like someone hasn't been going to group,' she said.

'What kind of group?'

'Did you sleep through your orientation or something?'

'I missed it,' I said. '*Someone* neglected to tell me about it.'

'Oops.' She fished around in her bag and slipped a card into my pocket. 'A support group. It's really helpful.'

'I doubt it. Tell me something. How did *you* die?'

'Me? I was raped and murdered.'

'Oh god. I'm sorry.'

'That's okay, it wasn't you.' Her lips formed a weak smile and she seemed to be making a mental note of something.

I felt like I was going to cry so I started laughing instead. The cigarette made me feel like I was hovering above my own body, watching myself covertly, and I thought of that old description of human beings—that 'we are atoms contemplating atoms'—and wanted to add *with puzzlement, with bemusement, with disgust.*

'Are *you* okay?'

'It's hard to tell.'

'Do you want to be alone?'

'No. I just need some air.'

I downed my beer and went outside; she followed and strolled beside me. It was a moonless night and the street lamps cast angular shadows on the brick buildings. Dozens of people rode bicycles silently in the dark. On the footpath, a girl was scolding her boyfriend, who had his hands up in mock surrender. In the distance, a burst of orange light in the sky.

'What the fuck *is* that?' I asked.

'The dead passing over. You really should've gone to orientation.'

'You know what?' I said to her. 'You were terrible at your job and I think you deserved to get fired.'

'Truth be told, yours wasn't the first complaint lodged against me.'

'I didn't complain.'

'I didn't like the work conditions anyway. I had to spend my days dealing with hysterics and catatonics.'

'Which was I?'

'The first.'

Up ahead, there was an insanely lit McDonald's, like a beacon in the night; I moved towards the light and went inside. The counters were so slick they look lubricated. I ordered fries and the taste was the first utterly familiar experience I'd had since dying. I imagined I was alive and drunk in Kings Cross.

My companion explained that Starbucks, McDonald's and other transdimensional corporations were started here by people unrelated to those organisations in life. First in, first served, she said, as neither patents nor copyright extend beyond the grave.

'I don't care.'

'I can see that.'

'What's your name?'

'Valeria.'

'Goodnight, Valeria,' I said and walked out of there.

Three blocks later, I tripped and stretched out on the footpath. I began an unmelodic, sentimental version of the silly song that my one-time foster father, Dr Fitzsimmons, sang to me in my darkest lonely-child hour. 'Show me the way to go home, said the girl on Bondi Beach, I lost my clothes about an hour ago, and now they're out of reach.'

A man's savage face jutted out of a window: 'Don't you know there's a war on?'

I did, but I didn't know where or why or for how long or with whom, and what's more, I didn't want to know—I didn't want to know anything.

'Degenerate!' The man slammed his window shut.

I looked beside me. Valeria was sitting there, smoking a cigarette, as if we'd never said goodbye. She had a listless smile on her face.

'Still,' I said, 'you can't live in a society without inadvertently learning certain things, even against your will.'

'What?'

'I said, I know some things.'

'Like what?'

'Okay. As far as I understand, this god-awful town, Lagaria, is a provincial outpost between two medium-sized cities, neither of which is a capital.'

'Correct.'

'To the north are swamps, to the east is desert. To the south is forest. To the west . . . I don't know what's there. The pits of hell.'

'No. Just more forest.'

'And it seems like the stinky dustbin of history overflows here.'

'That it does.'

'I'm going to guess that once there was a mad king, then a feeble king, then inquisitions and a bloody revolution and a monarchy toppled, then invaders, colonial brutality, rebellions, war, occupations, resistance, border problems, famines, land disputes, genocides, human rights violations, with just a little smidgeon of peace. Sound about right?'

'Not too far off. Decades ago, this was actually a police state.'

Valeria pointed to the dusty loudspeakers and the smashed cameras—the surveillance infrastructure of the old regime.

'And I'll bet being bested by a supernatural force hasn't made anyone a better person.'

'You're not wrong there either.'

'I just can't turn off my ears. At the Bitter in Soul, all people do is whine about underfunded public services and food shortages and resource mismanagement.'

Valeria gave me a loaded smile as a precursor to an unwanted lecture. She explained that, forty years ago, the government was decentralised; peace reigned for decades, until low-intensity warfare broke out between our southern and northern neighbours. Even before the K9 virus outbreak on the earthly plane caused an influx of deceased that had stretched resources in every area to breaking point, a battle was being fought to see if Lagaria would be carved up between our warring neighbours or placed under joint control.

'They call it a forever war, but it's only been twenty-five years off and on, with really long ceasefires.'

'Stop right there,' I yawned. 'Sounds like death sucks and then you die again.' Her black, haunted eyes gazed into mine. 'Actually, answer me this. Why are there so few children?'

'Nobody comes here from earth unless they've hit puberty.'

'Puberty? Why should scrotums and breast buds matter to the universe? You know what? I don't want to know.'

She seemed to be moving closer towards me. 'What else do you know about this, our sad little afterlife?'

'Nothing,' I said. 'And don't tell me.'

She moved closer still. 'Our major export is wheat and iron ore, crime rates are low, unemployment is high, euthanasia is encouraged, there's no rainy season and the leading cause of death is murder–suicide. Do you want to borrow my book on Lagaria and the surrounding regions?'

'Why doesn't anyone ever believe me when I say I don't want to know something?'

'What's the matter with you? You like being uninformed?'

'Yes! The more I know, the less I understand. It's something I've always felt. Knowledge is not worth knowing. It's possible to be *over*-informed. A full engagement with the world feels like a retreat from reality. Does that make sense?'

'Sort of.'

She smiled lazily, and I smiled back foolishly, and when this woman who was not my wife leaned in, I didn't turn my head or avert my lips, I allowed her to kiss me right there in the gutter.

22

Among the ferns in the breezy garden, a row of white folding chairs faced a pagoda festooned with carnations; a few dozen guests were already seated, and a long-legged, spindly groom was bounding down the back-verandah steps towards Gracie.

'Hey. We left you a dozen messages,' he said.

'I'm not screening messages right now.'

'Willow!'

The bride—soft-spoken and beautiful—was half his size. She smiled timidly as she made her way to Gracie. 'We heard about your loss. We're so sorry.'

'Thank you,' Gracie said.

'And thank you for offering to push ahead,' said the bride. 'But really, please, you should get some rest.'

'We've found a replacement, see,' the groom said.

'My cousin Jared.'

'We'd prefer if he was the one who performed the ceremony,' said the groom, with more insistence. It was clear they thought a recently bereaved widow officiating their wedding was a bad omen.

'I've already written your sermon,' Gracie said.

'I'm sure you can use it for another wedding,' the bride said sweetly.

'I wrote it for you.'

'Listen, Gracie,' the bride said. 'It's our special day, okay?'

'It's my special day too,' Gracie said. 'It's the day I get paid.'

Thirty minutes later, Gracie was centrestage between the couple, facing a semi-circle of friends and loutish cousins. 'All right, everyone. Sit down. Hurry up. I'm just going to narrate until everyone's ready. Here we are. The mother of the bride looks in fear for her personal safety. The parents of the groom have the sweats. The bride and groom are hyperventilating. That aunt-looking woman is wondering why her husband's hands have been in his lap so long.' To a particularly slow-moving elder, she said, 'Come on, Father Time, we can do this the easy way or the hard way.'

He gave out a breathy laugh and hobbled faster to his seat.

'The lover,' Gracie said, once a hush fell over the assembled guests, 'in Latin, is *amatore*. That means amateur. It's fitting. Let's admit it, you're a couple of amateurs embarking on a task that takes a seasoned professional to pull off. Who do you think you are?' She inhaled as if through a straw. 'Most of our lifelong romantic partners aren't even our second choice, right?' She paused. 'Most marriage proposals are either a diversion tactic or made to fill a wounded silence. Most wedding days go ahead because it's too late to turn back, agreed? Some couples only see their wedding as a necessary step towards their true goal of home ownership, others view this day as their childhood's official end.'

A short silence followed—everyone could hear the sound of Gracie breathing through the microphone. Guests grew uneasy at the prospect of what she might say next.

'Sometimes I develop intense crushes on the couple I'm marrying,' she said. 'Not this time.'

Gracie gently jabbed first the bride then the groom in the chest with her finger.

'Most marriages are kept artificially alive because consolidated assets are a nightmare to disentangle. Have separate bank accounts, just in case. Maintain a tidy roster of common enemies to keep you on the same side. Also, killing spiders is not a gendered task. Willow, get in there. And Gary. Don't be one of those deluded married men who look at every beautiful woman as The Road I Totally Could've Travelled. And here's a big one: Fight or flight? The smart ones always pick flight! You can't lose a flight. I mean, come back eventually, but sometimes—run.'

Gracie kept her face expressionless to conceal her urge to pull the pagoda down with her bare hands. She was also thinking that she wanted to use the word *defilement* but didn't know how to work it in.

'What is love even for? That's easy. The redistribution of the burden of living. It emerges as the by-product of intimacy. Should we bother with it? That's not entirely clear.'

She hummed a funeral march and abruptly stopped. She considered telling the audience her news. That, on the way here, she'd found out the sex of her child. In the waiting room, a woman expecting triplets had been telling the receptionist how wonderful it would be if her womb could be ethnically diverse, so she could have one Asian, one African and one white baby. A dreadlocked nurse had ushered Gracie into the room for the ultrasound, smeared cold blue gel on her belly and ran what looked like a gel-coated dildo over her stomach; on the monitor, the baby resembled a seahorse, a tadpole, a magic bean.

'Do you want to know the sex?' the nurse had asked.

When we'd discovered Gracie was pregnant, I had been adamant on keeping the sex a surprise, and she'd respected that. Now that I was dead, my wishes were null: it was going to be a girl.

'Gracie.'

Willow was looking at her with drowning eyes. How long had she been standing there daydreaming, muttering to herself?

'Probably the main advice I could give you is to enjoy your differences,' she said, 'like I did with my late husband, Mooney, bless his soul. Here's how we were different: I was talkative, Mooney always lost his keys. On the other hand, he used forks at Chinese restaurants, and in chain stores he repeatedly mistook customers for store clerks, but in restaurants it was *me* accidentally bothering customers for hot sauce or the bill. We were really in love. I always knew I would bury him, not the other way around.'

She stood perfectly still. She could hear the languid thumps of her heart. An afternoon sunlight hit the hushed and perplexed crowd. Her eyes were burning with hot tears.

'Here's what I want to know. Why does Death always tackle me to the ground and make me watch?'

The father of the bride now had his arm around her and was gently guiding her off the pagoda. Gracie aimed a pointed smile at the happy couple.

'You two are a fucking juggernaut. Your disintegration will be compelling. Invite us, please. Invite us!'

Gracie didn't know how many hours she'd walked before she was aware of the weirdness of physical motion. She felt scooped-out, voided. That was the last wedding service she would ever perform, and this decision seemed to wake her up.

The day was still warm and bright; she was on a busy street, amidst a peak-hour surge of bodies. Stone-faced men made her shudder, while the women—she could not see anything sisterly in a single one.

At Taylor Square, beside the fountain's spasmodic bursts, a barefoot maniac in a mouldy suit was shouting, 'We'll envy the dinosaurs their quick death!' It had come to this: cartoon hobos shrieking their end days predictions. She felt overcome with a desire to go into all the houses of God to blaspheme, to piss on church altars, to touch a Torah with jam on her fingers, to tread shit-encrusted boots into mosques.

Instead, she strutted along, comforted by her anger, until her pathway was impeded by an impeccably dressed couple slow-walking hand in hand in front of her. In order to overtake them, she was forced to step off the footpath onto the actual road. She glanced back at the moneyed couple who were still oblivious to her and, not two minutes later, Gracie was blocked by *another* loved-up couple.

It seemed a person couldn't walk down the street without encountering these itinerant, egoistic, two-headed lovebeasts with their low chuckles and interlaced ring fingers, secret looks and secret smiles, coded language and easy silences, taking up 92.5 percent of the narrow pavement. This time, Gracie flung herself at them, shouting, 'Out of the way, fuckers!' and charged through their barricade, savouring the physical contact while mean-laughing like she hadn't since adolescence. Their appalled faces were the first delightful thing she'd seen in a month.

That night in the bedroom, kneeling before an incense stick and a dashboard Jesus, Gracie prayed. It was an aggressive, petulant prayer, in which she demanded the return of everyone she'd ever lost. She opened her eyes; Owen was standing in the doorway as if leaning into a strong wind. Who was he, to be witnessing this? She gave him a dirty look.

'Have you heard of the widowhood effect?' he asked.

'Yes.'

'You have?'

'I have a sixty-six percent increased chance of dying in the next three months.' She closed her eyes tightly and gasped—she felt movement among her organs. It didn't feel like the baby kicking so much as a prowling and rustling about, making her feel unbalanced.

'Are you okay?' he asked.

Her swollen belly looked fake and rubbery, like the prosthetic silicone bumps that women wore in China to disguise an adoption.

'I'm in mourning, I have morning sickness, and I'm in withdrawal. Love is a form of addiction. I quit Mooney cold turkey. The comedown is a bitch. So leave me alone.'

That night, she crept into Owen's room and stood at the foot of his bed, watching this rogue individual who seemed to hesitate even in his sleep. Who *was* this man dying in her house? Most nights she lay unsleeping for hours in her bed, counting how many times Owen lumbered off to the bathroom to empty his bladder—four, five—sometimes only dribbles, his enlarged prostate unrelated to his fatal brain disease, the very definition of adding insult to injury.

Gracie went downstairs and knocked at the front door from the inside. Who is to say this is not how you summon ghosts? She vowed to knock once every morning and once every night, in hope that I might answer.

She was convinced my presence still remained and she moved around the house glancing hopefully at all anomalous shades of light. She was imposing her will on shadows, forcing them alive; every curtain flutter, every gust of wind or floorboard creak, she attributed to my wafting spirit. She swore she could hear me in whatever room she wasn't presently in.

'What are you doing?' said Owen.

Gracie was waving her hand haltingly through the air.

'I can feel him, he's here.' Her voice was full of love and pain. 'I think my hand passed through a fragment of him.'

She believed that if she gathered enough of these fragments, the whole me could be restored—such sweet nonsense! Owen felt a repugnance towards the whole notion and sneered. He was enraged by the idea of my return and, at the same time, scoffed at the obvious absurdity of it.

'Your scepticism is preventing his materialising,' Gracie said accusingly.

He said, 'This is bullshit. I'm going back to bed.'

After a few minutes, Gracie crept down the hallway to Owen's open door. The curtains were pulled back and moonlight filled the room. Owen was sitting up in bed; he gave her a smile that exposed his gums.

'You've come to me at last,' he said.

'I don't want to be alone.'

'Hop in.'

'I'm not sleeping in your fucking bed. I need my space.'

Owen climbed out of bed and got to work. He went into her bedroom and moved the side tables and armchair into the hallway, pushed her bed against the window, dragged his mattress and bedframe from his room into hers, arranging the two beds side by side until the room was entirely taken up by what looked like the world's biggest bed.

'Here's your space,' he said.

Gracie and Owen crawled into their respective beds and looked out the window at the starry night.

'Good night,' she said.

'Good night.'

Owen turned off the lights.

Gracie said, 'I remember when I was a kid, watching one of those American TV shows from the fifties, where couples slept in separate beds, and I turned to my mother, I was eight, and I said, "How do they decide whose bed to fuck in?"'

Owen chuckled. 'That's hilarious.'

'Is it? I don't know. Memories are pointless.'

Thinking about her mother was a lightweight style of mourning, a gentle betrayal to dwell on someone who died so long ago rather than the recently dead. She sat up in a hot panic.

'Are you okay?' asked Owen.

'No, I'm still in mourning.'

'I know. I'm sorry.'

'You are too.'

'No,' Owen said. 'I'm just depressed.'

'Depression *is* mourning, dummy—only it's for your dumb self. You're grieving for the better you that you failed to be.'

She reached over and grabbed her phone and unlocked it; she realised with shock that she hadn't been on social media once since my death. With bleary eyes, she scrolled through friends' updates and photos and shared news articles—our little fortress island was still safe from the K9 virus and boasting about it, but elsewhere a pattern was emerging. In China, France, the Philippines, India, South America: outbreak, containment, breach.

She was doomscrolling through incredible stories of cities engulfed, video footage of parents trying to break into quarantine to be with their children, Russians posting tips on how to commit suicide painlessly. Yet worldwide chaos wasn't tempering the resentful tone or altering any of her friends' and followers' trenchant positions. It was more or less the same unbearable people, with their unbearable opinions and the unbearable manner in which they expressed them—the morally bankrupt on the right, the morally confused on the left, and one least charitable interpretation after another.

She wondered when one human being had last given another human being the benefit of the doubt—2005? And why were all the most selfish people on earth pretending to have empathy burnout? And why were so many people boasting that vulnerability was their only accreditation? And why were people still engaging in the taxing promotional duties of selling themselves as happy? The whole discourse now seemed like someone's overreaction to someone else's overreaction to a hysterical response to an innocuous comment. She thought: surely the wisdom of crowds would not be a phrase if someone tried to coin it today.

For the first time in a month, she posted something: 'We're supposed to believe that there are five stages of grief, and not one of them is Terrified?' That elicited a string of condolences with accompanying emojis—'I'm still sorry for your loss' with a frowny face, or a frowny face with a single tear—links to widow dating sites (hook up with hot widowers!) and links to Widow Getaways for the 'widowed to come together for support and inspiration in the recovery process'. On their comments board, Gracie posted: 'What if mourning is just a dignified version of sulking?'

'Gracie.'

'What?'

Owen gazed at her adoringly from his bed. 'Have you taken your prenatal vitamins today?'

'No.'

'You're getting big.'

'Thanks for the heads up.'

Gracie thought it was annoying how a pregnancy was always described as either wanted or unwanted. These are not absolute states. A pregnancy can go from *quite* wanted to *desperately* unwanted and snap back again in a single hour. Right now, all she knew was that for her to be emotionally ready to deliver, she'd need the ninety-week gestation period of an elephant.

'Maybe you shouldn't look at the news right now.'

She ignored him. On Abby Flynn's post about how the tragedy of the worldwide outbreaks had made her look inward and given her strength to transform and find peace, Gracie posted: 'Self-actualising on social media is the new flossing in public.' On an article about how unjust it was that the working class in high-density urban centres were wearing paper masks while the rich wore masks made of impermeable graphene, she posted: 'Everyone believes they deserve better. They're wrong. They barely deserve what they have now.' Then she added: 'The real inequality on earth is that some faces are easier to love than others.' That instigated a lively and vitriolic discussion on Gracie's limited understanding of the world as a white woman. She posted: 'It's as Confucius says: "One dog barks at something and a hundred bark at his sound."' That elicited a barrage of *Fuck yous* and *STFU cunts* in response before blocking and unfollowing her.

Something about this reminded Gracie of how penguins will push their fellow travellers into the sea to make their own path clear of predators. Aimee posted: 'Check your privilege.' Gracie responded: 'I checked it about three days ago and again this morning. It's simply not practical to check my privilege AND confirm to you that I checked it as a preface to each and every sentence I write.' Aimee posted: 'You have no idea how hard it is to be a Chinese woman in Australia.' Gracie posted: 'I've known you nearly all your life. The worst thing that ever happened to you was when a waiter poured tap water into your sparkling water.'

Now Hamid wrote, admonishing Gracie for questioning Aimee's lived experience, and Gracie posted: 'Why do we give credence to "lived experience"? All the time people misperceive intentions, misread facial expressions, misunderstand tone; they project, transfer, carry a history of past troubled confrontations with them into benign interactions, and then you have to factor in confirmation bias, negativity bias, inter-group bias, the availability heuristic, the fundamental attribution error, the bandwagon effect, the clustering illusion, the empathy gap, salience, herding, selective attention. How can anyone know enough about every individual's psychological state to confirm how much of their inner subjective experience corresponds with objective reality? Maybe it's seventy percent. Maybe it's eighty percent. Maybe it's thirty percent. Let it be said once and for all: lived experience as an evidentiary standard is mostly garbage.'

Bruce posted: 'Log off and go to sleep.' Gracie responded: 'Why are you even chiming in? Your profile photo makes you look like a convicted sex offender caught in the act of erasing himself from the register.'

It has to be said, Gracie loved violating community standards. It gave her the same feeling she got crashing through hand-holding couples on the pavement.

She posted on a particularly ugly baby: 'Physiognomy is destiny.' On a photo of Emily and Andy Gilbert on their honeymoon, she posted: 'When you see a couple on a tandem bicycle, everyone thinks, Fuck off, you smug cunts. That was true in the 1890s and it's true now.'

It was easy to weaponise people's inability to hear a dissenting view; she was haemorrhaging friends and followers at a dizzying rate. Although people's low opinions always nauseated her, right now she wanted their opinions to be even lower, and so she soldiered on with nervous delight.

Owen said, 'Gracie. Are you going to put your phone down soon?'

'What business is it of yours?'

She looked back at the phone and smirked. She had lost her entire 'friend group' in one evening, all 5000 of them, except one:

a single miserable bastard named Julian Delahunty. She didn't know who he was! At three a.m., she received a message from him: 'Do you mind if I share this?' Gracie didn't know which of her posts he was referring to, but she wrote: 'I don't care what you do.' Mission accomplished. Satisfied, Gracie put her phone on silent and closed her eyes.

When she woke the next morning, Gracie had 47,503 followers. She posted: 'The greatest fear of being unmasked is that it often reveals an identical face underneath.'

23

On Saturday, Valeria took me to a post-traumatic death disorder support group. It was held in a squat brick building on a deserted stretch of Industrial Drive. 'I spent almost my whole adult life in therapy talking about death,' a beefy man was saying when we walked in. 'And here I am, dead *and* in therapy again. It's unbearable.'

'And yet, we bear it,' said a curly-haired woman who paced the room with authority. She spotted Valeria and me lingering in the doorway and tilted her head as an invitation to enter. 'Okay, I think we can start now.'

There were at least fifty people sitting on plastic orange chairs. The curly-haired woman clapped her hands. 'Most of you know me, but for those who don't, I'm Molly, your group guide,' she said. 'We have a few new members among us. Please introduce yourself.'

Valeria nudged me. I stood up. 'I'm Angus Mooney. Australian.'

'Hi, Angus,' said Molly. 'And how did you die?'

'I was murdered by a doctor who was in love with my wife.'

'Thank you. Can everyone else please state their name and cause of death, and can we start with the plague victims?'

About half the room raised their hands and introduced themselves. As if to set themselves apart from the rest of us, these historic fatalities gave each other knowing glances.

'So many!' she said. 'What else have we got?'

Each person raised a trembling hand and spoke. 'Gary. Stage-three Hodgkin's lymphoma.'

'Johannes. Mudslide.'

'Cynthia. Massive stroke.'

'Sumal. Old age.'

Everyone let out a whistle of admiration.

'Tamara. I think the hair-dye I used was toxic.'

Molly nodded with approval. 'Good. Thank you. Anyone here die by elective surgery? Any liposuction fatalities? Sun-bed morbidities? Anyone's silicone implants leach into their bloodstream?'

One tentative hand rose up.

'Chronic smokers?'

'I died during a colonoscopy,' offered a woman.

'I died sucking poison from a friend's snake bite,' said a ginger-haired man. 'I guess I accidentally ingested some.'

'What bad luck!' said Molly.

'Fabrizio. Cystic fibrosis.'

'Any suicides?'

Twenty-two men and one woman shot up their hands and spoke over each other like siblings in a large Irish family. This odd collective seemed sharply divided: some gloomy fuckers seemed broken by the shame of having killed themselves, but the rest acted superior, as if they'd sped to this afterlife on urgent business.

'Who here was in the wrong place at the wrong time?'

Several hands went up, including a glistening-eyed woman who held up both hands. 'Carol. Car accident. And no, I wasn't killed on impact. I was engulfed in flames. Nice to meet you all.'

It wasn't hard to see that this was as much a pissing contest as anything else.

'Who here died from self-inflicted wounds? And you can interpret that any way you like.'

More raised hands. The room felt heavy with one-upmanship and the need many seemed to have to prostrate themselves before a room of self-interested strangers. Maybe therapy's not for me, I thought, and began strategising my exit. Valeria sensed this and whispered, 'Give it a chance.'

The only interesting part of the whole evening was meeting a fidgeting unknown soldier. His name was Frank. He stood up and said, 'I stepped on an IUD. It was a real bummer. I never wanted to die young and leave a good-looking corpse.'

'Don't worry,' I said. 'You didn't.'

He cackled and scooted a couple of seats closer. 'Watch this.' He shot his hand up in the air; it looked like he was trying to hold his own arm at arm's length.

'Yes, Frank?'

Frank eased his gaze over the gathered whiners. 'Was any one here collateral damage?'

No one raised their hands, and a few folded their arms for emphasis. He looked at me and grinned. 'Every dumb fuck here thinks they were the intended target.'

He wasn't wrong. You could hear them doting over their self-image, worrying about their 'name and reputation', businesses that would be run into the ground without them, legacies trashed by the incompetents they left behind. People either couldn't put their ancestral grievances to bed or they couldn't shut up about diets and being fat-shamed. The former anorexics, still with their incorrigible body-image issues! It was all so embarrassing and endless. The ones who never had kids were gloating that they didn't leave anyone behind. It's uncanny how human beings never miss a chance to miss the point.

Molly gave a bent smile and shouted, 'Is there anyone we missed?'

A silver-haired woman's hand wavered in the air.

'How did you die?' asked Molly.

'Unknown causes.'

'Oh! Is there a story there?'

'No, not really.'

We sighed in disappointment. Molly said, 'Thank you, everyone, for sharing. Now I would love to pick up where we left off. Brett, you were talking about how you felt about the virus, remember?'

'No.'

'Remember you got upset when I suggested that when you die with millions of others, it's hard to know what to do with the sense of your own importance, once so core to your sense of self?'

That really got things going. For the next two hours, I mostly listened. We weren't the most moral specimens, but we weren't the worst either. We were superstars only in our own orbits, categorically boring, merely average. Some had a horrible life progression from victim to abuser, others were upbeat underachievers with or without criminal backgrounds. We gave to charity, but so rarely and so little that we could tell you the dollar amount. We were vanquished by our betters and could laugh about it, or we were zeros on a professional front and couldn't. We were taken by force, natural causes or freak accidents. The only lesson one could possibly derive from all this was that almost nobody died on their own terms.

Then we moved on to fears of exclusion. That's what burned—wondering what the other dead were up to, the suspicion that there was a better afterlife somewhere else. Now we were getting down to it.

A woman kneeling on her chair said, 'To have finally reached the end of a long road, only to find it connected to *another* long road . . .?'

Everyone had their own metaphor they were eager to air. I couldn't take any more. I got up and stumbled through the chairs, banging on knees and treading on toes, with Valeria following after me. I felt comical, the others looked mystified, and the only thing that had been clarified was that dying brought many of us to the brink of suicide. We were ashamed of our lives, and now we were ashamed of our afterlives. We blew it.

Once outside again in the bustling ghost town, sun-blinded in the warren of narrow streets and alleys, I learned that in life Valeria had been a brand manager, an event planner and a product coordinator, in that order. Before her own murder, she had lived in an apartment building in LA with a dog named Bones. She spoke in clichés: 'The sky's the limit.' And: 'I'm no wallflower.' She used the word 'literally' literally a dozen times.

A bus halted in front of us, a hot wind blowing dust, and a hesitant group disembarked. Valeria admitted she'd been obsessed with being single and overweight, and just at *the* breakthrough moment that she'd decided to enjoy a life not defined by what she didn't have, she came to a sudden and violent end. Apart from her murder, she'd had a pretty uneventful life.

The last person off the bus was a wide-eyed man who seemed surprised to be on solid ground.

'Good morning!' Valeria shouted at him. 'How was your passing?'

'Stressful. I was trampled in a riot.'

'That's too bad.'

We walked to a café that served gourmet doughnuts and coffee, settling on a red wooden bench outside. We were only a bite in when an old man in tortoiseshell sunglasses accosted us. 'Can you spare a couple of dollars?' he said. His mouth was black and half his teeth were missing. He held up a palm-sized machine: 'Quick transfer?'

Valeria turned to me and said, 'When you wake up here you get your teeth back, so when you see someone toothless, that means they've gone and lost them all again.' The man spat and turned away, insulted to be spoken about like that. Valeria said loudly after him, 'You really have to give zero fucks to lose a second set of brand-new adult teeth!'

Valeria and I drank our coffees, watching the slow-moving crowd pass by. 'Personally, I think you can tell those who were left for dead,' she said. I looked to see if that was true. There was an ambient fury about them. 'I used to be pretty angry too,' she said. 'But I feel okay now.'

'Me too.'

'Are you sure?'

'I'm fine, why?'

'You're crying.'

Was I? I reached up and felt my sodden cheeks. Well, who wouldn't cry, looking at all those dead folks. Poor us! But so what? And who was I? What right did I have to pity *anyone*, let alone *everyone*?

I wondered if death had broken me into many pieces and this piece I was here was the smallest piece of all. 'I'm stuck in death and meanwhile my baby is growing inside the woman I love.'

The thought of it felt lethal—yet here I was, mourning the living. How absurd! How much longing can a person take? What was I supposed to do? How was I supposed to behave? Gracie would know—that was the irony. I needed *her* to explain it to me.

'When we first met, I thought she was book smart and I was street smart, but it turned out she was both and I was neither.'

'Come on.' Valeria grabbed me by the wrist and pulled me to my feet. 'I have something I think will cheer you up.'

It wasn't a theatre exactly—we were inside a darkened auditorium. On stage was a small glass-enclosed room where a naked man was strapped to a metal table, illuminated by crossbeams of light. A dour white-coated man entered, wheeling an oxygen machine.

'That's the anaesthesiologist,' Valeria whispered.

'What is this?'

'An execution.'

'What?!'

She browsed the program. 'He killed a priest. Here's the executioner now.'

A man dressed in a black suit and gloves confidently entered the room. 'Do you have any last words?' he asked the naked man.

'Not off the top of my head.'

The sprightly anaesthesiologist, smiling affably, placed a mask over the naked man's face. The amber light on the two of them was cold and strange.

After a minute, Valeria whispered, 'He's asleep now.'

I gave her a hard, vacant stare.

'What?' she asked.

'Why would you take me here?'

'I thought you'd find it interesting.'

I got to my feet and banged every set of knees on my way out. 'Wait!' I heard her say. 'He hasn't flatlined yet!'

Outside, the skies were a metallic blue and the sunlight so glaring I had to shield my eyes. I started walking, desperate for the crisp, breezeless air to wash the dark, black-curtained room out of me.

'Hey. Are you upset?'

Valeria had followed me; I charged angrily on, through a swarm of dazed citizens. The sick sun was shining brutally on the surly dead. Why should I stop for her? Other than being deceased, we had nothing much in common.

She said, 'Wait, okay? I'm sorry I took you there.'

'We just have different ideas of a good time.'

'I thought you'd feel the same way I do.'

'About seeing a man die?'

'About being denied justice,' she said.

I stopped. My slow-moving brain finally caught up. Underneath her bright smile and meandering chatter was a woman who'd been raped and murdered. I hadn't considered she'd be daydreaming of violent retribution. I felt disgustingly obtuse.

I turned away and looked at the hundreds of walking fatalities as far as the eye could see, not a single incontrovertible fact to soothe them, each one reliving the terror of dying while anticipating a future death—it was all too much.

'Do you want to see my church?' Valeria asked, almost desperately.

'I don't think so. I don't believe in . . . whatever.'

'You mean like you didn't believe in life after death?'

She had me there. And besides, she was offering to take me on a tour of her soul—it would be rude to refuse.

The small, ancient-looking stone church was pizza-oven hot inside, with one large stained-glass window behind the altar and eight tinted ones along the nave, which dulled the sunlight. The images in them were gory; in one, priests were feasting on each other's throats, in another, a supine woman was pulling a blood-soaked baby from her own abdomen. There were lit candles everywhere and a mirrored ceiling. The priest may or may not have been wearing hair extensions.

Valeria pointed to a lurid portrait of a naked, bearded Christ with a spear that pierced his face and went out the back of his skull. 'All He wanted to do was live a quiet life and trim his beard and repair sandals, but He couldn't be late for his own resurrection,' she said.

'Nonsense,' I said.

'Shhh,' a congregant hissed.

The priest said: 'God wants you to pat yourself on the back for a life well lived. The surprise of God is that he had low expectations of you.' The priest was trying to look every member of the congregation in the eye, and alternated between using the microphone for emphasis and using it by accident. 'You should all feel flattered to be here. We are unique among our species. Our souls have been through a lot.'

He seemed like he was trying to flirt with the entire congregation, all genders, and I couldn't help but think of Gracie and how much she would enjoy this.

'We cycled out of our own obsolescence and our souls were pulled here like iron filings towards Our Magnet and Saviour. Now we are waiting for the Lord to state his business. Yet God's silence is a hurt silence. It's excruciating,' he said. 'Our deadly cancers are behind us.'

'Amen,' said the congregation.

'Our exit wounds have closed over.'

'Amen.'

The priest said: 'Let us complain.'

The congregation answered: 'Why us?'

The priest said: 'Let us put it into perspective.'

The congregation answered: 'Why not us?'

The priest said: 'Let this be a lesson to you.'

The congregation said: 'It is. And so we let it be.' They finished off with a chorus of exuberant *amens*.

I thought, If there is a God and he doesn't apologise for the inconvenience, then fuck Him. There's literally nothing He could do that would change my low opinion of him.

The priest said: 'Accepting God into your life is a heavy undertaking. Our existence feels improbable, but is inevitable—and perhaps ineradicable. We cannot go in the opposite direction. We cannot relocate ourselves. Our eternal silences are short-lived.'

I looked at the congregation. It shouldn't have surprised me that some people here were still trying to get back in God's good graces. Man, did I have zero respect for unshakable faith.

The priest directed his vibrant gaze skyward. 'Well, Lord, it seems we are at an impasse, yet we love Your off-hand way of expressing love. I get that we are going to heaven, but in stages.' He waved his hands over the congregation. 'How do we see Him? Our Emotionally Unavailable Lord and Saviour only appears to mankind in dreams, as that is the source of his immortality. Moses was asleep when he saw that burning bush. And so, let us sleep.'

Everyone closed their eyes in secret knowing. The silence lasted over a minute. The priest whispered into the microphone: 'When He created the earth, you don't think He had any other irons in the fire?'

I opened my eyes. Standing at the altar was a completely different man. This second priest had shaggy hair and looked genuinely insane.

'This is a twenty-four-hour church,' Valeria explained. 'The sermons are continuous. They tag team.'

'He built you a cathedral and you couldn't stop talking about the hinges on the doors. He's embarrassed for you. You were drunk on yourselves. He didn't mean for you to feel special. He didn't think exteriority would be such a thing, that you'd make such a big deal out of bare flesh. He really didn't foresee that you'd define yourself by the other, or that your self-perception would fill your field of vision. It was really weird, the things you were ashamed of. He gave you minds to think about the manifestation of the invisible, and He's been blown away by how you worried about your body-mass index. He made you age as a reminder to focus on the brevity of your life. Self-love was only meant to be a jumping-off point. You were performing your lives, but not for Him. Why did you feel so exposed? Why did you dread a faux pas more than His wrath? He didn't know that unwanted attention of the wrong kind would drive so much of your life choices and behaviour. You worried about a pimple *and not the looming stench of your rotting corpse*. He totally did not predict that.'

That's when I stood up to go. Valeria looked panicked. 'You have to wait until the next changeover,' she whispered.

I made my way towards the exit where a third priest was already waiting in the wings with an irresistible force-of-destiny smile, and where more parishioners were huddled under the arches in hopeful prayer. I thought: These dopes couldn't have a road to Damascus moment on the actual road to Damascus or any other fucking thoroughfare.

As I stepped into the street, I heard the priest say: 'What is the point of having daily lives now? What are the implications of a life bestowed again? Be grateful, would you? The Lord has carried you to term.'

FIVE

'The reverse side also has a reverse side.'

Japanese proverb

24

'I've got some news.' The supervisor was standing in a pile of half-finished umbrellas. 'Time to move on. You've all been reassigned to construction.'

'I don't know anything about construction,' I said.

'You're able-bodied.'

'Everybody here is able-bodied.'

'That's true, but everyone from constructibles has been reassigned to temporary housing. Hurry up. There's a bus waiting for you outside.'

'Aren't you coming with us?'

'It's under the purview of the DEM. You work for them now.' Prompted by our blank faces, he clarified: 'Disaster and Emergency Management.'

I wanted to know more, but his tone suggested work itself was some kind of a mysterious cult you didn't ask questions about.

There were forty of us squeezed onto an old bus, which carried us out past farmland, through dark, wooded hills, and down a broken road where every now and then we saw hardened mudslides or a crumbling brick wall—remnants of a former civilisation. Then we moved along a dusty road until we arrived in the middle of an open field, where men in green shirts were installing power lines.

Our new supervisor, Griffin, greeted us as we stepped off the bus. He had sandy hair, stared into the middle-distance while rolling cigarettes with his massive hands, and looked like he was at all times contemplating an abrupt mood swing.

'The ranks of the dead have swelled beyond our capacity to accommodate them,' Griffin said. 'We'll be making temporary shelters for the new arrivals. I want to personally thank you all for joining the humanitarian effort.'

'How many dead are these shelters supposed to accommodate?'

'A lot.'

The sleeping quarters were to be a hodgepodge of emergency canvas tents, prefabricated housing and old shipping containers. We loaded bricks off the back of trucks, drove in posts and erected tents. The only one who wasn't working was Farhad, who sat on the ground and refused to lift a finger. Griffin blew a whistle and marched over.

'Are you going to pitch in?'

'We're putting human beings inside storage facilities,' said Farhad.

'That's right.'

Farhad kicked at the containers. 'This is not a refugee crisis. This is a housing crisis. Why are they building temporary camps instead of just expanding the town and creating new suburbs?'

'I don't know.'

'We need affordable housing solutions!' he yelled.

'What do you care?'

'What do you mean? This is an emergency settlement at best. How long are people expected to live here in these conditions? And then where do they go?'

'Maybe they stay here,' said Griffin.

'That's unacceptable.'

'Just get back to work!'

After lunch, we dug pit latrines until sundown. I doused my head in the freezing water from a bucket, then joined my co-workers at the edge of the meadow to share a beer and marvel at our dubious achievement. Farhad again harangued Griffin about how many of the displaced dead would be expected to reside here.

'No idea,' Griffin said.

'Do you know anything about plague projections?'

'Not my department. But I can tell you there has never been this many dead.' Griffin squatted down and dug into the dirt with his fingers. 'Obviously we've had periods of heavy influx: the Mongol conquests, the Great War, the Spanish Flu, World War II, China's Great Leap Forward, the Second Congo War, COVID-19, but those were only blips compared to this.'

We fell silent as the massive scale of the situation began to dawn on us. Farhad was furious: those poor people, undertaking the difficult journey from life to death—and *this* is where they'd end up? They'd think they'd arrived in hell. And what about those who died *in* refugee camps?

'Will they be allowed to come into town?' asked Kira.

'Some might,' said Griffin.

'Which ones? Who decides?'

'That's obvious,' said Amir, who hadn't spoken all day. His face was creased with a down-to-business look. 'Why don't we just put the Jews into the camps and let the others into the town.'

'Why the Jews?'

'Why not?' he said. 'Why should we spare the Jews over other people who are not Jews?'

'You're dead, fuckface,' yelled Kira. 'What's the point of still hating Jews?'

'Because they're Jews!'

Joseph said, 'We still have to decide how to split the others up. Maybe the Sunnis, the Chechens and the Turkish over here, and the Shiites, the Russians and the Greeks over there . . .'

The rest of us exchanged eye rolls. It was so embarrassing to have dragged the narcissism of small differences all the way across dimensions, and so anachronistic to go on pretending there had *ever* been a single meaningful distinction between human beings worth making.

That night, at the Bitter in Soul, I drank in anguish. The clientele looked like they'd taken a wrong turn during a pilgrimage. A man walked around patting everyone on the shoulder, asking, 'How's your husk today? How's the old shell?'

There was more talk of dead doctors and engineers shanghaied at the arrival point, and an all-out war that could end either in one town enslaving the next or in a peaceful unification and the creation of a super state. These frenzied discussions went on and on: about cartographers who died under mysterious circumstances, looted granaries and firebombed casinos, and just how lame the failure of the Resistance was (resisting what, or who, I didn't know).

I closed my eyes and let the snippets of conversation wash

over me: 'The border always shifts on the anniversary of the third armistice' and 'You know "the angel of death" is just an honorary title, right?'

It seemed impossible to get the hang of the place. On my wanderings, I'd seen billboards advertising nightmare sketch artists, excess memory draining, murderers under bridges who would end your torment for a price. I'd shared park benches with embittered motivational speakers, good Samaritans in it for themselves, and first-life sceptics—those who disbelieved memories of earth, even dismissing their own recollections as mind-control propaganda.

Mostly, wherever I turned, I saw a traumatised population with an embarrassing number of epiphanies per capita, some with a siege mentality, others who were deathly quiet, as if afraid to give away their position. It was like we were living in the city version of a ghost ship, marooned inside a vanishing point. More than just a large, dreary town, it was a place of potentialities, and I was uncertain all our realities were consistent; I'd seen people gazing skyward, but when I looked up I saw nothing of consequence. I'd spotted men laughing at their reflections, whereas I found mirrors here totally dehumanising. The reflection looked queasily like me, but as if I could be anyone at all; it gave me the vivid sense of an animal that had strayed from the herd into an abattoir.

And the business of only three-fifths of the human dead arriving here; I'd heard many argue for wildly different amounts, half or even two-thirds, and a multiplicity of reasons. But no one knew if we were the forgotten or the creatures who gave up on love, if we were the chosen people or the unwelcome guests, or what we were beneath our human form, or if we were on another planet or the same planet in an alternative time period or merely still alive but on a well-trodden path to the psychiatric hospital.

People were still disputing how they got here; the man next to me at the Bitter in Soul insisted he had 'permeated some kind of hymen'. His drinking companion responded wearily, 'When it comes to the elixir of life—you can't give it away.'

I took another slug of whisky and said, 'I have no intention of ever learning any of the new astrological signs.'

I had resolved to remain incurious for practical purposes. The longer my existence went on, the more I wondered if my preference for not-knowing was merely a desire for a permanent state of plausible deniability.

Valeria came in and sat beside me, as if we had arranged to meet. We drank side by side in single-minded silence.

'I didn't ask to be reborn,' I said.

She raised a glass. 'The world is ugly, and the people are sad.'

'I'll drink to that.'

'Wallace Stevens.'

'Who?'

'Never mind.'

I thought about those wretched canvas tents and stuffy, windowless containers and felt ashamed of my good luck to have died on the right side of that razor wire.

Valeria said, 'Promise not to laugh.'

'Nope.'

'I've started to pursue my dream of becoming an actress.'

'Here?'

'Why not? I've been getting auditions. I haven't landed anything yet, but I'm saving up for some new headshots.'

Her optimism for a hopeful future was almost pornographic.

'I need to go home,' I said.

'I'll walk with you.'

Outside, the crowd hadn't thinned, despite the late hour. Nobody looked where they were going, and we saw three pedestrian-on-pedestrian head-on collisions. A church bell clanged incessantly—someone drunk had got to it again, probably the priest. A couple were going at it doggy style, up against a dumpster—street fucking was prohibited but rarely enforced, and then only during daylight hours. The admonishment 'get a room!' was often met with the simple rejoinder: 'No thanks. We're good.'

Valeria nudged me. 'How are you holding up?'

'What a loathsome question.'

'Here's a better one.' She lounged theatrically against the wall, implying an absent-minded sexuality. It was cute. 'Why haven't you fucked me yet?'

'I'm married.'

'Your wife's a widow.'

'What does that make me?'

'Available.'

Relationship choices in death were the same as in life: wearying monogamy, empty casual sex, doomed polyamory, unhygienic sex parties, soul-destroying solitude. Even here, there wasn't a single additional option.

Valeria told me that, should it factor into my decision, everyone had been cured of herpes, HPV and HIV. All the sexually transmitted diseases I had feared in life were gone. Our genitals were a blank slate. The women had their hymens back! Eggs were restocked, the infertile were fertile again, and even those who'd had hysterectomies had their reproductive systems returned in mint condition. All vasectomies were reversed. The birth rate was high, and so was the abortion rate.

At the door of my building, Valeria took my hand and raised it to her soft lips. It had always been a mystery to me why anybody found me attractive, let alone enough so to bother making a move, and I always put it down to certain women just playing the hand they believed they'd been dealt. She gave me a lascivious smile that I pretended not to see. I kissed her on the cheek.

'Good night, Valeria.'

'Good night.'

I went upstairs to my room and climbed into bed fully clothed and put the pillow over my face.

There was a knock on my door. Valeria, I guessed, had decided to make me an offer I couldn't refuse; now I probably wouldn't refuse it—after all, Gracie *was* a widow. And in this sustained fever dream of an afterlife, she wouldn't begrudge me companionship, would she? And why was I being faithful to my wife anyway? Was this about commitment, or denial of my own irreversible death? I splashed my face with water and brushed my teeth and dimmed the lighting. Valeria knocked again.

'Coming!'

I flung open the door. Two strangers—an elderly man and a woman—stood in a pocket of darkness in the hallway. They were sloppily outfitted, but as if they'd dressed up for the occasion; he wore a tie that hung loosely, she went from looking at me to peering into her purse. I don't know how I knew, but I just knew.

'It's us. Dawn and Joel. Your biological parents,' the woman who was my mother said.

'When we got a notification of your arrival, we couldn't believe it,' the man who was my father said. His pale, drawn face gave him the appearance of an accountant who'd died over a ledger. 'We don't expect you to invite us in, but we could buy you dinner. Now, or some other time?'

'Please, son,' the woman who was my mother said. She gave off the vibe of a librarian who'd just come from a book burning.

They looked like ordinary people, entirely unlike any of the strangers I'd often picked out of a crowd as my parents. I felt a cruelty welling up inside me. I wanted to slam the door in their faces.

'All right,' I said. 'I'll get my jacket.'

If there was a secret handshake that blood relatives do, I didn't know it. We made our way into a café, took a booth by the window and sat motionless, too afraid to speak. I couldn't work out what they expected from me—if they hoped I'd fawn over them, or if they wanted me to commiserate over their life choices.

The woman who was my mother said, 'Did you go on any special holidays when you were alive?'

'Did you ever get to see the Great Barrier Reef?'

The Great Barrier Reef? What were they on about? 'Coral's bleached now,' I heard myself say. 'The whole thing's pretty much ruined.'

'You're kidding.'

'Stoopid hoomins,' the woman who was my mother added.

They were nervous, and their clumsiness wasn't endearing. I had my own instincts to contend with—I felt like I was talking to a couple of collection agents. They were losers by anyone's definition.

'You seem really nice,' said the woman who was my mother. 'Doesn't he seem nice?'

'We could do a same-day DNA test if you want,' said the man who was my father.

'What for?'

'To prove to you that we are who we say we are.'

'I can see it for myself.'

It wasn't hard to recognise aspects of myself in their pinched, squirrelly faces. I didn't need or want any further verification.

'I have to ask,' I said. 'Why did you abandon me and disappear?'

'Well, we couldn't abandon you and then stick around,' the man who was my father said. 'How would that've looked?'

'He's joking. The truth is, we had a few bad years.'

'More than a few.'

'And then we did get sober,' the woman who was my mother added. 'We just had to move forward with our lives.'

'We regretted it intensely.'

'By the time we came to our senses, you were probably seven or eight years old.'

'By then we didn't think we deserved you.'

This was so banal, so mundane, I couldn't get my head around it. I'd expected an extraordinary tale of woe, but it wasn't like that at all. They'd just preferred not to keep me.

'And?'

'And that's it, really,' said the man who was my father. 'We were in a dark place back then.'

That's what was on offer: a brief account of their reasons, an insulting twinge of regret, and nothing more. What was worse was that, after rationalising every error in their lives to my face, they had the temerity to look relieved.

'So, what's going on with you?'

I wanted to bang their heads together—instead, I got to my feet.

'It was nice meeting you,' I said. 'But I'm just not interested. I wondered about you my entire life—but now I'm dead I don't have to wonder anymore.'

'We're a disappointment,' the woman who was my mother said, morosely.

'No, I'm just not in the headspace right now. Maybe in another life.'

They handed me a card. 'Please take this. It's got our address on it.' I stuck it in my pocket and stood there looking at their tight, sad faces in the ringing silence. I gave them a dreary smile and walked away.

Even my own reaction destabilised me. I wormed my way home through the thick shadows of the crowded streets and wondered where all my violent urges had gone. I missed them.

When I got to my floor, Valeria was outside my apartment. She could read the residue of dismay on my face.

'What happened?'

'I met my birth parents.'

'That's so nice! I have an aunt here and two cousins who I'm not even close to, but neither of my parents made it, unfortunately. It's so weird who makes it here and who doesn't. Don't listen to anyone who says they understand it because when it's their loved ones, people go on about how emotional connection is the binding force that draws souls together, but when it's someone they don't give a shit about, they'll insist that *indifference* is itself a force that goads the universe into action. In my opinion —'

'Why are you back here?'

'You know why.'

My own rapid breathing gave me away. She edged closer, her mouth on the precipice of a silky smile. It was useless to argue with my libido a moment longer. The voices in my head simpered Gracie's name, yet I took Valeria by the hand and, for my own sordid purposes, led her inside.

25

Gracie had a ouija board set up on the living room table and had been trying to summon me, only to be met by the familiar shape of empty air and the smell of dead silence. There was a knock on the door.

'Yes, what?' snapped Gracie at the thin nervous woman in a dark dress fidgeting expectantly on the doorstep.

'Does Owen Fogel live here?' asked the woman.

Gracie yelled out, 'Owen!'

Other than Dr Patel, Owen had never had a single visitor. Gracie beckoned her inside as Owen came down the stairs. He didn't hide his shock.

'Rebecca! How did you find me?'

'Nilesh told me,' she said. 'What are you doing here?'

'What are *you* doing here seems the more pertinent question. *I* grew up here,' he said. 'As you well know.'

She frowned as if she couldn't understand what he'd said.

'You never remembered the first thing about me,' he said. 'You never listened.'

'I wanted to talk to you.'

'There are phones for that.'

'Face to face.'

'Why don't we video chat at some later date?'

'Nilesh told me about your diagnosis. You should've told me.'

'Why?'

'Aren't you going to introduce me?'

'Gracie, meet Rebecca.'

'I'm his ex-wife.'

'Ex-wife! Owen! You never mentioned you were married!'

'Typical,' Rebecca said.

'You wouldn't know what's typical anymore,' Owen said.

'I doubt you've changed that much.'

'Would you like some tea?' Gracie interjected. 'Kettle just boiled.'

Rebecca noticed Gracie's baby bump and gave Owen an incredulous look.

'Are you kidding me?' she said.

'I'm not the father!' Owen yelled. 'Jesus!'

Gracie left and, a minute later, returned to give them no privacy whatsoever. Owen stirred his tea and stared unhappily out the window while Rebecca, perched on the armchair's edge, nibbled on the corners of an Anzac biscuit and looked earnestly into his face.

'Are you doing okay?' she asked. 'Emotionally?'

'I'm good. That's the God's honest truth. I've never been better.'

That was a lie. The last couple of weeks, Owen had been in a noisy, bored depression. He'd weighted himself to the couch with longnecks of beer and made gloomy toasts to no one in particular: 'To never being truly elderly.' And: 'To being run out of town by your own body!' And: 'To being alive—an offence punishable by death *every time*.'

Rebecca asked, 'Do you think this virus will get through the borders?'

'I thought so, but now I'm not so sure,' he said, sighing. The local apocalypse seemed to have entirely stalled, meaning there was now nothing to brighten his miserable day.

'I had to cancel a trip I'd booked to Bali.'

'What a tragedy.'

'I didn't say it was a tragedy.'

They were still and silent for a while, as if to drain themselves of defining characteristics. It was a battle to see who would reveal themselves last.

'So . . .' she said.

'So . . .' he said.

'I'm trying to recall . . .'

'Let's not get sidetracked.'

'Et cetera.'

'Ad nauseam.'

They spoke their own language, these two.

Rebecca turned to Gracie with a warm smile. 'How are *you* feeling, pregnant lady?'

Gracie told her the second trimester was a comparative breeze. She'd found an obstetrician at the Royal Hospital for Women. She read all the standard parenting books, then the professional ones, her favourites being *Obstetrics: Normal and abnormal pregnancies* and *A Pocket Guide to Clinical Midwifery*.

She wondered constantly if her body had made a mucus plug yet, and worried obsessively about the woman she'd read of in India who gave birth in a train toilet and whose baby dropped out directly onto the tracks. The whole upcoming event seemed alien and unspeakably grisly, but she supposed that, even to a horse, giving birth to a horse-shaped creature must seem to be the height of implausibility.

'I suppose,' said Rebecca.

Gracie went on to explain how occasionally she still burst into tears but couldn't distinguish whether its source was grief or hormones—probably some devious mishmash of the two. It's weird, in adulthood, to suddenly have a new identity, and she embraced two at the same time: stoic widow and expectant mother.

Rebecca turned back to Owen. 'I remember when I was pregnant.'

'It was a long time ago.'

'Not that long.'

Owen's face was expressionless.

'Remember the birth?' Rebecca asked.

'You know I hate it when people ask questions they know the answer to.'

Gracie looked at Owen, incredulous. 'You have a child?'

'Owen was a pain,' Rebecca said to Gracie. 'Hovering over the midwife, saying unhelpfully sarcastic things like, "Don't forget to wash your hands," and the midwife was gently telling him to fuck off, and then our beautiful baby girl was born.'

'Owen, you have a daughter! Where is she?'

'She died as a baby,' Rebecca said. 'Neonatal stroke.'

'Oh, Owen!' Gracie said.

'Thirty thousand children under the age of five die every single day,' he said dully. 'Welcome to slaughterhouse earth.'

Owen drained his cup while Rebecca sipped from hers somewhat awkwardly, eyeing her ex-husband. He stood rigidly. 'Finished your tea?' he asked her.

'Yes, I suppose I have.'

Owen opened the front door. Rebecca rose and moved to the door in slow motion. 'Goodbye, Owen.'

'Goodbye, Rebecca. Give my regards to future generations, if you see any.'

He slammed the door and sat back down very straight on the edge of the couch, next to Gracie, as if he might never make himself comfortable again.

'Owen.'

'When you're in the grave, it's back to nature.'

'What?'

'A coffin is glamping. When I die, just a shallow ditch for me.' There was an odour of frustration emanating from him. Now Gracie saw him as a husband and a grieving father. He had once been a doctor and teacher. Now, stripped of all his identities, what was he?

After a brief silence, Gracie said, 'You're not dead yet. What about, in the meantime, going back to teaching? Or giving students a last lecture? I've heard dying professors often do that, passing on all their accumulated wisdom.'

'Firstly, I have exactly nothing to say to the bellyaching, spoiled consumers that are today's generation of students. They're in love with themselves yet don't believe in individuality. Buggered if I understand the first thing about them.'

'And secondly?'

'The most pertinent life advice I have can be said in under five seconds: "Enjoy your bodies. Help a stranger. Fuck a friend."'

As he said this, Owen stared at her with a peculiar intensity.

'What?'

Before she knew it, Owen's face was a millimetre away from hers with a smile that looked like a disease of the mouth—then he quickly withdrew.

'Sorry. Sorry. Sorry.' He was whispering an incantation. 'Sorry. Sorry.'

'What just happened?'

She was still trying to decode this abrupt move when he fled to his room.

An hour later, a letter slid under her door.

'What's this?'

'Don't read it in front of me,' he said, from the other side.

'Okay.'

She made herself comfortable on the bed and began to read.

Dear Gracie,

Man's sexual desire only wanes in correlation to depression. If the human male of any age is in a good mood, he wants to fuck.

Gracie put down the letter a moment. 'Owen, I don't want to read this.'

'If you're talking, you're not reading.'

She kept reading:

After my diagnosis, I joined every single dating website and app: OkCupid, Match, eharmony, Tinder, Hinge, Bumble, Gluten-Free Singles, UglySchmucks, Mullet Passions. Why shouldn't I? I'm a thoughtful lover, within reason. (In my opinion, a network television half-hour of oral sex is the absolute limit. If you can't orgasm in twenty-two minutes, there's nothing I can do for you.)

I decided that not divulging my illness was an unacceptable deception, so I labelled my profile as 'Dying Man with Non-Communicable Disease Seeks Final Lover'. By lowering my standards to the point where I had to stop calling them standards, I sent out hundreds of messages, and received genuine responses that I parlayed into actual dates. To my surprise, not only was I not yet dead, I was not even obsolete (it's shocking how well even a dying man can do just by dating within his own age group).

'Owen.'

'Keep reading.'

She didn't want to, and so skipped a couple of pages and read on.

and almost all people on earth are bad actors except the professionally trained thespians, so when people see you watching them during sex, their faces take on a B-movie quality that I find hard to stomach.

I never once felt I was in bed with someone with an original sexual imagination. More than a few women asked me to slap or bite them. I went along with it, even though the truth is I've never experienced sexual rage of any kind. I mostly prefer to 'make love' with about eight percent hard pounding. That's too vanilla for most women. Their desire to be dominated has less to do with power dynamics, I now realise, and is more a tacit admission that, although we've built sex up as this ultimate adventure, there's nothing more mundane.

'Owen! I can't take it!'

'Okay, Gracie, just get to the last page.'

She turned to the last page:

an embarrassing declaration: I can't stop loving you, and you can't start loving me. But I'm a good guy, somewhat worthless, a wacky and harmless lover, also a depressing and morbid coward, and

I don't mind charity. I know you are very pregnant and you still love Angus, but I think the world might actually be ending and, even if it wasn't, I have three months left to live. Couldn't you snuggle for three months?

Gracie put down the letter and looked over to his shadow under the door. It creaked open. Owen was standing there with a small, expectant smile.

'Oh my God, Owen. Leave me alone.'

The following days, he seemed lighter. He bounced around the house, was uncharacteristically chatty, and told actual jokes that concluded with little bursts of laughter at himself when he forgot the punchlines. Something had changed in him.

Eventually, over dinner one night, he made a formal apology for his confessional letter. 'Spilling secrets of the heart is like draining cerebrospinal fluid from the brain to reduce swelling. A life-saving procedure, to be sure, but it's messy. Sincere apologies for putting you through it.'

'It's fine,' she said. She had come to understand over these past few days that his former cantankerousness was only a symptom of what happens when a short, miserable life finally stops masquerading as a long, happy one. Deep down, he was a kind man.

Later that night, in bed, something niggled at her. A surprising feeling—one that almost made her gasp when she identified it. It was a yearning. For Owen? She tried to contextualise it. We are such needy creatures that attention, she knew, if properly administered, can provoke feelings of affection—even love. And, as sorry as she felt for this dull-white, puny invalid slowly slipping into the abyss, she felt sorrier for herself. She was so alone; she hadn't been touched in so long, she had taken to rubbing up against towels to feel a soft caress.

And he really did love her; maybe she'd get a few seconds of bliss out of this arrangement? Why not take in a stray she could spoon? And if he wanted to kiss the tears right off her face, or lick her pussy in the dead of night—why not? And let's face it—Owen wasn't nobody. He *was* important to her. She had taken him in off the street, sure, but had she taken on the maximum amount of responsibility that she could bear? Did she even love him back a little? Maybe.

Gracie called out: 'Owen!'

'Yeah?'

'Can you come in here a second?'

He opened the door and stood curiously at the bedroom's threshold. Gracie thought, Maybe in this bargain I can stop pretending I don't want to be held by someone with an insatiable love for me. She lifted up the sheets and held them aloft in the universal gesture for *join me.*

26

My own living situation went from bearable to untenable. The neighbours were hedonistic, unhygienic maniacs. All day and all night long I could hear arguing, the sound of a person almost but never quite reaching orgasm, and a man's voice shouting, 'No, I won't lower my voice!' My shitfaced neighbours lurked in the dark corridors, held nightly drunken séances to contact the living, sang duelling national anthems in the shower.

A reckless aura hung over everything. Doors were left wide open and people with obscene, radiant faces tried to coax me into eightsomes. Sure, there's a case to be made that moving from languishing on one's deathbed to a sprightly midnight orgy gave one the right to act like a demigod, but I had a bad feeling that a lot of these folks had committed terrible earthly misdeeds that had gone unpunished and now felt they could get away with anything. The lights in the hallway had all been intentionally broken and some people on my floor decided to break down the barriers between them—literally—and began demolishing the walls. This was the frenzy of second life.

Maybe the broken-window theory applied here, and an openly insane man living inside the elevator created this chain of hysteria among the residents. Mostly, I used the stairs, but one afternoon I was too drunk and took the elevator. The lights flickered on and off, and Xander, the openly insane man living there, was crouching in his patch of fluctuating darkness, flashing his yellow teeth.

'In or out?'

'In.'

I stepped onto the overlapping straw rugs that covered the elevator's floor.

'Have you come to pay your respects?'

'No, just to get to the third floor.'

He hit a number that I hoped was three; the elevator's doors closed and we began the slow ascent.

'We should all walk around with pennies on our eyes. The ferryman doesn't take bitcoin.'

'Totally.'

'We're something much worse than dead. Aren't you embarrassed?'

'Should I be?'

'I'm talking about our failure to justify our heartbeats.'

I pressed myself against the corner to avoid physical contact. 'Yeah,' I said, 'we sure suck at that.'

He hit a switch and the elevator ground to a halt.

'Do you think we're avoiding the secret fear that we're all the same person?' he asked.

'Not sure,' I said. I wondered: Are we now going to fight?

'I have something for you.'

He switched on a torch and got down on his knees to go through his books, holding up titles. *Snug Harbor* by Herman Melville,

On Waking Dead by Henry David Thoreau, *Hexus* by Henry Miller, *Dreams and Nonsense* by Jane Austen. I felt as unlearned and poorly read in death as I had in life.

'You think only nobodies like us wind up here?' he asked.

'Where *do* the others go?' I asked. 'Are we all dispersed over various afterlifes? Do any of us get that holy grail of death—wholesale disintegration?'

'Hey, I like your questions.' Xander started tossing hefty religious tomes at me. The titles alone seemed intriguing: *The Apologists of Iscariot, Ergo Everlasting, The Merits of Oblivion, The Trinity Plus One, The Further Adventures of Jesus H Christ . . .*

'I'm not really in a reading phase.'

He didn't like that. 'Aren't you curious?'

I started scratching. Ignorance makes you itch. He eyed me coldly and tightened his lips. 'What about music?'

'What about it?'

He bent down and tugged a sheet of tie-dyed fabric off a milk carton filled with records, urging me to browse. I knelt down and flipped through them like I was at a garage sale. I found unfamiliar titles by recognisable geniuses: Miles Davis, Elvis Presley, Fats Waller, Johnny Cash. Then again, their late works already sucked, even before they passed away in their beds or on their toilets, and there was no reason to assume that brain death rejuvenated the spark of creativity. Maybe I could find something by an artist who had died young, before his time.

'Do you have any John Lennon?'

'I have George Harrison.'

It was curious that a visceral dislike of certain sounds stays with you throughout eternity. Turns out, I didn't want to hear slide guitar in this dimension either.

'Can you just restart the elevator?'

He kicked over a cardboard box and opened the flaps.

'One last thing. Go on, look inside.'

I felt a stab of fear. Xander was all wiggly; he seemed delighted by whatever was in that box—not a particularly good sign. I peered inside: there it was—a bloody knife and a couple of severed fingers. 'Do you like that? Does that satisfy your curiosity?'

'It sure does.'

I reached over and flipped the switch. The elevator groaned into motion and, a few terrible seconds later, its doors opened.

'See you later,' I said, and hurried out, shaking. It seemed gratuitous to scream.

Later that night, Valeria and I were in my bed, holding hands, like people on a ship during a storm, centring ourselves so the infinite didn't make us sick. As it transpired, my sexual desire was in perfect working order—over the last few weeks, we'd fucked a lot.

She'd say, 'Come inside me, don't come inside me—I don't care.' It still felt like a betrayal, but Valeria was correct: Gracie was a widow. And besides, celibacy is the only pointless human state.

I felt homesick, earthsick, lifesick, mouldy, ruined, you name it. I told Valeria about Xander and the extra fingers he'd set aside for a rainy day.

'You want to move in with me for a while?'

I tried not to seem amazed at the suggestion. Valeria looked at me with vague anxiety, playing down the import of moving in together.

'Why not?' I said, trying to sound casual. 'Might be fun.'

Her relief was instantaneous. 'Great,' she said. 'Let's do it.'

I didn't need a moving van—I didn't even need both hands. That night I threw a toothbrush, a razor, a stick of deodorant and three changes of clothes into a canvas sack and left my room forever. I didn't even lock the door behind me.

She led me through the business district, across train tracks, across a wide boulevard with well-maintained bright buildings and streets paved with a silver glint. The smell of pretzels blended with the scent of perfume in a cool breeze that blew downhill. Valeria lived in a beautiful, baroque building with an arched entrance and large metal door.

'Voila!'

A doorman stood straight and silent against a white pillar and eyed me distrustfully.

I asked her. 'Wow. You live *here*?'

The doorman smiled disapprovingly.

'Teddy. This is Angus Mooney. He's moving in with me. Isn't that exciting?'

'Very,' Teddy dryly replied.

Apparently being a former member of the state bureaucracy pays off: Valeria had a huge apartment on the ninth floor with high vaulted ceilings, tall windows, and deep balconies with a sweet view over the entire town. Valeria kicked off her shoes violently and was standing barefoot. I stood gawkily, trying to will myself into a state of calm. What does betrayal even look like in the context of eternity? Long-distance relationships *can* work, sure, but there's a limit.

Valeria kept smirking in a tranquil sort of way. She was a strange, traumatised woman; she talked from the corner of her mouth, the pretty corner, and her beauty didn't hit you instantly—it was on time-release. She lethargically unbuttoned her shirt, exposing her black lace bra. It was bewildering to yearn for two women at once. I floated slowly over to her.

They say only dead fish go with the tide. I'm no exception.

27

As Gracie's rebound, Owen's role was to never push or coerce her or present a single iota of desire or need, only to climb nervously into bed and await instructions. Gracie would encourage him—or not. Allow a kiss—or not. A slight incline of her head was enough to convey the message that she would allow him to please her.

Occasionally she returned the favour, mostly by hand, but otherwise Owen was more than content to spoon or stroke her hair, eliciting from Gracie a quiet moan of relief. It was a weird, sweet sort of coupledom. She helped ease his burden of dying, and he helped ease her burden of living.

He no longer tried to hide his infatuation, but neither could he hide the slow worsening of his condition—his deteriorating eyesight, leg spasms and coordination issues, and maybe because his decline was a pathetic, nerve-racking thing to behold, this pity-affection combination triggered all of Gracie's love to rush out of her. Owen felt it—it made him eager to reveal himself; in bed at night he talked about becoming a doctor for the status, the smell of his abusive father, the grin of his childhood bully, the agony of losing his daughter. Whatever the revelations, Gracie responded by giving him all the sympathy and understanding he could have ever dreamed of. In this way, dying exceeded Owen's wildest expectations.

One afternoon, they were on the couch watching, as Owen described it, 'the human race—elimination round'. Ashen-faced reporters debated the difference between Armageddon and the apocalypse over images of supermarket queues that looked like psychiatric wards, defiant rooftop parties, the chaos of the infected in makeshift hospitals. Owen was humming a little ditty, forgetting to stifle the sensual pleasure of the world dying to his exact timetable. Gracie squeezed Owen's hand so tightly he lost circulation.

When they could take no more reality, Gracie and Owen wordlessly left the house and walked to the beach, arm in arm, more to aid his balance than out of romance. It was sunset when they hit the rock pool's edge, and at Gracie's insistence they trod out to the ledge and let the waves wash over them until the sun fell into the sea. The sound of laughter made Owen turn to look behind them, where a small group of teenagers were drinking and smoking on the rocks. Beyond them, the yellow lights of the houses nestled in the hills burned like little fires. From this vantage point, civilisation seemed like a fool's errand.

Owen reached out and put his hand on Gracie's belly.

'How are you feeling?'

'Like I'm carrying unexploded ordnance inside my person.'

'I love you.' He took her hand and kissed her fingers.

'I'll allow it,' she said.

Of course she would allow it. In an austere world, being adored was the very definition of luxury.

'I mean—I love you too.'

28

Erecting housing for the new dead was such hard work—breaking ground, felling trees, sawing lumber, hauling brick, pouring cement—we barely talked metaphysically anymore. We'd all lost faith in oblivion anyway. We were out of ideas.

I was on a break, looking out at the beautiful countryside as a thunderstorm raged above the wooded hills. The cool, fresh wind carried the soft rain right into my face.

Griffin walked over to me. 'Break's over, don't you think?'

'In a minute.'

He stood next to me in silence, looking at the erratic rainfall, his thick, muscular arms folded in such a way that I could see his pulse.

I asked, 'How did you die?'

'I didn't.'

'What do you mean?'

'I'm indigenous to this land.'

It took me a minute to understand. He was a native? He'd never been alive? That blew my mind. If the rest us were dead, then who—or *what*—was this guy? It was a weird and fascinating idea.

'What does that mean? Are you different?'

'You know what I think it means? Not a goddamn thing.'

After we rode sweaty and tired back into town that night, Griffin joined me at the Bitter in Soul. He began to sound off on current events that, as was my way, I didn't understand or want to know about: The military presence was getting heavier. The rebels were at the western perimeter. A water-scarcity conflict ignited in the north-east and a border dispute flared in the south-west. They were siphoning off the electricians and plumbers, and transporting them to other towns, he said, which is why we had a disproportionate number of unskilled workers and DJs.

The latest rumour: some neighbouring city was using the newly dead as human shields. I twitched and tore at my coaster. So what was new? With limited resources, human settlements would always be at loggerheads. Also, I had a hangnail. I pulled at it and kept gazing at Griffin's face, trying to ascertain if we fundamentally diverged in body or soul. He was muscular and confident and balding. Under the dim bar lights, his oily skin made him look varnished. Despite not being earth-born, he was just another fully operational, conscious, man-shaped thing, like me.

He said, 'You want to see something hilarious?'

Griffin reached into his jacket pocket and pulled out a hideous, plastic devil's mask with a smouldering-red light-up effect. He placed the mask on his face and looked out the window.

'Here's one,' Griffin said, and headed outside.

I went to the door and watched as he strode over to a man in activewear, stepping off a rickshaw: a new arrival. 'I've been waiting for you,' Griffin said, in a raspy voice. The man fell sobbing to his knees and begged for mercy. It was immediately not funny, and

I could tell from his constant glances in my direction that Griffin was grinning madly under the mask.

Afterwards, he came back into the bar and finished his drink and said, 'I love messing with you dead fucks.'

'You're a piece of shit.'

That made his smile dribble away to nothing. He grabbed my beer, tipped it down his throat, and slammed the empty bottle on the bar. 'What are you deceased sons-of-bitches even good at?'

'You tell me.'

'Being infuriated, squeezing moral significance from a stone, walking around with unrealistic ideals you can't ever live up to and hating yourselves for it.' He snatched a drink from a passing stranger and downed that too. 'You come in here from your failed civilisation, moaning about your burial arrangements and expecting everything handed to you on a platter. Boo-hoo. You think your deep emotions make you heroic and you're never to blame for anything. Your favourite expression is: "through no fault of my own". Shit. You guys make me sick.'

He had a point. After he stormed out, the other patrons looked at me as though I was superspreading negativity directly into their lungs. It was unsettling, their tenacious glares like a precursor to group violence.

That night Valeria and I had sex in our usual manner—flopping around on each other's bodies until one of us came or both of us ran out of energy. Afterwards she said, 'I'm so happy God set you loose on me.'

I winced a little, as I did whenever anyone mentioned God in a positive light.

She said, 'Let's go to the roof.'

Everyone in the building had some degree of insomnia—nights were punctuated by chilling screams—and each night the residents trudged exhausted up the stairs and onto the roof to look at the unfamiliar constellations while comparing and contrasting nightmares.

It was cold out. We sat on the edge of the roof underneath a multicoloured string of fairy lights, dangling our legs over the side of the building, gazing at the necropolis laid out beneath us. The edges of the clouds were luminous, like sea foam in moonlight. We passed around a bottle of wine. The whole scene was drenched in melancholy.

'You know what this afterlife feels like?'

I looked beside me—it was Teddy, the sneering doorman. He lived in the building too, on one of the lower floors. He was talking to a short man leaning back in a banana chair who was drinking red wine out of a beer mug.

'What?' asked the short man.

'It feels like when a stranger sneezes and you say "bless you", and then the bastard just keeps on sneezing and you're stuck saying bless you over and over again, and you can't stop until he stops.'

Everyone had a metaphor or a simile—they were endless. I focused my attention on the view: the squat buildings, the stark outline of the old aqueduct against the moon. You could see the lights of the neighbouring towns flickering and sparkling. And further, intermittent whirling bursts of orange that collided with the moonlight and tore up the sky: more dead strangers crossing over. It was undeniably eerie and phantasmagoric.

A thunderstorm broke in the south and rain began to fall; we just stayed there and let it thunder around us, getting drenched. Not one of us would've complained if we were struck by lightning.

'To those we left behind,' somebody said, as a toast. We all raised our glasses and drank. Jesus, now we were all going to start weeping. Worse, Teddy started singing, with unexpected beauty. 'After you get what you want you don't want it. If I gave you the moon, you'd grow tired of it soon . . .'

His melodic voice was urging us to join in. But we couldn't—nobody knew what he was singing. 'There's a longing in your eye hard to satisfy, and here's the reason why: 'cause after you get what you want you don't want it.'

An angry voice from an open window shouted: 'Shut the fuck up! Some of us have to work in the morning!'

Teddy seemed to forget the rest of the song anyway, so he fell silent and we all kept our eyes on the dazzling coloured phenomena heralding the arrival of the newly deceased.

'It's so trippy,' Valeria said.

'Transmigration of souls has a lot in common with ultra-long-distance quantum teleportation,' said the short man in the banana chair. This information left me with a total blank. He continued: 'The idea that consciousness is an emergent property arising out of complexity was only ever an unproven theory. There was no mechanistic explanation for the hard problem. I mean, we *assumed* the soul isn't living matter, that consciousness was a pattern of information, but just because we never found it doesn't mean it doesn't tangibly exist at the quantum level. What if our soul is just the size of a photon, or *smaller* than point eight femtometres, a photon's effective radius? Remember when we thought the atom itself was the teensiest measurable thing? I think we can now safely deduce that the soul or the mind, or the ghost in the machine or whatever, was in fact invisible and undetectable *matter*, because it has evidently been transferred into your mirror body.'

'Maybe.'

He took a deep breath and made a show of patience. 'Instead of the soul, let's call it the soul particle.'

'Okay?'

'What if "they", whoever they are, read the atomic structure of your soul particle and sent the information through what *appeared to be* a tunnel of light.'

'It *was* a tunnel of light,' Teddy said.

The banana-chair man turned to him. 'Wouldn't the inside of a cable or optical fibre look much like a tunnel?'

'Meh.'

He spoke for a while of holographic universes and subatomic scales and quantum entanglement and Heisenberg's uncertainty principle. In other words—he lost me and Teddy and just about everyone else on the roof.

'Are you talking about aliens?' Teddy asked.

'Aliens? Do you have shit for brains? Nobody said anything about aliens.'

We sank back into silence and passed the bottle while watching the drama unfolding in the skies.

'If someone is beaming us here,' I asked, 'who's at the controls?'

'That's the big question,' said the banana-chair man.

'And if we were transported here, for what —'

'Common misconception. Teleportation is not transportation, it's replication.'

'Replication?' I thought about that a moment. 'So what happens to the original soul . . . particle?'

'Once the raw material of the duplicated soul particle appears here—it would be simultaneously extinguished at its origin point.'

'So our souls are reborn and murdered at the same time? Terrific,' I said.

The sky looked vandalised with fluorescent colours. Teddy grabbed another bottle of wine and took a swig from it. 'I died,' he said. 'I saw a tunnel of light, I moved towards it, and I was here.'

'How fast did you move through the tunnel of light?'

'Fast.'

The banana-chair man nodded vehemently. 'High transmission rates. Nice. Probably felt a bit shaky. Atmospheric turbulence in the uplink. That's one idea. What else could have been the light? Were *you* the light? Or was the light merely a compact ultra-bright source of multi-photon entanglement and narrow-beam divergence?'

I didn't think he knew his audience. Valeria had fallen asleep. I picked her up and carried her down the stairs. There's nothing like looking into the face of a person you're carrying in your arms to decide how you really feel about them.

I lowered her gently onto the bed, thinking that every theory was as insane as every other. The Heisenberg principle? Holographic universe? Teleportation of the soul particle? To be dead and still need to grapple with a mind–body problem? This kind of thing could go on forever. Valeria groaned; she was clearly having a nightmare, perhaps of her murder.

'Valeria.'

She opened her eyes and shook herself out of her trance.

She said, 'Let's quit smoking together.'

'Okay.'

In the dark we kissed a long while before she pushed me away with a sigh.

'You're distracted. Are you still thinking about Gracie?' I felt putrid. Lovesick in the wrong dimension. 'You're here. She's there.'

'I know.'

'Try to let go, okay?'

'I will.'

The indecent proximity of our faces made me feel warm, safe, at home. With our cheeks pressed together I felt, if not a flawed kind of love, then something almost indistinguishable from it.

'I love you,' I heard myself say.

We are not puppets but we are so predictable we might as well be.

SIX

'Each one wraps himself in what burns him.'

Dante

29

'In movies people always have back-up generators,' Owen said. 'Should we get one? From where? I've been in and out of stores my entire life and I've never seen a back-up generator stocked, advertised or sold.'

Gracie didn't glance up from her phone. The hashtag #byeeee was trending in the USA and she was scrolling through tragic farewell posts. She watched a video of a Christian evangelical leader saying, 'Love your neighbour as yourself—but don't let him near you.'

Her phone rang. She was so distracted by the news, she answered without checking the caller ID; the man on the other end was rambling and it wasn't clear what he wanted.

'Who is this?' Gracie asked.

'It's David Jennings! You married me and Darren! Remember?'

She did remember—this was one of the first couples she ever married: same-sex real estate agents from Cremorne.

'What do you want?'

'We just had a *baby*!'

'So what?'

David burst into laughter. 'She said, "So what?"'

Another person—presumably Darren—erupted in overwrought laughter in the background.

'We were wondering if you could do something. We're not religious, as you might remember. I mean, back in the day, I was christened, and Darren had a bris, but obviously we don't care about continuing either gross tradition, but we don't want to do *nothing*, so I thought maybe you could come by and do *something*.'

'Do what? What do you want?'

'I don't know. We want to do a service of some kind—something spiritual—for our little Chloe. Like a blessing? We'll pay you, obviously—your same rate?'

'I'm on a sabbatical.'

'*Please.* You're so brilliant and we just got really stoned last night and had this amazing idea. Please!'

She could hear Darren in the background saying, 'Please, Gracie! Do it! It'll be awesome!'

'It does present an intriguing problem,' she said. 'How to dignify, ceremonially, the spawn of secular meaning-seekers in this time of universal crisis.'

'What?'

'All right,' she said. 'I'll do it.'

Gracie hadn't been out in the world for weeks, and she had a panicky urge to turn the car around. Cars were double-parked everywhere, nobody worrying about tickets, mothers were smoking cigarettes while pushing strollers and people conversed a cough's length away from one another, picking up the old pandemic protocols where they left off. Added to this ominous state of things, at twenty-nine weeks pregnant, with the intense stresses of widowhood and looming motherhood, she was afraid she'd be grieving or nurturing indefinitely.

What about *her* infrastructure? Until now, her internal organs had been quite stable; now they were being pushed aside to make room for the baby, like something stuffed into an already overcrowded closet. Why didn't anyone give you an estimate of the structural damage to your body before you got pregnant? What would even be the cost of repair? Gracie could imagine a doctor holding up some broken part of her, saying, 'They don't even make these anymore.'

As she drove, she dictated random thoughts to her phone that were posted as text to her 175,000 followers, whoever they were, about the odd, anxious business of pregnancy. ('Has childbirth really been amazing since 1909, after the first caudal anaesthesia?' 'What if she's repulsed by my hairy pussy on the way out?' 'Is wilfully propagating an endangered or terminal species unethical or even obscene?')

'You're pregnant!' David squealed, as she got out of her car in their circular driveway. Darren ran over with his gangly arms outstretched and hugged her. 'I was hoping Mooney would be here to video!'

'He's dead.'

Darren's face turned ashen and David started to ugly-cry.

'We didn't know! Oh my God! What happened? Don't answer that! It's none of our beeswax!' Darren said. 'Can I be your baby's godmother? That's ridiculous. I'm so sorry. I wouldn't have bothered you.'

'I'm glad you did,' she said.

'You poor thing,' said David, sniffling.

Gracie took the pity unflinchingly. 'Let's get this show on the road.'

She headed to the backyard and threaded through sets of overweening friends and extended family members as they gathered solemnly around the garden-variety baby. She stood there like an insane ringmaster, using her superpower of universal eye contact, and began hollering.

'You've made a new nearest relative. What do you couples say? "Can we afford a baby?" They mean financially. But the subtext is, "Can we afford *not* to have a baby?" They mean existentially.'

Someone said 'What?', but most of the assembled crowd seemed prepared to hang on her every word. 'Some psychological scars come from the collective, from the recent and distant past. Some scars you carry cannot heal because they aren't from—strictly speaking—*your* wounds. Do you follow?'

They didn't. Perfect.

'In all religions worth their salt, birth is punishment. Why have you chained this baby to the cycle of life, death and rebirth? Don't answer. That's rhetorical. We know there is a dim possibility that the K9 virus will come to Australia despite our best efforts, and if it does, this will be the scrappy generation of survivors having unsupervised play in mass gravesites.'

Gracie took each parent's hand and gave them a shake.

'Darren and David, way out of proportion is the only way to love someone. Look at this ridiculous thing—a baby is a kind of comic foil for your self-seriousness. You are parents now, but even the saddest, drunken, most begrudging, dead-eyed pity-fuck can manifest a human life. Whether by accident, IVF, sperm donation or surrogacy, did procreation take into account the interests of this future person? Let's be honest—the fuck it did. We conceive with our own self-interest at heart. Let us acknowledge this and also observe a minute's silence for the non-existent person this baby was before you compelled her into being from the "safe space" of non-existence.'

Gracie ranted for another five minutes before she finished with, 'Now raise your glasses. That was a joke. Put your glasses down. Who toasts a baby? What are you, alcoholics?'

Four days later, Gracie received a request for another blessing.

'This baby has treated your body like an overnight bag,' she announced to the Newtown couple who'd hired her. 'Anyone do a background check on him? Here is a being crawled forth from a deep dreamless sleep. What's his name?'

'Jack.'

'Jack was born non-consensually, but let's not victim-blame. We love our children and bear them no ill will, at first. Being born is okay for personal growth, but aside from that, what's it good for?'

She took her eyeliner from her bag and drew angry eyebrows on the baby.

'Let's draw on this lonesome baby,' she said. 'Gather round! Draw something! Come on!'

Everyone wrote a little message, or doodled smiley faces or stick figures or love hearts. 'It's anonymous. Write your wishes, your curses.' Why not let this be a tradition? The human race is a blank slate; it was all open. The ground was shifting.

'All right, now step up and kiss the baby on the soles of his feet.'

She was making up traditions on the spot. It was ridiculous, and she knew it.

'Now. I want the parents to stand in front of me.'

She slapped the father's face, then the mother's face, got them both to admit their worthlessness as parents in training, and when they cried, she applied their tears to the baby's forehead. 'Tears and laughter are the only common language between all people on earth.'

Everyone liked that. Whoever had a tear was welcome to moisten Jack's precious brow.

Afterwards, Gracie didn't accept money from the parents but passed around a collection plate to the guests, announcing that the parents must not pay for her services. It's astonishing, she thought, how arcane rules lend any old bullshit an air of legitimacy. All it took was a little ritual for people to feel like they'd triumphed over death.

Owen couldn't understand why she was bothering with this new 'calling'. When a third event was booked, and it became clear that her non-denominational child-blessing business was about to take off, he put his foot down.

'Don't do this.'

'Why shouldn't I?'

'The country's gone batshit. Being cut off from the rest of the world is making people lose their minds. You don't need to participate in the crazy.'

'Everyone wants their baby blessed by the Pregnant Widow.'

'I don't think you should go back out there in your condition.'

'Why not?'

'It's here,' he said, and pointed to the muted TV. On the screen, images of an Australian suburb. Owen unmuted the sound.

'. . . loose in Perth and isn't answering her mobile phone, Instagram messages, emails or texts. Could Tara Wiggins be Australia's inaugural infection? And where is she? The AFP are using their state-of-the-art surveillance apparatus to track her down.'

Owen was rooting for her to escape; Gracie wanted to find her and let her live in the attic, like Anne Frank.

'It's Perth,' Gracie said. 'That's four thousand kilometres away. We're fine.'

'Okay, but tomorrow is December fourth. You're two days past your due date. Your baby's getting too big to be supported by your deteriorating placenta—no offence.'

'None taken.'

'You should make an appointment with your obstetrician to induce labour.'

'Good idea.'

She called the hospital and scheduled the momentous event for next Wednesday morning at nine o'clock. Gracie feigned calm by sipping cups of chai and writing a sermon for another woman's baby.

The ceremony was held the next day in a fragrant, leafy backyard in Watsons Bay. 'Please forgive me if I run to the toilet mid-ceremony,' Gracie began. 'My baby is up against my bladder like a hoodlum leaning on a lamppost.'

An aunt laughed, and her laugh morphed into a hacking cough—the other guests stared in a horror-struck trance.

'I have hay fever,' the aunt said sharply.

The mother ran and stood between the aunt and the baby.

'Please, perhaps you should just . . .'

'I'm not sick.'

'Get out.'

'I'm not going anywhere.'

Everyone shared the same look of primitive disgust that had evolved for this exact purpose. It wasn't exactly clear who pushed the aunt into the frangipani, but within seconds the guests divided themselves between those protecting the aunt and those attacking the aunt, those who thought it was okay to kick an old woman under special circumstances and those who found it totally out of line. The guests went at each other with a broom, a branch, a swimming-pool scoop. Someone turned on a hose and sprayed family members indiscriminately. The ordeal wasn't over for the aunt either—somehow, she'd wound up in the pool.

Gracie handed the baby to a sly uncle who'd stepped off to the champagne table. This was going to be a hard era for tactile people, she thought, on her way out.

The traffic was heavy, and the air conditioner was blowing heat. Two ambulances made mad dashes in opposite directions. Masked people were hurrying along the streets, darting suspicious glances at each other, on the lookout for sniffles and other flu-like symptoms.

What were they getting all worked up over? Didn't they know how far Perth was from Sydney? Even at traffic lights, Gracie detected a hateful throbbing of paranoia in the other drivers. Civilisation was showing its soft belly. She thought: Take a good hard look at yourself, humanity, you're making a scene.

The sun had almost set and there was a reddish glow in the sky. She sped through the suburban streets but when she hit the highway that traffic was almost at a standstill.

Then—it happened.

Her water broke—the liquid filled the seat in a puddle and splashed to her feet. This body had committed to its course of action, and she had no choice but to obey. She made a U-turn to get off the highway and drove fast along residential streets, careening towards the hospital.

She called Owen on the house phone. 'Who calls a landline?' he answered.

'You don't have a mobile.'

'So?'

'Owen, it's happening. Meet me at Randwick Hospital.'

'Are you sure?'

'There's amniotic fluid in my Converse!'

'Okay, okay! I'll leave now.'

On the radio, 'Que Sera Sera' began to play. It was a little too on the money, so she switched stations to the news. '... a cluster of infections in Katoomba and northern New South Wales.'

She switched it off and talked to the baby. 'You've caught me by surprise today. Let me see you to the door.' Eviction time. The baby had no business inside her body anymore.

The sun broke through the clouds as the hospital came into view. She was flooded with relief—but then the traffic ground to a halt. What was blocking the road? A man with a ginger goatee in the next car was banging his fist on the steering wheel, giving off staccato honks.

A policeman in a white mask, steering people away from the hospital, walked up to her car window and gave her a flustered look. 'Hi! That road's closed. You'll have to turn around.'

'I need to get to the hospital.'

'Randwick's quarantined. North Shore's quarantined. Westmead's open, but the highway's closed. You'll never get out there.'

'I'm in labour.'

He lowered his kindly face into the window. 'You're giving birth at a bad time.'

She didn't know what to say to that and tried to think of some convincing lie that would get her through. An irate crowd, sick and injured, had abandoned their cars and were running along the median strip, others pressing against the police barricade. The policeman maintained eye contact with Gracie, looking at her as if childbirth was unwholesome—and wasn't it? Her body was already doing unspeakable things. She stared sullenly at the hospital; she needed medical professionals.

'Can you just let me through?'

'You don't want to go in there, didn't you hear me? The whole place is quarantined. Hundreds of cases. It's a bloody shitshow. Your best bet is to go home.'

'But I'm going into labour.'

He looked at her without hope. 'I'll tell you what they're telling everyone: whatever you've got, whatever the problem, go home and google it.'

30

It was a cold morning as we rode the bus out of town, sipping our thermoses of coffee and staring out across the wooded hills, the fields of dried mud, the drab countryside. I was thinking, what if beneath the surface was just more surface? What if it was surface all the way down?

Near the old aqueduct, Kira said, 'Watch out!' and the bus lurched to a violent halt.

A line of protesters with linked arms had formed a human blockade across the road. The driver killed the engine. There was no way through, so we climbed out of the bus and stood dry-mouthed and helpless and examined their signs in the morning light: 'The Dead Are People Too' and 'Jesus Was A Refugee' and 'God Loves All His Dead Children Equally'. They chanted: 'Let the dead live—with dignity! Let the dead live—with dignity!'

It wasn't much of a chant. They draped their arms around each other and marched towards us, forcing us back. Their solidarity said almost everything there was to say about the human spirit—our mute cowardice said the rest.

Griffin nodded his approval and gave the protesters a taut smile. He wanted to be tolerant, but he had work to do. 'We get where you're coming from, but clear off, please, and let us pass!'

They let out a defiant howl and shouted insults at us, buoyed by the joy of resistance. They looked supremely alive. We seemed embarrassed and surprised by our own flat response. Their protest struck a sympathetic chord with us, and we could've easily joined their side.

'You're a traitor to your kind,' someone yelled at us.

'What kind is that?' Farhad shouted back.

A protester lobbed a small rock and it whacked the imperturbable Griffin square on the side of the head. A thin stream of blood trickled down into his eye. The protesters laughed and kicked their legs like chorus girls, resuming their chant with zealous devotion: 'Let the dead live—with dignity! Let the dead live—with dignity!'

There was nothing to be done but stand rigidly, ashamed by our role in this drama. Some of us even started mumbling the chant ourselves.

It grew hot; the sun beat down even as it was rising. Just when we were about to return to town, the chant was stopped short by the oncoming sound of vehicles. In the shimmering distance, two open jeeps sped towards us. They didn't stop or slow down—they opened fire, spraying bullets at the protesters' feet, raising clouds of dust. The protesters ran into the forest with a long-vowelled 'fuuuuck'. Finally, when the protesters were gone, the jeep stopped; the soldier manning the machine gun kept his weapon trained on the empty road.

'All good to go,' he said, a smile flickering around his mouth.

'Yeah—cheers,' Griffin responded.

We rode all the way to the site in silence and with the sinking feeling of being marooned on the wrong side of history.

That day, we threw ourselves into construction, harder than ever. By sunset we'd erected the northern perimeter of a chain-link fence with a long coil of barbed wire at the top. We stared at our handiwork in sickened silence. The idea of a person waking from death and being corralled here—all those K9-dead, the old-school crushed-at-work, the stabbed-to-death, the mauled-to-shreds, the fallen-from-elevation, the auto-erotically asphyxiated, the died in childbirth, those who died carving out a name for themselves, and those whose brain or heart ultimately failed them—it was an atrocity. I even imagined those who'd perished in similar camps all now obliged to start back at square one on yet another arduous quest to scrape together enough meaning to justify the suffering to come.

Come all ye dead. Up and at 'em.

31

'Owen!' Gracie flung open her front door, screaming. 'I'm having the baby here and now. Don't try to talk me out of it.'

The silence ticked like a clock.

'Did you hear what I said? My assets just liquidated. This is happening!'

Gracie conducted a frantic room-by-room search, charged up the stairs, flung open the bedroom door, and tugged at the bedsheets in case he had deflated there. The bastard was nowhere to be found. She only now remembered: she'd told him to meet her at the hospital and, Jesus Christ, she couldn't call him to let him know she was home and in desperate need of his expertise because he didn't have a fucking mobile phone.

She called the midwife but there was no answer. Bitch, thought Gracie. I hope she's okay.

She stared at the empty bedroom with tremendous fury and the grim realisation that she was going to have to give birth alone.

Fine. She wasn't the first woman to do that. For over two hundred thousand years, medical intervention during delivery had meant biting down on a fallen tree branch.

She laid towels and pillows on the tiled kitchen floor, filled hot-water bottles, lit candles and told herself to trust her body, but then thought: Really? The same body that encourages me to eat a tub of ice-cream in one sitting? She felt alone, so she posted a photo of her set up: *#homebirth #allalone #rightnow #feelingterrified.*

As the intensity of the contractions increased, Gracie made an effort to dull the pain, walking back and forth bent over like a hunchback, pressing icepacks against her crotch. She posted: 'Nature itself is misogynistic. A patriarchal think tank called ChokeaBitch couldn't have dreamed up a more diabolical scenario to beset womankind.' She wondered: Do otters go through this much pain? Or rats, with their hundred babies? She staggered to the window—nothing was moving on the quiet, sun-dappled streets. No raging thunderstorm—the ultimate insult.

She lay on her back on the blanket and pushed, wallowing in astonishing pain. She posted: 'Any tips on how you withstand a pain that's way beyond your pain threshold?' The regression to the primitive didn't take long; one moment later, she was on all fours emitting a slow scream; the moment after that, spreadeagled on the floor. She posted: 'I can almost hear the baby threateningly whisper: "Nice vagina you have there. It would be a shame if anything happened to it."'

This was utter madness—the pain was intolerable, worse than she'd ever imagined, and she had been certain she'd imagined the worst. She posted: 'I wish someone would come by and tell me to "calm down" and "relax" so I could kill them.' She posted: 'The miracle of birth? How can a miracle also be a life-threatening medical event?' She felt jangly and cold. She thought: I need images and videos of people less fortunate than me, stat.

The pain intensified, as did her hysteria. 'Your mother sucks cocks in hell!' she yelled, drunk with pain. She posted: 'It is not incorrect to say that mothers who die in childbirth have been fucked to death.' To the baby, she shouted, 'You're making a horrible first impression! I'm tired of this deadly game of hide and seek. Let's Freaky Friday this shit. *You* give birth to *me*.' Fear and pain rendered her insensible. 'Crown, motherfucker! Why won't you crown?'

The baby wasn't coming out. Something was wrong. Fuck it—there was only one thing to do. She posted: 'Anyone out there want to help me deliver this baby?' She got out the laptop and moved it between her legs so the camera was facing directly into her vagina. And then she hit: livestream.

Why not embrace this final humiliation? Giving birth is the ultimate sight gag. She looked at the screen and could see her vagina clearly, live footage broadcast to anyone who cared to watch. Comments were rapidly popping up in the on-screen chat.

Huffelpuffery: Woah.

Ummmm71: What am I looking at?

Babydaddyman: Is she serious?

oddlynormal: Are you serious?

lazarus001: Hot.

Huffelpuffery: Gross.

'Can you hear me?' asked Gracie.

lazarus001: Loud and clear.

Ummmm71: Yes. What's happening here?

'I'm alone in the house,' Gracie said. 'I've been pushing for an hour. She's not coming out!'

lazarus001: Are you serious?

Ummmm71: This is awesome!

'Yes, I'm serious!' yelled Gracie, ravaged by pain. 'Someone tell me—is she crowning? I can't tell!'

She suddenly felt an uncontrollable urge to push; she let out a primitive, grisly howl and pushed. She felt something dislodge.

Jones21: Holy shit.

Babydaddyman: She just shat herself.

lazarus001: I just threw up in my mouth.

Huffelpuffery: Be cool, baby.

Babydaddyman: You're doing great.

Her bowels had loosened in front of how many viewers? She looked at the screen and couldn't even register shock at the *three hundred thousand people* watching her. She tried to imagine she was one of those self-important conceptual artists giving birth on stage, or that the humiliation was happening to another version of her in a different universe. She took a towel and wiped herself.

'All right, world, what do you see?' she asked.

Noonoonoo: We can't see the baby's head.

Jetpack2001: I see a foot.

Ummmm71: She's got all her toes, that's good.

oddlynormal: Christ, Gracie, you need a cesarian.

'I'm alone.'

Huffelpuffery: You need a C-section. Or you will both die.

oddlynormal: Do it! You can do it!'

'Do what?'

lazarus001: Holy shit.

Huffelpuffery: I just googled it. A woman in Mexico did it and lived to tell the tale.

'Not even two successful cases? One?!'

Huffelpuffery: Inez Perez. In Mexico.

lazarus001: Her husband was drinking in a cantina with no phone.

'That son of a bitch.'

Jetpack2001: It took her an hour.

'An hour of cutting?'

Even if she managed to take the blade and cut her baby out, how would she not accidentally haul out the contents of her own stomach? How would she not bleed to death?

Huffelpuffery: She reached into her uterus and pulled out the baby.

Jetpack2001: It was a boy!

lazarus001: Before passing out, she cut the umbilical cord with scissors.

Huffelpuffery: 'After regaining consciousness, Perez bandaged her wound with her sweater.'

Huffelpuffery: A nurse later sewed it up with a household needle and thread.

'I'm going to pass out just thinking about Inez, let alone my own damn self.'

Noonoonoo: Here's another one, in the Philippines! Oh, wait, no, the baby died. Never mind.

oddlynormal: Okay? Inez made a vertical incision to the right of her belly button, going from under her rib cage to just above her bikini line.

oddlynormal: But she did this squatting with her pelvis forward, so she could cut straight through to the uterus. She didn't hit any internal organs, so make sure you don't either.

oddlynormal: Inez did it with a wooden-handled kitchen knife with a six-inch blade.

One night, several years ago, Gracie had impulse-bought from a late-night television infomercial a knife that could cut through cans and shoes; she now went roaring to the knife block and found the weapon she mainly used to cut the fat off meat.

oddlynormal: Get into position.

She followed oddlynormal's instructions and squatted with her pelvis forward.

oddlynormal: No, don't hold it by the handle. Hold the knife by the blade itself, take a pinch of skin, and start slicing.

lazarus001: Listen. Don't pass out from pain, don't bleed to death, and don't die from shock.

'You're being super helpful.'

oddlynormal: Start slicing!

Jetpack2001: Let's go!

Ummmm71: No. Wait!

'What?'

Ummmm71: Alcohol. Like 100% proof. Do you have any?

'Yes, should I pour it on the skin to clean it, you mean?'

Ummmm71: No, drink it.

'Right.'

She fetched the bottle of Devil's Springs vodka that Dr Patel had brought Owen on his visit. Strongest vodka on earth, he'd said—that should dull at least some of the pain. She resumed her position and took a long swig.

'Jesus Christ.'

Ummmm71: Keep going.

She gulped down a crazy amount and let out a purple-faced scream.

Huffelpuffery: Now get in there and rescue your fucking daughter!

oddlynormal: Slice your abdomen in the right paramedial region and cut the uterus longitudinally.

Gracie couldn't help thinking of the clairvoyant—was this the terrible event she didn't quite allude to, or did it *still* go further downhill from here?

Jetpack2001: Just get on with it.

She clenched the instrument by the blade. 'This is medieval.'

oddlynormal: You can do it!

'This is happening to me.'

Ummmm71: What is she saying?

'I had to remind myself. It's easy to forget.'

oddlynormal: Do it.

Ummmm71: Do it.

'I can't do it.'

oddlynormal: You'll die if you don't.

'I'll die then.'

Ummmm71: Your baby will die too.

'FUCK!'

Hufflepuffery: You are a badass.

'No, I'm not.'

Hufflepuffery: Say it.

'I am a badass bitch, and so is my daughter.'

Hufflepuffery: Say it again.

'We're an embarrassment of bitches!'

Horrified, she pressed the blade into her skin and looked her now seventeen million viewers in the eye.

'I hope this won't leave a mark.'

32

'Upon death, our souls are skipped across a black lake to wind up on these shores, under a sky so low you feel cramped in an open field. Is there any less edifying resurrection than ours? Oh, this nasty dream . . .'

'No,' I said. 'Your line is: "If this nasty dream be true . . ."'

'Dammit,' Valeria spat.

Valeria was rehearsing for a play called *Daniel Miller*—by Arthur Miller—in which she played the playwright's first wife, who just learned that their disabled son was shut away in an institution back on earth. It took me only ten minutes to realise that Valeria's physical gestures were overly performative and she couldn't stop hysterically emoting. I thought, I can't be in a serious relationship with a bad actress, can I?

I looked out the window at the streets overflowing with enraged protesters; the dissent against the inhumane treatment of new arrivals had evolved into a generalised anti-government march.

Hundreds of disgruntled dead were chanting in unison, shopfronts were being smashed, armed militias wrestled protesters violently to the ground. When exactly, I wondered, does a protest snowball into a revolution?

'Come away from the window and please finish helping me run lines?'

Concealing my irritable mood with a smile, I walked over and yanked the script from her hands.

'You've made an unscheduled stop,' she read overemotionally. 'What's so hard to understand?'

'I feel lost.'

Her voice suddenly dropped into an unnaturally low register. 'You were born grief-stricken into an endless maze.'

'How do I find the exit?'

'Why are you so sure there is one?'

'It's embarrassing to realise, Inge. If you believed in God, you dabbled in the occult. The invisible has become visible and we don't like what we're seeing. Most of all, we searched for origins when we should have searched for endings.'

There was something about the way I delivered that last line that made Valeria drop her script. Her lips moved but no words came out.

'What?'

She sucked her teeth and tapped a forefinger on the top of my head. 'What's going on in that coconut of yours?'

Did she mean besides the constant feeling of inconsolable loss? Besides going mad wondering about my child? This whole relationship felt wrong—couldn't Valeria see? I was on the rebound from another dimension.

'Nothing,' I said.

Valeria aggressively exhaled. 'I want you to tell me the truth. What are you thinking now?'

'You don't want to know.'

'Yes, I do.'

'You think you do, but you don't.'

'Don't tell me what I want or don't want!'

'I'm thinking how Gracie would always examine my lips before she kissed them.'

'Oh.'

'And how a bag of frozen peas was her cure for every complaint. And how she used towels so sparingly she'd often jump into the bed dripping wet and let the sheets dry her.'

'Okay.'

'And how she would lie across my lap, like she was much smaller than she was, and I'd pretend that she weighed too much—which she did.'

'ALL RIGHT!'

'You said you wanted the truth!'

'You're not going to forget her, are you?'

'No.'

Valeria made a weary, sickened grimace; as if she was hating herself for her overall taste in men. Then, suddenly, her whole face loosened; she knitted her brow in a mischievous sort of way and tried to suppress a sly smile. Here she was, a terrible actor, making a show of concealment—something was definitely up.

'Get dressed,' she said. 'I'm taking you to see someone.'

'Someone?'

'Think of it as a kind of therapy.'

'I'm not going back to group. It wasn't for me.'

She waltzed to the door and turned to me again, beaming ghoulishly. It was as if she was in character, performing another role entirely.

'Trust me, Angus Mooney,' she said. 'You haven't tried this.'

33

When Gracie came to, Owen was stitching her up.

'What are you doing?' she asked.

Owen was sweating and seemed unsure of himself.

'Medical school was a long time ago. I think I'm repositioning your bowel loops.'

'Okay.'

'Then I'll repair the uterine incision and, I guess, close up the abdominal walls.'

'That's kind of you.'

'I turn my back for one moment and you eviscerate yourself?'

'Where's Inez?'

'If that's the girl's name, she's sleeping,' he said. Noticing the look of fear on Gracie's face, he added: 'She's also perfectly healthy. Nothing wrong with her at all.'

'Let me see.'

'I've got my hands full. Turn your head to the right.'

Gracie turned her head to see tiny plump Inez with her old

lady's crabby frown, wriggling away on viscera-soaked blankets. Her beautiful daughter, powerfully alive!

'You're going to have to take it easy for a couple of months,' said Owen.

'I can't feel myself.'

'I've given you a shitload of morphine. How did you know to position yourself so the uterus was against the abdominal wall instead of the intestines?'

'My online assistants. Can I hold her?'

'I've got to finish this.'

Neither of them could believe she'd dragged her screaming daughter from her own wreckage.

'Neither of you should be alive,' said Owen, shaking his head. 'But you are.'

Gracie was depleted by the ordeal. Her head rolled to the side, and she saw her laptop open, still livestreaming, comments appearing at a breakneck pace:

Huffelpuffery: Champion.

Babydaddyman: Unbelievable.

Ummmm71: Fucking yeah!

JesusElSegundo: El elegido!

oddlynormal: Queen of the Apocalypse.

Babydaddyman: Unfuckingbelievable.

Ummmm71: All hail Gracie, Queen of the Apocalypse!

'Thank you thank you,' she said to whoever they were. Her mouth didn't feel like it was on her face. Her eyes closed. Owen sang some unrecognisable lullaby. 'Thank you,' she whispered again, and started reaching blindly and desperately for Inez, overcome with a surfeit of the oddest feelings—of being completely seen, of having surpassed all the expectations she ever had of herself, and of a premonition that an even more gruelling test was yet to come.

SEVEN

'He who does not answer the questions has passed the test.'

Franz Kafka

34

'How'd you die?'

'He was beaten to death and suffocated by a doctor who wanted his wife for himself,' Valeria said. '*In his own home*,' she added, with emphasis.

The beefy man looked at me like he couldn't deal with my facial structure right now. Valeria had introduced him as Marlon. He gave her a robust sneer.

'I can't believe you brought someone without checking first?'

'He really, *really* misses his wife.'

'Poor baby,' Marlon said, and they both laughed. I laughed too, having already made the decision to roll with whatever freaky therapy session Valeria had brought me to. She had led me through a graveyard and several filthy alleyways to this dilapidated warehouse, and every second there convinced me an illicit drug transaction was about to take place.

Marlon escorted us into a draughty room with thick concrete pylons. Machinery hummed, disassembled electronics were heaped in piles, and, in the charcoal shadows, overly bearded men hunkered over computers in dismal silence, the kind of people who could make a penthouse suite feel subterranean.

'This way, sad sack,' Marlon snarled.

Marlon guided me to the corner of the space and made a grand gesture towards a large oblong box made of steel—a floatation tank.

'Sensory-deprivation therapy? Why all the secrecy?'

'Think of it as an illegal border crossing,' Marlon said. 'You don't want to draw too much attention to yourself, do you?'

'I guess not,' I answered.

'First one's free.'

'The first what?'

Marlon glared at her in disbelief. 'He doesn't even know why he's here?' he asked, simmering in annoyance. She gave an exaggerated playful shrug and he exhaled bitterly. They both seemed put out by their mutual acquaintance.

Marlon stared at me, an ominous gleam in his eyes. 'Extraordinary grief calls for extraordinary therapy, wouldn't you say?'

'I suppose.'

Even his smile felt exaggerated. He handed me a beaker with a milky liquid inside. So—drugs. He was going to send me off on some psychedelic journey into the interior? Frankly, he didn't *not* look like a profiteering shaman.

I sniffed the liquid. I imagined this wouldn't be dissimilar to the ayahuasca ceremony Gracie dragged me to. That had been in some rich lady's Rose Bay mansion and, before it even began, every second person I didn't know had instructed me to be receptive and tolerant, as if they could intuit just from my face that I was naturally neither. Incense burned excessively, and I was peer-pressured into imbibing a gunky, earth-smelling brew.

'Are you ready for the disconcerting journey of a lifetime?' Gracie had asked me.

'I suppose.'

'Even though no horizon will remain untouched, don't panic. Remember: dissolution is not disintegration. Essence is not existence. You can afford to temporarily lose one of them. The truth is, the negotiations between you and your limits were over in childhood, and you settled for less than your worth.'

'Should we get on with it?' I asked.

'Sure,' said Gracie. 'Is your consciousness backed up somewhere, just in case?'

'What?'

'Joking.'

Being a vibrating sack hurtling through fields of fractal patterns and geometric shapes haunted me still. Frankly, it was not my favourite day ever, and I swore never to take hallucinogens again as long as I lived. Yet here I was.

'Bottoms up,' I said, raising the glass to my lips and chugging it down.

'Funny you should say that,' Marlon said, breathing heavily into my face. 'You'd better get in there quick smart.' He pointed to a nearby door.

'What for?'

'You'll see in about seven seconds.'

I felt it before he finished the sentence—my bowels!—and sprinted to the toilet, just sliding my pants down in time. Why had he given me the universe's most powerful laxative? I didn't bother asking. Questioning is itself a form of resistance, and why bother? The forces of malevolence were far outnumbered by the forces that just wanted me to play along. I was never a victim of injustice, if you don't count the time I was murdered. I mostly got what I deserved—and got away with more than that.

The burning, historic shit continued unpleasantly. Afterwards, I washed my hands like a surgeon and emerged feeling hollow. I didn't have the energy to be embarrassed.

'All good?' asked Marlon.

'Never better,' I said, eyeing the floatation tank. 'Is it swim time?'

'Take your clothes off.'

To debate the point would take energy I didn't have; I undressed.

'Underpants too.'

Why not? I removed them and he tossed me a plastic, transparent wetsuit. It was tight-fitting and difficult to slip into, and there was a hole at the crotch.

'Why's this here?'

'We need to put in a catheter.'

'Terrific.'

'Most people piss themselves the first few goes,' Marlon said, 'and we can't change the liquid in the tank every time. Valeria, do you want to do the honours?'

'With pleasure.'

She held the thin tube up as a dare. I shrugged consent, and she seized my penis in a pincer squeeze and slid the lubricated catheter into my urethra and strapped a bag to my leg.

'This is fun,' I said. 'Now what?'

'Have you ever sheltered your eyes from the dark?'

'I don't think so.'

The lid to the tank opened with a decompressing hiss. Inside was a protruding metallic cylinder, containing an absurd tangle of multicoloured wires and tubes and cables, connected to three monitors next to the tank. On the monitors, numbers ran backwards into the negative thousands.

'In you get,' Marlon said, with an aggressive smile.

Marlon peeled back a layer of fibre mesh to reveal an ominous pool of black water. I dipped a toe and the water began undulating. Actually, not undulating—convulsing. Then I realised: it wasn't water. I lowered myself into the warm, viscous liquid. It was thick as pudding and separated then coagulated around my limbs as I moved through it.

'Don't worry, we're not going to seal you in forever. Although you'll probably beg me to,' Marlon said, his face impassive.

'What?'

He let that hang there, his whole silly demeanour seemed to insinuate that it was a distinct possibility that this could destroy my mind. I thought: So what? A psychotic break wouldn't be the worst thing that had ever happened to me. Take it from me—when you get sad enough, you'll vote for the precipitous over the slow decline every time.

Marlon leaned into my face. 'You'll feel like you're being buried alive, but just for a minute.'

'Suits me.'

'If you try to hurt yourself, we'll instantaneously convert the liquid into a setting gel that will inhibit movement.'

He twisted dials, threw switches, and swiped his fingers across a touch screen. The machine emanated a low buzz and little clicks. A sluggish trickle of yellow piss snaked through the tube into the bag. I thought: What if this is my finest hour?

'Connecting the umbilical. This is your oxygen.' He held up a syringe filled with a brownish liquid. 'And this baby is an intramuscular injection. It's going to hurt.'

'Okay.'

'Aren't you going to ask me what it is?'

'Nope.'

'Dimethyltryptamine. It's the ultimate *gateway* drug. Get it?'

'Sure. Good one.'

As I suspected, it was a hallucinogenic. Marlon stretched a rubber helmet over my skull, with a lattice network of wires and a visor that blocked my vision. I could only hear his deep voice and my own deafening heartbeat.

'Another needle will be going into your brainstem,' Marlon went on in a monotone, 'right at the rostral dorsolateral pontine tegmentum . . .' His voice sounded oiled and slippery, difficult to catch hold of. 'Gotta be careful not to overload the cortex.'

Marlon's speech devolved into an exercise in free association and I couldn't connect the end of one sentence to the beginning of another—it was a harangue way above my pay grade. 'Flattened dispersion of punctured potentialities through the plane of distribution . . .'

Technical explanations made me sleepy. I started to drift off. I wondered: What journey was this psychoactive substance going to take me on? I thought: What always spoke poorly of psychedelic-induced hallucinations was the unchanging nature of their devotees' personalities. If they were communing with the universal spirit, why were they almost never markedly improved by it? Every tripper I knew almost immediately snapped back into the old thought habits they'd had before they embarked on their 'journey'.

'. . . inverse self-binding and agitation of matter into seepage . . .' The claustrophobia was intense. The dark looked like someone had painted black over it. '. . . should result in the widening of the thalamus . . .' What would my trip look like? I was expecting anything—a translucent goddess, or a bearded God-dude, or a giant Sauron-like eye, or—

'Are you listening?'

'No.' Frankly, I was beginning to lose my patience for this gloomy Gus. 'Like, whatever, Einstein,' I said. 'Let's just get this show on the road.'

'Okay, dumbfuck. Try not to have multiple organ failure.'

The lid hissed shut, and I was buried under the pitch darkness. I felt immediately bodiless; it was no longer clear if I had hands. I could hear my own laboured breathing and prepared for a visual, psychedelic diatribe.

I heard Marlon's low-pitched, disembodied voice: 'Think of your wife who you miss so excruciatingly and find the overlooked pathway.' I heard Valeria say, 'May I?' and Marlon say, 'Go ahead,' and Valeria say, 'Use your grief to crystallise the longing,' and Marlon say, 'You have to knead your yearning into existence,' and Valeria say, 'He won't know what that means.'

She was right; all I knew was that I was about to have my consciousness altered and I could think of at least three boundaries that could stand some dissolving.

'Are you ready?'

'I died ready.'

'Good one. Here we go.'

Other than my own breathing, there was dead silence. Nothing was happening in the undifferentiated darkness. If this was supposed to diminish the constant ache of missing Gracie and my unborn child, it wasn't working.

Then—everything at once. A deafening roar that sounded like public bathroom hand dryers blasting in each ear; an unbearable copper taste in my mouth; the agonising sensation of skin peeled from my body and a tightening in my bones, nothing much, just an overwhelming compression, as if I was being compacted or shrunk to a single point. Whether or not my eyelids were open, it was difficult to say. I was expecting dazzling colours and geometric patterns, but there was only an oscillating darkness that made me feel alone and unloved, lost on an unpleasant journey to nowhere. I think I passed out and regained consciousness multiple times.

That was the easy part. Next came the feeling of ascending and descending at the same time, plunging both vertically and horizontally in an uninterrupted freefall into a hot darkness that flattened me like a sandwich press. I feared for my central nervous system. I felt abstracted and disoriented, unable to separate my self from the blinding darkness. This was definitely going to be one of those therapies you needed to see a therapist about.

Something whipped past my eyes incomprehensibly fast; a tiny rectangle of halogen-bright white that gleamed thickly then disappeared. A few seconds later, the white rectangle reappeared again, hitting my eyes like hard sunlight.

I squinted into it. What was it? It looked like a door. I moved closer to it—or did it move closer to me?—and then I saw it clearly: it was the door—to my house!

Our little yellow house! I wanted to wallow in the sight of it.

It drifted away, and everything was all black again. I wanted to cry out, but I had no voice. Then the entire house slid into view, floating like a white island in a black sea of cold air. I was seized with a feeling of intense horror. I could hear the faraway sound of Marlon's voice, saying, 'You gotta steer it, man, like a boat.'

I tried to move to the softly glowing house, but I blew past it. It was dissipating into a haze in the black fog, then it returned, bleached out and vivid.

'We can see what you see,' said Marlon's voice from the depths. 'And we can pilot you remotely from here, at least until you get the hang of it.'

I was now being sucked into the house, into this beacon of light, accelerating through the blackness towards the door—*through* the door.

I was in my living room!

Now I understood—I was inside a simulation cobbled together from my memories. Whatever thought-decoding technology reconstructed these images from my brainwaves, this was high-priced virtual-reality entertainment, like being on Star Trek's Holodeck. I could finally locate my body in space, and I slowly turned around to take in the room—I had all 360 degrees to work with. The suit must have had fibre-optic internal sensors that positioned my body in a three-dimensional space that I could move around like a video game.

'It's so real,' I said.

Yet there was something slightly unnerving about it. This high-definition virtual world, taken from my unconscious mind, was like being inside a recurring dream.

'You can rotate at any angle. The user interface should be completely intuitive.'

I'm not a gamer; I've always hated video games, and I found it difficult to navigate.

'I can't move.' I said.

'You want to go up or down?'

'Up.'

'Via the stairway or through the ceiling?'

'What?'

'Ceiling it is.'

I glided up towards the ceiling and through it to the second storey. Now I was in my old hallway! I couldn't decide if this computer-generated environment was more like being inside a game, a home movie or a photo album. I drifted along the hallway, passing through the closed door into the bedroom.

And there she was.

All the tender parts of myself came alive for the first time since my death. In bed, there was a realistic-looking version of a sleeping Gracie, vividly and exquisitely depicted, precisely as I remembered how she looked asleep: from the adorable twitch of her left eye to her faint, open-lipped sleepy smile. It was almost too much. I rotated to take in the whole room, slickly rendered in incredible detail: puddle of moonlight on the armchair, the mouldering window frames, the unsteady towers of books. It was visually arresting; there was a weight to everything.

'This is immersive as fuck.'

I turned back to my widow replica sleeping with a sort of sadness. This was too much. Too vivid. Too poignant. Too maddening. Too blurry.

'It's so blurry.'

'You gotta pull focus.'

'How?'

'The lever on your right hand.'

I pulled the small lever on the right arm of the suit and Gracie abruptly filled my visual field.

'Not zoom,' said Marlon. 'Focus.'

Now the picture was so sharp, I could see the thin veins across the pink of her eyelids.

'The picture quality is amazing.'

It was disorienting to be inside a simulation this meticulously constructed—and yet, there was something off. It was incomplete. Where were the side tables and the wardrobe? Where were the floor lamps? Was this virtual bedroom smaller than the real one? It was then I noticed there was a *second* bed in the room, a double bed pressed against the queen.

Gracie sat up and yawned. I had to admit—this was worth it. It was crazy. Technology is crazy. I was in a kind of matrix. I was old enough to remember when a video-game character was a small stick that hit a ball to another small stick. Now I was floating *inside* a three-dimensional hyperreal recreation of my own beloved murder house, looking at a moving image of my own beloved widow.

Then—beside her, in the other bed, he rose into view.

Owen.

He was half-naked and small, lying alongside my wife. Now Gracie turned pale, her eyes shrieking. This was a bad trip, a nightmare Holodeck. The Owen simulation studied me with that familiar hardness in his eyes, and my fists clenched so hard I thought my bones might break. It was like dreams: you either got a roster of pleasant wish fulfilments or a noxious parade of outrageous fears.

Owen's mouth started moving but I couldn't hear anything.

'There's no audio.'

'I never said there would be,' I heard Marlon say.

Therapeutically, I knew I ought to interact with these glitchy three-dimensional simulacra and say whatever I needed to get off my chest. Wasn't that why I was here?

'I miss you,' I said to Gracie. 'So much.'

Gracie looked down, casting a troubled glance at something, but what? That's when I saw that between them, in a pillow trench, was a jaundice-yellow-faced baby—was this what my unconscious mind thought my baby would look like?

Before I could react, Gracie, Owen and the weird-looking baby—even the bedroom itself—wafted away like smoke.

'Connection's lost.'

Thick smoke piled up in my head, piercing the darkness. The visor was removed and someone was instructing me to keep my eyes closed. I could hear Marlon: 'We took a screenshot from the live feed. You might like this as a keepsake.' Something was pressed into my hand.

'She's not how I pictured her,' I heard Valeria say.

Then I passed out.

Valeria was asking if I knew my own name. I couldn't answer. We were in the back room of the Bitter in Soul. I felt diminished to half my size. My heart jangled like keys. In my mouth was a strange taste, as if I had licked the rust off an old car door.

Coming back from an immersive, artificial world was a sticky business. Valeria ordered us Coca-Colas and, after one sip, I spewed crushed ice before regaining control of my vocal cords.

'I don't want to do that again,' I said. 'I fucking hate VR or whatever mind-uploading tech that was.'

'Don't you get it?'

'Get what?'

'You raw-dogged the earth.'

'What?'

'You penetrated that little blue dot from behind. What do you think it was?'

'Some kind of simulation.'

'No, dummy. You permeated the boundaries between dimensions and witnessed the present moment on the living earth.'

'Speak English.'

'You went home.'

Was it possible? From my pocket I fetched the printout of Gracie and the baby. The baby. *My* baby? Was that really true? Was it mine? Had I come face to face with my own child? I felt like I'd just died anew. The screenshot was grainy and pixelated, but could it have been real? I replayed the events, the startled manner in which Gracie gaped at me.

'*She* saw *me*.'

'She saw a ghost.'

'That machine . . . It made me into a ghost?'

'Actually, the PC term is spectrenaut.'

Amazing, but—the dismal truth flooded my being from head to toe: I wasn't there for my child. I had broken my promise to look them in the eye. This afterlife I was inhabiting grew exponentially emptier. And this being real also meant that, in the springy pocket of my old bed, Owen, that brittle old stick, was fucking my wife! The pain of it was excruciating. I should have known. Worst-case scenarios always play out more or less exactly as you picture them.

35

Gracie anxiously stubbed out a cigarette into a dirty nappy and ran over to the window and looked out at the mad-faced moon: there were voices in the night. There were beings in the shadows. There was more to heaven and earth. There was life beyond the grave. There was an immortal soul.

She'd known it, sort of! She'd suspected it all along!

Trembling, she went to her computer. Her followers were discussing the warnings to remain inside their homes except to empty anything that collected water after a rain, to avoid virus-carrying mosquitoes breeding there. Then she watched a video tutorial on the handling of human remains, and read about rumours of a network of militias called EndTimers dedicated to exterminate with extreme prejudice the global one percent—once the death toll reached a critical level—so the billionaires didn't wind up being the only survivors. Unsurprisingly, it seemed resentment was going to be the world's driving force to the very end.

Gracie posted: 'Saw the ghost of my dead husband just now.'

In response, a string of ghost and shocked and mute-faced emojis. Gracie looked around the room, holding her breath. There was no reason to suppose that the ghost had gone.

'Not joking. There is life after death,' she posted.

The responses came fast: 'Photo please' and 'Take a video' and 'Say hi for me', along with more emojis: doubtful ones, eyerolling ones, a Pinocchio-nose one.

She looked at Inez, frowny and red-cheeked, ugly-crying in her cot. Then she posted: 'Inez saw her daddy for the first time today. #fatherdaughterloveforever'. That led to an outpouring of cat-with-love-heart-eyes emojis that may or may not have been sarcastic.

Gracie puzzled out her ongoing thought process on the supernatural phenomena: 'The presence of Mooney's ghost suggests that death is no freedom from the self, that is obvious, but is it consciousness with or without agency? Is it not dissimilar to locked-in syndrome?' That elicited even more emoji responses: zombies, skulls, devil faces, vampires, knives, hourglasses, and one that inexplicably hit home—an emoji of a magnet.

Meanwhile, Owen turned on the main lights in the bedroom, the lamps—lightbulb by lightbulb, he went about dispersing the dark in every corner of the house. Gracie came down the stairs with Inez in her arms.

'Jesus Christ, babies are embarrassing,' Owen said.

'What?'

'Within several hours of being born, a baby gazelle can outrun a predatory cheetah. Human babies can't do a fucking thing. It's just pretty pathetic, that's all.'

'Are you okay?'

'I'm fine, thank you. How are you?'

'You look like you just saw a ghost.'

'That's a weird thing to say.'

'And I did too.'

'Don't be silly. Let's watch TV.'

The news was on an American-style mass shooting at Williamstown hospital. Reports suggested the military were taking pot shots at the infected, the footage showing a parade of crazy haemorrhages; every eyeball bleeding; every mouth a hellmouth.

Gracie was still in shock, a weight of feeling immobilising her. Owen was wrapped in a blanket, holding in a scream, looking trapped in a perpetual shiver.

'You sure you didn't see anything upstairs?'

'Jesus!' he said. 'Can't a guy watch TV without being asked dumb questions? Don't forget who repositioned your bowel loops, okay? I think I've earned some quiet time.'

'Okay. Take it easy. You didn't see anything. I get it.' She let it go for now, and they stared at the TV together with knots tightening inside them. Neither ceased glancing around every few minutes to see if the spooky realm had opened up again and revealed the ghost standing right behind them.

36

For days, with the blackout curtains drawn, I sat in the armchair and listened to the ostentatious revolution on the streets banging its drum. The same thoughts kept swirling in my brain: My Gracie sharing a bed with Owen? Unbearable. The sight of my baby? Unbelievable.

I didn't shower, and only moved to tread a narrow pathway to the toilet and back. I couldn't even make it down to the Bitter in Soul; I drank in-house. First I was murdered, now I was being cheated on with the man who'd murdered me! My homicide had to be unsolved if Owen was still a free man.

How had he conned her into bed? Gracie would never willingly have sex with such an offensive fiend—was she in danger? And why wasn't Owen dead already? He should have succumbed to his well-earned brain disease by now. I couldn't wrap my head around any of it, and I couldn't physically or emotionally readjust to life after my transdimensional journey. It seemed that the lingering after-effects of haunting were dizziness and dislocation, and an indescribable yearning that felt like a possession.

'Are you going back to work?' asked Valeria.

'No way.'

How could I go? I had been changed forever. I had not discovered the unknown—I *was* the unknown.

'I thought if you could see her one last time, you'd get her out of your system.'

Talk about a backfire—it got Gracie back *into* my system, and at toxic levels. Whenever I closed my eyes, I saw her, along with that owl-faced bastard hooting at me.

Unable to stand building gulags any longer, I decided instead to eke out my existence by the oldest profession: mooching. I'd live shamelessly off Valeria until she summoned enough self-respect to toss me to the kerb. Seeing Gracie had also made me realise how mismatched Valeria and I were, so her idea flopped there too.

My mind was preoccupied with wondering if my soul really had been trafficked to the other side or if I had been the victim of some elaborate scam. This had all the hallmarks of an ingenious con: convince a mark he's a ghost and milk him for an exorbitant fee for 'haunting'. Was I a sucker or wasn't I? I couldn't decide. If I *had* been a hyperdimensional being, I could once again lay eyes on my baby daughter, gaze upon the face of my beloved Gracie, and haunt the shit out of my murderer. My God, how I wanted once again to be the occult gleam in his terrified eye.

'I should go back once more to check up on them,' I said.

'You can't afford it,' said Valeria.

'How much is it?'

'One thousand dollars.'

It was a heroin of an idea, and no obstacle would prevent me from going through with it. 'It's no problem.'

'Where are you going to get that kind of money?'

There was only one option I could think of, and it was going to push my heart to the limit.

37

The drab ground floor apartment smelled of conflicting air fresheners. The woman who was my mother made grilled cheese sandwiches. The man who was my father didn't like to talk when the TV was on, so the small talk between us was smaller than most: the consistency of wheat crackers, the relative weakness of the current stock of fridge magnets, whether glass eyes were ever better than an empty socket. The woman who was my mother kept her hands in a prayer position as she talked.

'So. Angus. What do you do for fun?' the woman who was my mother asked.

This was a question I'd never known how to answer in my entire life. 'I guess I try to enjoy myself in a general sense and never designate a specific time and place for it.'

'Very interesting approach, Angus! Isn't it, darling?'

'Very,' said the man who was my father.

It wasn't and they knew it. We'd already bottomed out. There was, I had noticed, some kind of feedback loop of self-pity travelling between them—the tie that binds.

'It occurs to me you might want to hear about your grandparents,' the man who was my father said, during the ad break.

'Actually—no.'

'I've got some doozies to tell you.'

'That's okay. I'd prefer to not hear about them.'

'Why not?'

It was hard to explain. Living a life with no immediate relatives had made me feel related to nobody, but also, in a strange way, potentially to everybody. Only since meeting my biological parents had I realised that the specificity of genetic family connection limits your conception of self to a depressing degree.

The woman who was my mother said, 'Well then, I bet you're wondering how *we* died.'

Not especially, I thought.

'We died one after the other. Didn't we, honey?' The man who was my father didn't respond. 'I said, didn't we?'

'I'm dead, not deaf. Can't you see, woman? He wants something.' The man who was my father let out a sharp, bored sigh that seemed to momentarily disrupt the TV transmission. 'I'm guessing it's money.'

The strained energy in the room turned prickly.

'He's right,' I said. 'Consider it reparations.'

The woman who was my mother crossed her arms sombrely. 'How much?'

'One thousand dollars.'

The man who was my father got to his feet and stood awkwardly beside the TV and scratched his beard. The woman who was my mother was breathing hard and wouldn't look away from me.

'Give it to him,' she said.

The man who was my father rose from his armchair, groaning. I almost promised to reimburse them, but it would've sounded unbearably hollow. From my inside coat pocket, I pulled out the magnetic card-reader Valeria had given me.

'We enter our cards at the slots at either end.'

'I know how it works.'

The man who was my father entered the requisite numbers and snatched his card back with a hostile flourish.

'Thanks, Dad.'

I don't know—I thought I'd try it out for fun. The silence afterwards became a fourth smothering presence in the room. I took the third click of my biological father's tongue as the cue to depart.

'You want to stay for dessert?'

'No, that's okay.'

'I see, said the blind man.'

I was embroiled in a family drama—my first—in which I was the black sheep. It felt absurd and I wanted to get out of there as fast as possible.

'Thanks for stopping by,' the woman who was my mother said, tearfully.

'No worries.' I stood to go, but got overwhelmed with a desire to make some kind of amends. 'You should know, I didn't have a bad life. I was fostered by some pretty decent folks, and I wound up married to a wonderful woman. She's had our baby. You're grandparents, I guess. Not that that matters here. Anyway.'

'Thanks for saying all that,' I heard the woman who was my mother say as I hurried out. When I glanced back, they were poised at the door eyeing me with sorrowful, kitteny looks. I might have been wrong, but I thought they got a little high off the sadness.

38

The second haunting was more physically demanding than the first, if that's possible, and began with Marlon greeting me with this weird admonition: 'You can't be an incubus, Casanova.'

'A what?'

'You know you can't have intercourse with that sleeping widow of yours, right?'

'I assumed.'

'I just want to be transparent about the limitations of our services.'

'Understood. I just want to see her with my own eyes. To be honest, I think this whole thing might be a cruel trick.'

He squinted at me. 'Do you know why we're anchored to places more than to people?'

'No. Why?'

'Our attachment to a formerly inhabited physical structure that had the primitive function of shelter *and* where we had a profound emotional connection to its inhabitants catalyses the reunification process in a space *already* made vital by having a part of you forcibly dispersed there, as ousting a human soul via murder functions like a botched exorcism. In other words, you're rejoining yourself.'

'In other words, I'm sorry I asked.'

'Let me get technical for a moment.'

'Please don't.'

Marlon ignored my pleas and breathlessly discharged a cascade of technical jargon with a vampiric intensity that made me crawl into an attic space in my mind: '... phylogenetic discharges and self-assembling dissipators peripheralised in the temporoparietal ...' It sounded like he was crushing words in his mouth and I quietly reverted to not caring about not understanding—my sweet spot.

Eventually Marlon tired of his own voice and secured my visor and it began: the various hurricane and volcanic eruption sounds intensified before dropping me into the unimaginably empty darkness where it was immediately impossible to know if my eyes were open or closed, if I was upside down or right way up. If I had to guess, I would've sworn I was either travelling from two opposite directions at once or I was descending in a spiral, or I *was* a spiral, or I was bending to the will of the formless dark that wanted me to be formless too.

I tried to conjure Gracie's face. Nothing happened, so I imagined Owen instead, sending me into a terrifying spin, until out of the inky fog came that squarish block of bright light, our little yellow house, dusted as if in frail moonlight; it grew larger and smaller, lurched back and forth. Maybe my burning hatred for Owen made me into some kind of a homing beacon. I was home—or was I? The house shrank to a pinprick of light and disappeared. This time I imagined Owen and Gracie entwined in bed together, and

I plummeted towards the house like a falling meteor through a dark squall. I aimed directly for the upstairs window, missed, and wound up in the upstairs back bedroom, Owen's room—the grisly site of my murder.

It was disquieting to glide into the actual setting of my worst recurring nightmare. The weirdness of it didn't rob the basic room of its power to terrorise. I also felt embarrassed to return to the scene of my murder, where I'd never once had the foresight to feel doomed. I didn't linger long there. I descended through the dusty floorboards into the living room downstairs, where it gave me a dirty pleasure to see a wheezing and waxy-skinned Owen sitting tragically by the window. He looked to be rotting alive.

The autofocus shifted in and out and gave me motion sickness. Was my soul really on earth or was I simply trapped inside my own psyche? I wouldn't put it past me.

Owen lurched to his feet and hurried out of the room and I glided after him, down the dark hallway, as if on an airport walkway. He hastened down the basement steps into the laundry room and slammed the door; I floated on through. He took a few quaking steps backwards until he hit the dryer.

I got all up in his grill. He rubbed his eyes cartoonishly then stared morosely at the floor. He should have been decomposing by now, but it was painfully obvious why he wasn't—Gracie had given him a new lease on life. That's why he hadn't succumbed to his fatal brain disease in a timely manner. Love was beating it back with her magic stick. What a distressing turn of events! I made ugly faces at him but his eyes were now squeezed shut, so I went to search the house for Gracie.

I found her in the bath with the baby, lips silently moving, looking happy enough yet more pixelated than last time. Was this the real Gracie, or a video image? I couldn't decide but, either way, the sight of her and our baby made me feel like a deficient being, an inadequate husband, a non-entity as a father. Only losers get themselves murdered, I was thinking, when Gracie sensed something in the air—that something was me.

Gracie ogled me sorrowfully and hoisted our rosy-cheeked child up in the air as if in sacrificial offering. Jesus Christ, this edible baby was mine. I wanted to wear her like a heavy necklace and kiss the little fingers on her impossibly tiny hand. I wanted to abscond with her into the ether.

Sentience is a life sentence, my child. Welcome to the party.

Gracie's smile twisted with animal pain and, as I drifted closer, I saw the aftermath of the birth written in clumsy stitching across the lower half of her abdomen. It must have been some delivery.

Gracie picked off colourful foam letters stuck to the rim of the bathtub and rearranged them: I-N-E-Z.

INEZ.

Was that our baby's name? Gracie's mouth moved in excruciating silence; I could never read lips—or hearts, for that matter. I wished I wasn't on mute so I could tell her that existence was not a sprint, it was a marathon. Pace yourself. I wanted to say that I was not from oblivion, yet I had travelled through it, and what awaited was worse than reincarnation but better than hell. You still had to floss and eat fibre and read non-verbal cues, and you still wound up using the silent judgement of others to exacerbate your own self-hatred. Basically, we did find out, after all, what it was like to wake up dead. And the whole idea of being 'put out of your misery' was totally false; misery endured. But so did love, so did the way I felt for her.

Gracie pressed her lips tight together and it occurred to me that I had no idea precisely what she was seeing when she looked at me. I rotated 180 degrees to the mirror and squinted at a milky humanoid shape—an absurd figure. I stared hard at the mirror; for a few seconds I morphed into a white splotch, then a white splotch with my own recognisable features, but I couldn't hold on and, without meaning to, I shapeshifted back into a milky gob of light.

When I looked back, Gracie seemed depressed. I had the vague sense I was doing something wrong—not just immoral but ostentatious, like I was a peeping Tom peeping with a disgusting amount of fanfare. Is haunting a perversion, like making someone watch you masturbate into a pot plant? Gracie had endured so much of my nonsense—my criminal manoeuvres, my ignorance and selfishness, not to mention the boneheaded move of getting myself murdered—now she had to endure this too.

Next thing I knew, the connection was lost, and with brute force Marlon was extracting me from the tank and lowering my carcass to the floor. It was an instant comedown. My eyeballs were burning in their sockets, I couldn't breathe, and I was flooded by a sadness so absolute the only way I could describe it was as the total physical embodiment of being unwanted. The only certainty was: I had to go back again as soon as possible.

39

Gracie perched herself on the washing machine and kicked it with the back of her heels to a hollow beat.

'Mooney's body was found in Darlinghurst, right?'

Owen was in a squatting position on the laundry floor, pretending to read the back of a box of detergent.

'Right. So?'

'Then why is his ghost here?'

'What do you mean?'

'Ghosts only haunt the physical space where they died.'

'Says you.'

'Wouldn't that mean he was killed here, in this house, and his body moved?' Her words left a ringing silence, and Owen stared mutely ahead. 'Owen! We need to go to the police!'

'Gracie! The police are busy right now. In fact, we don't even know if there *is* a police force anymore. And your evidence is somewhat insane.' He patted her hand and laughed softly. 'I mean, what are you going to say? *Excuse me, officer, I saw a white light with my husband's face, so ipso facto, he was murdered in my house?*'

'"A white light with his face"! You saw him too!'

'I can't have this conversation,' he spluttered, and with a violent jolt sprang to his feet. As he pondered his next move, there came the sound of doors slamming and engines thrumming and voices yelling outside. Owen and Gracie climbed the basement stairs and hurried to the living room. Out the window, they could see masked neighbours shouting in panic, cramming luggage and household items into their cars.

'Where are you all going?' Gracie shouted through the open window.

'We're evacuating the neighbourhood,' said Mrs Henderson.

'Why?'

'The man on TV told us to!' said the neighbour who lived on the other side of Mrs Henderson. People sure were pliable in an emergency. 'Haven't you been watching?'

'We're driving to Tassie!' Mrs Henderson said.

'We're driving to Alice!' shouted another neighbour, who Gracie had never spoken to.

'The mosquitoes here are undefeatable.'

'The whole place is a jungle swamp.'

'It's all the fucking swimming pools.'

'Look at what Maureen's wearing.'

'Where does she think she's going, to a formal dinner?'

The evacuees were getting in one last gossip.

'The desert, that's where we need to go.'

'Down the coast will be safer.'

There were two competing caravans of fleeing residents—one heading west, one south. Owen turned to Gracie with a fixed grimace on his face. 'I think we should go too.'

'I'm staying here,' she said.

'We'll run out of food here eventually.'

'What if he comes back?'

'Who?'

'You know who.'

'No, I don't.'

They stood solemnly, watching their neighbours chaotically fleeing.

'Not everyone will leave,' Gracie said.

'Probably not.'

'Especially the ones who just finished a home makeover.'

'That's *them*. I still think *we* should most definitely get out of this house. What if staying is certain death?'

'Death doesn't really exist,' Gracie said. 'We know that now.'

'I know no such thing.' He thought for a moment. 'I wouldn't mind dying in the desert, with the sand in my eyes, complaining of heat rash.'

They watched the long procession of cars drive down the street and vanish around the corner. There they went, the home owners! With their arrogant meat smells and heartwormy dogs, always renovating and vigilantly scrutinising interest rates as if they were the temperature of a feverish child. Gracie thought: You can be trapped in movement, just as inside a house. Come to think of it, she thought, this is how Homo sapiens has always spread out, beginning hundreds of thousands of years ago, from Africa to every corner of the earth. We were never really intrepid adventurers—all our magnificent migrations across the planet were just us running for our lives.

'Owen, maybe you should go.'

'If you're staying, I'm staying.'

'I *am* staying. He's trapped between this world and the next.'

'Don't start that again.'

'What if he's just floating in an empty void!'

They both imagined me like an astronaut dislodged from the exterior of a space station, unhappily whirling in space. Owen deliberated; any coldness he perceived from Gracie felt like jeopardy to him, and he couldn't risk losing her. Not now.

'Okay,' he said.

'Okay what?'

'You know what.'

'Say it.'

'I saw what you saw.'

'I knew it!'

Owen paced the living room with loud and sudden stomps as if he might just catch my spirit underfoot. 'He came back! As a ghost!' There was a look of pure revulsion in him. 'Is he a spirit of health or goblin-damned? If he really is a ghost, then he's a ghost with consciousness, and that consciousness is clearly not without malice, and that malicious intent to frighten can only be thwarted by a simple refusal to be frightened.'

'What?'

'If he comes back, lock down all emotions, even the primal ones. Take control of your fear reflex. Refuse to react, thwart the ghost's intentions with indifference and hope that the frustrated phantom gets bored and leaves us alone.'

'Owen, did you kill Angus?'

'What? No! That's absurd.'

'Don't lie. I won't be mad.'

'You won't be mad if I tell you that I murdered your husband?'

'Not if you did it for love.' Was she trying to trick him into an admission? Maybe.

'*Of course* I fucking didn't. Jesus, Gracie.'

Gracie studied this man whom she cared about—oh, why be stingy?—whom she loved. His death sentence, she considered, was a great asset to him; it had revealed him to be a devoted, kind and thoughtful man with a gentle heart, and he was sweet with her and patient with Inez. In bed, she enjoyed his melancholy kisses and how he reliably coaxed her to orgasm; he had a decent chest to fall asleep on and she'd even grown accustomed to his single-nostril snoring and the sharp intake of breath when he panic-woke after a bad dream. Moreover, she trusted him with her life and, while he was ornery, spiritually dead and preoccupied with himself, she simply couldn't bring herself to believe that murder could count as one of his foibles.

The last of the neighbours, loudly bickering over directions, backed their overloaded car out of their driveway and skidded out of sight. The street was empty now, a pregnant emptiness that frightened Owen and Gracie, though neither one of them acknowledged it. The timing was odd, they both knew that—the living had left just as the dead had arrived.

40

My only obstacle to returning to Gracie was the means to afford it. There was no fast way to make that much money legally—I couldn't scrounge any more from my biological parents—so my only option was to dine out on the chaos of civil unrest.

The transdimensional refugee crisis was coming to a head. Some group of dipshits that called themselves The League of the Militant Godless were marching and making their awful pronouncements to: 'Move Them On' and 'Transition to End Rationing'. Protesters holding 'Plague Dead Welcome' and 'We are all God's Dead Children' placards were trooping through the city centre to clash with them. At a barricade of overturned buses, I found the groups hurling insults across a line of armed police, and on a podium facing a jeering crowd, a squat man gripped a megaphone, shouting: 'How can we enforce law and order, let alone feed and house everybody?'

I sidled up to a protester and asked him, 'What's going on?'

He explained that a bunch of new arrivals were in a holding facility down near the canal, and an increasing number of senior government ministers were petitioning for them to be 'moved on'. I edged my hand into his pocket.

'We're going on a hunger strike!' he said.

'During a time of rationing and severe food shortages? Is that wise?'

'Fuck off.'

He walked off abruptly with my hand still in his pocket. That jerked him back towards me. By the time he shouted 'Thief!' I had already weaselled my way out of his pocket and disappeared into the crowd.

'They died in vast numbers,' a scrawny guy with a thick beard shouted through the megaphone. 'So why not let them keep dying? They're on a roll. Let's transition them humanely! Their numbers threaten our way of life!' That earned equal measures of cheers and boos. 'We are being swamped by plague-ridden dead who envy us our slow cancers and traffic accidents. Where will they sleep? What will they eat? We are on the edge of total social breakdown and these people will drive us into a revolution. They will form ghettos and they won't assimilate. We can no longer allow this debate to be muzzled. We must face facts. Resources are scarce and finite. We can't accommodate everyone! Let us simply send them on! I call for their integration to be halted in the short term. We must be allowed to say the unsayable! Can we seal off the tunnel of light at our end? Efforts are underway.'

I moved over to where smallish factions of protesters and counter-protesters were sternly making their cases, one side trumpeting the rights of the arrivals, the other the rights of those already here. I have to admit, I did enjoy hearing people debate the ethics of murder.

I reached into one pocket and felt only the thick outline of a flaccid penis. I quickly withdrew into the crowd at the same time that balaclava-clad men stormed the stage and threw the speaker to the ground. The new speaker waddled the stage with a defiant scowl and a fist raised in revolt.

'I speak on behalf of the dead in that facility. What gives *you* the authority to refuse us? Your date of expiration? I suffocated on my own blood. My friend went through decapitation. We have a man here who was struck by lightning! Just like you, we came here legally by the universal experience of death, and you sift through us for those with skills you deem useful to you and now guarantee "the rest of the swarming brood" safe passage to the other side—by means of murder?!' The speaker was moved to tears by his own words. 'Involuntary transit is murder! The forced migration of plague dead is murder! Process our brothers and sisters and release them into the community immediately!'

It was an impossible challenge to worm even two fingers inside a narrow pocket with so many bodies pressed tightly together. My hand was inside a third pocket when the crowd began to surge in violent spasms and nearly broke my wrist. Clearly, the madness of crowds wasn't working for me. I would need to use seclusion, darkness, and the threat of violence.

Two blocks away, in a dark passageway under a crumbling arch, I stood against the wall in half shadow and waited like a predator. I wished Ernie was there—I had never really stolen anything without his guidance. I heard heavy-booted footsteps and a huge figure emerged. The obese man's smile made him look like he was thinking pleasant thoughts—I thrust my knife in his face and shouted: 'Hand me your credit card!'

He reached into his pocket and offered me his card. 'Take it,' he said, his voice expressionless. The guy was stone-faced, a real pro. He sounded like he'd been robbed before. Kudos.

Then I moved to outside an empty office building and listened to the voices drifting over from adjacent streets. A rugged, red-faced man was strolling in my direction; he was whistling a happy tune, but I couldn't place it. 'Don't make me hurt you,' I said. He looked sadly at me and said, 'Awww,' as I pocketed his card.

My third victim was a drunk woman; I was very polite about it: 'Please give me your card?' Despite the friendly vibe, she hurled her card into the gutter and spat in my face.

My fourth and final target for the evening was asleep on the steps of the church in a puddle of urine—I managed to remove his card, siphon the credits *and* return it to his pocket without disturbing him.

Night after night I did this—in the dense shadows of cold alleyways, alongside the polluted canal, in the dead spaces between buildings, I'd take their money and flee, the sound of their curses or restrained sobs dwindling behind me.

Then a-haunting I would go.

41

The routine was as follows: I'd transfer Marlon the funds, guzzle the goblet of goo, defecate, catheterise, grimly offer up my arm for intravenous injections and, with my sphincter clenching uselessly and feeling like the hot part of a flamethrower, I'd sail off into the black yonder, exploding like a star.

Some nights—maybe because of the airplane-engine-like noise in my ears, and the twin sensations of tumbling *down* a waterfall and riding *up* a geyser—the gluggy darkness was impassable, and I couldn't navigate my way to the house. On those days, I'd spend the whole hour more or less gyrating wildly in the dark, with the occasional respite of floating like driftwood in the infinite black ocean with an unrelenting feeling of utter isolation.

Marlon grudgingly gave me a fifty percent refund on those days.

Other times I'd blast off into the shrieking chaos and make a straight shot to the house at a sickening velocity. I always knew when I'd breached the outer perimeter of the earthly plane because I could hear Marlon shout, 'Thar she blows!' Sometimes I'd overshoot and wind up in an even darker, boiled-urine-smelling abyss. Other times I'd decrease speed at just the right moment and make a slow careful orbit around the old homestead.

On these crossings I was still contending with crushing cranial pressure and disorientation, but I found my way to the house more easily each time. It sounds unlikely, but there was a certain paler patch of darkness, wetter and heavier, that I used as a landmark to find the house, and then it was like cruising downriver on an oil slick.

The feeling of arriving home was always one of intense relief, like touching the shore after a harrowing ocean voyage of typhoons and kraken. Not that my homecoming was always pleasant—I was compelled to witness my wife and my murderer in any number of depressing domestic tableaus: Gracie brushing her teeth while Owen was shaving, Owen clipping his toenails while Gracie expressed milk. The hardest was watching them parent together; tickling Inez's feet and tummy, reading plastic baby books and squeaking toys in her face and more or less playing house with *my* baby girl.

My inability to eavesdrop was infuriating, but their body language spoke volumes. Often, I would make that hellish journey only to see Gracie stroking Owen's forehead or Owen nuzzling her on the couch. Once I observed Gracie wiping her hands down Owen's shirt with such fun-loving intimacy that I almost died again. It was awful to observe, though not as bad as blundering in on their bedtime activities.

I'd arrive midway through some tawdry sex scene where they were mating in a sort of terrified wonderment. It was ghastly to behold. The sight of Owen's bony, long-fingered hands over Gracie's bare breasts, the arrhythmic thrusting and hard pleasure in his eyes, his misshapen flaking skull bobbing up and down between her legs, her approach to orgasm. Another time I materialised while he was simultaneously pleasuring himself and using a vibrator on her; we locked eyes and I stood, helplessly, watching Owen watching me watching them co-masturbate. You'd be hard pressed to convince me I wasn't in the tenth circle of hell.

Lest you think I could have done more to intervene, I sometimes floated around like I'd imbibed nitrous oxide; and I could barely make them out, like there was a thick membrane stretched across my eyes. Other times I'd just ricochet around the house with heart palpitations, or I'd wander disoriented, as if I'd suffered a stroke, or be completely immobilised, frozen as if inside a computer glitch. Sometimes it was all I could do to hang on, like a great current was trying to sweep me back out into the dark.

I'll admit, it was a sadistic pleasure to become the hobgoblin of Owen's small mind. It gave me enormous joy to be inside his wardrobe when he went to get his clothes in the morning or materialise behind him when he looked in a mirror—that never got old. I'd try to time the haunt so that I could get Owen in the toilet at night, wafting like mustard gas into the bathroom after he'd pointlessly locked the door behind him. I loved the sight of that breathless, emaciated, trembling fool; I'd slowly float straight through him, to haunt him from inside his own skin.

My overall goal was to get his amygdala really working for its money, but it didn't quite do the trick; only once did the stiff-necked bastard wave a crucifix at me and stamp his feet like I was a pigeon to flutter away; mostly, his reactions were a frustrating understatement: he seemed to approach ghosts with the same method he might bears or snakes—showing no fear and making no sudden movements. What a fucking prick. He made it seem as if his acute stress response required higher standards of fright than I was able to provide. I was already impotent as a husband and father; now, even as a ghost.

Gracie was clearly still recovering from her difficult birth; I watched her hobble to the bathroom, step gingerly to the cot, stoop painfully to pick Inez up or place her down. It was maddening that I couldn't help her, that I couldn't hear her pure melodious voice or kiss her bare sloping shoulder. When she'd imprison Inez within a fortress of cushions, I'd hover beside her to watch an episode of *Law & Order*, her guilty pleasure; it was thrilling how even across dimensions we could still watch bad TV together. Sometimes I hid so I could see her forgetful, dreamy smile, or to unobtrusively watch Inez suck her nipple like she had a grudge against that particular nipple.

Yet every now and then she shivered a little at the sight of me, as though I was a cold breeze that blew bitterly through her heart. Who could blame her? On those days I'd stare absurdly into the mirror to see how I was manifesting: I was either monochromatic, downright metallic or like whirling flakes of coconut—it wasn't predictable, sometimes a full-bodied apparition, every so often a shivering ball of light. On occasion Gracie confused me with the moonlight and couldn't sense me there at all.

Where was this going? I knew I couldn't haunt my widow forever, and not only because it was non-consensual. The journey itself was physically taking its toll; sometimes my mind seemed to be going. I'd say, 'Gracie, have you seen my keys?' and wouldn't understand why she didn't answer.

On more than one occasion I forgot I was dead. Other times I was an emotional wreck. Whenever my heart was unable to take the sight of my widow or my child anymore, I'd go to the window and look at the moon—that beautiful old frostbitten earth moon—and I'd stare at it and cry because that was my moon, and I wished I could find a real way back.

Not only that. I'd come back from this weekly excursion into the earthly plane feeling contaminated, bruised and sallow, my hair falling out in clumps. It took longer to recuperate each time. Once I woke up out of the tank with Marlon performing mouth-to-mouth on me.

'Thanks,' I spat.

Was it worth it? It was getting harder to justify. One night, I drifted insubstantially above her and Gracie *barely* looked up at me. I hovered closer and realised that she seemed put out by my visit. I said, 'Wow,' and my resentment must have registered, because she doubled down on a look of annoyance.

If only she knew how expensive it was, how much these visits were costing me. Shouldn't she be flattered? Shouldn't she take it as the highest compliment? Mortals didn't understand the monumental effort it took to traverse the occult space. And what accounted for this clichéd assumption that a ghost was stuck between worlds, anyway? Had it never occurred to the living that he'd broken the fucking bank and travelled vast distances to keep an eye on his loved ones at great physical and psychological cost?

How often I swore it would be the last time—but every week, even as my own face became strange to the touch, and little circles of light made a permanent home behind my closed lids, and my true self felt soon to be irrecoverable, I'd always say the same thing: just one more time.

42

Gracie caught Owen staring uncomfortably at his own gauzy reflection in the glass pane of the back door, poised to open it.

'Owen!'

Aware of the tension in her voice, his eyes glazed.

'What was I doing again?' he asked, bewildered.

'You tell me.'

'That's right,' he said. 'I was going to check on the wildlife.'

'What?'

Owen pointed at two cats pawing at each other on the lawn and started opening the door. 'The cats are already feral. Dogs don't go wild—they just moan over their master's corpse and then feel sorry for themselves to death.'

Gracie bolted the door.

'You think I'm going to get lost?' he said.

'We don't want to let in any mosquitoes.'

He mustered a laugh, as if that was a hilarious idea, and wandered back upstairs.

In the following few days, Owen was at the back door again three times, staring at the electric blue of the bug zapper. Panicked, Gracie moved the coffee table in front of the door to make access difficult. Late one night, when Owen didn't return from one of his frequent evening toilet runs, Gracie found him swaying by the front door, jabbing at his reflection.

'Where am I?' he asked.

'In your house,' said Gracie.

'Huh?'

'You grew up here.'

'What the fuck are you talking about? I grew up in Marrickville.'

'No. You grew up here. Remember? Your dad died out on those stone steps in the backyard because he had his hands in his pockets.'

'Hands in his pockets? That's the most ridiculous thing I've ever heard. The gigantic cunt who was my father died on his favourite stool in his favourite pub and it was the most delightful fucking day of my entire life.'

Gracie didn't know what to make of that. She wanted to deny the probability that Owen's end was nigh, but there were unignorable signs. He would lose the thread of his own tired anecdotes, as if memory files were being deleted in real time, he called Inez 'Jamie'—his dead baby's name—and he demanded Gracie stop dimming lights that were bright and undimmed. His left hand jerked all the time, he put coffee mugs down on thin air, missed steps each time he walked down them. The man who had not that long ago stitched up her abdomen could no longer convincingly butter bread.

One night I loitered semi-transparently at the foot of their bed for a spell and Owen made an *ugh* face and, I'll admit, it had never occurred to me to interpret his nonchalant ghostbusting shrugs to be symptomatic of a larger disease.

When I'd dematerialised, Gracie said, 'He looked a little yellow tonight.'

'That's kind of you to say,' said Owen.

'What?'

'Uh-huh.'

'You didn't see him?'

'Oh, yes Gracie, of course I didn't see him. You can give it a rest now.'

'What do you mean?'

'For a while the strange goings-on had me fooled, but what's more likely? That I'm seeing an actual ghoul or that I'm experiencing hallucinations attendant to a degenerative brain disease?' He pointed to his own head and tapped it. 'There's structural damage in the old attic, and this is a symptom.'

'How can it be a hallucination if I see it too?' she asked.

'That's my own fault.'

'What is?'

'I *told* you to indulge my dementia, I remember that much, when I first moved in, so —'

'I'm not indulging you.'

'I *told* you to step into my reality, whatever that would be. Remember?'

'What the fuck are you talking about? He's here! And he's been here dozens of times!'

'Infantilise me, don't infantilise me, I don't care either way, I'm not that easily demeaned. I was the one who told you about those German nursing homes where patients wait at fake bus stops for buses that never come until they forget what they're waiting for. I know the drill. I know what mischief lurks in the brain, *and* I know what lengths loved ones will go to just to be agreeable.'

'You're scaring me.'

'Gracie, please disregard my earlier request. I swear I won't lose my dignity if you just tell me you've been humouring me all along. And even if I *do* lose my dignity—who cares? I can spare it.'

'I'm not humouring you.'

'Liar. I love you.'

'Owen.'

The doctor inside him resumed control. 'Things are afoot in the frontal and auditory regions of the temporal lobe. The hippocampus is clearly affected now—that's memory. If I become aggressive, we'll know the frontal cortex is under attack too. Have I hurt you or been aggressive—uncharacteristically aggressive, that is—in any way?'

'No, not at all.'

This was true—what she didn't disclose to him was that, if anything, he'd been gentler. There *were* behavioural changes—the disease was changing his personality, for the better.

'Of course,' he said, 'I'd love to conclude that dementia is a gateway to the fourth or fifth dimension, and the destruction of brain cells is not a narrowing of cognitive ability but, rather, the removal of a cognitive obstacle. Wouldn't that be nice? Wouldn't that just be lovely?'

'Are you okay?'

'I'm fine.' He didn't move, and his whole body seemed to soften. 'Has this staircase always been here?' He quickly deduced the answer from the look on her face. He laughed. 'And the oblivion was inside you all along.'

Over the next couple of weeks, Owen started having visions of me when I wasn't there: often horned and riding black waves. He'd stare into empty space with bemusement, chuckling at his own brain, the rascal. 'It's esoteric yet dull, so dull.'

It infuriated him that he'd become conscious of his own deterioration, as if believing in the strength of one's illness strengthened it. 'The fucking nocebo effect has got me,' he lamented. 'It's the medical explanation for the worst self-fulfilling prophecy ever.'

Gracie taped signs on the doors: 'Owen, Do Not Go Outside. Do Not Open.' But what would happen when he could no longer read? He was already looking at teaspoons as if he didn't know what they were used for; he called his medical office to 'reschedule all of my appointments'; and, one terrible time, he confused Gracie with a prostitute, tried to pay her less than the agreed-upon price, and asked her if she minded waiting for her taxi outside. Reality was leaving him, piecemeal.

One afternoon, Gracie went online to peruse a Creutzfeldt-Jakob Disease forum for tips on how to manage symptoms. It had been weeks since she'd been online, and this appeared on the screen:

No internet
Try:
- Checking the network cables, modem, and router
- Reconnecting to Wi-Fi

ERR_INTERNET_DISCONNECTED

That was it. The internet was over.

She vaguely remembered going online for the first time—it was the mid-nineties, her browser was Netscape Navigator, and she had joined a Christian chat room where you could say horrifying things about Jesus and then sit back and reap the delicious whirlwind.

Now it was over, forever. Was it time for a postmortem, a debrief? Had it been a benefit to mankind? Had it brought us together? Hell no. It was like a game of *Cluedo*. Who killed humanity? It was the internet in the basement with the wi-fi.

'Hey, Owen, the internet's offline.'

'What?'

She walked into the kitchen to see Owen sitting on the counter, licking the inside of an empty tuna can.

'I think the internet is finished.'

He stopped what he was doing but kept the tuna can on his face, like it was a prop in a comedy routine.

'Owen, put that down.'

'We don't have any food left.'

Gracie yanked the cupboard doors open and could see it was true. 'Shit.' She looked in the fridge and nodded vigorously at the empty shelves. She lingered like that for a moment, before turning to Owen with a look of dismay on her face.

'You've got to look after Inez while I'm gone.'

'Gone where?'

She ran upstairs and covered herself with bug repellent; then she donned the outfit that she'd made from mosquito netting in anticipation of this moment—it was like a slim-fitting beekeeper's suit.

'You're really going out there?'

'Here's my take on post-apocalyptic society—it'll be child brides as far as the eye can see.'

'Call me if you run into any difficulty.'

She glanced at the screen of her phone. 'There's no signal.' The whole terrible experiment had been called off, just like that. Gracie thought: Surely we can all agree it was a massive failure. She tossed it across the room. 'Oh well,' she said. 'We'll have to go back to when global communications meant literally shouting from the rooftops.'

'Maybe you should stay here,' said Owen.

'We need what we need,' she said. 'Inez should still be asleep for another hour or so. How do I look?'

'Insane.'

The empty houses weren't as silent as she'd expected. The drip of taps, the ticking of clocks, a beeping to herald the death of batteries in smoke detectors. Gracie went in and out, filling sacks with fungal creams, sleeping pills, cough syrups, coffee, Saladas, tins of tuna, pasta sauces and organic muesli. She made a cup of tea in number forty-six—formerly home to the tedious Pluckroses, who'd once literally dragged her in off the streets to show her floor tiles—and lifted her netted veil just enough to take furtive sips.

It felt weird to be the sole witness to the emptiness where happy-ish lives were scheduled to have played out to completion. Now these structures were awaiting their return to nature. In the Yangs' upstairs bathroom, she found David Yang—geography teacher and Jimmy Barnes enthusiast—decomposing in the tub. His open mouth and wide eyes made him look like he'd died on the spur of the moment. Gracie thought: Remember when people wanted their death to be dignified? Whatever for?

Gracie walked back home, the quiet in the street sorrowful and threatening; even the birds' tweets seemed to be making sly comments about the frightful fate of bipeds. At her front door, she stopped and gritted her teeth; she couldn't bear to lock herself in that haunted house again just yet—she hid the sacks of goods under the porch steps and went back through the mute, unpeopled streets, towards the beach.

Gracie always felt that the ocean understood her, that there was real chemistry between them. She hit the promenade, moved along the clifftops, inhaling the salty wind, then clambered down the ledges and loose sandstone to the Mahon rock pool.

It was gusting and waves crashed savagely over the chains, white water churning in the pool, submerging the edges beneath view. Gracie ogled the endless sea beyond and almost forgot the terrible plight of the world. When we were bored with our lot, we used to think: Life is elsewhere. Now it really wasn't. It was nowhere.

It was in this mental space that Gracie allowed the idea to finally float into her mind: Extinction?

She quickly thought of Inez with love and a pang of regret. If only she had known . . . She couldn't even bring herself to complete the thought.

The afternoon grew humid and thundery, a storm ripening overhead. Gracie ambled along the windy slope that led down to the sand. How quickly a beach could transform into a wasteland, just in tone.

A group—or horde—of people were standing far off, on the southern end of the beach. Were they sea worshippers like her? Maybe. Should she go to them? No way. Would she? Yes.

Gracie heard deep humming and the clapping of hands as she tramped along the water's edge, the wind at her back. It was a kind of funeral: a half-dozen greasy-skinned bloodied corpses with bloated stomachs had been laid out on surfboards and draped in seaweed by mourners wielding rifles and kitchen knives and closed-off smiles. Some were down on their knees in the sand.

A haggard and hollow-eyed woman took a step in her direction. 'Are you infected?' she asked.

'No,' said Gracie.

'Don't get too close, love! We are! We all are!'

They gazed at her with the hard edge of hopelessness.

'So, what's the plan here?' Gracie asked.

'We're gonna give these guys a Viking funeral, and then we're going to take our own lives in the waves. You can stay and watch if you want.'

'Cheers.'

There were maybe fifteen of them who were alive, their bodies a haemorrhaging embarrassment. Gracie determined that the strong wind would likely blow their infectious coughs in the opposite direction, and just as long as she remained upwind, she should be okay. A man in a blood-stained t-shirt doused the bodies in kerosene and held a lighter aloft.

'Someone should say something,' a wraithlike man said flatly.

'I can do it,' Gracie said.

'Who are you?'

'I did this kind of thing, before.'

'*This* kind of thing?'

'Ceremonies.'

'Are you a minister or something?'

'Yes. I'm a minister.' Her participation in the landmark occasions of perfect strangers' lives was almost her defining mode of being. This will to meddle had first expressed itself in the commemoration of love, then to celebrate birth and, now, to pay tribute to death. Frankly, it made sense.

The impromptu congregation created a space for her with a respectful air as she stepped cautiously forward. What could she say? They were attentive and seemed to have instantly divested all authority to her.

'Bong! Bong! Bong! The Doomsday Clock has struck midnight. Welcome to the bitter end. Tomorrow is passing into history, and what we supposed was continuous turns out to have an actual end point—a sharp one. And just when we were on the brink of curing cancer. Only joking. We weren't even close.'

A groan went out from the infected. Gracie thought they had the look of judges presiding over a case in which the defendant had chosen to fart her closing argument. Should she share that observation? 'Wait. Let me try again.'

Gracie replanted her feet in the soft sand. 'We didn't dodge a bullet. We only dodged death by a thousand cuts. Is dying out so bad? Admit it. If we were to repopulate the earth, we'd have to fuck any number of terrible men. Am I right, ladies?' She wasn't herself. The sickening odour of corpses mingled with the brackish air was hampering her ability to formulate cogent thoughts. 'Only thing we know for sure—in the land of the blind, the one-eyed man is a cunt.'

There was a sort of generalised frowning among the group, but the inertia that rooted them to the spot allowed her to continue.

'We're here because some old frozen prehistoric doggy coughed in our faces, more or less, but isn't a highly contagious plague the perfect final ailment for a civilisation that had all but turned its back on face-to-face communication? I wouldn't even mind feeling a part of a noble failure, but our shortcomings as a species include ethnic cleansing, industrialised farming, and turning people into lampshades and bedsheets with a high thread count.'

Gracie pretended not to notice the rigid mourners bleeding onto the sand.

'I know it's hard. End times are tough all over, right? The question is, how did we not see where this volatile and unhappy interplay of negative amplifiers was heading? Overpopulation, ecocide, unchecked capitalism—check! Unheeded warnings, perpetual growth, unstoppable consumerism—check! What I'm trying to say is, a triumph of the human spirit was bad for the environment. We objectified nature. Our backfires spread like wildfires. We were custodians of the earth and we physically abused our charge.

Fishing the seas to extinction was as self-defeating as giving yourself a neck tattoo on the way to a job interview.'

The heaviness of what she was saying seemed to sink her deeper into the sand.

'I saw the best minds of my generation destroyed by unceasing self-regard and a dopamine-addiction feedback loop. Remember the brief period when we thought multitasking would improve the human race and when low self-esteem was considered one of the western world's greatest problems? We married our phones and waited for the external hardware to consummate the relationship. We evolved into a distracted species when our main task was watchfulness! Our bleakest doomsayers were too optimistic. How could a species hardwired with negativity bias not see this coming? The algorithms *couldn't* predict this because you can't commodify oblivion.'

One woman's shoulders shook with silent laughter and Gracie directed her sermon to her alone.

'Who even were we? We were courageous in the abstract, cowardly in the particular, hopeful in spite of all the impalings. The things we said with a straight face! The number of times we confused thinking and feeling! How unsatisfying were our windfalls! Maybe basing a society on "luck of the draw" wasn't the best approach after all.'

With a surge of energy, she began to shout: 'We were prey to our own predatory instincts! Human progress was fatal! The only thing we knew how to do was double down!' She liked how this line made her feel. 'We declared moral bankruptcy but kept on spending! Our sensual pleasures were expensive. We dehumanised some, over-humanised others, and barely managed to hide our jealousy of actual zombies with their outdoor living and their simple diets.' She considered this further. 'Admit it. We were only at our best when we were on MDMA. Can anyone say with a straight face that the earth isn't better off without us? Perhaps a small contingent of rich shitbags will make it to the Goldilocks Zone of a proximate exoplanet, but I fucking hope not. When you run the numbers, the expression "for the common good" only motivated three percent of us anyway. In any case, the upshot is, our options are finally limited to two. Do we want a good death, or not?'

'Yes!' a harrowed young woman shouted.

Gracie kicked sand in the air. 'Either all ground is consecrated or none of it is.' That made no sense but she liked the sound of it. 'I guess we do, so off you pop, into the sea with you, but not before we say our final goodbye.'

She raised her arms and lifted her face to the sky.

'Bye, self-esteem, you loser! Bye, patriarchy, you prick! Bye, marketplace earth, your goods and services were mostly shit! Bye, status quo—don't go changing.'

'That's enough.'

It was the man with the Zippo lighter; he looked like he'd just climbed out of a woodchipper.

'Time to get this show on the road,' he said. He staggered over to the corpses on the surfboards and began to set them alight; the corpses yielded quickly to the flames. There was bewilderment and tears. The mourners pushed the bodies over the breakers. Above, the smoke from the burning bodies was already filling the dusky sky.

'Okay. Now, before you all take your own lives, I want to share the good news, and it's not Jesus-related.' Gracie expelled a long breath. '*This* is not the end. There's a place—I don't pretend to understand it all, but *ghosts are real*. Our loved ones are not gone. They aren't always here, but they appear to be coming *from* somewhere. The heavens, or someplace like that, open up and allow them to return.'

'Oh, for fuck's sake.'

'She's just a crazy bitch.'

'What are we listening to her for?'

Ghosts—that was too much. She wasn't a minister—she was a crackpot. The gruesome array of haemorrhaging faces snarled in anger and kicked sand at her with open-sore aggression. A startled Gracie fell backwards onto the beach. They didn't need their weapons to threaten her—they *were* weapons. She twisted onto her feet and took off in a sprint, and they turned their attention back to the sea.

From the promenade, Gracie witnessed the infected knee-deep in the swell. By some prearranged order of events, the men stabbed the women, shoved their bodies into the sea, then each murdered the person to his left. It was briskly done. The sole survivor shouted a sweary goodbye to the Lord and shot himself.

White-faced and trembling, Gracie ran in the long tapering shadows of the afternoon. Back home, she closed the door firmly behind her. The windows rattled in the wind, and Gracie listened to Owen talk to Inez about how 'Mummy's finally home from her little walk and not dead at all,' and how he wouldn't mind wandering around the empty planet himself, enjoying the solitude.

'Earth really is a pretty great place without all those people in it,' she heard him say, as she collapsed on the couch and realised that she might never step outside again.

43

Gracie and Inez were in a deep sleep and unable to be roused, so I settled for unnerving Owen in the kitchen by darting through his midsection. Yet the tables had somewhat turned—it was *me* who found *him* to be the unsettling vision. He was drooling at me with a faraway look, then he bit down hard into one of his hands, drawing blood. There was nothing I could do to stop him or recapture his attention.

The session finished with sickening abruptness, as usual, but there was something wrong. When I left the pod, everything had a fuzzy dark halo around it; a mad roaring was in my ears. I was completely untethered from reality—I don't even know how I got back to Valeria's apartment. I only remember Teddy the doorman's mirthless grin, being dragged by the arms into the elevator, then waking up in bed with a disturbed-looking Valeria poised in the doorway.

'This is my fault,' she said. 'You're addicted.' I sat up and blew my nose, emitting a bleached, glutinous substance. 'Consider this an intervention.'

She took an exaggerated step backwards and slammed the door.

'You're going to stay in there until you get it out of your system,' she shouted, followed by the thud and scrape of furniture. She was barricading me in! Sure, I was a wretched thing to behold, but this form of old-school rehab, the coldest of turkeys, was degrading and melodramatic. I staggered to the door and tried to open it, but whatever was wedged there made it impossible to budge.

'This isn't necessary,' I yelled. 'But fine, whatever!' I returned to the bed panicky and flustered, already choking on the intense need to return to Marlon's warehouse.

For two days, I was hectored by hallucinations, smothered by the sick aroma of burning hair, and the delusion I was levitating in that undulating netherworld with synchronised feelings of melting and solidifying. I couldn't close my eyes without rushing headlong into one void or another, without the feeling of splitting in half, of being wishboned by a pair of powerful hands. The agitation felt permanent. I could hear Valeria pacing the apartment like a nightwatchman—or was that a hallucination too?

To be honest, I could easily have broken down the door, but I stayed in bed, pretending to be stuck. The truth was, I was embarrassed: as dazzling as it was to haunt the living, it was contemptible too. The ego it took to manifest on earth was reprehensible. Why make such a big song and dance about one individual destiny, even if it happened to be mine? My claim of ownership over Gracie's life was mortifying. To remain in a place where I no longer materially existed was pathetic.

It's always humiliating to admit your utter selfishness. Every accusation that 'you only ever think of yourself' is absolutely true. This is an uncomplicated matter. Ask the question: *cui bono?* (who benefits?), and if the answer is: Me! I do! Only me!—then stop right there, whatever you're doing.

Even my mean-spirited desire for my murderer/usurper to go mad from fear seemed infantile to me now. I made a resolution: my transient visitations would end. I had trafficked myself long enough. I had to embrace my living death, and never again surrender to the temptation to bother my poor widow; whatever their sad trials and tribulations, I would leave Gracie and Inez to their struggles. It would be painful, yes, but it was the right thing to do.

It took three more days of bed rest before Valeria acknowledged the change in me. I awoke one morning to find her sitting on the edge of the bed, drumming her fingertips on my thigh. She handed me a coffee.

'Are you done?' Valeria asked.

'Done and dusted,' I said.

'I'd like to propose a toast!' she said, holding her own coffee mug aloft. Historically, nothing ever dampened my spirit like enthusiasm, especially one accompanied by anodyne platitudes. 'To a new day, a fresh start, and a regrettable chapter closed!' Her contagious smile wore through my defences, and we clinked coffee mugs and celebrated my newly earned sobriety.

It has to be said, my favourite of all human states is when you're past the pain of illness but don't yet possess the energy to assume responsibilities. Valeria was almost obscenely sympathetic, indulging my 'recovery' even when it morphed into sloth. To be fair, she wasn't doing much either. Valeria was able to milk her government pension for another six months before being forced back onto the job market, and I luxuriated in how disempowered I felt to be entirely reliant upon her generosity.

This was our life: Valeria went to Pilates every morning and rehearsed her Arthur Miller play each night. We both became problem drinkers. Just because I had been consorting with my widow didn't mean we didn't draw the blackout curtains once or twice a week and gyrate on each other until we could chalk up a couple of happy endings.

We went up on her apartment building's roof only once in that period. The ochreous flashes of light that heralded the arrival of the new dead flashed so often now that it was like a veritable double sun strobing in the sky. Mostly, we sipped our drinks and observed the smattering of social unrest from the living room window. More protests. The mobilisation of armoured vehicles. Hundreds of soldiers marching flamboyantly. The detonation of a weak explosive device here and there. A crowd scattering in confusion. We'd huddle together and say, 'Wow,' or, 'Huh,' or, 'Look at that.' Whatever was going on below, we couldn't quite bring ourselves to care.

What frazzled Valeria more than the violent revolution was the looming of opening night. When she rehearsed, she was so sensitive, there was no sound or gesture I could make that she wouldn't take as a criticism. I wanted to say, 'We're all going to die again one day. What does any of this matter?' Of course, that line of thinking had never helped anyone the first time around either.

Besides, I had my own anxieties to contend with. Now that my haunting addiction was behind me, I began compulsively contemplating my impending second death. How would I go *this* time? The traumatic sense-memories of my final breath started to come back to me at odd moments, unbidden, and I began to obsess over the thought of bleeding out and suffocating again. I'm not sure if Valeria, swept up in her own singular fear of failure, observed this morbid change. I was still glued to the couch. One day, she found enough self-respect to order me out to buy groceries.

The number of confused arrivals had at least doubled since I'd last been outside—so many you couldn't commiserate even if you tried. At the supermarket, an absurdly long queue snaked around the block. A shirtless man was dragging another man up the street by his man bun. I took my place; someone gave me a violent push and I pushed back. A sort of restless insanity had set in. What was I going to do now? I felt lost and utterly bored. Existence was going to be really long.

I went back to the tiny-mouthed employment officer and reminded him who I was.

'You went AWOL.'

'Never mind that. I've come to try again. What else have you got for me?'

Without even browsing his files, he said, 'Security.'

'Like what?'

'Crowd control.'

'No.'

'You have the physique for it.'

'Not interested.'

He bit his lip a little. 'Come back in two weeks,' he said. 'I'll have something for you.'

'What?'

He leaned across the desk, speaking in a low conspiratorial tone. 'This is an open secret, but you didn't hear it from me, and I can neither confirm nor deny it,' he said.

'Okay.'

'The camps over by the western and eastern walls are already overcrowded ghettos. Tomorrow they're reopening the old mental hospital and cramming in some new arrivals there, but that'll be full in two minutes, and then what?'

'You tell me.'

'It's more fun if you guess.'

'My mind's a blank.'

'Come on. You've heard the rumours. About . . . *humanely* moving the newest of the new arrivals on to the next level.'

'What?'

'It's nobody's fault we're at capacity.'

'Wait a minute. You don't mean . . .?'

'Haven't you ever heard that expression, "last one hired, first one fired"?'

'What are you saying?'

'They'll need drivers to transport bodies. Diggers. Disposal. Same-day cremation.' Going off the astounded look on my face, he added quickly, 'I know what you're thinking! Large-scale cremations have a bad association. No one wants to be compared to *you know who*.'

'Hitler?'

'You're right. He's the opposite of Voldemort. Everyone *loves* saying his name.'

The employment officer's jaunty smile bothered me so much, I stomped out of there before I could commit a minor act of violence. Besides, I had to go to the fucking theatre.

The mundane production of Arthur Miller's weakest play—all three hours with no intermission of it—took place in an opulent theatre on the east side. About the performance, I had little positive to report: it seemed every actor had a friend in the audience he couldn't stop waving to mid-dialogue, and absolutely nobody knew what to do with their hands.

Valeria told me the director had told her to read the lines 'as if responding to repeated requests you were persistently saying no to'.

It was a weird direction, and undoubtedly the reason she herself gave a painful nine-second silence between every line.

The play was about how much you should punish a person for moral crimes that had been acceptable in the times in which they'd lived. It was a fair question. It made me think of everyone on the continuum from slave owners and rent-seekers to meat eaters and sexual outlaws. In any case, I was pleased I'd found an engaging train of thought to transport me to the final curtain, when the actors linked arms and even their bowing proved to be melodramatic. If applause can have a mood, this one was of genuine relief. One thing about old Arthur Miller: he knew where to end the play—literally seconds before the audience's breaking point.

Those who hadn't immediately fled the theatre hung around the cavernous lobby snatching flutes of cheap champagne from the trays of tuxedoed wait staff. They were a glamorous, chubby crowd of a certain vintage who seemed to be enjoying their deaths. Clearly, we were back to pre-twentieth-century notions of weight gain—big bellies for the rich, emaciation for the poor.

Then—my death's lowest moment:

I had been telling Valeria how much I'd enjoyed her performance, but critiqued her castmates, explaining how I had completely forgotten that most actors have all the outward signs of sociopathy. She didn't welcome that observation, so I gazed dully around the room—and that's when I saw him.

'Holy fuck.'

Valeria turned to me. 'What?'

'I don't fucking believe it.'

'WHAT?'

'That guy over there.'

'Who?'

I could barely say his name. 'Owen.'

'*Your* Owen?'

The first attempt to walk over was a fail. My feet, as in a nightmare, wouldn't move. Eventually, and doubting my own eyes, I managed a shaky approach.

It *was* Owen. He was holding court over a small clique of silver-haired patrons of the arts, recounting a long-winded anecdote that I'd heard half a dozen times—the one about his initial diagnosis. 'The doctor is dauntingly neutral,' he was saying. 'He has no skin in the game. For him, the difference between *it's terminal* and *it's benign* will be his mood on his evening commute home.' I edged closer and noticed that there was an outrageously beautiful woman on his arm; she couldn't have been more than twenty years old. What the hell was going on here? 'Anyway, as far as I remember,' he went on, pausing briefly to slurp his champagne, 'I called Dr Kosinski's mother a whore, whimpered in the elevator, and on the street reached out and grabbed a shopkeeper's hand. That was all the mourning I allowed myself.'

Those listening to his practised, tired anecdote murmured approval. I whacked him angrily on the shoulder.

Owen turned in a slow arc. 'Oh, hello! I wondered if I might run into you.' No words came out of my own mouth and I couldn't stop blinking, as if my eyes had to adjust to the sight of him. 'This *is* awkward,' he said. 'Haha.'

'You killed me.'

'Yes. It was uncalled for. I apologise.'

'Apology vehemently rejected.'

'That's your prerogative.'

Resentment leached into my bloodstream and I felt my body tremble.

'You *murdered* me.'

'I don't disagree and, again, I unreservedly apologise. Let me buy you a drink.' He grabbed a flute of champagne off a passing tray and handed it to me. 'Here you go.'

'Drinks are free.'

'Even better.'

I glared indignantly while he reached inside his jacket, removed a packet of butterscotches, and popped one in his mouth. He smiled in a businesslike manner. 'How about this afterlife,' he said. 'Isn't it exciting?'

'Not especially.'

'No? Rebirth isn't exciting? Immortality isn't exciting?'

'No one said anything about immortality.'

'At this point you'd have to admit it looks like the cards are stacked in favour of forever. Maybe it's an infinite loop, maybe it's not. But I get the feeling we die and we die and we die again.'

'When did *you* die?'

'Five, six days ago?'

'And you're at the theatre?'

'I'm a huge Arthur Miller fan.'

Arthur Miller? I wanted to lance his eyeball with a toothpick. 'Tell me about your final moments. I hope you were in excruciating pain.'

'Sorry to disappoint—I don't remember it at all. I guess I was asleep.'

'Typical.'

'To be perfectly honest, the last thing I remember was pleasantly drifting off to sleep in Gracie's arms.' He smiled toothily. I'd never seen the man when he was not actively dying, and now Owen's refreshed face made mine fare badly in comparison. 'Still,' he said. 'It wasn't all fun and games. I did die of a rare brain disease, you know.'

He said that part loudly, as much to the girl still on his arm.

'Poor baby,' the girl said. 'You want a scalp massage?'

'Thoughtful! Yes, please.'

She started to massage his scalp and Owen moaned with pleasure. 'So how about this? Life after death, eh? Gracie was right.'

'Keep her name out of your mouth.'

'You know who I keep thinking about? The cryogenically frozen! What a bunch of suckers!'

'Don't get too comfortable. I can always press charges, you know.'

'Whatever for?'

'What for? Uh, I don't know, *how about first-degree murder*?'

Owen laughed. 'Statute of limitations, fool. They don't prosecute crimes here from the other side. That's the first thing you learn in orientation.' I just let that sit there without touching it. He burst into mean laughter. 'You were an ignorant son of a bitch when you were alive and I can see nothing's changed. Anyway, so nice to see you.' He abruptly turned to rejoin the group.

'Hey,' I said and snapped my fingers in his ear; he turned to me, smiling in angry servility.

'Yes, Angus. What can I do for you?'

'How did you get rid of my body?'

'Oh! Have you been wondering about that?'

'A little—yes.'

'Do you remember my old colleague, Dr Patel?'

'I remember.'

'A brown gentleman.'

'Yes yes.'

'Do you ever remember me alluding to a nasty incident when we were interns together?'

'No.'

'I practically saved him from prison.'

'So?'

'So! I'd been saving the favour for thirty-six years, and exactly two minutes after you took your last breath, I called it in. Do you recall our musical collaboration?'

'Unfortunately.'

'He came over again with his cello and we pretended to rehearse Dvořák's cello concerto in B minor, with Gracie sitting right there listening. Although, in truth, there's no practical difference between pretending to rehearse Dvořák's cello concerto in B minor and actually rehearsing it.'

'Get to the point!'

'After Gracie went to bed, we put you in Patel's cello case.'

'You what?'

'It wasn't as simple as it sounds.'

'It doesn't sound simple at all.'

'We had to break your bones in order to fold you over so we could fit you inside it.' The thought of my bones breaking gave me vertigo and I almost had to grasp onto my own killer's arm to steady myself.

'And for my eternal punishment,' Owen said, 'mediocre champagne. Take this back.' He thrust his glass into a passing waiter's hand. 'Look. Obviously our unfinished business has drawn us to the same place. So, in the spirit of severing our sordid little bond, let me do something for you. Do you want this one?'

'This one what?'

He gestured to his female companion. 'She's on the clock until eight a.m.'

I looked squarely at the beautiful girl he was thrusting in my direction. She was lithe and lovely and swayed a little on her heels, as if unsteadiness was part of her charm. If she was a prostitute, then she was a high-priced one. I reflected on how, for the first month after my arrival, I had struggled to buy even a sandwich.

'Why do you have money?'

'Oh—well, that *is* an interesting story. Do you want to hear it?' Annoyingly, I did. Owen smiled victoriously. 'We died at a great time, did you know?'

'I've repeatedly heard the opposite.'

'All this overpopulation and turmoil? The police force here are not on their A game.'

'So?'

'So, the first thing I did when I got settled was to find my parents. Did you find yours?'

'Yes.'

'Oh. It wasn't a happy reunion?'

'It was fine.'

'Well. Mine was very happy—for me. Not so much for them. I told you about them, do you remember?'

I recalled a passing anecdote of little Owen whacked with beer cans and nearly smothered with a pillow. 'They were abusive.'

He went blank-faced, as if he'd activated old childhood defences. 'I did nothing that they didn't have coming to them.'

'What did you do?'

'They transferred all their savings to me and they'—here, Owen made air quotes with his hands—'"died by suicide", if you get my meaning.'

Owen was a murderer in the imperishable part of himself, the part that survived his own passing. I said, 'And what do you reckon you have coming to you?'

He said, without affect, 'You do what you have to do.'

Could this interaction be more astoundingly unsatisfying? I was at a loss; I couldn't just let it go, but I couldn't think of anything non-corny to say.

'Vengeance will be mine,' I said.

'Oh, don't be silly.' Owen looked like he wanted to make amends if it could be achieved with minimal effort and fuss. 'Listen. I get it. I removed you prematurely from the love of your life. My bad. I feel terrible. But there's not much I can do about it now.' He sighed tensely. 'Besides, don't think I've forgotten that you haunted me quite relentlessly, which kind of evens up the score, wouldn't you say? And if it's any consolation, I had terrible diarrhoea for forty-eight hours on arrival here. Now, of course, I feel amazing.' He softened his expression, a little too emphatically, and attempted a confiding tone. 'It's actually nice to see a familiar face. I don't know anyone here.' His voice lowered further to a gravelly whisper. 'And I miss her. So much. You're the only one who understands what I've lost.'

He thrust out his hand, an invitation to let bygones be bygones. I refused to take it. 'It's not coming out again,' he said. He looked down at his hand like it was some sort of accolade, then slipped it into his pocket. 'There. I've done my bit to make amends. If you won't accept it, that's on you.' At that moment, he noticed Valeria standing behind me. 'You were in the play. I've seen worse. Congratulations.'

'Thank you.'

'This is Sharmila,' Owen jerked the beautiful girl closer to him and gave her left breast a little squeeze.

'Jesus, Owen.'

'What, are you *judging me*? Here? Haven't you learned anything?' He scowled at me. 'I don't care anymore. Nothing here will be beneath my dignity. Why did I never understand in my whole time alive that the cost of being timid is too high? If I could, I'd piss in my dead face for behaving, my whole dumb life, as if social judgement mattered!' He was really getting worked up. Clearly, he was having an epiphany that made his blood boil. 'Anyway, I'd love to stay here and reminisce,' he said, grabbing his escort by the wrist, 'but these balls won't lick themselves.' Ignoring our faces of disgust, he dragged her out of the lobby in the direction of the disabled bathroom.

Valeria and I parked on the edge of the bed grinding our jaws like the morbid characters in her play. It had been a maddening encounter, and I couldn't believe how Owen had eased into his villainy, how he'd reaped such blissful rewards from his bad deeds; I already knew that there was no justice in the universe, obviously, but to have it rubbed in my face like that made my soul feel disgusting, like it needed to be sterilised. I laid my head on Valeria's shoulder, forcing her to soothe me.

'You should slit his fucking throat,' she said, patting my head. 'That's what I'd do if my rapist turned up here. No question.'

'I don't know.'

'Don't be such a pussy. Getting away with violent crime is really basic here. Especially these days. Go on. You'll feel better.'

'Maybe.' In truth, I suspected there was no way to serve revenge—cold, hot or room temperature—that was ever truly satisfying.

We worked our way through a bottle of cheap red wine. In the jittery quiet, thoughts of Gracie urgently surfaced: How had she coped with Owen's passing? It pained me to acknowledge that they had found comfort in each other and she'd likely be experiencing his death with genuine sorrow, and, worse—now she was alone with our baby daughter during a plague.

'Did you notice that I flubbed one of my lines?'

Valeria was elsewhere. Her endeavours to give me attention were thwarted by her obsessive concern with her performance and, in the next ten minutes, she managed to articulate twenty different versions of the question: *Was I really okay?*

'You were great,' I said, but I couldn't sufficiently animate my lying eyes. She noted that with a visible pang and we fell into a twitchy silence. That was it. We were fully selfish beings again, consumed by our own private dramas. In other words—utterly alone.

Once Valeria was asleep, I sneaked out to the warehouse, where Marlon greeted me with a look of wary surprise.

'Thought you must have died or got clean.'

I didn't answer—I just walked in and swallowed the gunk and shat out my guts and caught my own mad-eyed glint in the reflection of the tank's exterior. I slipped into the suit and jammed in the catheter without cleaning it. I couldn't submerge myself in the tank fast enough, and I was so focused on speedily locating the house I didn't wonder why there was a different hue to the darkness, an inky chemtrail that I intuitively followed.

Gracie was in bed, breastfeeding Inez. I made a heart shape with my hands and wiggled my foot meaninglessly. It was like a bad game of charades; I was straining to communicate that I was truly sorry for her loss, even if she was better off without the murderous Owen, that I apprehended the predicament of being entirely alone during the End Times and that, if there was anything I could do, I would.

Gracie gazed over my right shoulder and gestured to something. I turned around and my heart skipped multiple beats. He was there. Onion-skinned, diaphanous Owen, standing like a dim reflection of a bad projection—a vile intrusion into my sacred space! Not only that; he seemed to sharpen up at the sight of me. I could see Owen moisten his lips and smirk in astonishing clarity.

I know it's unhealthy to compare oneself to other ghosts, but I was of a much poorer resolution and he was so much easier in his movements; *he strolled* like he was on a prairie. For a novice, Owen was in his element—I was entirely outclassed.

Gracie silently watched us buzz around her like big sad grey moths, Owen on one side of her, me on the other, a couple of lovelorn Caspers. I could see in the mirror the reflection of our tableau: it was not unlike watching a horror movie through a neighbour's window.

And then—Owen reached his hand to the edge of the sheet and lifted it. In fright, Gracie pulled Inez to her chest and Owen dissolved like a morning mist. I remained on the spot, feeling inadequate, before the room trickled away into darkness.

I had to chew the air into digestible chunks before I could approximate breathing. My mind was getting poor reception. Marlon pulled me out of the tank, and it was hours before I could mumble in a simple-minded way.

'He was there,' I said.

'Who?'

'The bastard who murdered me.'

'Isn't he always there?'

'No, he died. He's here. I ran into him at the theatre. Now he's *there*. Haunting my widow in my own house.'

'The theatre? What did you see?'

'What?'

Marlon emitted an impatient sigh. 'I don't know what you want me to say. You think this is the only machine in town?'

'It's not?'

Marlon had insinuated a monopoly, and he knew it. Not only was Owen inhabiting my house, I told Marlon how he'd connected with the physical space, lifting the sheet with his phantom hand.

'Wow. He poltergeisted. That's pretty advanced tech. I wonder who has that?'

I felt a wave of self-pity so thick I couldn't breathe. Love triangles are bad enough when everyone's alive.

'I need to go back now.'

'I already took your last penny.'

'I'll owe you.'

'No credit.'

'Get out of my way.'

'Listen, Mooney. I feel your desperation, but you need rest and recalibration. Let me give you a free coupon to a brothel that's two buildings down.'

'I'm going back.'

'You can't do two haunts in a row—your mind will be indistinguishable from phlegm.'

'I'm going in!'

I scrabbled back into the tank and sank into the sludge. Not two minutes later, I was tearing back through the dark to the house.

Owen was there again too. He seemed to be just loafing around, this time in luminous vivid colour, looking like a loose collection of fireflies! Was he even inside a tank? Here I was, struggling to move in the restrictive glug of a black lagoon whereas he was practically doing headstands with his glossy physique; we couldn't even be classified as the same type of apparition. It was mortifying. I swiped at him; my hand went through his torso.

Gracie held Inez tightly and nodded crazily, as if saying, *Look at the state of my loved ones!*

Owen moved onto the bed and Gracie leaped off it—I hoped he was offended—and walked through me as if I was public property. She lowered Inez into her cot, then let a pillow sail through the middle of Owen. Weeping and raving, she hurled more at us; dirty plates, then forks, then coffee mugs, then a chair, then banana peels, then clothes, shoes and the guitar. Poor Gracie. We'd driven her to this.

Sometimes it takes another person's identical behaviour to show you the truth about yourself. Observing Owen, an echo of the past reverberating obnoxiously in the present, I saw again with clarity how selfish it was to exceed one's allotted lifespan. Even so—I had zero inkling we could actually be dooming her and Inez; that, for her former lovers to have the opportunity to stalk her, she might forgo the opportunity to be saved.

44

'My phosphorescent husband magically enters through one portal and through another comes my incandescent lover, both reduced to feeble rays of light yet wearing the same expression of longing.'

Gracie was on her laptop, writing in a Word document what she'd post if the internet ever came back online while Inez happily gummed a bunny's ear in her bassinet. The old boom box blasted a CD of nineties Swedish band Whale.

'Come to think of it, the Owen ghost was brighter and more agile. An older corpse, yet a ghost with less mileage?'

Gracie's thoughts were interrupted by a thud. She slithered off the bed and switched off the music: an abrupt noise from downstairs, followed by a plate breaking in the kitchen and a harsh whisper: 'Dickhead.'

She crept out of the bedroom with Inez and met two soldiers on the stairway. The tall one had a flamethrower on his back; the shorter of the two had a soft, dimpled face.

'Can I help you?'

'We're getting the last of the evacuees,' said the dimpled soldier.

'How did you know we were here?'

'Your music's really loud.'

'What are you still doing here, lady?'

'Just chillaxing. Where else should I be?'

The soldiers exchanged a look of confusion. 'At the Paddo barracks for one, that's where we're stationed. We're to pick up any non-afflicted survivors on our way back there.'

At that moment there was a loud creak from the kitchen. Gracie panicked. 'How did you get in here?'

'Back door was unlocked.'

Gracie barrelled down the stairs, between the soldiers, and hurried into the kitchen: the open back door was swinging in a southerly gust. Gracie slammed it shut as the soldiers strolled into the kitchen behind her.

'You left the back door open!' she shouted, afraid.

'Sorry, luv.'

'You could've let in a mosquito!'

'Is there anyone else in the house besides you and your baby?'

'Not . . . exactly,' Gracie said in a half-whisper. She saw something move in her periphery—a dance of light, a sparkle of dust. Were the ghosts back?

'Come on, it's time to go,' said the dimpled one.

'No,' she said stiffly. 'I'm not leaving.'

The soldiers took a step closer. 'This evacuation's mandatory, luv.'

'Just say you didn't find anybody alive,' she said.

'What if we just take the baby?' asked the tall one, reaching for Inez.

'What if I aim your own flamethrower at your ugly chin?'

'What do you want to stay here for?'

Gracie glanced longingly at the shadows around the kitchen.

'Come on,' the tall soldier said. 'Let's get you and your baby somewhere safe.'

Gracie plucked a carving knife from the magnetic knife block and started slashing the air between them.

'Jesus!' said the tall soldier.

'Fuck it. Let's leave her.'

As the soldiers edged out the back door, the dimpled one said, 'Good luck.'

After they disappeared from view, Gracie stood at the front window watching the empty street, swept up in a delusional wave of optimism. Things would get better, she decided. The human race would start again. This time we'd work out how to be in a community without having in-group paranoia and hostility for the out-group. We'd nail how to become mindful without a fixation on the self. We'd rebuild while resisting the temptation to develop a personal brand.

The sense of confidence almost lifted her off the floor. 'This time around, we'll *definitely* prevail over the shittier angels of our nature,' she said to Inez in a voice so tight it nearly squeaked. 'Almost definitely.'

45

To find the address of someone in Lagaria, you had to go to the fifth floor of an angular twenty-storey building and talk to a disdainful woman who sent you down to the basement and through a grimy tunnel to another building with a broken elevator where you had to walk up seven floors and along a passageway to a room where a possum-faced man sent you back to the first person you talked to.

The irksome woman in question wouldn't give me Owen's home address without the requisite paperwork. It was difficult to argue, still feeling mentally incapacitated by my back-to-back haunts; I had spent a day unconscious in Marlon's warehouse after he'd pulled me from the tank, and still my entire visual field was vibrating and in my ears were nonstop splashing sounds.

The only useful tidbit the woman could spare was that he was listed as a doctor at a nearby medical clinic. They must have forced him into it, I thought.

It was ten minutes away, inside a Victorian-style retail arcade with a tinted glass atrium. The clinic was on the second floor, between a hair salon and a luxury bridal store. On the thick wooden door was raised gold lettering: DR OWEN FOGEL MD. The door swung open automatically; inside was a spacious reception room, where a half-dozen bored yet healthy-looking patients sat on leather couches.

The receptionist was a young woman who leaned back and prepared to be unhelpful.

'Yes?'

'I want to see Owen.'

'Dr Fogel isn't taking walk-ins. Do you have an appointment?'

'No, but he does.'

'What?'

'With destiny,' I said.

She squinted at me, as if I was shifting in and out of focus. 'What did you just say?'

'Just tell him Angus Mooney is here to kill him.'

The receptionist rose slowly and hurried through a door. I took the opportunity to guess the waiting patients' ailments, and ultimately diagnosed them all as cadavers in good physical shape who had come for referrals to mental-health professionals.

The receptionist returned to her desk without looking at me. Owen emerged in his white doctor's coat and cast a contemptuous eye over the patients in his waiting room. This is what it means to have a vocation, I thought. It's fucking eternal.

'Mr Mooney,' he said with an unctuous smile. 'I'll see you now.'

He held the door open for me in a parody of gallantry. In his stark office, he sat down behind his desk and tilted back in his chair and put his feet up.

'An emergency appointment? Is that fair to the other patients?' A choking laugh flew out of his throat. 'You know what Gracie used to say?'

'Would you mind keeping her name out of your mouth?'

'Better catch the bear before you sell his skin.'

'Gracie never said that.'

'So you say.'

'You will not visit her again.'

'Maybe neither of us should—you ever think of that?'

'Of course.'

The two of us hovering incongruously over her living body obviously wasn't in her best interest, yet her very existence was a siren's song we couldn't resist.

'We could time share,' Owen offered. 'You haunt her mornings and I'll haunt her in the evenings.'

'No.'

'There is an argument to be made that one should only appear to the living in dreams. That's the Ethical Haunting Movement. Have you heard of it?'

'No.'

'I think I have a pamphlet around here somewhere.'

'How do you already know more about this than I do?'

'Your congenital incuriosity.'

He'd got me. I shifted uncomfortably in my chair. There were lies I always told myself—that simplicity was my goal, that I wasn't born as detail-oriented as my fellow man—but he was right. Most of my ignorance was out of sloth.

He suddenly stood up and slammed his fists on his desk. 'You say you love her—but have you even asked me about her? You've seen bits and pieces through the lens of your ghost visor, but you haven't the foggiest clue what it's like down there. Have you even considered what pure hell she's been going through?'

He held up a hand to silence me, even though I'd not opened my mouth to speak.

'Listen, Angus,' he said, softening his tone. 'I've been thinking about us.'

'What us?'

'You and me.'

'There is no us.'

'Are you sure?' He paced his office in a tight circle. 'There is a place we could go, a special place for healing, reconciliation and forgiveness.'

'What?'

He placed his hand on my shoulder. 'If you really think your murder rises to the level of a human-rights offence, then there is the Truth and Reconciliation Commission.' He removed his hand before I had the chance to bite it. 'It's set up so that life's losers and winners can put their violent past behind them and live peacefully side by side.' He paused and wobbled his head, as if to shake loose something that had landed on it. 'And if we need to talk about reparations, I'm open to the concept.'

I didn't say anything. Owen seemed to think his death was enough to cauterise my hatred and make us spiritual brothers.

'Angus, I went to check it out. It's got a rich history, slaves confronting their masters, the tortured face to face with their torturers, farmers versus foreclosing bank managers. Before the commission was instituted, there were daily bloodbaths and retribution, anyone with violent skeletons in their closet hoping to start their deaths afresh was beset by former victims, grudge-holders and those who wanted to indefinitely prolong blood feuds.'

He was enjoying himself, I realised, with this little lecture—delighted to demonstrate how he'd already absorbed the entire history of the place.

'Of course, I'm granted amnesty by virtue of the non-interdimensionality of the statute of limitations, as I previously mentioned.' Jesus. What a windbag. 'You could give your victim impact statement and, to be honest, I wouldn't mind the opportunity to publicly express remorse.' Owen finally stopped talking for a moment and gave me an uncharacteristically warm smile. It was obvious he thought he'd won me over. 'So, what do you say? Shall we?'

'No. I'm not doing that.'

All the wrinkles on his face converged in a frown. 'Well, thanks for stopping by. I'm sorry we couldn't come to an arrangement.' He opened the door for me. I didn't move. He exhaled loudly. 'Sorry if I wasn't clear. What I meant was, fuck off right now, will you?'

'I'm going, just not without you.'

'Oh. And where are *we* going?'

'To meet your fate.'

'Okay,' he said with a sigh. 'Let me get my jacket.'

Owen and I elbowed our way through the fetid mad circus of the dead. He said, 'You're no more interesting dead than you were alive.'

'I'm aware of that.'

'What's your job here?'

'I worked in construction for a while. Now I'm not doing anything.'

'Of course you aren't.'

The footpaths were crowded, so we turned down smaller streets; it was unpleasantly bright in every direction. A man with a nasty head wound stumbled by, shouting, 'Get out of my fucking way.'

'No wonder the unseen world keeps hidden. It's shit,' said Owen, and I couldn't disagree. Owen stared at me uneasily as we walked. 'I'm reminded of something. I went to school with these twins who often argued which of the two was unplanned.'

'What?'

'The one who came out first claimed that he was the child their parents wanted and the other was an afterthought,' Owen said. 'And the twin who came out second insisted *he* was the wanted one, but the usurper had pushed in line.'

'What's your point?'

'My point is that we are both Gracie's dead lovers. Why don't we just swap anecdotes and enjoy a sense of solidarity?'

'Too late. We're already here.' I gestured at the dark glass door of a narrow sandstone building.

Owen looked at the building dubiously. 'I'm supposed to go in here with you and meet my fate?'

'That's right.'

'Lead on.'

There were dozens of people milling around the lower lobby. At a snack stand, folks were buying popcorn and beer, and there was a near constant flow of foot traffic up and down the stairs. I led Owen up to the second floor. Along a platform, spectators gazed down into four long rectangular windowless rooms where men stood behind white painted lines.

'What is this place?' Owen asked.

'Before, you were talking about restorative justice.'

'And?'

'This is the other kind.'

'Retributive?'

'It's a duelling range.' I said. And then, more loudly: 'Dr Owen Fogel, I'm challenging you to a duel.'

The spectators in our immediate vicinity turned towards us with delight.

'You must be joking.'

'It's legal if both parties agree to it.'

Down on the four courts, each person stood behind a red line, pistol in hand, facing the other. Over loudspeakers, a commentator talked indecipherably close to the microphone. On one court a man shot his opponent before the countdown ended and on another, under strobing disco lights, a duellist was in mid-fall from a precise headshot and his vanquisher was doing a victory dance. There was no way of knowing who would prevail, but each court guaranteed at least one fatality.

'I've got to get back to the office,' said Owen.

'You won't duel?'

'No.'

'Have you no honour?'

'I think you know the answer to that.'

'For an extra seventy dollars we can duel in the hall of funhouse mirrors. Personally, I don't think it's worth it, but it's up to you. You're paying.'

'You want me to pay for you to kill me?'

'I can't afford this place,' I said. 'I'm unemployed.'

'Take care of yourself, Angus.'

He half-turned to walk away.

'You owe me!'

That stopped him; he *did* owe me—it was indisputable. He swivelled around and said something that I couldn't hear above the din of adjacent death threats. Together, we walked down to the booking desk, where I told the customer service representative that I wanted to kill Owen on court two. The representative looked at his on-screen timetable and said they were full and I needed to make a reservation.

I sighed. 'When's the earliest availability?'

'In six days.'

'But he's got to die today.'

'Sorry.'

I leaned forward and spoke quietly. '*Please*. You're embarrassing me. I told him he was coming here to meet his fate.'

'I can't clear the schedule.'

'And I can't wait,' I whispered.

'Then don't,' the clerk whispered back, conspiratorially.

'Oh Jesus,' Owen said. He'd had enough and I couldn't entirely blame him. 'Come on, let's get out of here.'

We strolled through the chaos of the streets as if we hadn't just walked away from a foiled murder plot.

'You notice the rain here isn't clean?' Owen asked. 'The clouds must be an accumulation of the filth of the descending souls.' Did he sense how humiliated I felt and decide that he had to resort to talking about the weather? He added, 'Your hair is much nicer now than it was before.'

'It is?'

'I'm not ashamed to say things like that. When I was alive, I wouldn't have dared compliment a male rival on his hair.'

'Progress, then.'

'You know what's sad? You're the person I'm most connected to here.'

'That is sad.'

He *looked* sadder too, now that we were somewhat uncannily in lock step, two enemies in perfect harmony waiting for some external force to veer them off in any other direction.

'Are you living your death to the fullest?' Owen asked.

'No.'

'Me neither.' He hesitated for a moment, then spoke loudly and emphatically. 'I want you to know something. If I ever see you again, I'm going to kill you as a precaution.'

I nodded with the realisation that we were each other's implacable nemesis and there was very little either of us could do to change that.

He said, 'Might I offer you some words of advice?'

'No—you may not.'

'Okay.' He wanted to leave but he couldn't leave. There was something still holding him to the spot. 'There's a lot about Gracie and me you don't know. And will never know. Unless I tell you. Should I tell you? We looked into each other's eyes a lot. It was romantic. Or was it faux romantic? Just an excuse not to talk? You know when you kiss someone because it's easier than talking? And you pretend it's passion? But really it's unease masquerading as passion?'

'What did I look like, lying there dead?'

'I don't remember.'

'Did I look peaceful?'

'Come on, you know very well how witless and rat-faced the dead look.'

'Admit you overreacted!' The sorrow in my own voice made me sick.

'Of course I overreacted! I panicked! I shouldn't have killed you! I'm sorry! Jesus!'

I smacked him in the face. 'You haven't even asked forgiveness!'

'I *just* said sorry.'

'Asking forgiveness is different from saying sorry.'

'I don't want your forgiveness.'

'Why not?'

'What I did was unforgiveable.' His expression softened. In his eyes was an encouraging smidgeon of self-hatred. 'But that doesn't mean I'm just going to let you piss all over me. Let me ask you once and for all: are you going to let this go?'

'No.'

'Fuck it.' He turned and disappeared into the crowd.

It was getting dark, and I stood staring fixedly into that darkness, bamboozled by my own thoughts, grimly processing the purity of his love for Gracie, astounded how my own feelings felt tepid in comparison. I couldn't help but think of some of the questions I had been asked in the post-work Evaluation of Record: *What is your longest lasting nagging suspicion? What formidable opponent did you most want to emulate? Did you ever have a holy cause during boom times or only in moments of deep despair?*

And I remembered how, when I was alive, I always wanted to die 'in my sleep': that made me feel ashamed now. How ludicrous to want to die without noticing it while never realising that you had lived without noticing it too.

46

'I've seen the fraternisation of rival ghosts. Yes, folks, death has a social dimension.' Gracie was at the kitchen table, an unlit cigarette in her mouth, typing disconnected thoughts on her laptop: 'I've been tag-teamed by them. I'm in some metaphysical three-way that's frankly less arousing than you'd think.'

She looked to the window where the moon was arrogantly big and the trees soaked in its white light. She wrote: 'If humanity survives this plague, we'll be whining about it forever.' She considered masturbating, but felt drained of fantasy. 'What of the EndTimers? Have they started their slaughter of the wealthy survivors? Is that real or some troll's fantasy?'

A tickling sensation on her arm, her heavy gaze drifted to a mosquito feasting there—an ambush.

Panic! She jerked her arm away and sucked out the mosquito's saliva and spat it onto the floor, poured over the bite what little was left of the magic vodka, both remedies for completely different ailments, but better than nothing as she attempted a mathematical equation: if a blood-borne infection is travelling along a vein at 7 centimetres per second, and the suction draws out the infected blood at twice the same rate in the opposite direction . . .

Gracie checked that every door was closed, every window sealed shut. She emptied canisters of bug spray in every corner until the air became thick and toxic. In the upstairs bathroom, she stripped naked and checked her body for other bites and assured herself that not *every* mosquito would be a carrier.

Inez, in the cot, was gumming the corners of a blanket. Gracie probed her tiny body for bites. Nothing. She realised Inez had never even been outside in all her short life.

'We tried so hard to have you,' Gracie told her. 'Well, not you in particular, but somebody. And you showed up. It could easily have been someone else.' Gracie stared into her face. 'What eye colour are you going to settle on?'

Only when she tasted them did she realise tears were running down her cheeks. She needed a drink—so what if she was still breastfeeding?

'Baby, let's do shots!'

Downstairs, she poured herself a tequila, dipped her finger in and let Inez suck it. Was the virus navigating the byways of her bloodstream at this very moment? Or wasn't it? It was a night of Schrödinger's Virus—she both had it and didn't have it.

She lowered Inez back into her cot, ravaged by a crazed slew of paranoid delusions. Even her sweet, adorable baby looked like someone awaiting trial. The ghosts, she decided, were only in her mind; she'd been liaising with fantasies. And the mosquitoes outside her window were loud, demanding their rights. She thought how female mosquitoes were responsible for spreading this disease—that was the sisterhood for you.

It was a hot night and, as Gracie felt her breath quicken in the darkness, she tried not to think of the freaky clairvoyant who had insinuated that something terrible was going to happen to her, or at least that she ought to keep low expectations of her future. Besides, the teeny pinprick of a bite on her arm looked benign, devoid of the irresistible force of destiny—she drifted uneasily to sleep. Until she woke gasping in the dawn light and sat woozily up and coughed, onto her pillow, a fine spray of blood.

47

Gracie sprinted from house to house, banging on doors, shaking wind chimes, kicking garden gnomes, overwhelmed with inchoate rage and an increasing terror at the lack of available options.

'Someone? Anyone?'

There was only a disquieting lull after the echo of her voice faded. The once sleepy suburban streets were now catatonic. She remembered when all you could hear was the murmuring of television dialogue or the verbal precursors to domestic violence. Now there was only the drone of cicadas.

Inez was heavy and the backpack she was in wasn't made for babies—Gracie had cut two holes for her little legs, and made a little burqa for her out of netting, for this primitive, sickening quest: to which nameless stranger should I entrust my daughter? Any kindly aunts or single mothers out there? A big sister? Sorry, gentlemen, you know you'll try to fuck her when she comes of age—or likely before.

Was she really hoping for adoption from the same uncaring people who had been annoyed when she was looking for her dog? She felt physically putrid, but adrenaline kept her going. There was pandemonium in her blood. The urgency felt paranormal.

'Hello?!'

The air was heavy, syrupy; the humidity had sucked the oxygen out of it. She peered through a wooden fence and saw Freddie, a young man she'd often seen lifting weights inside his open garage, dead on a banana chair, his body rotted through. A cloud of mosquitoes hovered above the swimming pool, their wings making tiny ripples in the surface of the water.

She ran across lawns and up driveways and into cul-de-sacs, screeching, 'Anyone alive?'

But there was nobody except those who had perished in their safe havens: the poolside dead, the tennis court dead, the investment property dead. All the judgemental women and insecure men she'd ever avoided were gone. She thought: What I wouldn't give to be penetrated by the male gaze.

She drifted down one residential street then swung left into the empty, four-lane highway, hoping to pick up a human scent. The roads were clear but for a few cars with cadavers inside, with or without cat and golden retriever carcasses on their laps—murder-suicides, most likely.

She walked down Marine Parade with its burnt-out cafés and shops, past the drive-through bottle shop emptied of its contents, past the pub famous for its single-punch fatalities, then she trundled up and down the contours of the hilly streets, where an ambulance had slammed into a utilities pole, and into the wealthier suburbs of once manicured lawns, dry fountains, and backyards with greenhouses and gazebos. She pounded on the doors of those heavily mortgaged sanctuaries and echoey McMansions with electric cars pointlessly plugged into their juiceless sockets. There must be *someone*.

'Hello?!'

She came to a tree where motorists had once died in good health—the withered roadside memorials seemed quaint now—and collapsed against the trunk. She thought how, for almost all of human history, being isolated from the group meant certain death. Then for a few hundred years we really, really wanted our personal space. Now here we were again, fatally alone and craving our fellow man.

Inez's faecal smell drifted up to her nostrils. She took a frangipani off the footpath and stuck it in Inez's hair. She said: 'It's funny. I always thought I'd be murdered by a man who whispered, right before I died, "It's nothing personal."'

It started to rain. The houses were lit up by lightning. The hail drowned out the cicadas. With only hours left to live, she berated herself for the precious time she'd wasted in her life: craving recognition; being hurt by insults to her dignity; traumatising herself in dressing-room mirrors . . .

At some point she must have fallen asleep, because when she opened her eyes the rain had stopped and the sky had grown darker. Inez was still sleeping, and Gracie was gazing up at the tree moving in the breeze when a snarl of a dog reminded her how a bad situation can always be worse.

She got to her feet and went onward despite the agony of her ruined body. Her legs felt like dead branches, and she limped along the median strip of the highway. Life was full of sudden reversals—there was no reason to believe this might not turn around for the best. She climbed onto a car bonnet and stood resolute in the setting sun, yelling out for help.

From the bonnet she saw a curtain part in a second-floor window of the nearest house. Someone must have been alive out of sheer perversity. She ran to the door and pounded on it in a rabid stupor.

'What do you want?' said a male voice.

'I'm infected. I've got my child here.'

'So?'

'Who's in there?'

'Me.'

'Who's me?'

'Who's asking?'

'Please open up. I'm trying to find someone to look after my daughter.'

The door opened and a man in a hazmat suit and rubber gloves stood behind a mesh screen. Gracie could see his steely grey eyes through the plastic visor.

'Are you alone here?' she asked.

'Yes.' How could she leave Inez with a strange man? There were a great many fates worse than death. The man understood her loaded silence. 'Try the Davidsons.'

'What?'

'Next door.'

Breathless and in searing pain, she shambled along the ferny path to the neighbour's terraced villa, leaned on the doorbell, and loitered on the welcome mat, listening to the low voices inside. She donned her face mask so as not to frighten them with her blotched and bleeding face.

The Davidsons, a handsome couple, stood imperiously behind a flyscreen door in their high-ceilinged entrance way, looking well-off and unperturbed, as if expecting their lifelong winning streak to continue. Gracie easily conjured up a future family portrait of them and Inez. She smiled at them from under her mask, trying to ferret out their darkest instincts.

'You infected?' Mr Davidson asked.

'I am, she isn't.'

'How do you know?'

'A mother knows.' Tears ran down her cheeks. The couple stepped back and scrutinised Inez. Gracie asked, 'Why didn't you evacuate?' She was operating under the sway of full maternal paranoia.

'Why *don't* we trust the *military* to take care of us? Is *that* what you're asking?'

'We'll protect her,' said Mrs Davidson. 'No mosquitoes getting in here. We had a daughter, Lilly. All grown up now. Well, before she died in the third wave.'

'I'm sorry.'

'We'll take her in, quarantine her for forty-eight hours.'

'If she doesn't show any signs of symptoms, we'll take care of her.'

'Promise.'

'Her name is Inez,' Gracie said.

'Step back, please.' Gracie shuffled back. The grated door opened, the woman bundled Inez up in her arms, and quickly shut it again.

'Don't worry, darling,' said Mrs Davidson.

'We got her,' said Mr Davidson.

A crawly sensation moved through Gracie and her body started shaking.

'We'd invite you in, but, you know.'

'Say goodbye to Mummy.'

'She's not talking yet.'

'Let us show you to your room.'

The door clacked shut. Gracie stood there, her eyes now like fogged glasses, listening to her heart thrash. What should she do?

She couldn't hear anything from inside—no footsteps, nothing but her own sharp intake of breath. What were they doing? Why were they so quiet? Were they already down in their sex dungeon, making up a cot of nails?

She pounded heavily and desperately on the door. 'OPEN THE FUCKING DOOR!'

The door opened—the Davidsons stood in terrible silence.

'Hello, Mummy.'

'I've changed my mind,' said Gracie.

'That's a shame.'

They placed Inez on the hallway floor and tiptoed back. Gracie scooped Inez up in her arms and ran back out into the diseased world. Blood was in her eyes now, clouding her vision further, and, despite the stabbing pain in her legs, she ran as fast as she could back to her own haunted house.

48

It was disconcerting to materialise from the colourless void into the striking squalor of the empty house. Owen and I arrived within minutes of each other, both noting the unsettling fact that Gracie and Inez were not at home, so we sort of hovered around, waiting up like worried parents, Owen self-consciously browsing the bookshelves while I just wafted near the couch, until Gracie stumbled in maskless and in a tremendous rage, clearly in no mood to tune in to whatever occult frequency we had manifested.

Gracie kicked out the flyscreens and flung open all the windows and doors and let the breeze roll through the house. A dried trickle of bloody tears streaked her hollow face. She covered Inez head to toe in distressing kisses and looked directly at me—that's how I knew what was about to happen; her eyes communicated the grim task ahead. In times like this, even if you don't believe in Him, you can't help but focus all your animosity on God and His loathsome opacity, unapologetic smiting, and amorphous reign of terror.

Gracie emptied all the opiates from Owen's large stash onto the kitchen counter and continued to eye me while she ground them up with the heel of her shoe, then added the powder to a glass. Her every move seemed to ask which parenting method—attachment? tiger mom? helicopter?—best prepares you to euthanise your healthy child. Gracie fought tremors as she added orange juice to this fatal concoction. The powder sat in the bottom of the glass, innocuous, like stool softener. She stirred it with a spoon.

Gracie carried Inez up to the bedroom, already feeling like the dark lord's emissary. We two spectrenauts followed close behind. The mood was biblical. A gloomy moonlight streamed through the window. Gracie laid Inez on the bed and made her laugh with raspberries that stained her cheeks and belly with blood. Owen was gazing at me with genuine sympathy and a hand over his mouth.

Now for the unbelievable moment: Gracie's smile looked gouged out of her face as she took the glass brimming with death and put it to our child's lips, the very child the universe had given us for safekeeping. Inez drank every last drop. How long would it take to ruin a body that small?

Inez laughed delightedly—a teddy bear was floating in the air. Owen was using his poltergeist capabilities to fly the bear to her outstretched arms. Inez squealed and giggled. He blew back over to the shelf and seized the bunny next, then levitated the kangaroo, after that sailing the furry sloth over to my rapt, dying daughter. Gracie broke into mad laughter and blew him a kiss. I was glad Owen was there, I'll admit. He really came through.

Where would Inez be going? Gracie mouthed the words slowly with half-demented eyes. To the same place where we'd rendezvous? Her look hardened, the question in her intensifying gaze implicit. Did I know Inez's whereabouts in the cosmos? At that moment, I was relieved I was unable to communicate the truth.

Inez's breathing grew shallower.

I needed to bear witness and even felt struck by a kind of dark privilege to watch my daughter die. I can only hope my presence consoled Gracie a little.

Inez's breathing shortened, then ceased. I didn't cry out—to cry out and have that cry unheard would have been more than I could bear.

Gracie stood over the body mutely. A wordless funeral and her unmade bed her unmarked grave. She kissed our daughter's eyelids with relief that she was free of harm. She staggered over to the window and opened it and stared at the moon, an old stone wheel that had stopped spinning long ago.

Everything was tomb-like. Gracie's harrowed face was bloodied, blunted by grief. All the rage had leached out of her; she had lost any residual fear. She couldn't have more than three hours to live—three too many.

Owen vanished, allowing me to have these final moments with my wife. That was decent of him, almost gentlemanly.

Gracie pulverised the remaining opiates and downed them with tequila. She lay down beside Inez, feeling boneless and already long dead.

I tried to lock eyes to commiserate so she wouldn't die alone, but co-dependence isn't symbiosis—the terror of the end was hers alone.

The pills weren't working fast enough; she started choking on her own blood.

And then—the thing that sat shivering inside her became still.

EIGHT

'Every atom belonging to me as good belongs to you.'

Walt Whitman

49

I am happy to report that whatever magnetic pull originally drew Gracie and me to one another was not weakened by our mutual deaths. We were a couple again; I had the spare set of keys to her heart, and she had mine.

Owen greased some palms and used his connections to get her off a doomed caravan scheduled for extermination and, in an uncharacteristic moment of conscience, brought her to his office and got a message to me.

Gracie was in Owen's leather swivel chair when I arrived, eyes wide in fright; whether it was the dementia of rebirth or the psychic torment of her recent act of infanticide, she was a mute, crumpled version of herself. For an hour we held each other so tight we looked like a fossilised couple from Pompeii. I barely noticed Owen standing awkwardly beside us with a palsied smile.

It seemed both impractical and indecent to bring Gracie back to share Valeria's apartment, so I took her to the broken-down building where I'd first lived. Fire-blackened walls indicated what had gone down in my absence. Xander remained in the elevator, no extraneous fingers on or about his person.

'Haven't seen you here in a while. Third floor, right? I never caught your name.'

'Angus,' I said.

It was disconcerting to hear him sound so ordinary. He planted his feet wide and gazed down kindly at Gracie, whose eyes were closed, face pressed against me.

'New arrival?'

'My wife.'

'Hey! Good for you!'

The elevator creaked with its usual slowness. Xander stared at Gracie, seized by curiosity. 'Good morning. Welcome to level two. It's quite annoying to be dead and continue to catch lint in your bellybutton, but you'll get used to it.' He reached over to Gracie and tried to prise open her eyelids.

'Hey. Hands off.'

He obliged and backed into the corner as if fighting a gravitational force.

'I know you!' he yelled at Gracie unexpectedly.

I was holding her upright and she began to sag. 'You don't know her.'

'Really? I guess not.' He let out a long whistle.

There he was, the old Xander—whatever danced across his field of vision wasn't in a reality I shared. The elevator stuttered to a halt. He smiled cordially as we exited into the dark, low-ceilinged corridor; I escorted Gracie to my old room and opened the door—there were two women naked in the bed.

'Come in. Join us.'

'Maybe later.'

We backed out and shut the door.

'Hey.' Xander's head was leaning out of the elevator into the corridor. 'Room 408's just opened up. Take her up there.'

For two days, we lay in bed gazing at each other, filling each other in on everything that had gone on. Gracie was having a bad time recalibrating and had an adverse reaction to dying: hives, uncontrollable bladder, persistent nausea. For that reason, I went easy on her, but still castigated her for blowing my murderer, of all people.

Gracie was shocked but not that surprised to hear that Owen had been the one who'd killed me. She classified her relationship with him as a state of inadvertent polyamory, and I went along with that. Besides, I'd shacked up with Valeria, so I was hardly the poster boy for fidelity.

She was overjoyed to see the screenshots I'd taken of Inez but they propelled her to demand clues as to her plausible location. She posed variations on the same unanswerable question: 'Where do the unaccompanied minors go?' Inez was all she thought about and nothing else mattered. She wanted to know every theory and was disappointed to know that I hadn't really heard any.

She wanted access to the internet, was frustrated when I told her most technologies were not accessible to non-military personnel, and irritated that I didn't know why. The truth was, I had never thought to ask.

Our hearts were set in a frozen cringe. At a minimum, she wanted to float in the ocean and was deeply depressed to learn that we were located inland.

'What about the here and now?' she asked.

'What about it?'

'I see the illusion of the passage of time is here too.'

'Twenty-four seven.'

'But we are not in our universe. We're in a wholly different space-time manifold, right?'

'Uh, that sounds right,' I said. I felt safer now that she was here and on the case.

Gracie climbed out of bed and stood naked before the mirror with a tight smile on her face. 'Our outward forms are a little uncanny, don't you think?'

'You think? I don't see it.'

Her eyesight was better now that she was dead, and while she was unfazed about the disappearance of her tattoos, she mourned the loss of her birthing scar, testament to the day she cut Inez out of her body. I thought: It's only a matter of time before she carves its replica and, what's more, it would be cruel to stop her.

'Gracie, should we sleep now?'

'I don't want to.'

Yet she came back under the sheets and we held each other tight, preparing for bed like we were arming up for battle. And we were. In her sleep, Gracie was harassed by dreams of infanticide; she thrashed like a drowning animal and I had to shake her awake and pin down her arms so she wouldn't claw out her own eyes.

'I think I won't ever allow myself to sleep again,' she said, before drifting off into the agony of another violent dream.

The next morning, I guided Gracie through the streets of the chaotic overcrowded necropolis among the last of the earth-born humans, an ungovernable populace if there ever was one. There were no guides to welcome the dead—there were too many new arrivals, and they'd mostly been left to figure it out for themselves. A foul, petrol-smelling rain was falling and the sun seemed perilously close. I explained to her how the weather here caused a mild derangement.

There were little fires in the streets that served no purpose, flickering symbols of civil unrest. Who *wasn't* plotting against the state these days? Military jeeps rolled through the city and Gracie didn't flinch at the sound of gunfire. It was as if she'd mastered fight or flight—or maybe her evolutionary baggage got lost in transit.

'Looky,' she said, pointing to a Nazi flag in a shop window. 'Why would anyone make creatures like us imperishable? It doesn't make sense.'

'I thought the same way.'

I showed her the duelling range, the public baths, the execution chamber, the strip clubs, the churches, mosques and synagogues; people exasperated in queues, drinking in bars, dancing in clubs, fucking in brothels, relaxing in spas, and otherwise escaping the present. She seemed bent out of shape that the endless caravan of the human race goes on and on, mournful and broken, scarcely improving, ricocheting off one plane of existence to another.

The novelty of walking on the surface of another dimension had worn off by mid-afternoon. She was emotionally maxed out. She'd never seen so many people who couldn't hold back tears. Next to us a woman was deliberately treading on the shadows of pedestrians. Gracie asked me to take her to the library: surely there was information there that posited a location of the children who'd died on earth.

The library was a single gigantic room, and we had to step over sleeping bodies to get at the various shelves that interested Gracie; she seemed to know what she was looking for and wasn't quiet about tossing irrelevant books across the hall in frustration. She made a hell of a racket, but other than the occasional pitying look, the woeful library-dwellers were surprisingly indifferent to her as she set up at a table with a staggering pile of physics, theology, and philosophy tomes; abstract and technical books she skim-read in a furious torment, turning pages so fast they tore, deploying her uncanny ability to read and ruminate at the same time.

It was fun to watch her until about eleven p.m., when I realised she intended to stay all night. The ceaseless snoring and noisy dreaming of the library residents was disturbing, but I understood that going home to be beset by Inez-poisoning nightmares would be worse for her. Eventually, with my head on the desk, I tumbled into a stormy sleep.

I awoke hours later with the sun coming through the east window. Gracie was still at it, a mountain of half-opened books around her, panic-reading texts on Euclidean space and differential geometry, as if the answer to everything was just a matter of angles.

By six p.m. the next day, the librarians threw us out—one night disturbed by a madwoman was about all they would put up with. We stepped out into the seething, haunted world and the hot silver moon hurt our eyes. Gracie looked like someone who was bracing for a punch.

'Baby,' I said, 'you look like you could use a drink.'

The Bitter in Soul was busier than usual. A fight had just taken place and the proprietor was busy uprighting chairs and sweeping broken glass.

'Come,' I said. 'Let's drink with our sad companions in the hereafter and the hereafters after that.'

'I thought you were in limbo, floating in some kind of ether,' Gracie said. 'All this time you were getting drunk in this shithole?'

Valeria was at the bar, staring at us. She recognised Gracie from the screenshots and dropped her jaw in mock surprise. It was immediately uncomfortable. Valeria and I mirrored each other's brittle smile. 'This is the woman I told you about,' I said to Gracie, as if we were swingers looking for a third.

'Valeria?'

'Yep.'

They exchanged appraising looks.

'I've heard a lot about you,' Valeria said. 'A little too much, actually.'

'I'll bet,' Gracie said. 'How are you?'

'Can't complain. You?'

'Can complain, and will. I alternate between feeling utterly hollow and feeling filled with bees. Does it stay like that?'

'It'll pass,' Valeria said.

'Will I get my period?'

'I just got mine.'

'I don't see why they needed to take anatomical correctness to this extreme.'

'I had a UTI last week.'

They were on the precipice of genuine smiles. Perhaps out of ill ease, Valeria told a long story apropos of nothing about a man she'd seen crucify himself a few days earlier. He had climbed up onto a cross and asked passers-by to nail him to it. 'I died for your sins the first time—this time I want to die for nothing,' he'd said. This was no Second Coming, Valeria had decided, just an ordinary dead man dying ostentatiously, or maybe a publicity stunt of some kind.

Gracie downed her drink and mine. 'Here he is!' she said. 'Look what the grim reaper dragged in.'

It was Owen, standing at the door, wiping his big dumb forehead. 'It's wet out.' Despite his efforts to reunite me and Gracie, I couldn't help but scowl at the sight of his sad, humdrum face.

Gracie walked over and confronted him: 'So you *did* kill him. Hm? Hm? After you told me you "most certainly did not".'

'Cat's out of the bag, then?' he said in a soft, mellow voice. 'Yes. Sorry about that. My bad.'

He had a cheeky look on his face. Gracie knew she'd been played, violated and, frankly, abused, but she felt all this at a remove. Owen made a vague hand gesture as if to say, should we forgive and forget? Let us not speak of it again? Would that be okay?

'Are your breasts bigger?' he asked.

'What did you just say to her?' I snapped.

'Thanks for noticing,' Gracie answered.

Now that it had been pointed out, I could see it was true. Her breasts were twenty percent larger than they had been when she was alive.

'What's that about?'

'Isn't it obvious?' Owen said. 'Sometime before you met her, Gracie had a breast reduction.'

'That's not true.'

'Actually, it is.' Gracie smiled at Owen. 'I was sixteen. I was just too embarrassed to mention it.'

Already I was on the back foot; lacking observational skills put me at a disadvantage, and I was also out of sorts about Gracie's gentle chastisement of Owen for beating me to death, as if he'd simply eaten the last Tim Tam in the packet.

For the rest of the evening, as Gracie got very drunk, Owen was in a near constant state of supplication—every round was on him, and he wouldn't stop talking about himself, mostly about how, against his best wishes and efforts, he had just been conscripted into working at an army hospital; he found it degrading to be in the service of others in the middle of what he imagined to be his eternal retirement.

Gracie remarked that none of his personality gains from the dementia remained; he was back to his old selfish awful self, a claim

Owen didn't refute. Instead he sat with his lips puckered and panted whenever Gracie said anything. Beside us, a man was loudly telling his life story to a woman who responded by saying, 'Sad face emoji!' On the other side, there was talk of life after death being a 'human right'. Wow. They'd never let that one go.

Gracie raised her glass. 'We've just been reborn and we're already rotten and decaying, while inside us lie new seeds of regeneration. Yes, we all are like Prometheus's liver—gnawed by an eagle, only to regenerate for the specific purpose of being gnawed again!'

'I'll drink to that,' Owen and I said in unison.

'Oh boy,' Valeria said.

It was a weird foursome, I'll admit.

Inside the bar, a man was selling some kind of opium-like substance in spray form, while outside there was a crazed and pointless tumult of yelling, music and gunfire—the stupor of infinity.

Gracie gave her general opinion on being reincarnated as ourselves. She thought people were confused about whether life was fleeting or not, fearful that we may never reach a logical conclusion, frustrated to realise that God could not appear in human form because the pressure of what race, gender and sexual identity They'd pick would send the human race into an interminable grievance fit. Otherwise, humans were the same as always: violent, loving, curious, self-interested, and made almost entirely of hope and denial. One surprising thing she'd noticed was a healthy lack of envy: folks seemed to have finally shed their obsession with inequality. Nobody wanted to be anybody else, mostly because everyone genuinely felt we were in the same mystifying boat.

'So true, Gracie,' Owen said, cackling. He was the picture of solicitude. I wanted to dry-retch. 'Remember when all the neighbours left?'

'When was this?' I asked.

Gracie and I were still catching each other up, and for hours we continued drinking and recounting our individual adventures, with shifty-eyed Owen always interrupting to correct the record or to look me in the eye and say, 'You had to be there.' It really was unbearable how quickly Gracie had forgiven him for my murder.

Around two in the morning, there was an actual firing squad outside the bar. Gracie asked the bartender to turn up the music, and we danced together for the first time in over a year.

We came home late and stayed up until dawn rediscovering our old sexual habits with our new bodies. I was so relieved and weepy to be back in her naked embrace, I had an irrational fear she was going to ask for a divorce.

It had quietened down outside; there was barely any sound of shooting or screaming from the street below. Gracie sat up in bed; her frown had commandeered her whole face. 'Somewhere is the source code, and why should the human mind need an unnecessarily complicated structure to hold it? Was Copernicus wrong? *Are* we the centre of something? Why persist? Where are our common ancestors? Are we our own descendants? If so, what did we inherit from ourselves?'

'Yeah, I had a lot of questions when I first came here.'

'We're overliving. Human beings have acquired some kind of living sickness—or did we always have it?'

'That's a good question.'

'To God, was human life one beguiling genocide after another from the get-go? Were we, in that tunnel of light, subjected to a form of prenatal testing before our rebirth at the other end? And can we conclude, then, that those who did not arrive here were aborted? Is the tunnel of light a technique of soul selection? Some kind of spiritual eugenics?'

Gracie's face was flushed and I let her wear herself out, making no effort to dissuade her from continuing: 'And why should subjective mental states be eternal? The question is not why is there something instead of nothing, but why is there so much of it? Does the chaotic inflation of an expanding universe happen right down to the level of the individual soul? In other words, are we spreading ourselves too thin?' Her hands grabbed either side of my face. 'Are we dealing with a God who doesn't have self-knowledge? A brain state unaware of itself? Is our mistake looking at Creation as a finished act when it's only at the beginning? Why was our resuscitated energy organised into its familiar shape? Is death a trial period? Was life a dress rehearsal? Was earth a stepping stone? Does the mind of God have its own neural basis that can be understood and replicated? Is the goal to become part of a single mind? Are we being used, cleaned, updated, so that when we're ready, we'll take our part in the Great Coherence?'

'Maybe. That sounds okay.'

'It sounds okay to you, to be an infinitesimal part of the undivided consciousness of an Infinite mind?'

'Yeah, I mean, maybe. Could be.'

'Is the maximum allowance one universe per god or one god per universe? Is life itself a pre-existing condition? Is non-existence the same as being transported to a universe consisting of nothing?'

'I don't know. What's the difference?'

'Exactly.'

This could go on forever. 'Gracie, you think you can uncover the meaning of the universe? You think God isn't smart enough to cover His tracks?'

'We were summoned here and forced to wait. Why? And why is there no religion that has God as a couple? Isn't God being a single dude *the* problem?'

'Maybe.'

'The clue in the lack of nothingness always rested on the human inability to truly imagine it. Is human suffering some kind of power source? Isn't the most depressing of all theologies that God being perfect means He is unimproveable?' She slapped her hands together, and a look of astonishment crossed her face. 'Or, fuck! Maybe Nietzsche was right! Is this the part of the eternal return before we return? ". . . even this spider and this moonlight between the trees . . . something something . . . the eternal hourglass of existence is turned upside down again and again, and you with it, speck of dust!"'

'Gracie, are you okay?'

She brought her fists down hard on the bed. 'It's this fucking itchy fabric of reality. Turns out, there *is* an infinite abyss—but it's bright and overcrowded. I'm not even sure the heat death of the universe is going to stop us.'

I said, 'Look, Gracie. I've been here a while. I haven't just been sitting on my hands. I've done some poking around and I can tell you, it seems more and more likely that the abyss of eternal nothingness was just a pipedream, and we're in an afterlife with a low entry threshold. We presumed finitude and we were wrong. Get over it. As to where this is all heading, I've got three best guesses. You want to hear them?'

'Of course.'

Gracie sat up and narrowed her eyes in a manner that betrayed a lack of faith.

'Guess number one,' I said. 'We will live and die repeatedly until we arrive in the galaxy of the son of a bitch who created our galaxy—we might even meet the Creator—but we will never ever learn the identity of the son of the bitch who created *his*.'

She blinked at me a few moments. 'And your second guess?'

'My second guess is that we're inside a dream and one person here among us is the dreamer. Question is, how can you discern the dreamer in his own dream? Maybe we're not meant to.

Maybe the Messiah does not descend from heaven, he goes from a state of dreaming to a state of lucid dreaming, and he must convince *himself* to awaken and only *then* will *we* cease to exist.'

'Okay, that's dumb, what's number three?'

I was leaning towards number three myself. I folded my hands together and pressed them under my chin to show her how seriously I'd considered it. 'Hear me out. Not everyone is here, right?'

'Right.'

'It's possible they just didn't make the cut, right? *Therefore*, the continuation of life occurs with a contracting cast of characters, right?'

'I'm with you.'

'A winnowing down of numbers. Not unlike what happens to Mike Teavee, Veruca Salt, Augustus Gloop and Violet Beauregarde.'

She looked at me emptily for a moment. 'Are you talking about *Charlie and the Chocolate Factory*?'

'One by one, they got taken out, until the only one left was Charlie Bucket, the only one who acted ethically. And what did Charlie get as a reward?'

'The factory.'

'The factory. That's my theory. One by one, as we go through the dimensions and universes and afterlifes, each go round there will be less of us, until the last man—or woman—gets to, are you ready for it? *Take over the whole place. Replace Willy Wonka, aka God.*'

She gazed at me with her hard-blue stare; there was something about this theory that had almost got to her. 'I need some air.'

Xander was not in the elevator and his absence somehow made the dark space even more claustrophobic. We trudged drowsily up to the roof, where Gracie stared sullenly at the unknown constellations.

'There are no more flashes of light,' I said.

Those signifiers of arrival had vanished. Nobody coming from earth. Nobody left to transport. Nobody left to die. The human flame had been extinguished; earth had just rid itself of the most troublesome of all apes. Frankly, it was hard to believe, and for some reason it made me think of how, if you drop a bullet at the same time as firing one from a rifle, both bullets will hit the ground at the same time.

It was getting colder, and there was the faintest white glow from behind the mountain.

I said, 'I've heard some people talk about how the orange flashes were some sort of energy source and, without the dead, it's triggered some sort of climate change.' The truth was, when I heard that, I shut down. I didn't want to know about it. But now I found myself regurgitating this eco gossip. 'Other people say the constant orange flashes were masking the white glow that we're now seeing for the first time. Maybe it's the ghosts of children trying to reach their parents.'

This idea was unbearably sad. We watched the peculiar lightshow in the sky, wondering if in the white glow was our Inez, reaching out, crying for us.

Her face was burning. 'We don't really know anything at all, do we?'

I wanted to tell her how much that wasn't true, that I had learned a lot here, maybe not about the laws of the hereafter but about life and how to live it. I had realised we were just walking barometers of other people's opinions, I told her. How often I used to misinterpret people's silence as judgement! It had occurred to me that all my self-criticisms were innuendo and hearsay, everything I'd ever pretended to be was for someone else's benefit, and if people were ever looking at you, it was actually to see if you were looking at *them*, and if they were paying you attention, it was only to gauge *your* level of attention. We craved approval so unreasonably, we didn't remove the labels others put on us, even though they were barely adhesive . . .

Gracie wasn't listening. Her mind was elsewhere. She lay down on the roof and stayed there. I realised: we couldn't save each other. Too much had happened. Our black veils were permanent. Gracie was weighed down by the impossible distances we're expected to cover over innumerable lifetimes.

'Let's go to bed,' I said.

'I can't move. Ever again.'

It wasn't like her to give up, but then she wasn't really her, any more than I was me. We were thin veneers, devastated versions of ourselves.

I picked her up and carried her downstairs—she cried all the way. I thought how our fears weren't just fundamental and primitive; they were supplemental, complicated and modern. This was going to come to no good.

I placed her on the bed and lay next to her.

'Do we also exist elsewhere *simultaneously* as well as *not at all*?' she asked.

'Uh-huh. Shall I turn the light off?'

'Is there something artificial about our *own* intelligence? Wherever Inez is, can our existences be synchronised? Why should the anthropic principle extend all the way to this hereafter? The God who created the universe isn't keeping tabs on us at all. Doesn't it seem, at best, an honour system?'

'Okay. I'm going to close my eyes and block my ears now.'

While I loved to see her mind work, even if it was no longer a mind I knew or understood, I couldn't hear any more of her thoughts. I pulled the covers over my head. Our traumas were too different, each demeaning and sickening in their own ways. I was just about to drift off to sleep when I heard Gracie say, 'What is the standard model of cross-dimensional reincarnation anyway?'

I kicked the covers off me and walked to the window and

looked out. Rising slow over the mountains was that dumpster fire of a sun. Below, the people on the street were cast in shadow; they were shouting but their voices folded into their echoes, making their babble incomprehensible. At my feet, a tiny cockroach scuttled across the floor. Where had it come from? I couldn't remember if I'd seen a cockroach before in this afterlife, and, if not, had the universe suddenly become more porous? If so, what did that mean? What was coming next? Just what a weakened population needed among it: beasts of prey.

'Mooney, come to bed.'

'No more talking if I do.'

'I promise.'

I climbed back into bed and Gracie tore off my pyjamas in a frenzy; I was readying myself for sex only to find she was forensically examining my body.

'What are you doing?'

'I want to see the Lord's bite radius.'

'Oh, Gracie.'

'Is reality a drug we take for its God-suppressing effect? Can we find the source of the illusion and turn it off?'

Her mind was stuck, and I was scared now, listening to her uncontrollably ponder the ungraspable metaphysics of it all.

'Are children now in liquid form? Are they gaseous? Can we triangulate her position? Can we find the right coordinates to input? Can we get to a place where we three overlap or correlate or occur simultaneously? We want to look homeward, we just don't know what direction it's in. How, then, can the prodigal parents return?'

50

The next night, the four of us went back to the Bitter in Soul for another evening of drinking to forget. The bar was alive with rumours: the revolution was in its terminal phase; there was going to be an incursion; they were fortifying the town; further rationing was mandated, which meant the washing-out of old condoms.

Owen had the decency to give me an increasing number of apologetic looks—he finally had the space for genuine remorse, and better late than never. We chatted amiably enough; the only thing we didn't talk about was life on earth. We didn't reminisce anymore—nobody did. It was an unspoken agreement that nostalgia was off limits and anyone who started a sentence with 'remember when' would be tossed out onto the street.

I only broke the rule once: 'When Owen first removed his knee-high socks in our living room, I remember thinking that his legs were so uniformly pale and hairless and plasticky, they looked like a prosthesis.' Nobody thought that observation was funny or interesting.

Owen said, 'Speaking of which, in this wartime moment, does anyone else agree it's actually something of a relief to see amputees? It's begun to resemble more the world we've come from.'

Valeria's hand sneaked up onto my shoulders and guided me to a corner table. It was weird between us—we didn't know how to physically relate. Platonic hugs? Carnal high-fives? Valeria said she wanted to check in with me, and with a great heaviness she admitted to being hurt that I hadn't checked in with her, and had our relationship meant anything to me?

I told her that she was very special to me while thinking how her love had always felt like an abstraction anyway, like it didn't pertain to me but rather the space I occupied.

Out of the corner of my eye, I watched Gracie and Owen deep in conversation. He was still obviously besotted with her. Gracie clasped her hands on his face, and Owen did a nod that was a veritable bow before he hurried out of the bar.

'Excuse me a sec,' I said, and rushed back over to Gracie. 'Where did he go?'

'He's coming back later.'

Gracie gave me a vaporous smile and started downing shot after shot of whisky. Twenty minutes later, she drunkenly climbed up onto a stool and began making nonsensical toasts: 'To the principle of mediocrity: we share half our genes with a banana. Cheers!' And: 'Life was a war fought and lost on four fronts—eight, if you count the diagonals.' And: 'It is often said that Death is the secret door and Heaven is a two-way mirror, but the truth is we are one component of a complicated mechanism that does not know its part, function or purpose.'

'Hear, hear,' I said, trying to get her down off the stool.

A couple with a baby hovered in the doorway of the bar.

'Hey!' the bartender shouted. 'We don't serve their kind in here.'

Gracie booed the family while trying to keep her balance on the stool. 'Why are we still mindlessly replicating our genes? I demand sterilisation be the very first order of business upon arrival!' Gracie wiped unexpected tears from her cheeks. 'I'll tell you all something. When I first got here, my urine was black and I literally farted a puff of smoke.'

There was a flash of light from outside and the sound of an explosion tore through the air.

Gracie shouted: 'You hear that? That's the abortions! They've all grown up, this furious race of unwanted beings, and now they've formed an army that's come to crush us!'

The window of the bar was shattered by a volley of bullets that missed the crowd it had tried to disperse. Only one patron screamed—the rest of us couldn't be bothered. A moment later, an old man ran in with a vicious smile: 'Come outside, everyone, and see! A man has flayed himself to see if our skins are reversible!'

'You go if you want,' Gracie said to me, still atop the stool. 'I'm just gonna stay here and —'

'Sit down!' the bartender shouted.

'Don't you disrespect me! Actually, you can. It's fine.'

Gracie plopped down on the stool and downed another whisky. I ordered coffee to sober her up. Her attention was caught by the man on the stool next to her, who wouldn't stop smelling his finger.

'Look at your face,' she said with disgust.

'What about it?' said the man.

'Notions of beauty are socially constructed, to be sure, but ugly is ugly.'

'What the fuck?'

Gracie put her head down on the bar, muttering, 'I didn't want to be more sinned against than sinning. I wanted to sin too.'

Just as the bartender turned up the music that was obviously his personal sex playlist, Owen returned.

'I'm back, Gracie.'

She lifted up her head, eyes now alert. There was a heaviness suspended in the air and it gave me an uneasy feeling. Gracie let out a laugh devoid of mirth, and she took my hand. 'We cannot know if Inez was blessed with nonexistence. We have to keep looking for her.'

'Agreed.'

'So then I'm not wasting any time.'

'What do you mean?'

'I have to attempt the expedition and make my approach on the only road onward,' she said.

'You mean . . .' I said.

'Owen?'

'M'lady.' Owen pulled out of his jacket pocket a black revolver. 'Dying by suicide is sort of like crossing a picket line,' he said, and handed the gun to Gracie, who handed it to me.

'What am I supposed to do with this?' I asked.

'Shoot me.'

'Baby . . .' I said, my heart cracking down the middle.

'Shoot me and I'll look for her.'

'No way.'

Gracie gave me a tipsy half-smile and whispered in my ear. She didn't have the emotional space to live right now, she said, to just hang around to see the seasons change, to watch the revolution unfold—maybe there'd be genocides, maybe orgies, definitely war, and, if not famine, then disease and rape. People around us would fall in love and get married and die. In short—nothing unthinkable. All the while, not knowing about Inez would fester and rot her insides.

I said, 'I'll come with you.'

'Oh, yes!' Tears came to her eyes—she'd needed to hear that. 'This time,' Gracie said, 'I'll go first.'

Gracie took my hand. Valeria took my other hand and Owen held Gracie's free hand. None of us might ever see the others again.

'Not in here, guys,' the bartender said.

That was fair. I bought a round of drinks for the house and over-tipped the bartender. Then we took our drinks outside. The alley stank of garbage and urine—it was the perfect place for a murder-suicide.

Owen said, 'The moon looks hairy tonight.'

We all gave the night sky an appraising look; the stars gave off a crisp glare. For a dreamlike moment, the four of us stood motionless, staring up.

Valeria said, 'You shouldn't do this.'

Gracie asked, 'Why not?'

'You're playing God.'

'God isn't. Somebody has to.'

Valeria asked if she could kiss me goodbye.

'I don't know,' I said.

'Oh, go on,' Gracie said. 'I don't mind.'

Valeria leaned in and I gave her a so-long kiss.

Owen drooled to Gracie, 'In that case, may I kiss you?'

'No you fucking can't,' I snapped.

Owen stood there blinking at her, then smiled like he was trying to swallow something indigestible. We looked dumbly around. The plan was I'd shoot Gracie in the head, and then I'd shoot myself, but whether it was the last vestige of the fear of death, or the will to live, or some combination of the two, I was shaking. We'd all died once. This should have been no biggie, but I couldn't deny I was scared.

'Make it quick,' Gracie said.

'Someone should say something,' I said.

'Fuck no. Let's make this as unceremonious as possible,' she said, and she was right. There was nothing left to say. Death as an unsentimental journey. I could get on board with that. 'When you're right, you're right.'

Gracie looked at the clock tower. 'Time of death, twelve-fifteen a.m.' I looked at the clock. It was twelve-fourteen a.m.

I pointed the gun at Gracie; she stood tall and dignified and stared into the barrel. If we don't find Inez, I thought, maybe the next world will at least offer some clarity.

'What are you waiting for?' Gracie asked.

'You know what the Vietnamese say?' I said.

'What?'

'I don't know. I thought you knew.'

'What?'

'I'm just trying to psych myself up.'

'Try not to overthink it.'

She didn't seem afraid, just impatient. Were we asleep and about to wake—or was it the other way around? I understood I might as well be strapping her to a rocket and blasting her into the unknown.

'Mooney, come on.'

My hand holding the gun began to shake uncontrollably; I used my other hand to wipe the tears from my eyes. Shooting Gracie in the face or in the heart was unimaginable. I could put a bullet in the base of her skull, maybe.

'Turn around.'

She turned around, and it quickly dawned on me that shooting my beloved from behind wouldn't work either.

'I can't do it,' I said.

Gracie sighed loudly. 'Oh, for . . .' She snatched the gun out of my hand and pointed the barrel awkwardly under her chin. She winked.

'Ciao.'

'Wait!'

Too late.

The blast knocked her violently off her feet and her body fell hard to the ground. It was painful, the piercing tone a gunshot made in the inner ear. This was the second time in less than a week I'd watched her die.

I stood swaying for a few minutes, trying to process; maybe she was already enjoying an enthusiastic welcome into a superior afterlife with an aperitif, or was she now squirming in embryonic form in some rando's womb? Had she arrived at the place where she could personally rebuke the Creator for his sloppy methods or had she found a perfect counter-example to existence? It was infuriating not to know whether her death was heartbreaking or not.

I took the gun and pointed it at my own head. I wondered if I could overtake her, exceed the speed limit in the tunnel of light and arrive before her.

'I can't watch.' Valeria kissed me on the cheek and went back inside the bar, stopping briefly at the door to look back at me hammily. I had a real soft spot for that terrible actress.

Bye, Valeria.

I turned back to the task at hand—why I still couldn't cultivate sufficient indifference to dying was genuinely beyond me. I couldn't pull the trigger and was ashamed of my hesitation.

'I'll do it,' Owen said. 'I killed you once, I'm happy to do the honours.' It was true. He was a whiz at murder. 'Would you like me to?'

I looked at his face and had to admit, the dregs of my hatred for Owen were only granular now.

'I could strangle you with or without gloves,' he offered.

I thought: the world is populated by two types of people—those who think it's hilarious when someone dies in an ironic way and those who think all death is sad, even when a hunter suffocates in a rabbit hole. 'Then I'll just shoot you,' he said. 'Make it quick.'

I turned away and gazed upwards at the night sky, where the stars blurred like the lights of an underwater city.

'Any last words?'

I shook my head and wondered whether I'd end up going from a lower realm to a higher realm, or progress horizontally to a side realm, or go nowhere at all. Or—just then I had a weird thought. What had Gracie said about Nietzsche's eternal return? A closed system in which we recur innumerable times, reborn as ourselves and everything playing out exactly the same way. *The eternal hourglass of existence is turned upside down again and again, and you with it, speck of dust!* What if some of us—a very rare number—were allowed to remember? What if I returned to the point of origin with my memory intact so I could tell the whole story? Would I even *bother* warning everybody? I doubted it—and, to be perfectly frank, who would believe me?

I held out the gun to Owen. 'Would you mind?'

'This is perfect. It proves a theory that I've been toying with. Would you like to hear it?'

'Not really.'

'Angus,' he said, 'I think that we're meant for each other in this exact way.' Owen smiled unpleasantly and put his arm around my shoulder, as if trying to make murder a convivial experience. 'Just as everyone has a soulmate, one person meant to love, maybe everyone has a deathmate—the person they are meant to kill.'

'Oh my God. Shoot me now.'

'Okay, I'll stop.'

'No, I mean *actually* shoot me now.'

'Of course. With pleasure.'

'Or with pain. I don't care. Just do it.'

I turned away and set my eyes towards the sky dripping with stars and, in the watery moonlight, I set free a deep breath of relief and was flooded with an unexpected feeling of mastery.

'You got this,' I said to myself and smiled.

It was to be quick, no slow fade to black this time. This murder would be the least important moment of my death. It was what I had literally been born to do. There was a strange white light across the sky.

Owen said, 'Here we go.'

You got this.

STEVE TOLTZ was born in Sydney in 1972. His first novel, *A Fraction of the Whole*, was shortlisted for the Man Booker Prize and the Guardian First Book Award. His second novel, *Quicksand*, won the 2017 Russell Prize for Humour.